The
Center
of
the
Action

The Center of the Action

by Jerome Weidman

Random House
New York

First Printing
9 8 7 6 5 4 3 2

Library of Congress Catalog Card Number: 68–28559
Manufactured in the United States of America
by Kingsport Press, Inc., Kingsport, Tennessee
Designed by Andrew Roberts

"The higher
the flame
has leaped,
the colder and
deader the ashes."

Olive Schreiner,
From Man to Man

A Note for
One Particular
Reader

This is a story about a recent American phenomenon: the change in our communications media, as they are now known, from the days when each went its separate and eccentric way, to this morning's headlines. These, as any newspaper reader knows, will include the announcement that yet another old and venerable book publishing house has become less venerable, meaning extinct. It was purchased yesterday by a newspaper chain which, only last week, was itself purchased by a television network which, the week before that, became the property of what the purchaser—through his vice-president in charge of public relations—chooses to have himself called: a communications colossus.

I do not deplore this. I merely note it. "Progress," wrote Emerson, "is the activity of today and the assurance of tomorrow." He was, of course, getting into Gibbon's act: "All that is human must retrograde if it do not advance."

For me the core of this advance has been one corner of these vast new financial empires. As a short-story writer, a novelist, an essayist, and a playwright, I have known many editors and producers. Some, I regret to say, intimately. But it is the book publishing business, into which I stumbled when I was twenty, where most of my last thirty years have been spent; where most of my interests lay; and where, now in my fifties, most of my friends function. They are all solvent. This pleases me. Insolvent friends are a nuisance. But some of my friends are dead. Progress killed them.

It is because I miss them, and because I believe they would be alive today, or at least would have lived longer and happier lives if progress had not caught them in its web, that I was moved to write this book.

It is a novel. By this I mean it is a combination of observed reality and imagined expansion. The novelist does not bring his imagination to bear on hard fact merely to cover his tracks. He does so because he can't help it. Without imagination he would not be a novelist. Without imagination he would not completely understand what the photographic plate of his mind has recorded. He would merely reproduce it. I have been a novelist too long to be content with mere reproduction. I have to do it my way.

All the characters in this book are invented. So are the incidents that make up the story. But both come out of a time through which I lived, a time when the growth of the communications colossus was just beginning. I did not, of course, in those days know this.

Politicians are constantly saying, as they bully us for our votes, that we must hand these votes over because we are living through a period of history. I don't believe this. I don't believe anybody knows he or she has been living in history until, much later, he or she looks back. When I looked back, I was astonished by what I saw: the moment in time—I am tempted to say the point of infection: "What we call progress," said Havelock Ellis, "is the exchange of one nuisance for another nuisance"— when the whole incredible phenomenon began. I have chosen in this novel to tell the story of only that brief moment.

Others will, of course, tell the story of the succeeding thirty years, from that first moment until today, the story of the slow, steady in-gathering of the outer provinces, often to the bewildered astonishment of their citizens, into the centrally governed empire ruled over by men who frequently do not know, and often do not care, what it is their provincial subjects do all the way out there beyond Madison Avenue. These other books, no matter what they are called, will not be novels. They will be accumulations.

The method I have chosen will not be universally admired. The man who owns a distillery today does not like to be reminded that once he was a rumrunner. But the rumrunner's story, scrawled in the cabin of his heaving Chris Craft, is bound to be closer to the truth than the aging distiller's recollections dictated from the opulence of his tower suite offices.

After examining some of the distillers, and hearing their versions of what took place thirty years ago, I decided I would be on safer ground if I allowed a rumrunner to tell my story.

Jerome Weidman

The
Center
of
the
Action

1

" There's No Point in Being Angry with a Dead Man"

This much I've learned. If you're going to be a son of a bitch, you'd better go all the way. There's no money in being a half-hearted bastard.

I didn't learn that out of a textbook. It was drilled into me at Mattlin & Merritt, on lower Fourth Avenue. In the days when I could still get away with shaving only twice a week. The lesson might interest you. If it doesn't, do me a favor. Put this down, and go back to your TV set. I hope it's color, which is what you deserve. I'm not writing this for schmucks.

I'm writing it for the record. Which is another way of saying: to stay out of jail. Not that I've got more to hide than the next guy. But the district attorney's office sometimes has a funny way of interpreting things that were done in a strictly legal way, and already there are several versions of this story. Before any of us is much older, there will be more. You don't have to be Norbert Wiener to figure out that they can't all be true. This is your chance to read the only version that is.

It starts at ten minutes after seven in the morning on the first Tuesday in April. The year is 1954. I am still in my pajamas. I am sitting in my study with a cup of black coffee and the *New*

York Times. I am waiting for the two Empirin tablets I have just swallowed to take charge of my hangover, and I am wondering why a newspaper with all that money wants to waste so much of it on writers for the financial section who clearly have never seen a share of stock. Eight feet away, under the Larry Rivers that set me back three big ones at Parke-Bernet last November, my wife Evie is sitting with her cup of coffee and the *Daily News.* She breaks the silence.

"Guess who died?"

Some people talk. Others speak. My wife Evie breaks silences.

"It's too early," I said. "My head hurts."

"It's going to hurt worse when I tell you," Evie said.

"All right, who died?"

"Walter Idleman."

"Oh, Jesus."

"I told you," Evie said. "Ready for your second cup?"

"Make it hemlock," I said.

Evie went out with both cups. I thumbed from the financial section to the obituary page. In one way, this was a waste of time. Evie doesn't make mistakes about things like dead people. It's a subject she knows more about than the statisticians at Metropolitan Life. But I always need a couple of minutes between the moment when I get hit, and the moment when I make up my mind who it is I'm going to hit back. The man who slugged you isn't always the most profitable target. On the obituary page, across a two-column box, the *Times* let its readers in on the source of my brand-new headache:

WALTER IDLEMAN DIES AT 64;
RAN GROVER CLEVELAND HOTEL
20 YEARS

I didn't have to read the rest. I knew as much about Walter Idleman's life as I wanted to know. But now that the son of a bitch had put me up the creek by dying on me, I had to find a paddle. I tackled the two columns of graveyard prose:

4

Beverly Hills, Calif., April 6 (AP). Walter Idleman, President of the Grover Cleveland Hotel in New York from 1940 to 1952, died here today. He was 64 years old. Mr. Idleman moved to Beverly Hills in 1953. Survivors include his widow, Alice Dietz Idleman, and a daughter, Mrs. Claude Wakefield, Jr., formerly of Scarsdale, N.Y.

I stopped reading long enough to wonder about these two broads. I've come out ahead in more than one financial wrestling match by avoiding the guy I was fighting, and tackling the tomato whose rent he was paying. Unfortunately, I couldn't recall ever meeting Walter Idleman's wife or his daughter. I went back to the *Times*. The subhead read:

SPOKESMAN FOR INDUSTRY

"The guest is always right" was the motto Mr. Idleman maintained during his 20-year association with, first as manager, then as president of, the Grover Cleveland Hotel at Seventh Avenue and Thirty-second Street.

He devoted himself to attracting business both for the hotel and the city. He was treasurer for many years of the New York City Visitors Association and spokesman for the hotel industry here. Mr. Idleman's interests ranged across the entire spectrum of the city's activities, embracing the theater, the financial district and the sporting world, in all of which fields he had many friends. The Custom Tailors Guide of America named Mr. Idleman in 1949 among the nation's ten best-dressed men. He professed great surprise at this distinction, and when asked for a statement by the press, he said, "A man can't be well dressed unless his pants are pressed." Mr. Idleman was known as a wit in the circles he frequented.

Mr. Idleman's remains will be flown to New York so that he may be buried in the family plot in Scarsdale. A service will be held at Campbell's Funeral Church, Madison Avenue at 81st Street, at 3:00 P.M. tomorrow."

Evie came back into the room with the two coffee cups. "What are you going to do?" she said.

"Stay out of Campbell's," I said.

"Nobody will know you're doing it," Evie said. "It's not the

5

missing faces people remember at funerals. It's the ones that show up that get mentioned in the papers."

I took the second cup of coffee she was holding out and carried it across to my desk. "I'll also remember not to send flowers," I said.

"There's no point in being angry with a dead man," Evie said.

"The son of a bitch stayed on his feet for sixty-four years," I said. "Why couldn't he do it for another three weeks?"

"Oh," Evie said.

"Oh, what?" I said.

"You didn't tell me you were that close to winding up the Sissenwein thing," Evie said.

There were a lot of things I didn't tell her. I'd always figured that was why our marriage had chugged along for sixteen years without any major derailings. But now there was something in her voice. Like a warning whistle when the engineer starts bringing Old Ninety-eight into the turn. Except that Evie doesn't whistle. She has a voice like a cat. I mean one of those uptown cats. The kind that knows it doesn't have to slink around the garbage cans for its next meal. Evie's voice purrs.

"I didn't know you were even interested in the Sissenwein thing," I said.

"I'm interested in everything you do," Evie said. "Even the things you don't tell me you're doing."

What wife isn't?

"Now listen," I said. "Are you implying that I've deliberately kept this thing away from you? The work I've been doing on the Sissenwein estate?"

"I'm not implying anything," Evie said. "I'm saying something. You'd better listen."

My God, the things a man can find himself in, while he's still in his pajamas, at ten minutes after seven in the morning!

"What else can I do?" I said. "I'm a captive audience."

"You've been a captive audience since we got married," Evie said. "But I haven't been very happy with the applause I've been getting."

6

"You married a businessman," I said. "Not a claque."

"That girl who married Henry Ford," Evie said. "She married a businessman too. But there are people outside her own family who know she's alive."

"Nobody thinks you're dead, Evie," I said. "Nobody who knows you."

"I'm interested in the people who don't know me," Evie said. "We've been married sixteen years. That's a long time for a girl to be waiting in the wings. I'll be thirty-eight my next birthday."

"You don't look it," I said.

"In a year or two I will," Evie said, "If you pull off this Sissenwein thing, I won't mind looking thirty-eight. If you don't pull it off, I'm not going to wait that year or two."

"This is a hell of a note," I said. "Here I am, in my own home, early in the morning, nursing a hangover, and my wife starts to threaten me."

"It's the only time I can get you to listen," Evie said. "The rest of the day you're talking so fast, you don't even hear yourself. So pay attention. My feelings about this Sissenwein deal are simple. It's more than money. It's the sort of thing I thought you were going to do when I first stared into those gray-blue eyes that look like the bullets my kid brother used to load into his BB gun. I thought then you were a winner. That's why I said yes. It's been sixteen years, but you haven't won yet."

"You haven't exactly been living like a starving Armenian," I said.

"Thanks to my father's money," Evie said.

"It hasn't been all his," I said. "I make a buck now and then too, you know."

"You're not listening again," Evie said. "I've told you it's not the money that interests me in the Sissenwein deal. It's what it will do to our position in this town if you pull it off. So you'd better pull it off."

"I'm good and close," I said. "Byram Noonan said yesterday at lunch we'd be ready to put the package on the surrogate's desk next week. Four months of work, not one minute of it easy, so this bastard Idleman has to drop dead in the home stretch."

"I'm sure he didn't do it just to cause you trouble," Evie said. "Walter Idleman probably liked staying alive as much as you do. There's nothing to be gained by knocking a corpse. Drink your coffee and start thinking."

I took a sip, dialed Byram Noonan's number and swiveled around in the chair to look out at Central Park. On East Fourth Street, where I was born, the only green things I saw until I was twelve years old were the faces of my classmates in arithmetic class at P. S. 188. Now that I'm forty-one, I pay seven eighty-three a month in maintenance, on a co-op that set me back a hundred big ones, because looking out on trees helps me think straight. This is a commentary on life. You might jot it down.

"Helloo?"

"Juliette," I said into the phone, "Ted here."

"Ted who?"

"Cut it out," I said. "How many Teds do you know?"

She laughed. No, she giggled. At a quarter after seven in the morning, it takes a Frenchwoman to be able to do that.

"Aah, but thott is tellink!" she said.

Byram had found her in France during the Battle of the Bulge. Since then he'd paid for some pretty expensive teachers, so Juliette had learned to talk English. But she'd also learned something else. If you add a cute French accent to your obvious assets, you're way ahead of the girls who have nothing to offer but the contents of a Number Four Cup. Juliette Noonan always sounded like Renee Adoree whispering in John Gilbert's ear on top of that haystack in *The Big Parade*.

"This is Ted Leff," I said. "Could I talk to Byram?"

"Only on zee long distahns, Teddy dollink."

"How come?"

"He ees in California."

"I had lunch with him yesterday on Fifty-third Street."

"Perhaps that iss what drove heem out of town?"

"Impossible," I said. "I've been using that new mouthwash. The green one on television. Where is Byram now?"

8

"Lahsst night, dollink. I wass crayzee about the old mouthwash."

"As soon as I finish this new bottle," I said, "I'll go back to the old one. When is Byram going to be available?"

"He deed not say, but I know he mosst go to a funeral here at Campbell's tomorrow at three o'clock." She giggled again. "What tar you dewink theess ahfternoon?"

"Stay home and see," I said. I hung up. I swiveled back to my coffee cup. Evie was giving me that look across her own cup. "All right," I said. "If my lawyer's got a wife who twitches her tail even on the telephone, what do you expect me to do about it?"

"Stay out of the Noonan apartment while Byram is away," Evie said.

I gave her a look of my own. Most men get married because they're impressed by what a girl carries around in her blouse. Not me. All women have two of those. When it comes to marriage, the thing to go by is what a girl carries around between her ears, or what her old man has in the bank. I've been lucky. I've never met a girl yet who had as much up there as Evie, and her father keeps the stuff in a bank he built for himself. I intended to stay lucky. Evie had just laid it on the line.

"Just for the record," I said, "I've never been inside the Noonan apartment without you, in case you're interested."

"I am," Evie said. "Very. And I intend to stay interested. So whenever you find you've got an irresistible impulse to visit the Noonan apartment, you call me, and we'll go together. Hand in hand. Now then. Why wasn't Byram at home?"

I gave her another look. I don't know how many men who have been married sixteen years still find themselves giving their wives looks. At twenty minutes after seven in the morning, yet.

"How do you know Byram wasn't at home?" I said.

"Better take two more Empirin tablets," Evie said. "Some of your brain pores are still clogged. Who do you think I thought you went to the phone to call? In front of me? Juliette?"

"I dig," I said. "That would have been dumb."

9

"And you're not," Evie said. "So you obviously called Byram about this Idleman thing, and Juliette answered the phone because Byram is not at home. Why?"

I told her. No. I told Evie why Juliette had said why.

"Hmmm," Evie said. She not only breaks silences. She says "Hmmm," and it doesn't sound like a bonehead filling empty spaces in a conversation. It means her brain is turning over. "Byram obviously flew to the Coast because he knew about Walter Idleman's death before the *Times* and the *Daily News* knew about it," Evie said. "How come he got on a plane without telling you?"

"Maybe he tried," I said. "Last night we were with your parents at Loew's State, watching a black-tie hundred-dollar-a-seat preview of M-G-M's version of Deuteronomy as directed by John Huston for the benefit of the Muscular Dystrophy Chopped Chicken Liver Fund."

"There's one way to find out," Evie said.

"As Humphrey Bogart used to say to Effie, that's right, precious." I swiveled back to the phone and dialed our answering service. "Ted Leff calling," I said to the girl who came on the wire. "Any messages for me or Mrs. Leff last night?"

"One moment, please." During the pause I took a sip of coffee. That's another place where Evie is ahead of most women. She makes great coffee. Why not? Her old man imports enough of it every year for his supermarket chain to keep Brazil in business. "Mr. Leff?"

"Yes?" I said into the phone.

"Mr. Noonan called? Mr. Byram Noonan? He said it was urgent?"

"What time did he call?"

"Nine-twenty, Mr. Leff?"

At nine-twenty, as I remembered it, Cain was swinging forty pounds of cardboard rock at Abel's head in glorious Technicolor.

"Was there any message?" I said.

"Yes sir," the girl said. "Mr. Noonan said he'd just had bad news from the Coast? No, I'm sorry, Mr. Leff. Bad news from

10

his Coast *office* is what Mr. Noonan said? And he was catching the ten o'clock plane from Idlewild?"

"Anything else?" I said.

"Yes, Mr. Leff," she said. "Mr. Noonan said would you please not go to your office in the morning? That's now, of course, this morning? You're please not to go to your office until he calls you at home? From the Coast, that is? He'll call you from the Coast?"

"Did he say when?" I said.

"Yes sir," she said. "Seven-thirty, New York time?"

"Anything else?" I said.

"No sir," the girl said. "That's all, Mr. Leff."

"Fine, okay, thanks," I said. "I'll check you later."

"Yes, Mr. Leff."

I hung up.

"What?" Evie said.

"Things may not be as bad as they could be," I said. "There's no real evidence of a double-cross. Not yet, anyway. Byram tried to reach me last night before he flew to the Coast. He left a message he'd call me this morning at seven-thirty."

The phone rang. Reaching for it, I looked at my wrist watch. It's a Patek Philippe. I picked it up in Zurich for half a big one two years ago, when Evie and I went over to celebrate Passover by seeing if there was anything to this skiing crap that all our gentile friends were creaming about. There isn't. Not for Jewish boys from East Fourth Street who value their legs as much as Marlene Dietrich values hers. Four-wall handball is still my game, even if I no longer play it in the Jacob Riis settlement house on Rivington Street. But the watch proved to be a winner. It loses ten seconds every two weeks. Never more. Never less. Right now it showed twenty-nine and a half minutes after seven. Byram Noonan was still on my side. I picked up the phone.

"Hello, stupid," I said.

2

" If You're Going to Be Buried out of Campbell's, the Only Time to Die Is in the Spring"

"You certainly pick some peculiar places to hold your business conferences," Evie said.

"All the pieces of this Sissenwein deal have to be put together quietly," I said. "If the surrogate suspects even a hint of finagling we're dead. Until the whole package is wrapped up I don't want to be seen going into Byram's office, and he doesn't want to be seen coming into mine."

"Most of New York will see you getting together at this thing," Evie said. "Not to mention watch you talking your heads off."

"That won't matter," I said. "When two men run into each other and start chatting at a funeral, nobody gets suspicious. Everybody figures they're just comparing their latest blood-pressure readings, or checking their age against the number of years the guy they've come to bury managed to get under his belt before he cooled. You just make sure you corner Juliette, and see to it she doesn't start waving her pennants at the pallbearers. I'll take care of the rest."

"How much of the rest is there?" Evie said.

"Jesus Christ," I said. "You're more steamed up about this damn thing than I am."

"I thought I made it perfectly plain yesterday morning how I feel about the Sissenwein deal," Evie said. "How much of the rest is there?"

"I don't know yet," I said. "It depends on what Byram learned in California. He's coming here direct from the airport."

Snaking in and out of the Madison Avenue crowd to the Eighty-first Street corner, it occurred to me that if you're going to be buried out of Campbell's, the only time to die is in the spring. All the rest of the year the building looks the color of spit-out tobacco juice. Then comes the middle of March, and the management goes crazy with the first-floor window boxes. They slap on bright yellow paint, and then stuff the boxes with fire-engine-red geraniums. Watching the Cadillacs fighting their way up to the Madison Avenue entrance under all that color, a stranger in town might get the idea somebody inside is giving away a bride. A dumb stranger, that is. Assuming there's any other kind, he'd see right away what I saw: all those Cadillacs had the Z on their license plates that tells you right away it's a hired car. Naturally, Evie noticed it too. The last thing that got by my wife Evie was Halley's Comet.

"I don't know why," she said, "but hardly anybody bothers to hire a limousine when they're going to a wedding. For a funeral, though, look at them. They obviously think it's the only way to go."

"The reason is simple," I said. "When you're heading for a wedding it's usually in a church or a synagogue. In a church or a synagogue you know damn well there's that boy upstairs looking down from His cloud that you're not going to be able to fool, so you might as well save the twenty bucks and take a hack. Or like us, if you live around the corner, you walk."

With funerals, though, it's different, and I could see right away that Walter Idleman's funeral was no exception. The men and women unloading from the hired Cadillacs all looked as though they expected to be recognized. Before we got off the sidewalk and into the lobby, Evie was obliging them.

13

"The *Times* wasn't kidding," she said.

"You mean it's true that the Jefferson Davis crowd has started lobbing shells into Fort Sumter?" I said.

"No, Teddy dear," Evie said. "What's true is that Walter Idleman's interests apparently did range across the entire spectrum of the city's activities unquote. Over there? Standing next to Mrs. La Guardia? The woman with her back to Walter Pidgeon? No, not the one with the Mexican jewelry. The one with her head tipped up, like she's calling instructions to somebody on a fire escape. That's Katharine Cornell talking to Jack Dempsey."

"I hear when he was on his tail during the long count at the sesquicentennial in Philadelphia," I said, "Tunney quoted a fast stream of Shakespeare at Dempsey to keep him from getting up. You go over and find out if it was from one of the plays or one of the sonnets. I see Byram."

This is not difficult to do, even in a crowd and when he's sitting down. It's not unusual, if you're at a restaurant table with Byram, for some stranger to come up and make a couple of admiring remarks about one or all of the three Yale teams on which Byram Noonan played left tackle not too many years before Pearl Harbor. He's put on a little weight since then, but he still stands six-feet-four in what Grantland Rice used to describe as his "stockinged feet."

"Okay, fine," Evie said. "I see Juliette waving, which means she's either sighted the French stand-in for Dustin Farnum, or she's saving a seat for me. Where do you want us to meet you after this clambake is over?"

"On the sidewalk," I said. "The Eighty-first Street side. And do me a favor. Keep her on the subject of cremation or contraception. All I need is to have that French accent making remarks in this mob of big ears about some of the late Hubert Sissenwein's properties."

"You handle Byram," Evie said. "I'll take care of the Rita Hayworth of Ninety-sixth Street."

She took a reef in her broadtail and headed down the aisle.

14

Mink, I once heard my wife Evie explain to her father, is for U.J.A. rallies, not funerals. Her father paid for the broadtail. Why not? I pay her rent. I waited just long enough to see Evie and Juliette make contact, and then I went up the aisle toward the back of the chapel.

Byram was sitting where I had told him to sit: on the last bench at the left. Byram always does what he's told. That's why he's worth the stiff retainer I pay him every year.

A few people who were already seated turned to look at me as I passed, but they didn't look long. Whatever score I've managed to make, the size of which is nobody's business but mine, I've done it by keeping my picture out of the papers.

"Hello," Byram said. He moved over to make room for me on the bench. Right away I knew there was trouble. When things are going well, Byram Noonan's greeting is "Hi."

The reason for this is that when things are going well he has time to think about how he is going to say what he wants to say. This is very important to Byram. Not because he is fussy about grammar, but because he is the Silas Marner of our spoken language. There are people who don't like to waste words. Byram Noonan is a miser about syllables. He treats them as though he has a turnstile in his throat, and for every sound that comes through he has to drop a coin in the slot. By Byram's calculations, "Hello" costs twice as much as "Hi."

"What's the trouble?" I said out of the corner of my mouth. Out of the corner of his, Byram said, "Oy!"

Nobody uses Yiddish words with more passion than gentiles. The short words, anyway. You take a member of Porcellian. All his life he's heard his father refer to the slob at the next desk to his in the bank as a numskull. Then our boy comes down from Harvard and he gets a desk of his own in the bank. One day into the bank comes a boy from East Fourth Street, lugging a satchel full of hundred-dollar bills. All he wants to do is start an account. After a few minutes with the numskull he stalks out in disgust, carrying his satchel full of hundred-dollar bills to the bank down the street, muttering as he goes the word "Putz!"

15

The razor-sharp accuracy of the description has an effect on our friend from Porcellian. He says to himself: My God, how long has this been going on?

When I first met Byram Noonan it had not been going on at all. For him, I mean. In fact, Byram didn't even know he was meeting me. I was a kid of seventeen at the time, just out of Thomas Jefferson High, shoving a hand truck through the streets of the garment center for the groceries that managed to make it up onto my mother's table on Vyse Avenue in the Bronx. There was nobody else around to get them there. My old man had coughed out the balance of his left lung across his sewing machine in a pants shop on Allen Street while I was still memorizing my valedictory speech for the Thomas Jefferson High graduation exercises. When they were over, I invested two cents in a copy of the *New York Times*.

Now that it costs a dime I still read it the way I used to read it when I was a kid. Working my way backward from where John Kieran used to be, to where Brooks Atkinson was letting somebody have it, to a book reviewer named John Chamberlain who wrote the kind of simple English I like, and ending with a red-hot headline on the front page about NINTH PLANET, PLUTO, DISCOVERED AND NAMED AT LOWELL OBSERVATORY, FLAGSTAFF, ARIZ. Actually, the morning after I graduated from Thomas Jefferson the big headline on the front page of the *Times* was: HAWLEY-SMOOT TARIFF BILL SIGNED BY PRESIDENT HOOVER, but I never got to read it. I never found out what Kieran and Atkinson and Chamberlain had to say on that day, either. On that day I opened the paper to the want ads.

That's how I became a key member of the firm of Schmeichel & Zetzer, Inc., Form-Fitting Frocks, 498 Seventh Avenue, at ten bucks a week in official salary, plus as much as I could get out of the petty-cash box and Lila Pincus, the bookkeeper who was in charge of it, by writing fake vouchers. A lot of other members on the staff of Schmeichel & Zetzer must have been doing the same thing because one morning when I came to work, there was an old man in the office, talking to Miss Pincus. He had a face like the place in a gutter where a lot of trolley tracks cross, and the kind of voice that Graham MacNamee used when he was broadcasting the Dempsey-Firpo fight and he was having trouble figuring out which one of them had just gone through the ropes. This old creep, it turned out, was something called a custodian. He had been appointed to take charge of the Schmeichel & Zetzer premises by the Irving Trust Company, the Receiver in Bankruptcy for the Southern District of New York, while the accountants and the lawyers audited the books and records.

Thus I learned that the flow of my ten official bucks, as well as my off-the-record take from the petty-cash box, had come to an abrupt end. While I was trying to figure out what to do about this, a lawyer named Noonan, who had been hired by the Irving Trust Company, came into the office.

He did it the way a medical student who is a hypochondriac might step into his first leper colony. Mr. Noonan didn't exactly shrink, but you could almost see him pulling the bottom of his coat a little closer around him. It was obvious that he had never before been in a Seventh Avenue loft, but it was equally obvious that he wasn't going to let this interfere with the job he'd been hired to do. Mr. Noonan did it so well that both Messrs. Schmeichel & Zetzer became guests of the federal government for three years. These two putzes—in Scarsdale, I am told, the Young Marrieds now say "petz," but it's the sort of innovation I prefer to disregard—had sent a false financial statement through the mails.

Six years later, when I was a seasoned veteran, I took a whirl at the end of the dress business in which Schmeichel & Zetzer had failed. I was so excited about running my own business that I was a little careless about whom I did it with. For instance, I sold a shop on Grand Concourse $3,600 worth of spring taffetas at 8/10/EOM, and six months later the son of a bitch still hadn't paid. So I hired a lawyer named Golig and sued.

The day I walked into court I met Byram Noonan for the second time, even though he continued to remain unaware that we were meeting. He represented the bastard from Grand Concourse. I found this interesting. Mr. Noonan still looked like he'd just come from a session in the Bachrach studio where all the members of his Yale team had posed for a group photograph to be presented at a testimonial dinner to Tad Jones. What the hell was he doing, defending cheap little crooks in the openest and shuttest kind of open-and-shut case—namely, a failure to pay for goods delivered? I soon found out what Mr. Noonan was doing. He was winning the case my lawyer should have won.

I was not as smart at twenty-four as I am today, but I was smart enough to read signs written in large letters on barn walls. The next time I needed a lawyer, I hired Byram Noonan.

For my purposes, he's the best in town, and my purposes would sometimes cause the eyebrows of a Porcellian to go up. What I like about Byram is that his eyebrows stay put. Another thing I like about him is that he's a downtown lawyer. The deals I get involved in, you retain a lawyer with offices north of Forty-second Street, and before the deal is on paper you learn your lawyer also represents the choreographer who is going to do the Tahitian number in Act II, or the printer who is going to get up the brochure for the bond issue, or the widow of the former owner of the apartment house you're about to add to your real estate parcel on Lower Park. This never happens with Byram. He's strictly a 120 Broadway man. In seventeen years of deals that have done what the *Times* said Walter Idleman's interests did—namely, ranged across the entire spectrum of the city's activities—Byram Noonan never wore two hats at a conference he was attending as my representative.

But the best thing about Byram is that he's a square. Or, as he would prefer to put it, if he knew he was one, which he doesn't, Byram Noonan is a putz. His legal talents are enormous, but they are no help to his basic stupidity about human beings. This is very good. What you want in a lawyer is what you want in an automobile. You want it to get you there. You don't want it to do your thinking for you. Anyway, I don't.

Not even Judge Brandeis could have pulled together so skillfully the tangled threads of the Sissenwein deal. And yet the man who managed to do it could also bring back from France a bimbo like Juliette, and for a dozen years, during which she has been slipping in and out of beds like a hot-water bottle, remain happily convinced that he's married to Martha Washington. Only Byram could sit in a pew at Campbell's, arms folded across his blue serge suit, staring at the casket up front as though he were Fulton Sheen listening to Cardinal Spellman laying out for the boys a new set of rules for handling the traffic at St. Patrick's on Easter Sunday, and at the same time report to his client and partner on a business trip to California by saying with complete seriousness out of the corner of his mouth, "Oy!"

"Talk English," I said. "This is a Jewish funeral."

"When I spoke to you on phone yesterday morning from California," Byram said, "I didn't yet have entire picture of situation."

"Now you have?"

"Think so."

"What do you mean you think so?" I said. "You either have the entire picture or you haven't. What's there to think about?"

"You," Byram said.

"Don't waste your time," I said. "All the thinking that has to be done about me I'll do myself, and there isn't much of it left I have to do. I've been working quietly for four months to pull the pieces of this Sissenwein deal together. I've got every executor to agree that the price I'm offering is fair and reasonable. You told me at lunch only day before yesterday I was ready to come out in the open by making my offer for the whole package to the surrogate next week."

"When I told you that," Byram said, "all four executors of Sissenwein estate were alive. Death of Walter Idleman reduces number of living executors to three."

"Byram, if you asked me to meet you here to give me a lesson in arithmetic," I said, "I'm going right back to my office and tear up your next year's retainer check. I know there are now only three executors. And I know I can't go to the surrogate with my offer until a new executor is appointed to replace Idleman because I've got to approach this new executor the way I approached Idleman and the other three. I've got to have time

19

to work on him and convince him that it's in the best interests of the estate to sell the whole shooting match to me. All I want to know from you is who the hell is he, this new executor?"

"That is why picture of situation is not entirely clear," Byram said. "New executor is not a he."

"You mean the surrogate has appointed a woman to replace Idleman?"

"Not necessary appoint anybody," Byram said. "According terms of Sissenwein will, if any or all of four executors dies before estate is settled, alternates must be appointed by surrogate from list included in will by Hubert Sissenwein himself, and choice must be made in order of precedence laid down by Sissenwein."

"And the name at the top of the list is a woman?"

"Yes and no," Byram said.

The odds were getting close to even money that on this particular day Campbell's would be burying two stiffs before the organ music stopped.

"Byram," I said, "I understand yes, and I understand no. When you put them into the same sentence, I go crazy. Did the surrogate appoint a woman to replace Idleman, or didn't he?"

"He did," Byram said.

"Congratulations," I said. "We'll get there yet. Next question. What's her name?"

"Mrs. Claude Wakefield, Jr.," Byram said.

The name hit a note. I could feel my forehead crease as I listened to it while staring across the heads in the pews toward the casket up front. A picture of me in my study with Evie the day before came sliding into my head. Into sharper focus came a piece of detail that was part of the picture: the *New York Times* obituary.

"Mrs. Claude Wakefield, Jr., formerly of Scarsdale," I said. "She's Idleman's daughter, isn't she?"

"Correct," Byram said. "Trouble is she used to be something else before she became Mrs. Claude Wakefield."

"What?" I said.

"You mean who," Byram said.

"Don't tell me what I mean," I said, "Just tell me what *you* mean?"

"Before she married Claude Wakefield, Jr.," Byram said, "Mrs. Claude Wakefield, Jr., was the widow of Ralph Mattlin."

"Oy!" I said.

"Precisely," Byram said.

"Where the hell has she been all these years?"

"My Coast office dug up fact Wakefield important figure in foreign-end TV film distribution," Byram said. "Headquarters in London. He and wife apparently living in England last dozen years."

"She in London now?" I said.

"No," Byram said. "She flew to Beverly Hills from England day before yesterday to bring her mother here to New York for the funeral. They were on same plane with me this morning from Los Angeles. I'm sure she's here in building right now. Probably in room over there on right, where they let family wait until eulogy starts. I'll point her out to you."

"Don't bother," I said.

"She's quite attractive," Byram said.

"She always was," I said.

"You know her?" Byram said.

It was like asking Christy Mathewson if he knew the New York Giants.

"I once worked for her husband," I said.

"Of course," Byram said. "You started with Mattlin & Merritt on Fourth Avenue."

"No," I said. "I started with Schmeichel & Zetzer on Seventh Avenue, but let's not go into my biography at the moment. We've got Mrs. Claude Wakefield, Jr., to take care of."

"How will we do that?" Byram said.

"Not we," I said. "Me. But I'm going to need some help, so listen."

21

3

" You, You, You, You and You— Follow Me, Please"

The next morning, as soon as the Empirin started taking charge of my hangover, I looked up from my copy of the *New York Times*. "Evie," I said.

"Wait a minute," she said.

I could tell from the way she was scowling and the way her lips were moving that she had the *Daily News* open at the page that carried an account of the Walter Idleman funeral.

Finally Evie looked up. "The bastards," she said, "They mention everybody from Sitting Bull to Vincent Impellitteri, but not us. How about the *Times?*"

"The *Times* doesn't even mention Vincent Impellitteri," I said. "Are you in a mood to listen? I have something to tell you."

"I don't know what mood I'm in, after the workout Juliette gave me yesterday," Evie said. "She's got this French idea men find her irresistible if when she's sitting down she acts like a plate of jello caught in a high wind. What's on your mind this morning?"

"Juliette," I said.

"Aren't you getting a little long in the tooth to be thinking about things like that at ten minutes after seven?" Evie said.

"The time for you to start complaining," I said, "is when I stop thinking about things like that at ten minutes after seven. What's on my mind at the moment is not actually Juliette. It's the promise I made to you about her two mornings ago."

"What promise?" Evie said.

"That I would never go to the Noonan apartment without you," I said. "I've got to break that promise."

"My God," Evie said. "I didn't know you were that crazy about jello."

"I'm not," I said. "And when I go to the Noonan apartment this afternoon at one o'clock Juliette won't be in it."

"You're going to have to prove that," Evie said.

"I don't have to," I said. "You'll be proving it for me. While I'm at the Noonan apartment you are going to be lunching with Juliette at Tony's. Byram's reserved for you his favorite corner table."

"And while I'm listening to Juliette's steam-heated account of her adventures with the U.S. Army during the Battle of the Bulge," Evie said, "where is Byram going to be?"

"At his apartment," I said. "Introducing me to the new executor of the Hubert Sissenwein estate."

"Who is this new executor?" Evie said.

"You won't believe it," I said.

"Try me and see," Evie said.

I did.

"My God," Evie said. "That's coming full circle, isn't it?"

"Yes and no, as Byram would say," I said.

Benita Mattlin was not really the starting point. Even though I did meet Ralph Mattlin's wife the day before I met him.

My tour of duty on Seventh Avenue ended pretty much the way Schmeichel & Zetzer's had ended, with one exception. I did not become a guest of the government. It doesn't sound like much of an achievement, but 1937 was Count Your Blessings Time. The fact that I managed to stay out of jail after my bankruptcy was the only blessing I had to count, so I counted it.

Then I did some thinking. I was not a kid any more. I was closer to twenty-five than to twenty-four, and all I had to show for my almost seven years on Seventh Avenue was a closet full of Kolmer-Marcus suits, an apartment at the Montevideo on which I could no longer pay the rent, and a lesson about life learned the hard way: if you're going to issue a false financial statement to get credit in the form of piece goods, don't send it through the mails. This leaves you wide open to a federal rap. The way to handle the situation is to walk down the street and deliver the statement in person to the shmiggeggies you intend to fleece. If you're in a jotting-down mood you might make a note of that. Life is full of surprises. Even men as solvent as Samuel Insull find themselves on occasion in the position of having to issue a false financial statement. It's like bad breath. It could happen to you too. If it does, you might as well know how to do it right.

This very good rule, however, has one serious drawback. Landlords will not accept it in exchange for rent. Not in 1937, they wouldn't. So I hocked all but one of my suits, sneaked out of the Montevideo in the one I saved, and again invested two cents in a copy of the *New York Times*.

On that day you didn't have to read the headlines. They practically came screaming off the front page with details about the explosion of the dirigible *Hindenburg* at Lakehurst, but I never heard a sound. I was buried in those want ads again.

I had placed a few want ads of my own during my days as a dress manufacturer. So I knew a little more about them than I'd known on the morning when I became a delivery boy for Schmeichel & Zetzer. The ads that imply if you come to work for the outfit that placed it you will not only be a Morgan partner by eleven o'clock next Tuesday, but you will also grow taller, more handsome, and a full head of hair, these you can disregard. Unless you are crazy about meeting the authors of four-line short stories, and you have a lot of carfare to throw away on this hobby. I didn't. Not in the spring of 1937. So I looked for the kind of ad in which the fictional content was small. In the Office Help section I found one that didn't seem to have any. It read:

> Young Man Wanted to Do Very Rapid Addition of Columns of Figures. Must Be at Least Twenty-five. Boys and Older Men Not Wanted. Must Be Presentable. No Pimples. No Physical Deformities. No Mustache. Must Look Educated. Must Be Well Spoken. Above All Must Be Able to Add As Rapidly As an Adding Machine.

While the author of this ad had left out a number of my more important characteristics and talents, as far as he went he had written my biography. In addition, I didn't even have to spend any carfare to get to see him. I walked over to the Knicker-bocker Building at the corner of Forty-second Street and Broadway, took an elevator to the ninth floor, and at the end of a long corridor found a door marked in gold letters:

909–910

ARNOLD ZOHN

CERTIFIED PUBLIC ACCOUNTANT

ENTER THROUGH 911

I did that and found myself in a small room that seemed to be heaving like one of those newsreel shots of an earthquake. I don't remember if that was the year the boys whose daddies were paying their tuition in the Ivy League were swallowing goldfish, or seeing how many of them could crowd themselves into a single telephone booth, but it's the latter that Mr. Arnold Zohn's outer office reminds me of now, when I think back to that day in 1937. There were so many guys crowded into the room that for a few seconds I didn't realize what a triumph it was merely to have got through the door. Then I saw that the room was divided across the middle by a wooden fence, and I was on the crowded side. At the other side of the fence a good-looking girl at a desk was saying over and over again, in one of those purring voices that doesn't exactly bite but makes its point, "Mr. Zohn will be with you in a few minutes. Mr. Zohn will be with you in a few minutes. Mr. Zohn will be with you in a few minutes."

I took a quick look around. It's pretty hard to tell from the way a man's nose tilts whether he can "Add As Rapidly As an Adding Machine." Pimples, however, you don't need reading glasses to spot. I could see, from looking at the faces around me, that if Mr. Zohn had meant what he said about complexions in his ad, about half the guys in this outer office would never get to see his inner. Furthermore, a few of them either could not read, or did not believe he meant what the ad said: they had mustaches. In addition, at least half a dozen looked old enough to have marked their ballots for Woodrow Wilson, and while there were some who might have looked better educated than I did, I was all the way out in front on one specification in the ad: I was wearing the best suit in the room.

This assessment must have been pretty close to the one Mr. Zohn made when he came out of the inner office behind the girl at the desk and silently looked us over for what seemed to me a long weekend, but probably was no more than two or three minutes.

"You, you, you, you and you," he said finally, stabbing his forefinger across the wooden fence into different parts of the room. "Follow me, please."

I wasn't sure that one of the stabs was aimed at me. Only a bonehead, however, would have asked for clarification. So I elbowed my way through the crowd with the other four *you*'s. Mr. Zohn held the gate in the wooden fence open for us, then led the way into the inner office. At one end, under the windows that looked out on Forty-second Street, two desks sat side by side. Both could have been bought for the amount I'd paid for the bottom half of my suit. Both were unoccupied. At the other end of the room, under a wall of bookshelves loaded with volumes of the Prentice-Hall tax service, there was a long mahogany conference table with a glass top. Six chairs were set around the table: one at each end, two on each side. On the glass table top in front of each chair there was a sheet of

26

accounts-receivable ledger paper and a freshly sharpened pencil.

"If you will sit down, please, gentlemen," Mr. Zohn said.

As soon as I saw he was heading for the chair at the far end of the table, I steered for the one at the bottom end, and I made it. I wanted to keep an eye on Mr. Zohn's puss during whatever was going to happen, but I didn't want to have to turn my head to do it. People who interview other people for a job assume the interviewees are nervous. The guy who will stand out, therefore, is the boy with the Screw You attitude.

The four nervous *you*'s took the chairs at the sides of the table, which meant they were facing each other. That made me feel I was a couple of notches ahead already. Nothing in the shape or arrangement of any of those four faces could possibly be helpful to anybody, including their owners.

"When I give the signal," Mr. Zohn said, "you will turn over your ledger sheets and start adding. As soon as you have written down your total at the bottom of the column of figures, please raise your hand. Is that clear?"

While the others were mumbling their "Yes sirs," I noticed that Mr. Zohn had set a gold pocket watch on the table in front of him.

"Okay, then," he said. "Ready? Set? Go!"

I picked up my pencil and turned over my sheet. The debit side was blank. The dollars-and-cents column on the credit side was crowded with figures all the way down to the blue total line at the bottom. I scribbled "$1,247.38" under the blue line and raised my hand. Since I was staring directly at Mr. Zohn, I could see what my hand going up did to him. It gave him the look of a man who has been goosed with a pickle dipped in axle grease. "You're finished?" he said.

"Nonplussed" is the word Dickens would probably have used to describe the sound of Mr. Zohn's voice. I've found, however, that it's a mistake ever to borrow anything but money. So I'll let Dickens hold onto "nonplussed," and I'll stick to my own recollection that Mr. Zohn sounded like a small dog when you come up from behind and stamp down good and hard on his tail.

27

"Yes sir," I said.

I don't know how Dickens would have described what this reply did to the four jerks on my right and left. In the words of a more contemporary writer, who shall be nameless here because he possesses all the other attributes of a bastard, they looked as though they had been caught with their pants down.

"Very well," Mr. Zohn said. He dropped his popped eyes to the gold watch and made a note on his sheet. "I'll mark your time and wait until the others are finished."

The others went back to work. Keeping my eyes on my wrist watch, I noted that the first of the four to finish came in two minutes and ten seconds behind me. The other three then came in spread out. All the way from that first slob's two minutes ten, to four minutes and twenty-five. When the fourth shvantz finished, Mr. Zohn stood up, circled the table and picked up all our papers. He carried them back to the head of the table, sat down, studied the sheets for a while, then looked up.

"What is your name?" he said. He sent the question straight down the table toward me like a bowling ball heading for the pins.

"Leff," I said. "Theodore Leff."

"Will you remain here, Mr. Leff, please," Mr. Zohn said. "You other gentlemen, will you please go out and wait in the outer office, please? Thank you." When they were gone and the door was shut, Mr. Zohn said, "This figure you placed at the bottom of your ledger sheet, Mr. Leff. This one thousand, two forty-seven, point three eight. Is it your impression that you have set down the correct total for this column of figures?"

"Of course not," I said. I stood up and came down the table toward him. On the way I scooped up one of the chairs used by the guys who had just left the room. I set the chair at Mr. Zohn's elbow, sat down, took the ledger sheet on which I'd scribbled the cockamaymey total, and said, "Time me, please."

Mr. Zohn looked down at his watch and said, "Ready? Set? Go!"

I went. Without any doubt about the result. If I'd ever had any doubts in that area, I lost them all the way back in P. S. 188

while Miss Wien was telling the other members of my class that I was the fastest adder she had ever met. Without bragging, I can say I think her statement was accurate. I am a very fast adder. I always was. I stink on subtraction, but I can add like a Monroe calculator. I have never found this to be an inequitable balancing of talents. Men who can add usually do so. Guys who are good at subtraction, they end up with a row of zeros. On that day in 1937, in Mr. Zohn's private office, I ended up with a total of $2,532.91.

"Is that correct?" I said.

Mr. Zohn looked at the bottom of my sheet, then glanced at his own sheet and said, "Yes."

"How long did it take me?" I said.

Mr. Zohn examined the figure he had jotted down when I dropped my pencil. "Two minutes, eighteen seconds," he said.

I did the calculation in my head.

"That means," I said, "I beat the fastest of those other four chaps by almost a full minute."

Mr. Zohn stared at me in silence for a few moments. This did not surprise me. It's that word "chaps." I found it in the work of a very funny writer named Wodehouse. The first initials are P. G. You might jot them down. They will help you find his books. His books will help you deal with shlomboes like Arnold Zohn, who now said, "Did you know you could add this column of figures in two minutes eighteen seconds when you came into this room?"

"Not to the exact second, no," I said. "But I knew I could add it pretty damn fast. I've been a fast adder all my life. What I didn't know was how fast those other four chaps could add."

"In other words," Mr. Zohn said, "what you did, just jotting down any old figure at the bottom of the column, that was a trick? A trick to surprise the other men? Maybe even to scare them? So they'd get rattled and lose time?"

"You could put it that way," I said.

"Can you think of any other way to put it?" Mr. Zohn said.

The way he said it made me look at him more closely. I don't always remember to do this. I try to remind myself never to forget. Because there are people who tell you not to judge a book by its cover. Some of these people are probably right. I notice, however, that very few of them end up as chairman of the board at General Motors. The trouble is that there are times when the only thing you've got to judge that book by is its cover. There are times when you have to make a decision before you can read what's inside the book.

Mr. Zohn had just asked me a question. If I'd known more about Mr. Zohn than the way he looked, I'd have known better how to put together an answer. But all I had was the way he looked. This was not very helpful. Mr. Zohn looked the way most members of the human race look: a basic boob with peripheral variations.

Mr. Zohn's first noticeable variation was the kind of mustache I'd first seen on the upper lip of a man named Chaplin in a movie called *The Kid*. Mr. Zohn also had a long, thin head; the kind of beard that makes you think the owner mixes Waterman's blue-black ink with his shaving cream; a skullcap of tight little kinky black curls; eyes that looked like licorice gumdrops; and sucked-in cheeks.

There was, however, one other thing I knew about Mr. Zohn. The want ad he had written for the *Times*. In it, to what he wanted Mr. Zohn had devoted twenty-five of the fifty-three words for which he had paid out coin of the realm to the descendants of Adolph Ochs. *Young Man Wanted to Do Very Rapid Addition of Columns of Figures. Above All Must Be Able to Add As Rapidly As an Adding Machine.* To what he did *not* want, however, Mr. Zohn had devoted twenty-eight of those fifty-three words: *Must Be at Least Twenty-five. Boys and Older Men Not Wanted. Must Be Presentable. No Pimples. No Physical Deformities. No Mustache. Must Look Educated. Must Be Well Spoken.*

What this distribution told me was that inside the book called *Arnold Zohn* there might just possibly be a brain that worked a little bit like mine.

"You can put it this way, Mr. Zohn," I said. "Just from reading your ad, I could tell you were interested in someone who had more on the ball than just the ability to add figures fast. It sounded like the kind of job I'm looking for. The way I figured it, I figured if I played fair, if I just sat down and added away like those four other men, one of them might turn out to be a faster adder than I am. I'm glad to learn that this is not true and I'm faster than they are, but I didn't know that when I sat down at this table with them, and I didn't want to take a chance on losing a job I wanted to have very much. What I mean is, Mr. Zohn, after all, I didn't do anything these other four men couldn't have done. It's called thinking."

Mr. Zohn stared at me for a few moments out of those black gumdrop eyes. I noticed something else. His eyelids didn't blink. Not even when he turned to the phone and picked it up.

"Miss A," he said. "Clear the outer office. The position has been filled." Mr. Zohn put down the phone, turned back to me and said, "Where did you get that suit?"

"Kolmer-Marcus," I said.

"They don't have anything on their racks for less than seventy-five dollars," Mr. Zohn said.

"This one didn't come off the racks," I said. "It's custom-made. One-two-five, with one pair of pants."

"How come a young man in a hundred-and-twenty-five-dollar suit is applying for a twenty-dollar-a-week job?"

I took another chance.

"I'm not," I said. "I don't work for twenty dollars a week." I stood up. "But I want the job because I've always been interested in accountancy. I intend to make accountancy my career. Thanks for giving me so much of your time. I'll go look for somebody who can afford to pay what I'm willing to work for."

I turned and started for the door.

"Stop the crap," Mr. Zohn said.

I turned back in surprise. The schmuck talked English.

"I don't think my mother would like me to work in an office where people use language like that," I said.

"Is your mother alive?" Mr. Zohn said.

"No," I said. "But I am guided by her principles."

"So how much will you work for?" he said.

"How much can you afford?" I said.

"At the moment," Mr. Zohn said, "not too much. But I'm moving into an area where I'm sure things are going to be better. They might even become very big. I think they could get big for whoever is with me. If you don't squeeze me for too much now, I'll more than make it up to you later."

"I may not live till later," I said. "Right now it costs me sixty a week to get through from Monday to Monday. You can have me for that, Mr. Zohn."

"Okay," he said. "But don't tell Miss A."

"Why not?" I said.

"She's my wife," he said. "And I promised her I wouldn't pay more than thirty."

4

" You Don't Look to Me Like the Sort of Man Who Does His Own Cooking"

She should have made him promise not to tell me what I was supposed to do for the money. It might have changed his life. But he did tell me, and it sure as hell changed mine.

"I've got this new client," Mr. Zohn said to me. "Mattlin & Merritt, down on Fourth Avenue."

Again there was something in his voice. It threw the switch on my memory box. Mr. Zohn reminded me of the way my mother had sounded, years ago, when she was telling our neighbors down on East Fourth Street that we had decided to move to the Bronx. Whoever Mattlin & Merritt were, they clearly represented a step up in the world for Arnold Zohn.

"What do they do?" I said. "This new client?"

"They manufacture puzzles," Mr. Zohn said.

If puzzles were a step upward, there could be only one place out of which my new boss was moving.

"You have any clients in the garment center?" I said.

I don't know how, with that face and the equipment attached to it, Mr. Zohn managed to look surprised, but he did.

"How did you know?" he said.

How did Stanley know it was Livingstone?

"I've worked in the area," I said. The look on his face indicated pretty clearly that he did not consider this a recommendation. "That's why I decided to become an accountant," I said quickly. "The accountants were the only people I met on Seventh Avenue who had any class."

From the way the look on this walyo's face changed, I knew I wasn't going to have any trouble handling Arnold Zohn.

"It's a profession that attracts good people," he said. I figured he could say it again. After all, look who it had just attracted. "They can't always choose their clients," Mr. Zohn said. "I mean when you're a young man, and you're just starting out, you're grateful for anybody who comes along and wants to pay you for your services, no matter what business they're in."

I suddenly found myself wondering how young a man this specimen was. Death's-heads are not like trees. You can't slice out a cross section and count the rings. Arnold Zohn had obviously looked the way he looked now on the day he was circumcised. He would probably look this way on the day FDR stopped running for President, which could be never. My new boss might have been twenty. He could have been fifty. My mind jumped to Miss A in the outer office. I hadn't paid too much attention to her on the way in because of the scrimmage I'd walked into. Now the old memory box flashed a slide on the screen inside my head. There she was, all one hundred ten pounds of her. Every ounce in exactly the right place. Miss A, or Mrs. Zohn, I was willing to bet, had not yet voted in a national election. Why, I was suddenly asking myself, would a twenty-year-old chick who looked like that, marry a man who looked like my new boss? I made a mental note to find the answer. I do it all the time. It's a better habit than calisthenics.

"You mean," I said, "you're dropping your garment-center clients for this Mattlin & Merritt?"

"Not exactly," Mr. Zohn said. "But ultimately I hope to."

"In that case," I said, "I'd guess there must be more money on Fourth Avenue than there is on Seventh."

"That's what my wife thinks," Mr. Zohn said. Then he

seemed to think he had said too much. He touched the little square of mustache under his nose as though to stop it from twitching. "Well now, look," he said crisply. "We might as well get down there."

He stood up. I followed him into the outer office. The scrimmage was over. Miss A was alone in the room. She looked up from her typewriter.

"This is Mr. Leff," her husband said. "Theodore Leff. He's our new assistant. Mr. Leff, this is my wife. Here in the office we call her Miss A."

"Why?" I said.

Mr. Zohn managed to do it again. He looked surprised. Not his wife. "Because my maiden name is Applebaum," she said.

"There's an Applebaum's around the corner from where I live," I said. "I buy my groceries there."

"You don't look to me like the sort of man who does his own cooking," she said.

There was something about Mrs. Zohn that I was beginning to like, and it wasn't just what she was carrying around in her blouse.

"I don't," I said. "But when a friend drops in who does, I like to have the makings on hand."

"Stay out of Applebaum's," Miss A said, "and you'll find whatever salary my husband has agreed to pay you will go further. They have an unwritten store rule that whenever a bachelor or any man is shopping alone, a penny is added to each item as the checker punches the price into the cash register."

"No kid?" I said.

"Fact," Miss A said.

"How do you know that?" I said.

"My father owns the Applebaum chain," she said.

I began to like Mrs. Zohn better. Even at that time there were close to a hundred Applebaum stores in the New York area. It said so in their ads.

"What do you think?" Mr. Zohn said. He said it to her.

35

"Can he add?" Miss A said. She said it to him.

"He beat the other four men by almost a full minute," Mr. Zohn said.

"That's a pretty sharp suit he's wearing," she said.

"Do you want me to leave the room?" I said. "I don't want to inhibit you in this frank discussion of my virtues."

"You're not inhibiting me, Mr. Leff," she said. "And I'm not discussing your virtues. I'm discussing that suit."

"What's the matter with this suit?" I said.

"I'm sure it knocked them dead on Seventh Avenue," Miss A said. "I'm also sure my husband told you why he hired you. On Fourth Avenue that little number might knock him out of the box."

I not only liked her. I didn't know how to figure her. Miss A looked like one of those girls you saw in the Sunday rotogravure sections, weaving the daisy chain on the Vassar campus. It had never occurred to me until this moment that maybe they made those girls take a course in "How to Talk Like James Cagney Telling the Mob What's What."

Miss A snapped her fingers and turned to her husband. "I've got it," she said. "Arnold, take off your tie."

"My tie?" he said.

"If you repeat everything I say," she said, "you'll be late for your appointment. Take off your tie." He started to loosen the knot. Miss A turned to me. "You take off yours too," she said.

"Why?" I said.

"I want you to exchange ties," she said. "Just for the day."

I hesitated, then figured why not? I could go back to work on my pride after I'd reestablished a nice steady incoming flow of blintzes. Sixty a week was sixty more than I'd had coming in for a long time. I took off my tie.

Miss A stepped across to a green metal locker and opened the door. It was full of stacks of letterheads and pads of analysis paper and boxes of envelopes, but it was also obviously her dressing room. A dime-store mirror was hanging on the inside of the door.

"You first," she said to Mr. Zohn. He stepped to the mirror, put my tie around his neck and went to work on the knot.

"Now you," Miss A said to me.

I stepped to the mirror, put her husband's tie around my neck and knotted it. A funny thing happened. Even before I finished tying the knot, the suit began to look better. It was a gray Glen plaid. I'd picked the Spitalfield to go with it because I thought the matching colors were just right on a guy applying for a job. Mr. Zohn was wearing a brown herringbone, and he'd obviously chosen the black knitted tie to go with it because he knew as much about clothes as he knew about the people he hired. Once a dope, always a dope. His wife, however, this sexy Mrs. Zohn with the ball-bearing trap, no dope she. The black knitted tie went with my gray Glen plaid the way Ruby Keeler went with Al Jolson.

"The suit is still sharp," Miss A said. "But now you look a little more Fourth Avenue than Seventh."

"They could use you on the staff of that magazine," I said. *"Esquire."*

"They could use someone," she said. "Everybody in their ads keeps looking like Clark Gable."

"I never thought I looked like Clark Gable," I said. "But I'm closer to it wearing this tie than the one I came in here with."

She gave me one of those looks that seem to start from a windup at the other side of the room. When she figured it had picked up enough speed, Miss A aimed it right at my bull's-eye and said, "That's not close enough, Mr. Leff."

Her husband started spitting out a series of small coughing noises. He could have had one of those New Year's Eve noise-makers in his throat. Mr. Zohn had obviously seen his bride in action before. "We better get going," he said.

"Add good, boys," Miss A said as we went to the door.

I waited until her husband and I were outside and around the bend of the corridor. Then I said, "What are we going to add?"

"A set of books," Mr. Zohn said.

I let it go until we were out in the street.

"You said this Mattlin & Merritt, it's a new client," I said. "So I guess you want to make a good impression."

Mr. Zohn gave me one of those looks his wife had just pitched upstairs. Anyway, he tried. But he wasn't in her league.

"Naturally I want to make a good impression," he said. "What kind of remark is that?"

It's known as a left jab, stupid. Now here comes the right cross.

"You're walking in on a new client with a new employee like me," I said. "I don't think you want to tell them I'm a new employee because it'll look as though you hired me just to impress them. Or even worse, they'll think a completely inexperienced guy is being put to work on their books. If I was Mattlin & Merritt, or even one of them, I don't think I'd like that. You see what I mean?"

"Sure, of course," Mr. Zohn said. The mustache did another little jig. "But I don't understand where you're going with all this."

To the bank, schmuck. To the bank. If I could only find the way.

"I'm just trying to put myself in the picture a little more clearly," I said. "So I'll know what I'm doing when I get to this Mattlin & Merritt. What I mean, Mr. Zohn, if you'd answer a couple of simple questions I feel I can do a better job for you."

"What kind of questions?" he said.

"Like how come you say you can't afford to pay me even the sixty a week you're going to pay me, but your wife, Miss A, her father owns the Applebaum chain of grocery stores?"

By this time we were going down the subway steps, so I couldn't see his face. When we reached the turnstiles, he said, "Pay your own fare and keep a record of it. At the end of the week, you make out a petty-cash slip and give it to Miss A, and she'll pay you back all your expenses."

He went through first. Just then the warning bell rang for a shuttle train about to get going. He started to run. I ran after him. We made it. But it wasn't until we were sitting down in the half-empty train that I could see his face. Mr. Zohn looked

38

embarrassed. Lots of people look like that when they find themselves doing something unfamiliar. Like thinking.

"It's this way," he said finally. "My wife's father's money is my wife's father's money, not mine. I'm going to make it on my own. The two years we've been married, we've managed pretty well. Especially with I don't have to hire a secretary or somebody to answer the switchboard. My wife's father, he's offered lots of times to help, but I always said no, and my wife agrees. Even though she's been raised very fancy and she's all her life been accustomed to money, also real luxury, she feels it's her duty to stand at my side. No help with money, that's her motto as well as mine. Helping out with money, that's definitely out. But helping out with business? He can throw a client my way? That's different. I'd be a fool not to take it, and my wife agrees. She's a very unusual girl. Not many girls raised the way she was raised, with a college education too, would come to an office day after day and work as their husband's secretary. Her mother thinks she's crazy, and so does her father, but my wife doesn't care. She makes up her own mind."

I had a feeling this didn't take her long, and Miss A spent at least some of her spare time making up his. The train banged into the Grand Central end of the most efficient little liver shaker put together by Western man. I could hardly wait to get rich so I could start riding around in taxis again.

"Is that how you got this Mattlin & Merritt?" I said. "Through Mr. Applebaum?"

But I was talking to the back of his brown herringbone. Mr. Zohn was running again. Maybe if Bebe Daniels had met this guy she wouldn't have lost her head over Charlie Paddock. I sprinted after my new boss. When we were sitting beside each other in the downtown local, I tried again.

"Is that how you got this new client?" I said. "Through your father-in-law?"

"Mr. Applebaum has a very diversified portfolio," my new boss said. "The grocery stores are merely the one property he owns on which his name appears. This Mattlin & Merritt, when they went into business three years ago, Mr. Applebaum put up one third of the money, and he took stock for it in the corporation. Unfortunately, the company hasn't been doing well, and nobody seems to know why. I mean, they got off to a great start, and they're selling an awful lot of puzzles, a real substantial gross they've got, but they're always short of cash. Last week, when they came to Mr. Applebaum for a loan, he said not until he had the books audited by a new accountant. He doesn't trust the man Mattlin & Merritt have been using. So Mr. Applebaum told them I was coming in to do a complete audit."

I could see my sixty bucks a week beginning to disappear over the horizon like a dog sled in one of those Warner Brothers movies about Jack London and the Yukon.

"Then it's really not a client?" I said. "It's just a kind of test? If you turn in a good job, maybe they'll keep you on as the regular accountant?"

"No, I'm positive Mattlin & Merritt will keep me on," Mr. Zohn said. "There's no maybes about it."

"Because they're scared of Mr. Applebaum?" I said. "Is that it?"

He said something, but I didn't hear the words, because the train was slamming into the station and the doors were banging open, and Mr. Zohn was breaking away from the barrier again. I raced after him.

"I'm sorry," I said when I caught up with Mr. Zohn on the subway steps leading to the street. "I didn't get that."

"You asked if I was positive I had the Mattlin & Merritt account nailed down on a permanent basis because they're scared of Mr. Applebaum," he said.

"Well," I said, "maybe I shouldn't have used a word like 'scared.' All I meant, Mr. Zohn, I meant—"

"I know what you meant," he said. "And I don't blame you for drawing that conclusion." He touched the mustache, as though to make sure it hadn't fallen off during the last heat. "My father-in-law owns one third of the Mattlin & Merritt stock, so naturally you assume they'll do anything he wants them to do, especially since they've already agreed to his insist-

40

ing that they take me on for this investigation audit. But that's not the reason why I'm positive they will keep me on as their regular accountant."

"What is the reason?" I said.

"Mr. Mattlin is a gentleman," said Arnold Zohn.

5

The Reward of the General Is Not a Bigger Tent, But Command

Perhaps he was. No. I'll do better than that. I'll eliminate the "perhaps." After all these years I think I can stick with the word Arnold Zohn used. Ralph Mattlin was a gentleman. It's not much of an achievement. Anybody will call you a gentleman if you lend him money at a reasonable rate, use a handkerchief when you blow your nose, and refrain from goosing his wife in public. What surprised me on that day in 1937 was a good square look at the arena in which a gentleman like Ralph Mattlin functioned.

They've changed the name to Park Avenue South. And they've put an island down the middle of the street to separate the northbound traffic from the southbound. And they've dotted the island with cement tubs that look like septic tanks full of last year's thrown-out Christmas trees. But they're not fooling anybody. Not me, anyway. It's still Fourth Avenue. And it still looks the way it looked before they started tearing the city apart. The way it looked on that day in 1937 when I met Ralph Mattlin for the first time: like a length of not very good salami connecting one of the city's garbage pails, Union Square, with one of its medals: Park Avenue.

It was the sight of this street, when Arnold Zohn and I came up out of the subway, that suddenly made me come awake. Not that I'd been asleep. In those days, before I knew what a hangover was, I came out of bed on my toes and stayed on them all day long. What I mean is that I had just landed a job, and I was interested in where it was taking me. The sight of Fourth Avenue suddenly made me realize I might have to revise my thinking about the places jobs could take you.

I'd known Fourth Avenue all my life, but I'd never thought about it. Until that day Fourth Avenue was just a place through which I walked once in a while when I was a kid saving carfare on my way uptown. A street through which, when I was making it for a while in the garment center, a taxi sometimes carried me on my way to one of the big downtown piece-goods houses where I was going to do some fancy talking in the hope of lining up some more credit.

On this day in 1937, however, it was different. I'd just spent a couple of hours with Arnold Zohn and his wife, Miss A. He had made it plain that he couldn't wait to get rid of his crappy Seventh Avenue clients and start life all over again among the classy inhabitants of Fourth Avenue. She had made me change my tie so my Seventh Avenue suit wouldn't offend the delicate schnozzolas that did their sniffing on Fourth. Without being aware of it, all the way downtown with Arnold Zohn, I had been feeling like Orphan Annie heading for her first interview with Daddy Warbucks.

Then I came out into the street, and I took a good square look at Fourth Avenue, and I asked myself: *This is moving up in the world?*

It looked exactly like Seventh Avenue. The same dirty old loft buildings. The same great big store windows full of bolts of piece goods. The same kind of beat-up big square trucks parked on the side streets. The same smell and feel that you'd walked into a great big armpit.

"Mattlin & Merritt are in three ninety-six," Mr. Zohn said. "On the Twenty-ninth Street corner."

He started for the Twenty-ninth Street corner like Reigh

Count coming into the stretch at Churchill Downs. By the time I caught up with him at the revolving door under the foot-high brass numerals "396," I'd passed a bank, a luncheonette, a manufacturer of paper boxes, a display of pink and green paisley silk fighting it out for my attention with a bolt of blue velveteen, a window full of beaded passementerie, a button company, and a store that sold outboard motors. Mr. Zohn pushed me into a pie slice of the revolving door, hopped into the one behind me and shoved so hard that I came shooting out into the narrow brown lobby the way a wet orange pip comes out from a squeeze between a thumb and forefinger.

"Are we late?" I said.

Mr. Zohn looked at his wrist watch. "No, early," he said. Then he seemed to catch up with the sandpaper in my voice. On any other face, what happened would have been described as a blush. On Mr. Zohn's kisser it was more like when you're watching an eclipse of the sun through a piece of smoked glass and the two balls cross. "I'm sorry," he said. "I guess I'm a little nervous."

This gave me something to wonder about as the elevator carried us up to the sixth floor. Here was a guy married to a tomato whose father was not only loaded, but kept trying to spray the stuff all over his son-in-law. He had just been handed a client in which the old man owned one third of the stock, and apparently all Mr. Zohn had to do to hold onto the account was not stop breathing. As for the physical surroundings in which this new client functioned, I had just discovered they were no different from the ashcan called Seventh Avenue which until now had been to Mr. Zohn what those signs in the museums call a natural habitat. What the hell was there to be nervous about?

"Remember," Mr. Zohn said as we got out of the elevator. "Let me do the talking."

"You bet," I said.

I had no idea yet when the time would come for me to do the talking, but I was pretty sure it would. At the moment I had nothing to say. All I had to do was follow. I followed Arnold Zohn into a long and narrow hall. At one end, toward the back

44

of the building, there was the sort of dark green metal door through which I had spent the first seven years of my life, after I got out of Thomas Jefferson High, shoving my way back and forth. It had a single word painted on it in black letters: SHIPPING.

If you ever get invited to deliver a commencement address, and you want to give the boys and girls Standing on the Threshold a piece of advice that will do them some good, here it is: "Any time you see a door marked 'Shipping,' don't go through it." Doors marked "Shipping" do not lead to the rooms with wall-to-wall carpeting in which the boys who split financial melons gather for the cutting-up ceremonies.

Even today, now that I've got my eating money safely tucked away in tax-free municipals, when I see one of those doors I do what I did on that day in 1937: I turn and head in the opposite direction.

This led to a set of double doors at the Fourth Avenue side of the building. On both of them appeared the same set of words, arranged in a small arc, like the little crown you see Napoleon putting on his head when he made himself Emperor in the textbook out of which Miss Schlissel taught me Modern European History. The words were: MATTLIN & MERRITT, INC. I followed Arnold Zohn through these doors into a reception room.

In the garment center there's no such thing as a reception room, except maybe for the few doctors in the area who handle workmen's compensation cases. In the average dress house you go directly from the elevator into the showroom. Sometimes, if the firm is cramped for office space, they'll stick a switchboard into a corner of the showroom, just inside the front door, and invest a dollar in a "Reception" sign so when you come in, the girl handling the plugs can hit you with a "Whom did you wish to see?" It's a pretty foolish question, of course. Nobody comes to a dress house to get their teeth filled. But you give a broad from Bushwick Avenue a chance to say "whom" and she gives it a lifted-pinky workout that could raise the rent.

The girl who was sitting behind the Mattlin & Merritt reception desk looked as if she'd never heard of Bushwick Avenue. And what she was sitting behind was only partly a reception desk. She looked like one of those plump little sexy numbers you see in the grocery department at Macy's who offer the passing customer a sample of some new kind of cheese a Danish firm is trying to get the American public hipped on, and what she was sitting behind was a small fort. The sort of thing we used to build out of old lumber in an empty lot on East Fourth Street.

One side of the fort, the side facing the front doors, was a billing machine. The side to the right was a secretary's desk, with the kind of typewriter that sinks like a sidewalk elevator at night, and comes up for action in the morning the way Jesse Crawford's organ used to rise at the Paramount. The side to the girl's left was a window cut into the wall at the level of her head, and through it I could see what looked like part of a Ping-Pong table covered with stacks of mail.

"May I help you?" she said.

I began to get a hint of what it was that made Mr. Zohn think he was moving up in the world by coming downtown. On Seventh Avenue I had never heard anybody say, "May I help you?" Maybe they were scared of the answer. I certainly know the one they would have got from me.

Arnold Zohn said, "I have an appointment with Mr. Mattlin."

"And your name, please?"

"Zohn," he said. "Arnold Zohn."

"As in temperate?" she said.

"What?" he said.

"*Z-o-n-e?*"

"No," he said. "*Z-o-h-n.*"

"And this gentleman is with you?"

"Yes, this is Mr. Leff."

As in torrid. I liked the look of this little Scandinavian butterball.

"One moment, please." The girl picked up a phone and said, "Miss Eitner, please." Pause. Then: "Maud? Two gentlemen to

46

see Mr. Mattlin? Mr. Zohn? And Mr. Leff? All right." She hung up. "Won't you sit down for a moment, please?"

"Thank you," Mr. Zohn said.

What we sat down on was a fumed oak bench that could have been lifted from the waiting room outside the office of Mr. O'Connor, my old principal in P. S. 188. In fact, if it were not for that window next to the left ear of the girl behind the billing-machine fort, I could have been back there in P. S. 188, watching O'Connor's secretary, Miss Brust, typing the old bastard's letters, wondering what he had on me today, and waiting for the buzzer that always goosed Miss Brust into saying, "All right, Ted, you can go in now."

On the wall in Mr. O'Connor's waiting room there had been a framed statement in Gothic type: THE MEASURE OF A MAN'S REAL CHARACTER IS WHAT HE WOULD DO IF HE KNEW HE WOULD NEVER BE FOUND OUT. On the wall facing me now in the Mattlin & Merritt waiting room hung a framed sentence in the same kind of type:

THE REWARD OF THE GENERAL
IS NOT A BIGGER TENT, **BUT**
COMMAND.
O. W. Holmes, Jr.

On a table under this framed sentence there was a curious structure that looked like one of those houses of cards that a bored guy with a casino deck in the movies builds on the old green baize while he waits for the other players to arrive. Except that these cards were about five or six times as large as the ones with which suckers I've met are always trying to fill an inside straight. Also, these cards did not have spades, hearts, diamonds or clubs on their faces.

What they had on their faces were scenes. The sort of scenes you see in paintings, or in newspaper photographs, or in movie fan magazines. There was George Washington on the steps of the Sub-Treasury Building in Wall Street, taking the oath of office as our first President. Under him Pocahontas was saving

Captain John Smith. On Smith's left Carole Lombard was in a clinch with Clark Gable. Above Clark, Shipwreck Kelly was eating a sandwich on top of one of the flagpoles he was always climbing. In front of the flagpole Babe Ruth was pointing to the fence in Chicago over which he was about to clout the next pitch for that famous homer. And the card nearest me showed Judge Samuel Seabury putting the hard words to Jimmy Walker on the witness stand.

There were lots of other scenes, but these were the only ones I could recognize from where I was sitting, and I didn't want to get up for a closer look. I wanted the girl behind the fort to think I visited offices like this every day in the week. What she actually was thinking I did not find out until much later, because just then a door at the left of the fort opened and another girl came in. "Mr. Zohn?" she said.

He stood up. So did I.

"Yes," Zohn said.

"I'm Maud Eitner," she said. "Mr. Mattlin's secretary? I didn't mean to keep you waiting, but I wanted him to see you, and he's been delayed uptown at the doctor's. Since I don't know how long he'll be, it occurred to me there's no point in waiting any longer and wasting your working day, so won't you come in? I'll put you in Mr. Nachman's office, and you can get started."

"Thank you very much," Mr. Zohn said. We went through the door Miss Eitner was holding open for us. "You said he's at the doctor? Mr. Mattlin?"

"Yes," she said.

"I hope it's nothing serious?" Mr. Zohn said.

"Oh no," Miss Eitner said. "Mr. Mattlin stops in three mornings a week on his way down to the office. When he made this appointment with you, he probably forgot that this was one of his Dr. Yustin days."

Three times a week to the doctor? Mr. Mattlin sounded pregnant.

"We don't want to put Mr. Nachman out of his room," Mr.

48

Zohn said. "Mr. Leff and I can work anywhere, so long as there's enough space to spread out the books and records."

"There's no better place to work than the room in which the books and records are kept," Miss Eitner said.

"But won't we be in Mr. Nachman's way?" Mr. Zohn said.

"Not today," Miss Eitner said. "I told him last night Mr. Mattlin had decided to repaint the offices, and I felt it would be best to start with the Bookkeeping Department, so I told him he could have the next three days off."

I was suddenly struck by the number of *I*'s in that sentence. Miss Eitner was pushing open a door with a glazed glass panel on which was painted: BOOKKEEPING DEPARTMENT. She did it the way I was sure she opened the door of her house: without any hesitation about whom it belonged to. The garment district is full of secretaries who run their bosses as well as the joints they work in. It began to look as though I'd bumped into another similarity between Fourth Avenue and Seventh.

"Is there anything I can get you?" Miss Eitner said when we were inside the Bookkeeping Department.

It was about the size of the waiting room. There was a tall iron safe against one wall, a worktable in the middle, a coatrack in one corner, and a few cheap straight-backed chairs around the table. Between the two windows that looked out on Fourth Avenue was the only piece of furniture that interested me. The kind of roll-top desk I had seen only once before: in the picture of the Cheeryble brothers' office in the copy of *Nicholas Nickleby* from which Miss Marine used to read aloud to us in English class at Thomas Jefferson High.

"No, I don't think so, thank you," Mr. Zohn said. "If the safe is open, I guess we can get started."

"Fine, yes, I opened it a few minutes ago," Miss Eitner said. She went back to the door and turned. "Do you think you can complete your audit in three days?"

"I'm not sure," Mr. Zohn said. "Does Mr. Mattlin want it finished in three days?"

"No, no," she said. "I merely meant if you need more time, I can arrange to have Mr. Nachman stay out of your way for another day or two."

"Thank you, but I really don't think that will be necessary," Mr. Zohn said. "There's plenty of room in here for him as well as us."

Thus I knew that when I guessed, in those first minutes of our meeting, that I had just been hired by a putz, I had guessed right. Anybody can miss a point. It takes a Stupidity Major to put English on the miss.

"Well, just the same," Miss Eitner said, "I think I'll keep him out of your way."

She said it with a smile. Smiles do not necessarily always improve a face, and there were probably people who felt Miss Eitner's face did not need improving. At the risk of losing my reputation for chivalry, I must say these people could not have been in the majority.

Miss Eitner was no Toby Wing. But she was no Lon Chaney playing Quasimodo, either. Her hair was black, and she wore it piled high on her head. This exposed her ears, and showed how smart she was. They were good ears. At first glance her face was not so good, but if you took a second glance you saw something interesting. It was all lines, no two of them running parallel, so that her face looked as though a kid had dropped a handful of pieces from his Meccano set on the floor, and somebody had said that's it, don't touch the arrangement. Miss Eitner wore no make-up, and if she had let Stan Laurel borrow her figure, nobody would have known the difference. But anybody who didn't know something else was as dumb as my new boss, who clearly didn't know it: Miss Maud Eitner didn't take crap from anybody.

There are homely people, and there are homely people, and she clearly could have been ticketed in either group. But because it was even more clear from the way she held herself that Miss Eitner didn't give a damn about what anybody thought of the way she looked, you looked twice. If you had any brains, that is. Don't write off these plain Janes with no meat on them. They start from further back, so they learn to run faster. When they get there, and if you happen to be standing around when they do, you could learn a few things. You might jot that down.

"If you want anything, just pick up the phone and I'll be along," Miss Eitner said. "When Mr. Mattlin arrives, I'll have him stop in to say hello."

She walked out and closed the door.

"That's some broad," I said.

Mr. Zohn took the little stab at his mustache. I was beginning to see that this was his signature. Like Pierre Laval's white tie.

"What do you mean?" he said.

"It's like you're asked to come to the palace in St. Petersburg to do a little sweeping," I said, "and when you get there you're met at the door by Catherine the Great with instructions how to handle a broom."

Mr. Zohn took another swing at the blob of black fur under his nose, but it didn't help. "I don't understand," he said.

He could say that again.

"I mean she seems sort of bossy."

"Well, she's been here since the firm started," Mr. Zohn said. "Let's get started."

He took off his coat and hung it across the back of one of the straight chairs. Then he went to the black iron safe and pulled open the heavy door. The shelves inside were jammed with the sort of red and white sprackle-edged ledgers my safe used to be jammed with when I was in the dress business. I began to feel more at home. I took off my coat. As I turned to hang it across a chair, my eye caught something standing on top of the roll-top desk. It was leaning against the wall under a framed print of a guy with white side whiskers who clearly did not belong in this century. I stepped across to the desk and saw from a small brass plate in the frame that the guy with the fuzz was William Makepeace Thackeray, and the thing leaning against the wall under him was one of those cards I'd seen out in the reception room on the table near the fort. I picked up the scene showing Pocahontas saving Captain John Smith, and I saw two more things. The card was not a card. It was a jigsaw puzzle, and it was wrapped in cellophane. "Is this what they sell?" I said.

Mr. Zohn was pulling a ledger out of the safe. "Who?" he said.

Where did this idiot think we were? In the office of Alfred P. Sloan at General Motors?

"This outfit," I said, holding up the picture of Pocahontas and Captain John Smith. "Mattlin & Merritt?"

"I don't understand," Mr. Zohn said.

Those three words seemed to be this boy's *e pluribus unum*.

"When you said they sold puzzles," I said, "I thought you meant like two twisted nails, locked together. See if you can pull them apart. Or those things with a glass top. You have to tip the little balls into the holes."

"Oh no," Mr. Zohn said. "Only jigsaws."

"How come I never saw them anywhere around?" I said. "You say they sell a lot of them."

"They sell them only in bookstores."

That could explain it. The last time I'd been in a bookstore, I'd gone down to Barnes & Noble during my sophomore year in Thomas Jefferson High to buy a trot for *Tartarin de Tarascon*.

"Why don't they sell them in other kinds of stores?" I said. "Like toy stores, say? Or drugstores? Or even in Applebaum's? Any kind of store?"

"Because Mattlin & Merritt are publishers," Mr. Zohn said. "They don't make toothpaste or cornflakes. They make books. Anyway, they started to."

"What stopped them?"

"They were all flops," Mr. Zohn said. "The first few books they published, they lost their shirts."

"Including your father-in-law's?" I said.

"He's got extras," Mr. Zohn said.

I gave him a quick look. Could it be, under all that brain fat, a sense of humor was hiding?

"So how come they switched from publishing books to turning out these things?"

"It was Mr. Mattlin's idea," Mr. Zohn said. "He's got this friend, he's crazy about jigsaw puzzles. Mattlin was visiting him one day—I think he put up some money when Mattlin and Mr. Merritt started the firm—and he was working one, a jigsaw puzzle. I think the way Mr. Applebaum told me the story, Mr. Mattlin was actually up there to explain to his friend why they'd lost so much money, and he said to him—Mr. Mattlin's friend —he said he wasn't surprised they'd lost money, nobody reads books any more. There was so much dust and soot and carbon monoxide in the air, he said, people's eyes were getting ruined without reading, so why should they spend money on books to ruin them some more? What people wanted, he said, they wanted something to do that wouldn't hurt their eyes—and right there in front of him, in front of Mr. Mattlin, there right in front of him was his friend doing one of these things that didn't hurt the eyes. The next morning, when Mr. Mattlin came into the office, he had a conference with Mr. Merritt and, well, like my father-in-law, Mr. Applebaum, says, the rest is history."

"What part of it?" I said. "Waterloo?"

"I don't understand," Mr. Zohn said.

You tell a boob he can say it again, so he does.

"I mean this outfit can't be doing very well with these puzzles, or we wouldn't be here doing this audit."

"If we don't get started," Mr. Zohn said, "we'll never get it done." He put the ledger down on the table and opened it. "This is a cash-payments books."

It was like pointing out Manila Bay to Admiral Dewey. But I wasn't ready yet to reel this boy in, so I said politely, "I see."

"The first thing I want to establish is that all the entries made in this book are added up correctly," Mr. Zohn said.

During my time on Seventh Avenue my own bookkeeper had filled up half a dozen of these books with figures about my own business, but I said even more politely, "May I ask why?"

"It would take too long to explain," Mr. Zohn said. "I'll tell you some other time. Right now, just start adding."

I did, and he tackled the general ledger. I thought this was a mistake. By noon I was sure of it. In doing an audit, the story is not in the monthly totals posted from the subsidiary records to the general ledger. The story is to be found in the subsidiary records themselves. In this case, the cash-payments book. It's a trick I learned on Seventh Avenue when the accountants for the Receiver in Bankruptcy tied the tin can to my tail. The lesson had cost me plenty. I decided to keep it to myself.

After a while Mr. Zohn looked up, glanced at his watch and said, "How about a sandwich?"

When a boss makes this democratic remark, what he's really saying is: in this outfit, buster, there's none of this full-hour-for-lunch crap.

"I never eat in the middle of the day," I said. Not when I'm on the track of something that looked as though it might be fun after sundown. "But you go right ahead, Mr. Zohn," I said. "I'll stay with this, and maybe I can wrap it up by five o'clock."

"I forgot to tell you," Arnold Zohn said. "In my office the hours are nine to six."

"I won't forget," I said.

He went out, and I stepped on the gas. By the time he came back, twenty minutes later, chewing a toothpick, I was beginning to get a picture.

"Mr. Mattlin show up?" he said.

"Nope," I said. "Maybe he's being operated on?"

"What?"

The words came out on the wings of a belch. Before the smoke cleared away, I'd practically shared his corned beef on rye with him. He'd put on too much mustard.

"Miss Eitner said he drops in on his doctor three mornings a week before he comes to the office," I said. "It's now a quarter to one. Looks like a pretty long morning."

"Maybe he had to stop off in some other place today," Mr. Zohn said. "Let's get to work."

I bent over and picked up the toothpick he'd lost with the belch. "Here," I said. "I believe this is yours."

"That's all right," Arnold Zohn said. "I've got another."

He took the toothpick I was holding out, dropped it in the wastebasket, and sat down. He pulled a fresh toothpick from his pocket and stuck it into his mouth. He bent over the general ledger. I went back to work on the cash-payments book. When the phone rang, I looked at my watch. Five minutes to six.

Mr. Zohn took the call. "Hello? Yes." Pause. Then again, "Hello?"

The difference in tone between the two hellos told me the first one had gone to the office operator, and now the voice at the other end belonged to Mr. Zohn's wife.

"Well yes, we made a pretty good dent," he said to Miss A. "Yes, I think he's going to work out. He adds very quickly, and he doesn't eat in the middle of the day. That's right. He didn't go out to lunch. That's right. He worked right through."

It was a funny feeling. I could have been a slab of steak they were examining in a butcher shop and trying to make a decision about buying.

"No," Mr. Zohn said into the phone. "Because he didn't show up today. No, not even in the afternoon. Miss Eitner said he was stopping off at the doctor on the way to the office, but he didn't show up all day. No, I don't know why. What? Well, I'm not so sure that's a good idea. In fact, I don't think I'd better. She sort of runs the place, you know, and I don't want to antagonize her by asking questions. She could say it's none of my business why her boss didn't show up today. What? No, I won't be late. It's almost six. We'll be leaving in a few minutes. What? Okay, sure. I'll tell him."

He hung up.

"Tell me what?" I said.

"She wants you to give me back my tie." He started to loosen the one around his neck that I'd swapped with him in the morning.

"Couldn't I keep yours overnight?" I said. "I'll give it back to you tomorrow."

"Why?" Mr. Zohn said.

55

"I've got a date tonight," I said. "I'd like her to see how much better this suit looks on me with this tie your wife made me wear."

He hesitated, then said, "We're having dinner with her parents. Maybe she feels this tie, I mean yours, Mr. Applebaum won't like it."

"It's from Al Lewis," I said. "Seven bucks. Mr. Applebaum probably gets his own ties there. I'll bring your black knitted into the office in the morning."

"Okay," he said. "Let's get these books back into the safe."

"You go ahead," I said. "My date isn't until eight o'clock. Another hour or so, and I think I'll have this licked."

He gave me a look. "I don't pay overtime," he said.

"Did Louis Pasteur pay overtime?" I said. "Or Justice Oliver Wendell Holmes? If I want overtime, I'll go out to Detroit and say to Henry Ford put me on an assembly line. The reason I took this job, Mr. Zohn, the reason I'm willing to work for sixty a week, I'm trying to get into a profession. I want to be like you. An accountant. A professional man. Forget the overtime. You go ahead. I'll finish this cash-payments book. Do I meet you here in the morning?"

"No," Arnold Zohn said. "We always meet in my office at eight-thirty. We discuss what our program is for the day, then we go to the client, whoever he is, we go there together. It makes a better impression."

"I'll see you in your office at eight-thirty," I said.

He put the general ledger back in the safe and punched his way into the brown herringbone. He tapped his mustache as though he were touching a mezuzah on the door. He said good night and went out. I went to the door and listened. In a few minutes, from the other end of the floor behind the waiting room, I heard the elevator door slam open and then shut. I went to the roll-top desk, where the Manhattan directory was sitting under the telephone. I thumbed the pages to *M*. Just as I'd suspected, there was no listing for Ralph Mattlin. Mattlin & Merritt, yes. Ralph Mattlin, no. I'd never known anybody on

Seventh Avenue with a privately listed number. I saw now that ever since noon, when the picture painted by the cash-payments book had begun to take shape in my mind, I'd known without even thinking about it that Ralph Mattlin would have a privately listed number. It was part of the feeling that had hit me when I climbed out of the subway with Arnold Zohn. The feeling that I was going into new places. The feeling that I'd moved into an area that I didn't quite understand. Now, a few hours later, I knew something else: it would take all the marines we had down in Nicaragua to keep me out of it. I can smell money the way a dog can smell a bitch in heat. I picked up the phone. "Miss Eitner, please," I said.

The butterball at the outside phone said, "Is this the accountant?"

"Yes," I said. "Mr. Leff."

"One moment, please.

Miss Eitner's slow Eskimo Pie voice came on with "Yes, Mr. Leff?"

"I wonder if I could see you for a moment?" I said.

"You don't have to wonder," she said. "That's what I'm here for."

"I'll come to your office," I said. "If you'll tell me where it is."

"No, you wait there," Miss Eitner said. "I'll come along to you."

Miss Eitner was clearly a No-We'll-Do-It-My-Way type.

"What can I do for you?" she said when she came into the room.

"You can answer a question," I said. "If you don't mind."

"I won't know whether I mind or not until I hear the question," she said.

"I was just wondering," I said. "This bookkeeper. Mr. Nachman you said his name was?"

"Is," Miss Eitner said. "Yes, Mr. Nachman. What about him?"

"Is he a fast boy?" I said. "I mean a snappy dresser with a little black book full of girls' names?"

"Not in the least," Miss Eitner said. "He's a sort of pudgy man with gray hair. Elderly I guess is the word. In the neighborhood of a hundred and seventy or eighty pounds. With about, I'd say, sixty or sixty-five summers to his credit. Maybe more. He could be your father, Mr. Leff. Does that answer your question?"

It answered one I hadn't even asked: how Miss Eitner felt about Mr. Nachman.

"You've answered it too well," I said.

"How do you mean?" Miss Eitner said.

"You've pulled the rug out from under my theory."

"Explain your theory," she said.

"I had a theory that there's some connection between, I mean I thought there was some connection between Mr. Nachman having the day off today and the fact that Mr. Mattlin hasn't showed up all day. I sort of had a picture in my mind of both of them out at the race track."

Miss Eitner folded her arms across the place where other women had a bulge, and she leaned against the edge of the roll-top desk. She tipped her head to one side, and her eyes closed down until they looked like slits in a subway turnstile. She stared at me as though she were sighting a gun. "Tell me, Mr. Leff," she said. "It is Mr. Leff, isn't it?"

"Yes," I said. "Ted Leff."

"Let's stick with mister for a while," she said. "I want to ask you a question, Mr. Leff. Fair exchange, sort of. You know?"

If I didn't, this sure was the broad who would see that I did. "Shoot," I said.

"My question, Mr. Leff," she said. "This theory of yours. Did you arrive at it from the work you've done here today on our books and records?"

"That's right," I said.

"Did you tell this theory to your boss?" she said. "Mr. Zohn?"

I didn't even hesitate. "Of course not," I said.

"Of course not you say," Miss Eitner said. "I am impressed

by the way you say 'of course.' I like your reading of the phrase."

You were intended to be impressed, honeybunch.

"Why?" I said, dripping innocence all over the word like a leaking faucet.

"It implies that you either don't think too highly of Mr. Zohn's intelligence, or you feel you're onto something with which you can make a bit of hay for yourself rather than for him."

I was beginning to like this undecorated tomato almost as much as, in the morning, I'd begun to like the knockout Arnold Zohn was married to.

"Miss Eitner," I said. "You sound to me like a girl who operates in an arena of which I am very fond."

"What's that, Mr. Leff?"

"The No Crap Department."

"I couldn't have put it so delicately," she said. "But since there's no denying the basic truth of what you say, I'll just say yes, I think we do."

"In that case, I'll be glad to answer your question," I said. "Provided I get something from you in exchange."

"If I can provide it," Miss Eitner said, "I think the answer will be yes."

"No," I said. "Don't think. I want a straight yes."

"Okay, Mr. Leff, you've got it," she said. "A straight yes."

"Okay, Miss Eitner," I said, "I'd like you to give me Mr. Ralph Mattlin's unlisted home phone number."

"Okay, Mr. Leff," she said. "You've got it if you answer my question about Mr. Zohn."

"Mr. Zohn is a dope," I said. "Not a small one. Mr. Zohn is a dope with earlaps, Miss Eitner. If you're on my wavelength?"

"I am not only on your wavelength, Mr. Leff," she said. "I may be a little ahead of you."

"Well, don't get out of sight," I said. "As Mr. Odets arranged for Gary Cooper to say to Madeleine Carroll in *The General*

Died at Dawn, I think we can make beautiful music together."

"Why don't we start tonight?" she said.

"Because I'm a little short of cash," I said. "I don't want to take you to dinner except in the sort of setting where I think you belong."

"Don't be a dope like Arnold Zohn," Miss Eitner said in that calm voice that sounded as though she were setting type. "You pick out the saloon," she said. "I'll pick up the tab."

"Is this a way for us to start our relationship?" I said. "With me looking like a gigolo?"

"Don't worry about how you'll look," Miss Eitner said. She shoved herself away from the desk. "This is strictly business," she said. "I'll take it out of petty cash."

6

" Everybody Thinks
Australia Is Just
a Lot of Sheep"

One thing can be said for being born in a tenement. You get handed at birth a yardstick about real estate.

Take a boy who has spent the first twelve years of his life in a sixth-floor cold-water railroad flat on East Fourth Street. "With toilets in the hall," as my mother used to say, sinking the shiv into our less fortunate relatives who lived "with toilets in the yard." The point is that from then on, everything that happens to this guy in the way of living quarters is bound to be a step upward. From East Fourth Street you can move in only one direction.

There is, however, an element of danger: the tendency to believe, when you enter any habitation with walls that don't leak, or rooms that don't smell of stale urine, that you've stepped into the Taj Mahal.

On the other hand, it's a little like the Constitution. There's a built-in system of checks and balances. Nobody born and raised on East Fourth Street is going to lose his head and think of Greenwich Village the way Marco Polo thought of Cathay just because some of the inhabitants were a little unbuttoned. The stories about John Reed jigging in the streets with Edna St.

Vincent Millay, while Floyd Dell and Maxwell Bodenheim kept time by pounding a couple of bassoons on Mabel Dodge Luhan's rear end, are glamorous legends only to out-of-town hicks. To a born-and-bred New Yorker, a dump is a dump, even if you get Frank Lloyd Wright to build you a gold-plated *pissoir* in the middle of it. That's pretty much what Ralph Mattlin had done, as I discovered the morning after I had my petty-cash dinner with his secretary.

Using the privately listed number Maud Eitner had given me the night before, I called Mattlin's house at six. That's six in the morning. It's a great time to make phone calls. No matter who answers, you're one up on them. If you're wide-awake, that is. I always am. Not because I'm more virtuous than other people. I just happen to get along on less sleep than most people. Some of those people will tell you everything you're taught in school is a lot of malarkey. I've found that only part of it is. Take the old adage about early to bed and early to rise. I've never been able to swing the first half. But neither have I ever been able to break the habit of the second. When the sun comes up, so do I. The best rules for living are the ones you work out for yourself. Here's one of my favorites: *Late to bed, and early to rise, makes jack.*

"Who wants Mr. Mattlin?" a voice said at the other end of the phone.

It was one of those voices that has no sex. I couldn't tell if it belonged to a man or a woman. Since Miss Eitner had told me Mattlin was not married, I could have been talking to one of his obliging girl friends. But I doubted it. Women who spend the night in a bachelor's bed don't answer the phone at six in the morning. Not the way this woman had answered it. If she was a woman. This woman—no, this person—sounded crisp, wide-awake and impatient. As though I'd interrupted her or him in the middle of the day's baking. At six o'clock in the morning, the only person I ever knew who could do that was my mother. Besides, the person at the other end sounded as though he or she was accustomed to taking messages. I figured I was probably talking to a servant.

"I'm a cousin of his," I said. "From Melbourne."

"From where?"

"It's in Australia," I said. "It's a big city."

"I never knew Mr. Mattlin had a cousin in Australia."

"Neither did he," I said. "But he's got several. Aunts and uncles too. Maybe even second cousins. It's the branch of the family everybody's been ashamed of for a long time, because Great-great-great-grandfather Sholto—he's the one settled in Australia—he was a criminal."

"He was a what?"

"Oh, it's perfectly okay now," I said. "I mean Grandfather Sholto didn't escape from prison or anything like that. He went out to Australia after he served his term in Dartmoor, and since then we've all done very well. We're in rabbits."

"What did you say?"

I wasn't quite sure myself. But I kept on going. I had to. As some bright boy once pointed out, invention is the offspring of necessity.

"Rabbits," I said. "Everybody thinks Australia is just a lot of sheep. But it isn't. Our branch of the Mattlin family, we made it in rabbits. You see, the truth is, what you do, you coax them to cohabit."

"To do what?"

Whether it was a he or a she, I was certainly holding his or her interest.

"It's a form of mating," I said. "You coax them to go at it in a big way, which is not very hard to do with rabbits, since you might say they have a sort of inclination in that direction, and then you shave their fur and you sell it to American hat manufacturers in Danbury, Connecticut. Anyway, we Mattlins do. Any time you see a man walking down the street, wearing a fedora, you can bet ten to one, or you can even give higher odds, because you're perfectly safe—you can bet the thing is made of Mattlin rabbit."

"Listen, whoever you are," the voice at the other end said. "I don't know what this is all about, but Mr. Mattlin is still asleep."

63

"Wake him up," I said. "I'll be there in half an hour."

Actually, I didn't get there until a few minutes after seven. The address Miss Eitner had given me was on East Thirty-eighth Street. I was beginning to wonder if the plan I'd cooked up the day before wasn't a dream sequence that had come not out of the Mattlin & Merritt cash-payments book but out of Miss Eitner's petty-cash martinis, when I saw the graystone town house in the middle of the block. I stopped wondering.

I'd seen dozens of houses like it, maybe hundreds, but they were all in the Sixties and Seventies, between Fifth and Madison, or Madison and Park. The kind of houses you see in the Cadillac ads. Where the front door, which looks like it's been borrowed for the night from the Metropolitan Museum of Art, is being held open by an eight-foot-tall butler. So the man in tails and the woman in ermine, who have just stepped out of the limousine at the curb, can move smoothly into the golden-yellow glow spilling down from the crystal chandeliers on the other guests. These are already wading through the pools of champagne toward the birdbaths full of caviar. All wearing on their unused faces the same sort of antiseptic little creaseless smiles invented by Winnie Winkle.

Seeing a house like that on East Thirty-eighth Street was like seeing Queen Marie of Rumania on East Fourth Street. It made you wonder. But I didn't wonder long. Moving up the steps to ring the bell, I was once again getting a whiff of my favorite perfume: the smell of money.

"Are you the man from Australia?" said the man who opened the door.

So at least that much was settled. I had not been talking to a woman.

"Not all of Australia," I said. "Just Melbourne. We pronounce it to rhyme with Well Bin."

I wasn't exactly sure I was talking to a man, either. He—it —was old. Old and fat. He kept his head down, as though his back hurt. He was wearing slippers, a pair of dark gray unpressed pants, and a black alpaca jacket. No tie. No shirt, either, I suddenly realized. He reminded me of Irish janitors I'd

64

seen in the movies. The kind that are always swapping Sean O'Casey dialogue with Una O'Connor.

"I don't care how you pronounce it," he said. "Just come on in."

I came in. He closed the door behind me as though he were putting the lid on a coffin. Something told me if I ran for mayor, I'd be smart not to count on this boy's vote. He led me across the hall into a living room on the left. It was not like those rooms in the Cadillac ads. But it wasn't exactly an army barracks, either. The room had that same smell of money. This puzzled me, because the furniture was old. But not old in the way our furniture had been old on East Fourth Street. This stuff was expensive old. I got the feeling somebody had spent a lot of money to make it look that way. I had never had this feeling before. It made me a little uncomfortable.

"You don't look to me like you come from Australia."

I turned back to the man who had let me in. He looked a lot the way my father had looked toward the end. Except that my father had never been so fat, and my father's hair had not been so white. Also, even though my father had not been the sort of person over whose eyes a great deal of wool ever got pulled, he had never looked at his son as suspiciously as this old man was now looking at me.

"Don't go by the clothes," I said. "When I got off the ship yesterday, I peeled myself out of everything I was wearing and I burned it. To get rid of the smell of rabbit. Then I bought myself a complete new outfit here in New York. How do you like the cut of this jacket? It's conservative, sure, but you'll notice it's also snappy."

"I wasn't going by the clothes," he said. "I was going by your accent."

"I thought you'd notice that," I said. "Tell me what you think of it."

"It sounds like you picked it up in the Bronx," he said. "Not in Well Bin, Australia."

"Have you ever been to Australia?" I said.

"Of course not," he said. "Why should I go to Australia?"

65

"If you're interested in rabbits," I said, "it's the only place. If you'd ever been there you'd know everybody in Australia sounds like they picked up their accents in the Bronx."

His round fat face pinched together in a way that made him look more suspicious. "Wait here," he said. "Mr. Mattlin will be down in a few minutes."

It wasn't until he was out of the room that my mind caught up with the sound of his voice. I thought what I'd heard was irritation mixed with maybe a little suspicion. I now realized what I'd heard was fear. Some servant. If he was scared of a nice Jewish boy in a hundred-and-twenty-five-dollar suit, how would he react when Jack the Ripper rang the bell and asked if he could use the knife sharpener?

Hearing his footsteps move up the stairs out in the hall, I suddenly had the feeling I was not alone in the room. I turned and found myself facing a large oil painting over the fireplace. It was a picture of a woman with white hair in one of those dresses Lydia E. Pinkham has been wearing on the side of that bottle ever since I was old enough to look into a drugstore window. The woman in the painting had probably been a knockout as a girl. She'd certainly been a good-looker when the painting was made. This could have been when she was in her fifties. That could have been when Teddy Roosevelt was yelling "Bully!" at the slowpokes who were following him up San Juan Hill. After a couple of seconds, I realized what had given me the feeling I was being watched. It was the woman's eyes. They were very bright. They seemed alive. I moved to the left. The eyes in the painting moved with me. I moved to the right. The eyes in the painting followed me.

"What are you doing?"

I turned. A tall man in a blue silk robe was standing in the doorway. There was something about the way he was doing it that seemed a little unreal. I wondered why. Then I realized it was the way he was holding himself. Like a walking question mark. Slightly hunched over. As though he was ashamed of his height and was trying to hide it. He had plenty to hide. This boy was at least six-feet-four. The next thing I noticed was his

66

hands. Or what he was doing with them. One of them was sunk
in a pocket of the robe. I had the feeling he wanted it out of
sight because he couldn't control it. He didn't want anybody to
see it start twitching. In the other hand he held a cigarette. Not
the way most people hold a cigarette. He held it the way an
actor holds it just before he delivers a line he knows is going to
bring down the house. All in all Ralph Mattlin reminded me of
a Second Avenue Noel Coward about to hang one of those
brittle lines on Gertrude Lawrence in *Private Lives*. At that
moment I realized something that took me by surprise. It had
never occurred to me before that the first half of Mattlin &
Merritt was a landsman.

"The painting," I said. "The way the eyes follow you. It's
very unusual. Unusual and moving. It's sort of—I don't exactly
know how to say it—but it gets you. It really does."

His face seemed to change. I realized he had been scowling.
Now that he'd stopped, I realized something else. He looked
like the woman in the painting.

"You like it?" he said. "You really like it?"

With that kind of opening, how smart does a guy have to
be?

"It's beautiful," I said. "I don't mean to sound corny, and I
don't know much about art, but that's one of the most beautiful
paintings I've ever seen. I mean not only the painting, the
artwork. I mean the person."

His face changed again. I was on target. I'd hit him where he
lived.

"Thank you," he said. "That's my mother. Grubensteller did
it only a few months before she died."

Good for Grubensteller. He was a gentleman. Van Gogh
would probably have waited a few months until after she died.
Mattlin walked over to look at the painting. While he did that I
looked at him. On Seventh Avenue you would have spotted him
at once as a salesman. Ralph Mattlin was a good-looking man.
Tall guys sometimes are not. Even when their features are okay.
Because their heads are out of proportion. Ralph Mattlin didn't
suffer from that problem. His head was just the right size for his

six-foot-four frame. So were his shoulders. Except for a few differences, he could have been Byram Noonan. Byram's hair is as black as Theda Bara's used to be. Ralph Mattlin's hair was the color of good mink. Both men had short, straight noses, blue eyes and strong jaws. But the combination, in Byram's case, made you think of a happy harp who played football. In the case of Ralph Mattlin the combination made you think of a sad rabbi who played the fiddle.

I couldn't understand why. I still don't. I mean how you know just by looking at him that a man is a member of your club. Even when what you're looking at, taking him piece by piece, is an Irish halfback.

Evie, who always understands everything, including the shape of the Guggenheim Museum, says it's like the theater. If you knock every play before it comes to Broadway, you're going to end the season with a batting average that could make Di Maggio look like a sandlotter. The reason is simple: most plays that make it to Broadway in any season prove to be flops. Evie says it's the same with what she calls Our People. If you start with the assumption that everybody you meet is Jewish, no matter what they look like, or what handles they've hooked onto themselves, you're going to be right often enough to run up an impressive score. Evie may have been right. But on that day in 1937 I had not yet married Evie, so she wasn't around to give me advice.

I have nothing against people being members of my club. I just wish some of them wouldn't confuse me by looking like WASPs. That morning in 1937 when I first met Ralph Mattlin I wanted my head clear. What I'd come for had nothing to do with his religion. It was his business I was interested in.

"Now then," he said. He turned away from the painting. He still looked sad. But he also looked refreshed. As though he'd just put away a glass of iced lemonade on a hot August day. "What's all this about Australia?" he said.

"It's a lot of crap," I said.

He was lifting the cigarette to his mouth. His hand jerked. The ash splashed down on the head of a faded mandarin in the rug. It must have been oriental. Would anyone weave a faded mandarin into an occidental rug?

"What did you say?"

"Mr. Mattlin," I said. And then, "Excuse me. It *is* Mr. Mattlin, isn't it?"

Something happened to those pale blue eyes. All of a sudden this sad Jew didn't look sad or Jewish.

"Of course it's Mr. Mattlin," he said. All of a sudden something else. All of a sudden there was sandpaper in the voice. "You've come to my house," he said. "You know my unlisted phone number. What sort of nonsense is this about it is Mr. Mattlin, isn't it? Who else could I be?"

The warning bell went off inside my dome. This was no Arnold Zohn.

"I'm sorry," I said. "I was merely—"

"Don't waste my time by being sorry," Mattlin said. He zinged the cigarette into the fireplace like a guy at Coney trying for the bull's-eye in a darts game. Without shifting gears, on the same swinging movement, he scooped a fresh cigarette out of a thick cut-glass bowl on the coffee table in front of the fire. "You've managed to get my unlisted number, and you've announced yourself as a cousin of mine from Australia, and now you say that's a lot of crap. Who the hell are you?"

"I'm your accountant," I said.

The match flame on its way to meet the fresh cigarette stopped moving. "What accountant?" Ralph Mattlin said.

"The one Mr. Applebaum assigned to do an audit of your books before he'll shell out the loan you want."

The blue eyes did another shift. Now Ralph Mattlin looked sad and Jewish again. I made one of my mental notes. This guy had stuff on the ball. But he also had a weakness. When it came to money he scared easy. I had run into this on Seventh Avenue. It's a fatal flaw.

"You're Mr. Zohn?" he said. "Arnold Zohn?"

"No, I'm Mr. Leff," I said. "Ted Leff. I work for Arnold Zohn."

"Where is Mr. Zohn?"

I looked at my wrist watch. "Probably in bed," I said. "Or maybe his alarm has gone off and he's shaving. He looks like a man who believes in things like early to bed and early to rise."

The blue eyes changed again. Ralph Mattlin took a long drag on his cigarette. He did it the way a runner, after busting through the tape, might take a swig at the water bottle. It was easy to see that without tobacco this boy couldn't get through a revolving door. I noticed his fingernails. They were manicured. I began to feel a little more confident. Not that up to now I had been what you could call unconfident. But I have a pretty good knowledge of the places where my fast one will nearly always cut the corner of the plate. For example, I've always been able to handle guys who sit around in barbershops with one hand soaking in a basin, making lousy jokes that the broad in white painting the fingernails on his other hand has to laugh at. I don't know why I have this ability. It's just a gift. Maybe you have it too. Next time you see a guy with fingernails that look like little greasy mirrors, try it. I hear that's how Cortez took Mexico.

"You don't seem to know very much about your boss," Ralph Mattlin said finally.

"Why should I?" I said. "I never laid eyes on him before yesterday morning."

"Yesterday morning?"

"He hired me at nine o'clock," I said. "For the specific purpose of impressing you. He wanted you to think he's a big shot, with a staff. I'm the staff."

"I'm going to make a guess, Mr. Leff," Ralph Mattlin said. "Do you mind?"

"Go ahead," I said. "It's your house."

"If Arnold Zohn knew you were here right now, you'd stop being his staff. Is that correct?"

"On the button," I said. "But also unimportant. By the time I leave this house Arnold Zohn won't need a staff."

"Why not?"

"He won't have a client worth impressing."

70

Ralph Mattlin waved to a chair near the fireplace. "Sit down, Mr. Leff," he said. "You're beginning to sound interesting."

I sat down. He dropped into a two-seater couch facing me. He put his feet up on the coffee table between us. They were not small feet. If this boy wore anything less than a Twelve Charlie, I could get both my feet into a demitasse cup. His slippers matched the robe. Blue leather. I could tell it was his favorite color. I could also tell it was his mother who had pointed out to him why blue should be his favorite color. Because of his eyes. Grubensteller had given her an identical set in the painting that was watching us.

"I hope what I have to say will be more than just interesting," I said. "I hope it will solve your problem."

"What is my problem?" Ralph Mattlin said.

Me. But he didn't know that yet.

"According to Arnold Zohn," I said, "your firm is doing a lot of business but making very little profit. So little that you're always short of cash, and when you went to one of your stockholders, this Mr. Applebaum, when you went to him for a loan, he said nothing doing until you allowed his son-in-law to do an audit of your books and find out what's wrong."

"And you've completed the audit?" Ralph Mattlin said.

"No, of course not," I said. "Mr. Zohn and I, we only started the audit yesterday morning at ten o'clock. I don't think there's an accountant in the whole world who could finish an audit this size, going back three full years, to the very beginning when you went in business. Nobody could finish an audit that size in one day."

"So I take it you and Mr. Zohn have not yet completed your audit?" Ralph Mattlin said.

"We haven't even scratched the surface," I said.

"You're a coiner of phrases, Mr. Leff."

The alert signal went off again. That Ralph Mattlin was not a schmuck like Arnold Zohn, I had learned before we sat down. Now that we were both on our tails, examining each other across his blue leather rowboats, I had just learned something else. Inside this handsome six-foot-four package, which alternated between looking like a yeshiva student and an Arrow collar ad, there was something else beside a brain. There was also a bastard.

"Words are not my business," I said. "Figures are."

"Am I to understand you feel you're doing your business by coming here to see me at this ungodly hour when you haven't yet completed your audit?" Ralph Mattlin said.

"I don't have to finish this audit to justify my coming here," I said. "I came here because I've found out what's wrong."

"With Mattlin & Merritt?" he said.

"Precisely," I said. Then I added, "If you don't mind my coining a phrase?"

He looked puzzled. As though he was trying to connect up what I'd said with something that had happened. Then he apparently made it, because he laughed.

"I'm sorry," Ralph Mattlin said. I could tell that he was. This surprised me. Most guys, when they act like a bastard, if they follow up fast by saying they're sorry, you can be sure they're just using words. All they're doing is making hasty sounds in the hope that they won't get the shot in the mouth they've just earned. Or lose the sale they've just jeopardized. Mr. Ralph Mattlin was beginning to shape up as something new in my experience. A son of a bitch who didn't like acting like a son of a bitch. And was genuinely sorry when he found he had. "I shouldn't have said that," he said.

"Why not?" I said. "It's still your house."

"It's yours too," he said, "when you're a visitor in it. I apologize for that bit of uncalled-for sarcasm. Now tell me what's wrong with Mattlin & Merritt."

"You have a crooked bookkeeper," I said.

Three things happened in quick succession. Like one of those precision double plays that used to be part of the day's work for Tinker, Evers and Chance. Mr. Mattlin's eyes jumped wide open like those of a burlesque comic in the first stage of a Four Wings and Scram. Then his feet fell from the coffee table and hit the carpet as his long body came forward on the couch like a blade snapping back into a pocketknife. And finally, Mr. Ralph Mattlin screamed. I don't mean shouted, exclaimed or ejaculated. He screamed. What he screamed was "Abe *Nach*man?"

I don't astonish easy. Especially in setups where the explosion takes place because I've pulled the trigger myself. But for a few startled moments I couldn't help giving this guy the hairy eyeball. A few seconds ago he was a great big long elegant man of the world. Lying back in his silk robe and puffing his cigarette like William Powell playing Nick Charles for a group of Myrna Loy's girl friends who had dropped in for a cup of oolong. Now, all of a sudden, he looked and sounded like an Avenue C pushcart peddler who had caught some yenta trying to sneak a few extra spuds into her shopping bag while his back was turned.

"Mr. Mattlin," I said, "I didn't know your bookkeeper's first name is Abe. But your secretary did say the man who kept the Mattlin & Merritt books was a Mr. Nachman."

"You talked to Miss Eitner about this?" he said.

Said? No. He was still screaming.

"I had to," I said.

There was no reason for me to scream. I was handling the tiller.

"What does that mean?" he rapped out. "You had to. I don't understand what you're talking about. I can't imagine what your game is. It's absolutely disgusting. These shameful accusations against an innocent man. It's shocking. Positively indecent. I ought to call the police. You should be arrested. Coming here in the morning like this, breaking in here and saying things that—"

At this point he ran out of steam. He sagged back in the couch. He passed his hand across his eyes. It was a gesture I recognized. I saw Lewis Stone do it once. He was playing Menelaus in *The Private Life of Helen of Troy*. Helen had wrapped it up with Paris. The fun was over. So she'd come home, and she wanted to be taken back on the payroll. Menelaus was understandably a little reluctant to reinstate her. So she flashed open the front of her robe and showed the old man what he'd been missing. It was a little too much for him to absorb in one glance. So the old geezer had to cover his eyes for a moment. He'd done it with a limp wrist. The way Ralph Mattlin was doing it now.

"I'm sorry," he said quietly. Mattlin, not Menelaus. "I don't know how to absorb all this. Mr. Nachman is— He's my oldest — I mean he's been with us from the beginning. I would trust him with my life. He's more than an employee. He's my— I mean he's a decent, hard-working, serious, loyal, very devoted person."

"So was Jesse James," I said.

Mattlin leaned forward. He took another cigarette from the glass bowl. I could see why he didn't keep them in boxes. He obviously couldn't live through the extra split second it took to lift a cover. Three tries and he managed to get the cigarette going. He leaned back.

"Please tell me what this is all about," he said. "Tell me what you've found out."

"What Samuel Seabury found out about Jimmy Walker," I said. "Mr. Zohn set me to work on the cash-payments book. Checking the additions. You turn page after page in a cash-payments book, thirty-six months' work of expenditures, three years of a firm's life, you'd have to be awfully dumb if you didn't begin to see sort of what you could call a kind of a pattern emerging. Certain recurring expenses, I mean. And what I began to realize as I added the figures on the pages, I began to realize Mattlin & Merritt, they're spending an awful lot of money on postage."

"Postage?" Ralph Mattlin said.

He sounded like a guy who had never seen a two-cent stamp.

"For mail," I said. "Letters. Every week, I noticed, there was an entry. Four hundred dollars for postage."

A little more starch seemed to come into Mattlin's wilted face. "That's impossible," he said.

"Exactly what I thought," I said. "So I had a talk with Miss Eitner. I asked her how things worked in your shop. Right away

I knew my suspicions were well founded. If you'll excuse my coining another phrase, Mr. Mattlin?"

The look he gave me now would have turned a piece of litmus paper cherry-red. "Don't bother to entertain me," Ralph Mattlin said coldly. "Just give me the facts."

"Miss Eitner said you do all your shipping out of your warehouse on West Fifty-seventh Street," I said. "And that stuff is all metered, or it goes Railway Express and parcel post. So this four hundred a week was for stamps. Ordinary mail. Letters going out of your Fourth Avenue office. A man doesn't have to be a Monroe calculator, Mr. Mattlin, to figure out that four hundred dollars a week comes to twenty thousand two-cent stamps. That's a hell of a lot of stamps. It's probably more than Alf M. Landon's headquarters used all during the months they were sending out campaign circulars. What I mean, Mr. Mattlin, common sense said to me right away, hey, wait a minute. This is a small firm that sells jigsaw puzzles. Like any firm, small or medium or large, they have a certain amount of correspondence. Which means they use two-cent stamps. But how the hell can they possibly use twenty thousand a week? The answer, from the common-sense standpoint, is they can't. So I discussed it with Miss Eitner."

"Did you discuss it with Mr. Zohn?"

Mattlin shot the question at me like Sergeant York picking off a Kraut in the Argonne Forest.

"No," I said.

"Why not?"

"Two reasons," I said. "First, when I came to my conclusion about this thing, it was almost six-thirty last night, and Mr. Zohn had already gone home. Second, I had a hunch you wouldn't have wanted me to discuss it with him."

"How could you have that hunch?" Ralph Mattlin said. "You'd never met me. You knew nothing about me."

I knew a bookkeeper had been taking him to the cleaners for three years. So I knew he had to be at least just a little bit of a dope.

"I knew you were hard up for cash," I said. "I knew you'd tried to borrow it from Mr. Applebaum. I knew Mr. Applebaum had forced Arnold Zohn's audit on you. I figured if I were in your shoes, Mr. Mattlin, I'd hate Arnold Zohn's guts, sight unseen, one gut at a time. I'd only started to work for him a few hours earlier. That was long enough for me to realize between Arnold Zohn and me it would never get to be like it was with Troilus and Cressida. He's a schmuck, Mr. Mattlin."

"And you're not?" he said.

The sandpaper was back in his voice. I hadn't yet figured this guy out. But once I learned the combination, how and why he moved back and forth from the marshmallow to the sourball, I knew I could work with him. I suspected the key was in what I'd discovered a few minutes ago—namely, that when it came to money this boy scared easy.

"No, I'm not," I said. "A schmuck would have run to his boss with my discovery."

"But you," Ralph Mattlin said. "You ran to the place where it would pay off better?"

"I'm going to use a phrase I coined a couple of minutes ago, Mr. Mattlin," I said. "Precisely."

He banged the cigarette into the fireplace. He lit another one. He stood up. For a few minutes he paced back and forth behind the couch, glaring at the mandarins in the carpet. It occurred to me that I had never actually seen a mandarin. Maybe what was woven into the faded carpet was a bunch of Talmudic scholars with slant eyes?

"Tell me this," Mattlin said suddenly. "What makes you feel that those four hundred dollars a week were taken by what you call our crooked bookkeeper?"

I didn't have to think. I knew. It was exactly what I'd been doing on Seventh Avenue before the lawyers for the Receiver in Bankruptcy nailed me. But I thought I'd better keep that explanation to myself.

"Miss Eitner got your bank statements and canceled vouchers out of the safe for me last night," I said. "It wasn't hard to find the checks. There's one for every week you've been in business.

Four of them every month. All drawn to cash. Even though they're all posted in the cash-payments book to postage. And they're all endorsed 'A. Nachman for Deposit' in the National City at Fifth Avenue and Thirteenth Street. Four hundred a week. Say he actually used fifty of it for stamps. Miss Eitner agrees that would be a generous sum for handling the firm's postage. This leaves Mr. Nachman with a take of three-fifty a week, or eighteen thousand two hundred a year. For three years, what it comes to, Mr. Mattlin, your bookkeeper, he's gotten away with a little over fifty thousand dollars. And that's why your firm has been short of cash."

Mattlin stopped pacing. He came to my chair and stared down at me. He reminded me of Houdini at the Palace, trying to guess the number on the dollar bill a member of the audience was holding in his hand. The blue eyes looked like highly polished small windows that opened out on nothing. It was as though he'd suddenly become a shell. All the flesh and bones had been scooped out of him. Like the meat out of a baked potato. Only the skin was left. Staring into those ice-blue eyes, I had the screwy feeling I was looking into an absolutely empty man. Then Mattlin did that thing with the cigarette again. He smashed it into the fireplace. He scooped up another from the glass bowl. He headed across the room like Hugo Zachini coming out of one of those cannons at the circus. Mattlin pulled up in front of a mahogany secretary. A phone was standing on it. He whipped it up as though it were red-hot. While he dialed a number, in a series of complicated movements that reminded me of a kid making a cat's cradle with a looped piece of string, he managed to set fire to the cigarette. This boy obviously owned stock in the American Tobacco Company.

"Dr. Yustin, please," Mattlin said into the phone. "Ralph Mattlin calling. Yes, it's very urgent." There was a pause. Mattlin drew deeply on the cigarette. He blew out the smoke and examined the burning end as though he distrusted it. "Bernard?" he said finally. "Yes, Ralph. I can't tell you on the phone. I've got to see you right away. Please, Bernard. It's very urgent. I'm sure you can shift one of your other patients. You must, Bernard. I don't think I can get through the day unless I see you at once. Thanks, Bernard. I'll be there as soon as I'm dressed."

Mattlin slammed down the receiver. He kept his hand on it. He leaned forward, hunched over the instrument. He dragged deep on the cigarette. He seemed to be staring through the mahogany top of the secretary at something in the next house or the next block. Also, he was panting. As though he'd just run up a few flights of stairs.

"I'm sorry about this," I said.

Mattlin whipped around. "What was that?" he said.

"The doctor," I said. "I was just giving you the facts. I didn't mean to make you sick."

"Sick?" The glare changed slightly. "Oh," Mattlin said. "No, Dr. Yustin isn't that kind of doctor. He's my analyst."

The empty blue eyes slid over my head. Back to the secretary. Mattlin remained like that for a few moments. Hunched over. Supporting his weight on the hand that rested on the telephone. Then he seemed to reach some sort of decision. He shoved himself up straight. He reached the door in four long, slashing steps and opened it. "Abe!" Mattlin shouted into the hall.

He turned, one hand on the knob, and looked at me. Now his eyes were very bright. The way his mother's eyes were in the Grubensteller portrait. He could have been smiling. He could have been glaring. I couldn't tell. But I could sense the excitement boiling up inside him. I could feel it all the way across the room. The Jewish fiddler was gone. Ralph Mattlin now looked like a goy halfback. Whatever the play was, it was the son of a bitch inside him who was calling it.

The fat old man who had let me into the house appeared in the doorway. "You wanted me, Ralphie?" he said.

He sounded the way he had sounded when he was talking to me. Scared.

Mattlin seemed to like that. He smiled. "Yes," he said. "While I go upstairs to dress, would you mind entertaining this gentleman?"

"Entertain him?" the old man said.

"All you have to do is listen," Ralph Mattlin said to him. "Mr. Leff has something interesting to tell you." He turned to me. "Do you mind, Mr. Leff?"

"No," I said. "Of course not."

"Come in, Abe," Ralph Mattlin said. The fat old man moved nervously into the room. "Mr. Leff," Mattlin said with a small, courtly bow, "I'd like you to meet my bookkeeper, Mr. Nachman."

7

"Bridge Players Don't Care About the Character of the People Who Supply Them with Their Heroin"

"Where are you?"

"In a phone booth," I said.

At the other end of the wire Maud Eitner said, "No, I mean where like in geography."

"In a United Cigar Store," I said. "At the corner of Lexington and Thirty-eighth."

"Then you really did it?"

For a moment I listened to the echo of her voice. It had lifted as though she'd been hit. A little bit of that feeling of strangeness came back to me. The feeling I'd had when I stepped out of the subway with Arnold Zohn the day before. As though I'd started downtown on a routine business visit, and found myself in a strange country where a guy in uniform was suddenly asking to see my passport. She didn't sound the way I thought she'd sound.

"You're just around the corner from Ralph Mattlin's house," she said. "You must have just come from there." Then her voice dropped. "Or are you on your way *to* his house?"

It wasn't a question. It was an accusation. I didn't get that, either. These Fourth Avenue people were a little bit like gentiles. Even when they were friendly, even when you felt they liked you, even when you were sure you understood the combination, all of a sudden you weren't sure.

"Weren't you listening last night?" I said. I don't like anybody implying that when the starting gun goes off I suddenly start fussing with the laces on my sneakers. "I told you I was going to do it this morning around seven o'clock," I said. "It's now a quarter to eight. Why do you have to waste time with questions did I do it?"

"A lot of people say they're going to do things," Maud Eitner said. "Especially at night when they're full of martinis and lasagne. Then in the morning they have second thoughts."

My second thoughts she'd need a code to translate. I may have been right. Seventh Avenue and Fourth Avenue may have been the same under the surface. But they talked a different language. I had to learn it, if I was going to do my fishing in these new waters.

"Forget those other people," I said. "You're in a different league now. The thought you want to hold now is when Ted Leff says he's going to do something, it doesn't matter if he's drinking martinis or milk. Or if he's eating lasagne or lox. I do it."

"You sound like that boy in the Kipling poem."

"Which one?" I said.

"I don't know," she said. "I've never read much Kipling."

"Then why bring him into it?"

"Because all of a sudden you were making the sort of noises I always hear when I'm reading one of his ballads. Like 'McAndrew's Hymn.' Or 'The Mary Gloster.' The noises of men bigger than the kind you see on the street every day. I guess that's what makes them writers."

"Who?" I said.

"Kipling," she said. "You and I look out the window and we see Irving's Luncheonette. They look out the window and they see far-off Cathay."

Female wise guys. That's what slows a man down in his struggle to the top.

"Miss Eitner."

"Maud, please."

"All right, Maud please, but will you stop hocking me?"

I didn't even know the rate of exchange in far-off Cathay.

"I thought you liked to hear me talk," she said. "Last night you were hanging on my every word."

"When I have more time I'll chin myself on them," I said. "Right now there's work to be done. Where are you?"

"In bed," she said. "Where do you expect me to be at this hour?"

My God, the questions a guy has to keep himself from answering if he wants to get ahead in life!

"I also mean like in geography," I said. "Where is your bed? You gave me your phone number last night, but I don't know where you sleep because you wouldn't let me take you home."

"I'm a good girl, I am," she said.

"What?" I said.

What would you have said?

"I'll send you a copy of *Pygmalion*," she said. "It's quicker than answering questions."

It's one of the problems, I learned slowly on Fourth Avenue, with people in the publishing business. They don't live life. They sell written descriptions of life. I got to know editors who couldn't balance their checkbooks. But they would speak with authority about a scene in a manuscript in which J. P. Morgan is making glaring financial mistakes while organizing U.S. Steel. I have known broads on Fourth Avenue who never saw a naked man, but they will tell you with a, b, c precision where Havelock Ellis got it all wrong.

"Miss Eitner," I said.

"Maud, please," she said. "I live with my mother, an acidulous old lady pushing eighty. She is as respectable as Rabbi Stephen Wise. She wouldn't like it if the doorman of our apartment house told her I was brought home last night by the shortstop of the DeWitt Clinton High School baseball team."

"I went to Thomas Jefferson," I said. "And my game happens to be four-wall handball. Now will you do me a favor and dry up? There's one more thing to be done, and it has to be done by nine o'clock this morning, baby. Nine-thirty the latest. So will you please tell me where your apartment house is?"

"Eighty-eighth Street, near East End," Miss Eitner said. "I have a terrific view of Doctors Hospital."

"How long would it take you," I said, "to get to some place near the Mattlin & Merritt office where we could have a slow cup of coffee and a fast talk?"

"By taxi I could meet you in half an hour," Maud Eitner said. "By subway it could be next Tuesday at noon."

"Take a taxi," I said. "This thing really must be done but quick. I'm serious. Speed. Speed. Speed. I'll pay for the cab."

"Will I benefit from this breakfast session?" she said.

"Of course you'll benefit from it," I said. "From now on, you and me, we're like the top and bottom of a B.V.D. combination. Inseparable."

"Then I'll take the taxi ride out of petty cash," she said.

"Where to?" I said.

"In the book business down there on Fourth Avenue," she said, "that depends on your tastes. You must have kidneys and plovers' eggs to start the day with? Then it's the Hotel Walpole, Horace of course, on Twenty-eighth, just off Fourth, going toward Madison. You're satisfied with a toasted bagel and perhaps a smear of cream cheese? Then it's Nathan's Noshery just across the street."

"Do the kidneys have stones?"

"What?" she said.

Even the jokes worked just as well on Fourth Avenue as on Seventh.

"Don't send me that copy of *Pygmalion*," I said. "Read it yourself. We had to write a report on it in Thomas Jefferson High for English Four. I'll meet you in Nathan's in half an hour."

She made it in twenty minutes. Which meant she'd left something out. I hoped it wasn't a shower. From here on in we were going to be close.

"What happened?" Maud Eitner said as she slipped into the seat at the other side of the red leather booth. "Tell me all."

I did.

"How did it end?" she said.

"When Mattlin came back downstairs," I said, "minus the blue silk robe and dressed for the street, he was carrying a coat for Abe Nachman as well as for himself. They went uptown together, and I went into a United Cigar Store phone booth to call you. I know he was heading for this Dr. Yustin's office, but where Honest Abe was going I don't know."

"If Mattlin has any brains he was taking him to the A.S.P.C.A. and having the old idiot put away," Maud Eitner said. "But I'm sure Mattlin took him along to see Dr. Yustin."

There was something in her voice. A layer of bitterness under the kidding. It opened a window. If your taste runs to good-looking broads, it comes as a jolt that an average looker can have the same taste in men. Jolt or not, I had to face it. Maud Eitner had a thing for Ralph Mattlin. She was even jealous of his bookkeeper.

"What about this Dr. Yustin?" I said.

"He's Ralph Mattlin's analyst."

"I know that," I said. "Mattlin told me. What bothers me is how it works. I told you how when I finished telling him where his dough had been going he went to the phone and called Yustin. What got me was his voice. Mattlin's. He was like a kid begging this Yustin to let him come see him. Practically on his knees. I always thought these analysts, you have regular appointments. A few times a week, and that's that."

"That's pretty much the normal way," Maud Eitner said. "But Ralph Mattlin is different. He uses his analyst the way a bad cook uses ketchup. To cover everything. Nathan, you take this bagel right back and see that it's toasted properly."

"You bet, Miss Eitner," the waiter said. "It's that new cook." He picked up the plate and started back to the kitchen.

Maud said, "He's never going to get to be an old cook if he doesn't learn how to treat a bagel." To me she said, "There ought to be a law against toasting bagels improperly. What's this thing that has to be done by nine or nine-thirty?"

84

"It won't get done by nine-thirty," I said, "unless you tell me about this Abe Nachman."

Maud Eitner looked down at the table. With her long blood-red Fu Manchu fingernail she began to poke tiny holes in the square of butter on the little paper plate. "There's really not very much to tell," she said. "Abe Nachman is Ralph Mattlin's uncle."

I thought about that for a moment, then realized what I was thinking about. The Grubensteller portrait in Mattlin's living room.

"It must be on his mother's side," I said. "Nachman looks like Mattlin's mother. I mean in that painting over the fireplace. Mattlin's fireplace?"

"I've been to the house," Maud said. "I know. It's a German Jewish family. You've met them. The only thing they worry about is why President Wilson got so fussy over the sinking of the *Lusitania* that he would start a war over it. Berlin Jewish, if that means anything to you."

"I'm East Fourth Street Jewish," I said. "My mother was a Galitzianer, and my father was a Litvak. So on the subject of German Jews, I heard plenty while I was growing up. Especially the prize packages from Berlin. What I'm saying is I'm on your wavelength."

"Good," Maud Eitner said. "Then the rest of it will be easy. Ralph Mattlin's father was in the import business. Surgical instruments. Lenses. Optical goods. That sort of thing. Even I, when I was a little girl, I remember the firm name. Mattlinberg & Nachman. My mother used to say they were the only people who made proper lenses. When you got your glasses changed, my mother said, you told the optometrist I want Mattlinberg & Nachman lenses."

On East Fourth Street you were lucky if you had glasses to get changed.

"That explains the name," I said. "Our friend dropped the 'berg.'"

"They also seem to have dropped whatever talent they had

for optical goods," Maud Eitner said. "Someone told me once that when Mattlinberg & Nachman went into bankruptcy around 1925, the partners handled it with as much grace as anybody ever did. Old man Mattlinberg dropped dead of a heart attack, and old man Nachman moved into the Mattlinberg home as a boarder, I suppose you'd have to call him. Then Mrs. Mattlinberg died, and Ralph just kept his uncle in the house ever since. Not exactly as a boarder, I think you'd have to say. A boarder is a person who pays rent. Abe Nachman didn't have anything to pay anything with. He sort of ran the house for Ralph is about the closest thing to paying for his keep that I can come up with as an explanation. When Ralph and Gene Merritt started Mattlin & Merritt, Ralph moved his ancient uncle in as our bookkeeper. If you give it a moment's thought you get a picture of how Ralph Mattlin's mind works. After all, his Uncle Abe's housekeeping services can be performed before or after working hours. Instead of paying him for these services, Ralph gives him a job in the office. By doing that, Ralph gets his partner in effect to pay half his housekeeper's salary."

"Abe obviously didn't think he was being paid enough," I said. "So he helped himself to that four hundred a week."

"I don't think that's the reason," Maud Eitner said.

"You know a better one?" I said.

"I think Honest Abe started to get scared," Maud said. "After all, he's well into his sixties, and my guess is he didn't think he could afford to waste more time, so he decided to build himself a little nest egg against the time when Ralph Mattlin gave him the gate. Anyway, that's my guess."

"My guess is you're not guessing," I said. "You're basing your statement on some hard facts."

Maud Eitner started stabbing her fingernail into the butter again. "Well, not hard facts exactly," she said finally. "Hard information would be more accurate. I've been playing bridge for years with a loud-mouth named Bernie Yustin. That's how I got my job as Ralph Mattlin's secretary. Dr. Yustin recommended me."

I thought about that for a couple of sips of coffee, then said,

"What I always heard, I heard these analysts, it's like what you tell a lawyer or a doctor. It's confidential. A man on the leather, he's spilling his guts, isn't he?"

"Usually with blood pouring out in spurts every inch of the way," Maud Eitner said.

"So how come this Yustin he told you all these confidential things about Ralph Mattlin?"

Maud Eitner shrugged, and using the paper napkin like a broom, she swept the last bagel crumbs from her lips. "You know anything about Wagner?" she said.

"The senator?" I said.

"No, the composer," she said.

"Like music?" I said.

"Yes, like music," Maud Eitner said. "He wrote some of the greatest the world has ever heard. But as a person, this Wagner was a fourteen-carat, dyed-in-the-wool, triple-X son of a bitch. The same with Bernie Yustin. He's a first-rate therapist. I've heard people, some of them doctors, I've heard them say Bernie is one of the most brilliant analysts in America. Unfortunately, he's also a bastard and a show-off."

"With a bastard and a show-off a nice girl like you has been playing bridge for years?" I said.

Maud Eitner opened her purse and took out a small mirror. "You know anything about bridge?" she said.

"Only the kind that takes you to Brooklyn," I said.

"Bridge players are like dope addicts," Maud Eitner said. She tipped her head left, right, back, and forward to catch different angles of her horsey face in the mirror. "They don't care about the character of the people who supply them with their heroin. All they care about is the quality of the narcotic. It's a snob's game. Like tennis. Good tennis players don't play with bums. The same with bridge. I'm the best bridge player you have ever shared a bagel with. If you ever meet Bernie Yustin you'll meet the only player who may be better than I am, but not by much." She dropped the mirror back into her purse, snapped it shut and looked at her wrist watch. "Now what's this thing that has to be done by nine or nine-thirty? It's now five minutes to."

"Last night, when I said good night to Arnold Zohn," I said, "I told him I'd meet him in his office in the Knickerbocker Building at eight-thirty this morning."

"You'll never make it," Maud Eitner said.

"I don't want to," I said. "He'll wait for me for a while, of course, but then he'll give up." I looked at my own wrist watch. "He's probably given up on me already, which means he's heading for the Mattlin & Merritt offices right now. When he gets there, I'd like you to be there to meet him."

"Why?" Maud Eitner said.

I looked her right in the eye. "I think I've done you a favor," I said.

"How?" she said.

"By tying the can to Honest Abe Nachman," I said. "The least Mattlin's going to have to do is fire him. Mattlin may even have to carry the thing to the cops, depending on how his partner feels about it. I don't know what this guy Merritt is like, but stealing fifty thousand fish is a big rap. Merritt could honestly say twenty-five thousand of it is his, and as a result Merritt could want to see Honest Abe Nachman get zonked for it. Whatever happens, it's the end of Mr. Nachman in the Mattlin & Merritt office. Am I right?"

The bones in the boney face went to work and arranged themselves for a long, cold look. "Suppose you are," Maud Eitner said. "What about it?"

"This about it," I said. "It leaves Mattlin wide open. Doing this to his own uncle, his mother's brother, Mattlin is going to be badly shaken. He's going to want to lean on someone. A smart dame could have her shoulder in the right place for a little leaning on. Do I have to spell this out any further?"

"No," Maud Eitner said. "Just tell me what you want me to do."

I told her.

8

" It Looks Like I've Done a Good Morning's Work for You"

A half-hour later the phone rang in the booth near the kitchen door in Nathan's Noshery. I watched the waiter go in and answer it. Then he stuck his head out. "Hey!" he yelled. "If you're Mr. Leff there's a call for you."

I took his place in the booth and said, "Hello?"

"Ted?"

"Speaking."

"Maud."

"How we doing?"

"Everything on shed."

"Talk English."

"I am," she said. "Shed as in schedule."

"Where's Zohn?" I said.

"He gohn."

"Trouble?"

"Some," she said. "But nothing I had difficulty handling. He came into the office promptly at nine-thirty. Benita tipped me off the moment he came in the door, and I met him in the reception room."

"Who's Benita?"

"Benita Adler. The girl at the billing machine in the reception room. I told Mr. Zohn not to bother taking off his coat. Mr. Mattlin had decided he didn't want the audit done, I said, and my instructions were to tell Mr. Zohn to leave our premises as soon as he arrived."

"How did he take it?"

"Difficult to tell," Maud Eitner said. "It's not the kind of face on which you can read much more than bad shaving technique. He said could he see Mr. Mattlin and hear Mr. Mattlin tell it to him in person. I said no, because Mr. Mattlin was not coming in today."

"He ask about me?" I said.

"Immediately," Maud Eitner said. "I told him you'd come in a few minutes after nine, and I'd told you the audit was off, so you left. There was still nothing in Zohn's face when he said thank you."

"That's all he said?"

"No," Maud said. "When he went to the door he added you will be hearing from me."

"Will we?" I said.

"Young man," Maud Eitner said, "I am nobody to ask. I don't yet know the answers to anything. I am merely following your orders."

She'd never get better ones.

"What about Mattlin?" I said. "Did you follow that one?"

"I didn't have to," Maud said. "As soon as I got rid of Zohn I went back to my office to call Mattlin at Bernie Yustin's office, as you suggested, but as I came in my door the phone was ringing. It was Mattlin on the wire. He wanted me to find Ted Leff and have him waiting in the office when he got there. That's here, from where I'm calling, so you'd better get up here. Mattlin will be here any minute."

He had not yet made it when I got there.

"Oh, good morning, good morning, good morning," the girl behind the billing-machine fort said. Or sang. On Seventh Avenue a girl as cheerful as that so early in the morning would have been arrested for soliciting. "Miss Eitner said you should go right into the bookkeeping department."

"Thanks," I said. "By the way, is your name really Adler?"

"Of course it is," she said. "What a funny question to ask."

"You don't look like an Adler," I said.

"What a funny, funny thing to say," she said. "What do I look like?"

"You put it that way," I said, "I think you look like Nancy Carroll."

Miss Adler laughed. "How do you know Nancy Carroll's real name isn't Adler?" she said.

"I don't," I said. "It's just I never think of her as an Adler."

"A lot of people would think that's an anti-Semitic remark," Miss Adler said. "But I don't because I'm not in any way prejudiced. I understand how people feel, and what I think you must do, you must not feel unkindly about the Adlers. Even Sherlock Holmes? The detective? In those stories? I've just started reading them. My boyfriend recommended them, and I notice the only girl Sherlock Holmes ever liked was an actress named Adler. What do you think of that?"

It was Maud Eitner I wanted to get with, and I had to do it fast, but I couldn't help taking another look at this dame. Was she kidding me?

"I think maybe I haven't given enough attention to the Adler clan," I said. "When things ease up—"

I never finished that remark because just then Maud Eitner opened the door from the inside office. "You leave Benita alone," she said.

"All I'm trying to do is sell her a twenty-payment life policy," I said. "It's for her own good. With a double-indemnity clause, which comes to only twenty-eight dollars a year extra, she'll be financially independent at seventy-seven."

"Benita is going to be financially independent by Decoration Day," Maud Eitner said. "She's engaged to be married. This way, Mr. Leff."

91

We went through a door, past the Ping-Pong table, and into the Bookkeeping Department, where yesterday the cash-payments book and I had made like Archimedes in the bathtub.

"There's one question I want to ask you," Maud said. "This thing you're cooking. Is it going to hurt Ralph Mattlin in any way?"

"If anything I had in mind had any chance of causing Ralph Mattlin so much as a torn cuticle," I said, "you'd be the last person in the world I'd ask to help me."

There's one thing about plain women. When you pull the right switch, they light up like the Con Edison tower on Fourteenth Street. I've always liked the way it looks on a Saturday night. It never looked better than Maud Eitner looked at that moment.

"Since yesterday," she said, "I've been trying to figure something out about you."

"Don't waste your time," I said. "There's nothing complicated about me. I'm all surface."

"No, you're not," she said. "On the surface you're a tall, skinny kid with curly yellow hair, pale blue eyes, and just enough freckles to complete the picture of a young Swede off some Midwestern farm who has just arrived in town from a hick medical school to take up his duties on the Bellevue ambulance. But underneath the surface I know better. Underneath the surface I'm trying to figure out if you're a smart Jewish boy with a touch of the bastard in him, or a full-grown bastard who happens to have just sort of incidentally a touch of the smart Jewish boy. Now this morning, I think you are—"

"Don't tell me," I said. "Remember what happened to the centipede when he was asked how he walked."

The phone rang. She took it from the roll-top desk.

"Yes, Benita? Okay, fine. He'll be right in." Maud Eitner hung up the phone. "Ralph Mattlin just came in," she said. "He's asking for you. Let's go."

We went back along the open space, past the Ping-Pong table, toward the section of the loft that faced the Fourth Avenue and Twenty-ninth Street corner of the building. In the garment center this is the part of a loft that is known as Mahogany Row. The reason is primitive. If the firm is fancy enough to include a private office for the boss, his door will be made of dark wood instead of, like the Shipping door out back, green tin. Ralph Mattlin's door was made of dark wood. Maud Eitner rapped her knuckles on it.

"Herein!" Ralph Mattlin's voice called from inside. The visit to Dr. Yustin had obviously calmed him down. The guy I had left two hours ago would have called a plain, ordinary and not very enthusiastic "Come in!"

Maud Eitner and I went in. The first thing I noticed was that Ralph Mattlin's office differed from his home in only two respects. There was no fireplace, and the Grubensteller portrait of his mother on the wall was smaller than the one on East Thirty-eighth Street. The eyes, though, they had that same look of Christmas-tree bulbs that had just been switched on, and they had that same trick of following you around the room.

"Come in, Mr. Leff," Mattlin said. "Maud, would you hold my calls? I don't want to be interrupted."

"Certainly," Maud Eitner said. She went back through the door and pulled it shut.

"Sit down, Mr. Leff," Ralph Mattlin said.

I sat down in an armchair facing his desk. Mattlin was wearing a dark gray worsted with a pattern that seemed a little too busy for Fourth Avenue. Somehow, though, it looked right on him. There are guys who can wear clothes and there are guys who can't. Even though Mattlin's office obviously contained at the moment two guys who could, there was something funny about his jacket. It was single-breasted, but the lapels were high and peaked. Like a rabbit's ears.

"I'm sorry about the hasty way I left my house this morning," Ralph Mattlin said. "Your revelations were rather upsetting, as I'm sure you can imagine, and my first thought was to do something about them."

"Naturally," I said. "That would be anybody's first thought."

"Was it yours?" Mattlin said.

"Naturally," I said again.

He laced his fingers together and leaned back in the chair behind the desk. He nibbled one of his knuckles gently as he stared at me in silence for a few moments. "Mr. Leff," he said. "Would you mind telling me what your first thoughts were?"

This boy was giving a new dimension to the process known as leading with your chin.

"Well, like this," I said.

I tried for the tone Rabbi Goldfarb used to use down on East Fourth Street when he explained to a father why it was better to take the fifty-dollar rather than the twenty-five-dollar training job for a boy's bar mitzvah. What the boy learned in those few weeks before he became a man would last him the rest of his life. Why not give him the best?

"My first thought, Mr. Mattlin," I said, "I thought, I've found a crook in your office. You find a crook, naturally you expect to see him punished. Then, after I left your house a couple of hours ago, my next thought, I thought but this is no ordinary crook."

"How do you mean?" Ralph Mattlin said.

I couldn't see the knuckle he was nibbling, but the nine others were white.

"Well," I said, "I mean how you talked about him. Mr. Nachman. He'd been with you from the beginning. He was a decent person. You've always trusted him. All those things you said. They made me think maybe there's more to it than met the eye. I mean I began to think maybe there's some sort of explanation behind the stealing that I didn't know about. Maybe I shouldn't go running to the cops before I find out what the explanation is. That's what I thought."

Mattlin unlaced his fingers. He took a cigarette from a glass tray on his desk and fired up. "When you say cops," he said carefully, then he seemed to decide to retool the sentence. "No, wait," he said. "You really intended to go to the police?"

"Not for real," I said. "I mean not directly. I don't know anything about the police. What I was going to do was tell my boss. After all, it was Arnold Zohn who was really doing the audit. I'm just his assistant. What I discovered, technically

94

speaking, I should have brought the information to him. It's just possible, after he told you about it, the thing could have ended up in the hands of the cops."

"But you decided not to speak technically," Ralph Mattlin said. "You decided to bypass Mr. Zohn and bring the information to me. For reasons you explained at my house earlier this morning."

"That's right," I said. "So naturally, after I left your house, my thinking continued along the same lines. What my thinking did, it said to me, look, you've kept Arnold Zohn out of it up to now, how about keeping him out of it until Mr. Mattlin decides what he wants to do. Does that make sense, Mr. Mattlin, or doesn't it?"

"Go on, please," Mattlin said through a belch of smoke as big as a leg of lamb.

"So I called your secretary," I said. "I told her something important had come up, and you knew all about it, and I said I thought you'd appreciate it if, when Arnold Zohn came in here this morning, she'd tell him to beat it until you called him to come back and continue the audit. Assuming you wanted it continued."

Mattlin did that funny thing he'd done down on Thirty-eighth Street. He examined the burning end of his cigarette as though he didn't trust what it was doing. "You were getting Mr. Zohn out of the way," he said finally. "Would you mind telling me why?"

"Not out of the way," I said. "Out of *your* way, Mr. Mattlin. There's a difference."

"Is there?" Mattlin said.

The only other boy I knew who could put the lifted eyebrow into his voice like that was Lew Cody, and old Lew wasn't making pictures any more.

"I think so," I said. "After all, I asked myself, what does Mr. Mattlin want out of all this? Two things, I answered myself. He'd like to get his fifty thousand bucks back, and he'd like to keep this nice person, his friend Mr. Nachman, he'd like to keep him out of jail. From the way you took him uptown to this Dr.

Yustin, I figured you figured Dr. Yustin could help you accomplish this. So why should I louse up your chances by letting a not too smart accountant like Arnold Zohn get in the way?"

Mattlin punched out the cigarette and went for another one as though he got billed for the amount of time between puffs. "As a matter of fact," he said, "that's almost exactly what happened. Under questioning by Dr. Yustin it developed that Mr. Nachman has never liked my starting this firm. From the beginning he was terrified, and convinced that I would lose every penny of my investment and go bankrupt. So he started siphoning off those sums every week and putting them into a special account in his name. When I went broke, he felt, he would have this money to give me to tide me over until I could find my feet in some other business. Every penny he took is in the account, and he's turned the entire sum over to me so I can deposit it in the firm bank account, where it belongs."

That could have been, as he put it, almost exactly what happened. The way I was putting it was: always keep your eye on the word "almost."

"Then you don't need Mr. Applebaum's loan?" I said.

"No, we don't," Ralph Mattlin said.

"Which means you don't need Arnold Zohn poking around in your books and records," I said. "Doing audits you don't need and don't want."

"That's correct," Mattlin said.

"Well," I said, "it looks like I've done a good morning's work for you."

He got the hint. I could tell from the way he tried to drive the cigarette through the ashtray into the desk. "You have indeed," Ralph Mattlin said. He paused to get the match and the new cigarette together. "And I wonder if there's any way that I can express my gratitude."

He could stop wondering. I had a program all worked out.

"You could remove me from the ranks of the unemployed," I said.

"In what way?" Mattlin said.

"Well," I said. "Arnold Zohn hired me yesterday for the sole

96

purpose of impressing you he has a staff when he came here to do this audit. Now that he doesn't have the audit, he doesn't need a staff. So I'm out on my tail. You, on the other hand, Mr. Mattlin, what you don't have is a bookkeeper."

"Don't I?" he said.

It was my turn to put the raised eyebrow into my voice. "I can't believe you intend to let Mr. Nachman come back to work here as your bookkeeper," I said.

"Can't you?" he said.

Now he was overdoing it. A man with two raised eyebrows loses his effectiveness. He just looks surprised.

"I don't see how you can let him come back," I said. "You may have succeeded in keeping what he's done from the cops, but you'll never keep it from the people who work here. These things get around."

"Do they?" he said.

You bet your ass they do, sonny boy. And he knew who would see to it that they did.

"Always," I said. "On top of that you've got a partner. I don't know anything about Mr. Merritt, but I do know that Mr. Nachman, what he was stealing here for these past three years, he was stealing it from both of you. Not only from you, Mr. Mattlin, but also from Mr. Merritt. On the other hand, he was stealing for only one person. For you. It's true the firm got all the money back, so Mr. Merritt has got back his half too, but if I were Mr. Merritt, from now on I'd be pretty suspicious about what an ex-crook was doing with my books and records. I'd be asking myself what's Mr. Nachman going to do next?"

Mattlin attacked the ashtray again with the cigarette that must have still had in it at least four good drags. "As a matter of fact," he said, "I've decided to send him to Lakewood for a few weeks for a rest." He set the new cigarette between his lips and talked around the flame he was lifting to it. "Mr. Leff," he said, "I think, if I understand your drift, you would like to take over Mr. Nachman's job here at Mattlin & Merritt?"

My analysis on Thirty-eighth Street was correct. A total schmuck he wasn't.

"That's right," I said. "I would."

"It doesn't pay very much," Mattlin said.

In a half-hour of trading punches, a moment of honesty always goes over big. I went over.

"According to the cash-payments book," I said, "Mr. Nachman was being paid eighty-five dollars a week. That's twenty-five a week more than Arnold Zohn promised yesterday morning he'd pay me."

Ralph Mattlin blew out the match. "Mr. Leff," he said, "the job is yours."

See how easy it is to take a giant step in the business world?

"Thank you," I said.

"On one condition," Mattlin said.

"What's that?" I said.

"That you keep to yourself what you discovered," he said. "I think it would merely make all our employees nervous to know the facts, and I'd rather not upset my partner. I mean, after all, no harm has been done. The money has been returned. Mr. Merritt is a sensitive man. His function to the firm is editorial. The news can only upset him. Why interfere with his function for no good reason?"

"I see your point," I said. "I won't say anything about this to anybody."

"Thank you," Mr. Mattlin said.

"On one condition," I said.

The concealed bastard began to shine through the gentleman in the pale blue eyes. "What's that?" he said.

"If you'll tell me where you got that suit," I said.

Mattlin looked surprised but also pleased, and it didn't stop him from talking. "I had it made in London," he said. "Why?"

Before I finished with him I intended to have a few made in the same place.

"No particular reason," I said. "It just looks good."

"It should," he said. "At the prices they charge over there." He stood up. "Now I think it would be a good idea if we went down the hall so you can meet Mr. Merritt."

9

"Did You Hear
the One about
the Chorus Girl
and the Bank?"

What puzzled me was how Mattlin had met him. There are combinations that just don't seem to make any sense. You meet a man and a woman. You're told they're Mr. and Mrs. Your first reaction is how in God's name did those two get together?

Ralph Mattlin and Gene Merritt reminded me of the magazine that the Shelley and Keats buffs in Thomas Jefferson High used to pass from hand to hand in English class like the stick in a relay race. I wasn't one of the runners, but these boys who make with the iambic pentameter don't always have twenty-twenty vision. That's why one day, on my way through the cafeteria, a member of the club handed me a copy of the magazine. Leafing through it, I didn't exactly understand what was making it so tough for the Four Eyes Set to hold their water. What I was examining looked like the Sunday roto section of the *Jewish Daily Forward*. Except that this *Vanity Fair* had more English words under the pictures, and you didn't have to read the thing backwards.

Then I came to a page marked *Impossible Interviews,* and I stopped leafing. The page was dominated by a cartoon showing Queen Mary of England facing Madame Lupescu of Rumania. When I say facing, I mean glaring at. Between the two women there was a poem:

> "The Court of St. James all detest you,"
> Said Queen Mary to Madame Lupescu.
> "I'm just doing my best,"
> Replied the toast of Budapest.
> "Why sneer with misgiving
> At what brings us our living?
> So be honest and tell me the truth—
> Try to remember how it was in your youth—
> It's such a bad thing
> To sleep under a king?
> I esk you? I esk you? I esk you?"

Ten years later, the moment Ralph Mattlin brought me into his partner's office, I remembered *Vanity Fair*. Not because of the poem. Let's face it, Robert Browning it didn't put out of business. In fact, I didn't even remember the magazine because of the cartoon, which was done by a guy named Ralph Barton, and I've yet to see anything better, or even as good. No. What made me think of *Vanity Fair* when I first saw Ralph Mattlin and E. Spinoza Merritt side by side was the caption at the top of that page: *Impossible Interviews*.

When you get right down to it, getting smarter is nothing more than a matter of keeping your eyes open as you get older, and getting older isn't really much more than a matter of meeting more people. You can't duck it, no matter where you go. Even Robinson Crusoe couldn't avoid it. The more people you meet, the less stupid you should get about what makes people tick. Or so it would seem. But it doesn't always work that way. Not for me, anyway. I've met as many people as the average guy, and probably more than most. And yet every time I meet a new one, instead of drawing on the stuff I've learned or should have learned with the years about human nature, I find myself falling back on the same old yardstick I picked up on

East Fourth Street before I was bar mitzvah. The way I remember my French class in Thomas Jefferson High, the Frogs have a saying that covers this. It begins *Plus ça change.*

"So what kind of schmootz are you running around with now?" my mother used to ask when I came home and happened to mention a friend I'd just met. "A Galitzianer or a Deitch?"

What she was asking was: are you spending your time with one of those greasy slobs from Eastern Europe, or one of those snooty bastards from Germany? With my old lady, there was no middle ground. For her the world was divided into two groups. Aristocrats and serfs. Since she and my father had both been born serfs, she naturally hated serfs more than she hated aristocrats. But not by much. It was this small gap that gave me my yardstick. A snooty bastard, no matter what his other qualities might be, was better than a greasy slob.

That was why, when I first saw Ralph Mattlin in his house on Thirty-eighth Street, I was impressed even though I didn't really want to be. A greasy slob he wasn't. And that was also why, when I first saw E. Spinoza Merritt in his office I was, as Dickens is always putting it, dumbfounded, incredulous and astonished. He meant I was surprised. A greasy slob E. Spinoza Merritt couldn't be anything but.

It was written all over him like "Spit Is a Horrid Word, But It's Worse at the End of Your Cigar" was written all over the Cremo ads. If somebody had put a dirty apron around his little pipestem waist, E. Spinoza Merritt would have been a dead ringer for Fahvel the Flicker, the half-witted Polish immigrant who for a nickel used to pluck the feathers off the chickens my mother and her neighbors used to buy in Shumansky's butcher store on the Avenue C corner of East Fourth Street.

It was from watching Fahvel when I was a kid that I picked up another one of those yardsticks that's as hard to shake off as a lisp. On East Fourth Street you could always tell a person had something wrong with the machinery between his ears from the way his eyeglasses sat on his nose. If they sat straight, parallel with his forehead, you were safe in assuming he could maybe

101

find his way across the street without help. If the glasses sat crooked, one lens higher than the other, you could be sure he'd never find third base. Fahvel's glasses had always sat crooked. So did E. Spinoza Merritt's.

When Mattlin and I came into his office, those glasses all of a sudden got crookeder. Merritt's head, which was dipped down over his desk, came up as though we'd caught him with his hand in his fly. Maybe we had. The glasses jumped. As they started to settle back on his nose, I saw his eyes. They were the eyes of Fahvel the Flicker at the moment when he began to suspect he was going to be screwed out of his nickel. Merritt looked frightened. I wondered why he was making such a big deal out of looking up from his desk. Hal Roach used to have Tige, the bulldog in the *Our Gang* comedies, do it as regularly as he had him stop at hydrants. Then I saw the top of Merritt's desk. It looked like the window in a pet shop. We'd caught Merritt cutting up newspapers into strips with a pair of long golden scissors. "What is it?" he said.

Even his voice sounded like Fahvel's. High-pitched. Like a frightened girl trying to sound like one of those dog whistles advertised by Abercrombie & Fitch for people who want to summon Rover but don't want to hear themselves doing it.

"Are we interrupting?" Mattlin said.

"I'm choosing the pictures for the Christmas list," Merritt said.

I was surprised he could speak. His voice seemed to be coming out of the bottom of a cylinder. He was wearing an ordinary shirt, but the collar looked like a sore-throat bandage in a comic strip. After a few moments I saw why: his head sat high on his neck, like a jelly apple on a stick.

"This won't take long," Mattlin said. "I just want you to meet our new bookkeeper."

Something swept across those frightened eyes. It could have been only that his head moved and the light in the room made a shadow across his face. Or maybe it was the eyes themselves that moved. Like in a gangster movie when the stool pigeon is talking to the boys he's stooling on, and the camera comes in on his face at the moment when he realizes, in the middle of what he thinks is a casual conversation, that the hard boys have caught onto who's been singing to the cops. "What happened to Mr. Nachman?" Merritt said.

"He's sick," Mattlin said. "I sent him to the doctor. He says it's Mr. Nachman's heart. He's got to quit. He's really too old, Gene. Luckily Mr. Leff came along. Mr. Leff, this is my partner, Eugene Merritt. Gene, this is Mr. Leff. Ted Leff."

Merritt stuck out his hand. I stepped back. If I hadn't, I would have been run through like a slice of onion intended for the skewer of a shashlik. Merritt was holding out the pair of long golden scissors as though he had taken up his position for the first move in a fencing lesson.

"Sorry," he said. He put down the scissors and tried again. "Pleased to meet you, Mr. Leff."

"Same here," I said. I took his hand. It was like lifting a matzo ball out of a plate of cold chicken soup.

"Have you worked in publishing before?" Merritt said.

The eyes did it again. But not in the same way. I made one of my mental notes. These two boys didn't trust each other. Then I added the obvious subhead to my mental note: because I had been hired by Ralph Mattlin, Mr. E. Spinoza Merritt would never trust me. The conclusion was even more obvious. If I was thinking of a free ride in this outfit, the ice wagon to which I'd have to hitch my sled was the one owned by Ralph Mattlin.

"Only as an accountant," Ralph Mattlin said. Not quickly. Or awkwardly. He did it as smoothly as a girl in the window of Child's putting a plate under a fresh stack of buckwheats. But I could tell Mattlin wasn't taking any chances on my answering his partner's question. He was getting there first. "Mr. Leff was auditing our books with Arnold Zohn," Mattlin said. "He discovered that Mr. Nachman was mixing up things so badly, because of his age and his illness apparently, that about fifty thousand dollars in cash was being held in a special emergency account that you and I didn't even know about."

Merritt's eyes jumped. I began to get the feeling of a guy wearing a mask. The only thing that was real was what you could see through the eye slits.

"We have fifty thousand dollars more than we thought we had?" he said.

Again I had the feeling I'd had about Ralph Mattlin the day before. The feeling that the man I was looking at, no matter what else I would find out about him, this much I would never be wrong about: when it came to money he scared easy. I began to see what it was Ralph Mattlin, the elegant almost-goy, and Gene Merritt, the greasy slob, had in common: they were both buck-hungry.

"Fifty plus," Mattlin said. "With that much in the bank, it seemed to me we could do without Mr. Applebaum's loan. So I told Mr. Zohn to go home and I asked Mr. Leff if he'd like to take Mr. Nachman's place. I'm pleased to say he said yes. I hope you approve, Gene."

Merritt giggled. Fahvel used to do that when my mother handed over the nickel. Buck-hungry people are pretty much the same, on Fourth Avenue as well as Seventh. It's not the geography that counts. It's just the amount.

"To a man who finds fifty thousand dollars for us," Merritt said, "I'd be a fool to say no. Nice to have you with us, Mr. Leff. Did you hear the one about the chorus girl and the bank?"

I pressed the right pedal. The thoughtful look slipped into place. It was the one thing about this nut that was suddenly familiar. Seventh Avenue is full of dress salesmen who think it's un-American to end a conversation without adding the latest hot one.

"The chorus girl and the bank," I said slowly. "The chorus girl and the bank. No, Mr. Merritt, I don't think I've heard that one."

"She was generous to a vault," Merritt said. He giggled again, and waited. The eyes jumped with worry. "She was generous to a vault?" he said. "She was generous to a vault?"

I laughed. No point in shaking him up too much. Not at this stage of the game.

"That's a good one," I said.

"It certainly is," Ralph Mattlin said. "Very good, Gene. Very good indeed. She was generous to a vault. One of your best, Gene. Really good. First-rate."

A smear of pleasure swept the fear from the eyes behind the crooked glasses. Merritt picked up a piece of newspaper. "What do you think of this?"

Mattlin and I bent over to look. It was a picture clipped from a rotogravure section. The picture showed the three wise men sitting on their camels and staring up at the star of Bethlehem.

"First-rate, Gene," Mattlin said. "Really very good. I mean that, Gene. Absolutely first-rate."

I got the feeling that Ralph Mattlin treated his partner the way a doctor at Payne Whitney might treat one of his patients who was not exactly violent but the party line was: on your toes, everybody, you never can tell.

"Thanks, Ralph," Merritt said. He turned those eyes on me. "How do you like it, Mr. Leff?"

I moved fast and slipped into my thoughtful look again. "Excellent," I said finally. "Really first-rate. I've never seen the wise men look so, I don't know how to say it. Yes, I know. So intelligent. You feel they're alive. That ought to make up into one of the best Christmas jigsaw puzzles I've ever seen."

It probably would too. I'd never seen a Christmas jigsaw puzzle.

"Thank you, Mr. Leff," Merritt said. "Well, I guess I'd better get back to work." He grabbed the golden scissors like Scaramouche snatching up his sword at the sound of an approaching enemy. "I'd like to have an editorial conference on this at three," he said. "If that's okay with you, Ralph?"

"Perfect," Mattlin said. "That will be swell, Gene. Three o'clock is just right for me."

"After I finish assembling the pictures for our Christmas line," Eugene Merritt said, "I'm planning to write a cookbook. Would you like to know the title, Mr. Leff?"

Go be a schmuck and say no!

"I certainly would," I said.

105

Merritt giggled. "Nobody knows the truffles I've seen," he said.

He was still giggling when Mattlin and I closed the door. He was also slashing away at the pile of newspapers.

"Did I understand that correctly?" I said to Mattlin when we were out in the hall. "You're going to have an editorial conference about that picture?"

Ralph Mattlin gave me another dose of the over-the-glasses look. I had the sudden feeling he liked me. I was willing to bet that if I didn't drop the ball, in a short time that over-the-glasses look might become a wink.

"Gene doesn't like to make crucial decisions by himself," he said. "On this one, you know how the three wise men are looking up at the star?"

I nodded and said, "What about it?"

"Well," Mattlin said, "Gene will want me to help him decide whether in our puzzle the camels should be facing right or left."

10

" You've Got a Better Chance Than You Had Before I Showed Up"

I waited until five minutes after three before I walked out to the reception room.

"Miss Adler?" I said.

"Oh, Mr. Leff." The inside of my head went *boing!* It was the sort of happy squeal you began to hear years later on TV commercials when the owner of the puppy tears off the top of the box of new-type dog food. "I've just heard the good news," she said. "Maud tells me you're our new bookkeeper."

With Maud Eitner's gift for accurate reporting she could very well be in the running when the Columbia School of Journalism decided to look for a new dean.

"That's right," I said. "I haven't met the entire staff yet, but speaking for the reception desk, I'd say it's in good hands."

"Why, thank you, Mr. Leff." She sounded like Kate Smith doing "Silent Night" on Christmas Eve. It looked to me all of a sudden like all those boys who were hunting for Shangri-La were wasting a lot of travel money. The answer seemed to be: find yourself a comfortable spot behind a billing machine in a reception room. "Just for that," Miss Adler said, "you can call me Benita."

"All right, Benita," I said. "Now could you tell me how I get to Miss Eitner's office?"

"With the greatest of pleasure, Mr. Leff," she said. "Except I think she's in with Mr. Mattlin, taking dictation. Let me check. One moment, please."

While she picked up the phone on her desk, I spent the moment wondering about the boy Miss Adler was engaged to marry. She must have found him in *Hansel and Gretel*. If he didn't like sugar he was heading for one hell of a great big bellyache.

Miss Adler held out her phone to me and said, "Miss Eitner wants to talk to you."

"Hello, bookkeeper," she said. "What's on your mind?"

The answer would have surprised her, so I didn't make it. It surprised me. Miss Adler's beautifully rounded outlines were suddenly interfering with what the wild waves were saying to one of their most attentive listeners. Me. I made a mental note to look into the matter. But not at the moment. First things first, Julius Rosenwald always said. And to Julius, even Montgomery Ward had enough brains to listen.

"What's on my mind is the exact location of your boss at this moment," I said. "Is he in Merritt's office?"

"No, Merritt just went into his," Maud said. "Merritt likes to have the editorial conferences in Mattlin's office."

I could understand that. If you spend your days slicing up newspapers into neat little piles, you don't want them pushed around by people opening and closing doors that cause drafts.

"Will they be tied up for a while?" I said.

"Hard to tell," Maud said. "Depends on what the subject is."

"Camels," I said. "Which way should they face?"

"Oh, dear," Maud said.

"You mean me?" I said.

"No," Maud said. "I mean that could take the balance of the afternoon. Our Christmas business is always the biggest of the year, so they like to be careful about all the details. Last year, when we did one that showed the scene in the manger, my boss and Gene Merritt spent two days trying to decide on the color of the straw."

"Just because I'm a bookkeeper," I said, "don't treat me like a hick. I happen to know about straw. I've watched it in the wind. Straw comes in only one color."

"Not in this business," Maud Eitner said. "We did it in shocking pink for the West Coast, puce with a touch of orange for the Northeastern states, and strictly magenta for the South."

It sounded like my spring line the year I was cutting taffeta on Seventh Avenue.

"You think Mattlin & Merritt will be in there long enough for you and me to have a talk?" I said.

"It'll have to be here in my office," Maud said. "Sometimes they buzz me to come in and take notes."

It suddenly crossed my mind that buzzing her might be fun. "No, I don't want to do it in your office," I said. "I don't want them to think you and I are getting chummy."

"Aren't we?" she said.

"Yes, but for a while let's keep it confidential," I said. "What do you suggest?"

"Let me think," Maud said. She either did, or she stayed off the phone long enough to give me the impression that she was. When she came back on the wire she said, "You're in luck, bookkeeper. It happens to be Friday, and on Fridays your new boss, Mr. E. Spinoza Merritt, always goes up to the Bronx to consume a bowl of Sabbath noodle soup with his parents, and he makes it a point to get there before his mother lights the candles at sundown. So he'll be leaving here around five."

"Now all we have to do is get rid of Mattlin," I said.

"He's doing that for us," Maud Eitner said. "He just poked his head out of his office to tell me to call his home and tell Mr. Nachman he'll be there by five to help the old creep pack and take him to the train."

"My God," I said. "Arnold Zohn told me Mattlin is a gentleman, but isn't this carrying things too far?"

"Not far enough," Maud Eitner said. "Honest Abe is only going to Lakewood."

"I'm surprised Mattlin's not carrying him there piggyback."

"If his parents were still alive," Maud said, "Mattlin probably would. He's really in deep with Uncle Abe Nachman. Anyway, the decks will be clear shortly after five. Whatever decision they reach on how the camels should face, I'll have to take it over to Production. This is always good for a half-hour at least, production people being slow talkers. So why don't you meet me for a drink at five-thirty around the corner in the Walpole Bar?"

"Why not?" I said. "How about dinner after the drink?"

"I'd love it," Maud said. "But Friday nights I, too, must tackle a plate of Mama's luckshin soup under the Sabbath candles."

"You are forgiven," I said. "When I had a mother I never missed a Friday night, either."

"Listen," she said. There was a change in her voice.

"What?" I said.

"Since you seem to be free," Maud said, "how about coming over to Eighty-eighth Street with me? I think you'll like my mother. If you don't like her, you'll certainly like the chicken soup and gefüllte fish. She's too old to make them herself any more, so they come out of a delicatessen, and if you were raised like me on the belief that your mother was the greatest cook in the world, you have a taste treat in store for you."

I hesitated. I don't do that often. But I don't do other things, either. Like put myself under obligation to people in areas where I don't need loans. I liked this straight, plain, unadorned broad. She had style. She had brains. She had guts. And I suspected she liked me. Maybe for the same reasons. I didn't know that yet. But I knew that ever since my mother died, Friday nights were bad. You can keep moving six nights a week without any trouble if you've got a place to spend the seventh where you can put your feet up and take off your girdle. I hadn't had mine off since the day I came home from the cemetery. Until I found out where I was going in this Mattlin & Merritt thing, it seemed sensible not to take it off in front of comparative strangers.

"Maud," I said. "That's the most tempting proposition I've

110

had since Sarah Bernhardt offered to take me back to Paris as her dresser at the end of her last American tour. But if I can't have you to myself tonight I won't break my date with Gertrude Lawrence."

"Tell her I loved her in *Susan and God* and I hope it runs forever," Maud said. "Some other time for Eighty-eighth Street, then. See you at five-thirty in the Walpole."

If she didn't, I realized as soon as I came in, it would not be the fault of her eyesight. The Walpole Bar looked like one of those French movies that get rave reviews because the producer ran out of money before he got around to the line on the budget marked "Lights." As a result, the whole thing seems to have been photographed in a cellar without windows during an eclipse of the moon. After Jean Gabin, peering around for a place to put his coat, accidentally hung it over the lens of the camera. While I groped my way across the room toward what I hoped would be a corner table, it occurred to me that the Hotel Walpole was part of my whole feeling for Fourth Avenue. Something I'd always known about but had never really looked at.

To me the word "hotel" had always meant one of two things. The Waldorf, which when I was a kid was keeping the corner of Thirty-fourth Street and Fifth Avenue warm for the incoming Empire State Building. Or the New Trelawney, just north of the garment center and west of Broadway, where for two bucks you could spend an hour or a night with any broad you came in off the street with. And no nonsense about carrying in a cardboard suitcase full of old telephone books, either. In fact, if you didn't have somebody to come in off the street with, but you had the five bucks, any bellhop in the joint could supply the omission.

The Hotel Walpole on East Twenty-eighth Street just off Fourth Avenue was something new. Correction. Something old. All I know about architecture is that if the place looks like the Parthenon, stay out of it, or you're liable to be mistaken for the poor slob who is about to be sentenced. And *Hudson River Bracketed,* which was once assigned as outside reading in my English class at Thomas Jefferson High, is the title of a novel by a tomato named Edith Wharton. Even without knowing any more than that, I could tell that the Hotel Walpole belonged to the Let's Paste On More School of Architecture. This school reached the height of its popularity about the time Diamond Jim Brady was just beginning to do some serious work on his belly.

From the street it didn't really look like a building. It looked like a ten-story slab of dirty graystone and dirtier red brick on which the builders had tried to see how many statues of naked broads with strategically placed sandstone veils they could hang before the whole thing toppled over. Here and there, when they remembered what the place was going to be used for, they'd cut a window. But they couldn't have been very enthusiastic about it. Because all the windows looked like portholes. And if there was any chance that these portholes might have admitted some light, this was fixed by surrounding the holes with bunches of complicated gargoyles.

The moment I stepped into the lobby, I knew the same man who had built the place had also decorated it. Either that or it had been done by a relative who was trying to show the builder how closely he was able to follow the basic plan. The faded old plum carpets looked like the outside brick. The naked chicks on the walls were made of bronze but held their veils in the same strategic places. And the electric light bulbs, all colored dog-turd brown, were Christmas-tree size.

When I made it to the corner of the bar and found that what I'd been heading for was what I'd hoped it would be—namely, a corner table—I also found four little old ladies sitting around it.

"Excuse me," I said. I backed away. This was a mistake. It brought the seat of my pants up against the drinking arm of one of the four little old ladies at the next table. What looked like the bottom half of a very dry martini went over her shoulder. "Excuse me," I said again, and made one of my mental notes: get out into the middle of the room, stupid, and let your eyes grow accustomed to the gloom before you make your next move.

One thing about my mental notes. As a rule, they're easy to

follow. Unfortunately this time the rule got dented. The trouble
was that in the Walpole Bar there was no center of the room. As
I found out after backing into two more tables. Every inch of
floor space was covered by a slab of dark brown mahogany.
Every slab was surrounded by four little old ladies. I was about
to grab the arm of a little old man in a blue mess jacket with
gold buttons and ask him to put an appeal for a St. Bernard on
the radio, when Maud Eitner came out of the darkness. She
scooped me up like a train picking up water on its way through
a station.

"Steady on," she said into my ear. Then, into the ear of the
little old man, she said, "Gregory, I've got North Northeast
nailed down with my purse and gloves. If you bring us two of
the usual, but very fast, I think Mr. Leff and I can repel all
boarders."

She steered me around the tables and eased me gently onto a
dark brown leather seat in another corner of the room. Maud
took the seat facing me. After my eyes came back to work I saw
we were facing each other across a slab of mahogany that
seemed to have been carved from a corner of one of the big
ones surrounded by the little old ladies.

"Why didn't you warn me?" I said.

"I've known you only since yesterday," Maud said. "You've
acted and sounded like a young man who knew his way around.
How was I to know you'd never been in a residential hotel
before?"

"Is that what I'm in?" I said.

"Up to your, well, up to your," Maud said. "And possibly
even higher."

I looked around the room. "Why are they all wearing those
funny little hats?" I said. "Like Queen Mary?"

"So everybody will think they've just come in off the street,"
Maud said.

"Haven't they?" I said.

"Of course not," Maud said. "They lie around in their rooms
upstairs all day, clipping bond coupons or whatever their money
is in, and then at five o'clock they put on their hats and come

113

pouring down the elevators to get stoned. Thank you, Gregory."

"Two for North Northeast," the little old man said. He set down two martinis and went away.

"What's with the North Northeast?" I said.

"Gregory used to be a scoutmaster," Maud said. "And I used to be a girl scout. I don't remember how we discovered this about each other, but once we did we started naming the wall tables by boxing the compass. North, North Northeast, Northeast, East Northeast and East take care of the five on this side. Over there, the five on that side, they're East Southeast, Southeast, South Southeast and South. Beyond that, over there where it's really dark, that's *terra incognita*. I don't go there without a pilot or at least a flashlight, but Gregory assures me the danger is really very small, because the drinks are stronger and they glow in the dark. What's on your mind now?"

She made it sound like a shelf in a closet. There was no getting away from it. This broad had something. Several, in fact.

"Is that how you always open a conversation?" I said.

"With certain kinds of people, yes," Maud said. "Benita Adler, for instance. If she'd said she wants to see me, I'd merely show up and wait, because Benita is the earth-mother type. She laughs and sings and skips about like a carefree child, seeing nothing all day long but shimmering decency in people and bathing in sunlight, even when the rain is coming down in sheets. All she wants out of life is just to have a house on a hill, preferably with a thatched roof, and weave mittens for the poor. So when Benita says she'd like to see me, it could be anything from whispering to me the red-hot stop-press news that life is beautiful, to urging me to think pure thoughts. With you, though, when you say you want to see me, your type, I know at once you've been thinking about something that involves the real world we all live in, which means you're thinking about money. So, then, what now, bookkeeper?"

I suddenly began to understand the advantages of badly lighted saloons in residential hotels. This homely broad was beginning to look not so homely.

"Two things," I said. "And they have nothing to do with

114

money. Ralph Mattlin took me into his partner's room and introduced me to E. Spinoza Merritt. What I want to know is why didn't you warn me?"

"Most people, I do," Maud said. "But you, why, frankly, you looked the sort of chap who could handle it."

Even lion tamers look like they can handle it, until they get mauled.

"Is he all right?" I said.

"If you mean is he mentally sound," Maud said, "the answer is yes, definitely. He looks a bit demented, but that's only surface. The crooked eyeglasses. That gaunt, skinny, starved face. The eyes that always seem to have small window shades pulled down just behind the irises. The Adam's apple bobbing up and down in that long, wrinkled, turkey-like neck. All that, yes, he does look like a fully matriculated candidate for Bellevue. Actually, though, Gene Merritt has a brilliant mind. He was cum laude at C.C.N.Y. Or maybe it was Phi Beta Kappa. I'm not sure except that it was something Greek, and as you know, that's a language they rarely use to flunk people out in. Then, I happen to know that when Merritt worked for the *World* for a while after he graduated, Herbert Bayard Swope said Gene Merritt was potentially the most brilliant editorial writer he'd ever known. At that time, I would like to point out, our Gene could have been no more than twenty-one or -two. Does that answer your question about is he all right?"

"It answers it," I said, "but I don't believe a word of the answer. That face. Those eyes. The way his mouth works all the time. Like Mae Murray pouting at you with those, and I quote, bee-stung lips. And those jokes. Oy!"

"Did you hear the one about the chorus girl who was generous to a vault?" Maud said.

"Twice," I said. "When did you hear it?"

"Yesterday," she said. "This morning he came in with a cookbook to be called *Nobody Knows the Truffles I've Seen.*"

"I got a dose of that one too," I said. "Now tell me where he got that cockamaymey name 'Merritt.' "

"When I was a shy little girl," Maud Eitner said, "trying to avoid the boys on the block who wanted to play doctor, cocka-maymeys were pictures you pasted on your wrist with spit. Your own spit, of course. So your mother could be provoked into screaming wash it off, wash it off before you get blood poisoning! If you mean is the name 'Merritt' invented, the answer is yes, but actually it's a sort of translation from our mother tongue. Merritt's real name, the name his parents brought over from Poland, is Wishnick. In Yiddish, as I understand it from my mother, wishnick is a form of booze. Something like brandy. Anyway, brandy is something you use only for celebrations. On state occasions, so to speak. When congratulations have been earned or, stand fast now, merited. Merited. Wishnick to merited to Merritt with two *r*'s and two *t*'s. You grasp?"

"I grasp, I grasp," I said. "Stop hocking me. Does this boy's mind work like that all the time?"

"I'm afraid so," Maud Eitner said. "It's what makes life at Mattlin & Merritt a little difficult at times. Take the editorial conference on camels this afternoon. After Merritt went off to the Bronx to see his mother, which I'm going to have to do likewise ere long, so drink up, bookkeeper, Ralph Mattlin told me what happened. He suggested having the camels face left, not that Mattlin had any convictions about it, but he knows that unless somebody gets the meeting started, Merritt will stall for hours with no decision one way or the other. Stall not as in stable but stall as in vacillate. You follow?"

"I'm right on your tail," I said.

"Good," Maud Eitner said. "The moment Mattlin suggested left, Gene Merritt stopped stalling or vacillating. His reason? One of those first five books the firm published, before they got smart and went into the jigsaw-puzzle business, it was a novel called *So Rose the Red*. A couple of those anonymous reviewers for the news magazines, those boys who don't care what they say, since in effect they're writing the sort of thing women receive in the mail once in a while from sex nuts who get a kick out of putting down on paper unsigned obscenities—these creatures wrote that they saw a hidden political significance in the

116

silly title. They said it was a concealed plea for communism. The news magazines have always been nervous about communism, so the boys and girls who write these anonymous reviews spend a lot of time finding the stuff in all sorts of silly books because it's an easy way to get a raise. Whether that was why *So Rose the Red* flopped I don't know, and nobody knows. But it didn't help. Ever since then Gene Merritt has been terrified of anything that even smells of communism. So today he told his partner if we do a jigsaw puzzle of the wise men and the star of Bethlehem, and we show the camels facing left, there will be people who will read into this a secret attempt on the part of Mattlin & Merritt to orient the puzzle business toward the political left, and some of these anonymous prostitutes who work for the news magazines will even say the firm is attacking Christianity. As a result we'll have not only the whole press in the country down on us, but also the church, because everybody knows the Archdiocese of New York doesn't make a move without consulting the current issue of *Time*. Yes, by all means, Gregory, another drink, please, and I have a feeling Mr. Leff could use one too."

"Make it a double," I said. When the waiter went away I narrowed my eyes like John Barrymore in *The Sea Beast* peering into the mists for a glimpse of the White Whale. "Maud," I said, "you are giving me a muscle, aren't you?"

"What a shocking suggestion to make to a graduate of Ethical Culture," she said. "My dear Ted, any Jewish girl who tells a lie on Friday night as the sun is going down should be forced to spend Rosh Hashanah in Mecca, and I don't mean the temple downtown. If you don't believe me, when Ralph Mattlin comes in Monday morning you ask him."

The advice you get from women is like some of the side dishes you get in cheap restaurants. It's better to let other people take it.

"I believe you," I said. "Now tell me how these two guys ever got together and went into business. I mean, it's Mutt and Jeff all the way, on every level."

117

"What's wrong with that?" Maud said. "The key to a good partnership is not necessarily that both partners should be the same sort of people. Mattlin & Merritt haven't exactly been so spectacularly successful that the firm can be used as an example for others to follow, but I wouldn't be at all surprised to learn that, let's say, Abercrombie was a tall, and handsome, aristocratic-looking man who went to Yale, whereas Fitch was a short, fat, pushcart-peddler type who prepped at the Ninety-sixth Street Talmud Torah."

"But I'll bet they were both nuts about fishing," I said. "Or they never would have gone into the business of selling rods and reels."

"You could say the same about Ralph Mattlin and Gene Merritt. Thank you, Gregory. I think I just saw Miss Adler come in. She seemed to be heading for South Southwest. She's undoubtedly meeting someone, so I'm sure she'll be all right. But she's going to be married on Decoration Day, and I wouldn't want her to be carried down to the altar with a broken neck. So would you give her a helping hand through the encircling gloom and see that she arrives at her table intact?"

"Certainly, Miss Eitner," the little old man said. "For you I would give a helping hand to Herbert Hoover."

He headed for the darkness like Marco Polo pointing toward the shelf of guidebooks in Macy's marked "China and Its Environs."

"What's this same thing you could say about Ralph Mattlin and Gene Merritt?" I said.

"Their backgrounds are different, of course," Maud said. "Mattlin is one kind of Jewish boy. German. Merritt is another kind of Jewish boy. Yours."

"East Fourth Street?" I said.

"Avenue B, actually," Maud said. "Between Sixth and Seventh Streets."

"Close enough," I said.

"His father had a small tailor shop."

"Maud," I said, "on Avenue B there are no big ones."

118

"This one was apparently big enough to get Gene through C.C.N.Y.," she said. "Then he worked on the *World* for a while, but he apparently wasn't happy there. Even though, as I said, the master of the hounds himself thought highly of the cross-eyed lad. A whole series of jobs followed. None of them very good, or very exciting, or very something, whatever it was that kept Merritt moving on to the next one. He was actually selling life insurance when he met Ralph Mattlin."

Why not? Miss Wien in P. S. 188 once told me Karl Marx was selling hot chestnuts when he met Friedrich Engels.

"How did that happen?" I said. "I mean, in the normal course of events guys from Avenue B don't meet guys like Ralph Mattlin."

"The normal course of events, I've discovered, is not always so normal," Maud Eitner said. "Consider, if you will, our present situation. Today a boy from East Fourth Street managed to meet Ralph Mattlin."

Because the boy from East Fourth Street had given the normal course of events a good hard nudge.

"I had help," I said.

"What I like about you," Maud Eitner said, "is your Chesterfieldian streak. When it costs nothing, you are generous. I once read somewhere that Lord Chesterfield wrote all those letters to his illegitimate son because since he couldn't give him a piece of his estate, he gave him a piece of his mind. You got my help because I wanted to give it to you. Somebody must have wanted to do the same for Gene Merritt, and I'll give you one guess who it was."

The pieces began to fall into place.

"Your old friend," I said. "The one, the only, the inimitable Dr. Bernard Yustin."

"For that demonstration of acute perception you can stay after class and help me wash the blackboard," Maud Eitner said. "Merritt had sold a life insurance policy to Yustin, and after the contracts were signed, when he asked the next question, which all these lads ask—namely and to wit, 'Do you have any friends who should be as bright as you are and buy an insurance policy from me?'—Yustin fixed up a date for Merritt to see Mattlin."

"What was Mattlin doing?" I said. "Standing around? Waiting for the right insurance salesman to come along?"

"Yes," Maud said. "Although Ralph Mattlin didn't know it, of course. A lot of people are standing around when in their own minds they think they're doing things and working their heads off. Like Grant in that grocery store at Galena. He didn't really know the Civil War was just around the corner. Mattlin is another case in point. He was thirty-two years old. He'd been out of Yale for ten years, and nothing much had happened. He wasn't starving, because his mother had left him the family house and everything that's in it. That wasn't much, but it was more than boys on East Fourth Street get left. Mattlin didn't have too much trouble finding work. Yale men who look like Ralph Mattlin never do. The father of one of his college chums owned a concert-booking agency, so Ralph went to work there for a while. He hung around with musicians and singers, which he seemed to like. Just when he stopped liking it, I don't know, but after the musicians and singers, he was involved in theatrical financing for another little while. Or a medium-sized while. You know the kind of thing. Helping raise money for what are known as Broadway Ventures. I guess they weren't very good ventures, but the financing experience led to where you would think it would lead. Wall Street. Mattlin was actually working as a customers' man for Scully, Frick, Cohn & McDowell when he met Gene Merritt at a bridge game. When he came into Mattlin's house on Thirty-eighth Street, Merritt was carrying *Lord Jim*."

His lordship must have been on a low-calorie diet at the time. "The book?" I said.

"Bookkeeper," Maud said, "I am beginning to wonder about you. Here I've had you indexed neatly under the column headed 'Unstupid,' and then you make a remark like that."

"I was merely expressing my astonishment," I said. "Surely, Maud, you're not so dumb that you think I'm dumb enough to think Merritt was carrying a man named Lord Jim? After all, Maud, where would a greaseball like Merritt from Avenue B meet a lord?"

"Tell me something," Maud Eitner said. "Did you ever lose an argument?"

"Once," I said. "It taught me a lesson."

Maud laughed. "Bookkeeper," she said, "I think you have earned another round."

"Petty cash?" I said.

"Naturally," she said. "But this time you will write the voucher. After all, you're now the bookkeeper."

She made a noise. The waiter came. She made another noise. The waiter left.

I said, "Why was Merritt carrying *Lord Jim?*"

"He was an insurance salesman, and they spend a lot of time in subways," Maud said. "Riding to and from the residences and offices inhabited by suckers. Merritt liked to fill the time reading something other than those car ads for Listerine that say 'Behind His Back They Call Him Hal, and They Don't Mean Hallelujah!' Gene Merritt liked to read books. It turned out not only did Ralph Mattlin like to read books too, but at the time he happened to be reading his way through Conrad."

"How many books?" I said.

"The Memorial Edition comes to twenty-three volumes," Maud said.

"I once started to read my way through the *Encyclopaedia Britannica,*" I said. "Twenty-four volumes."

"You're counting the index," she said. "That's cheating. How far did you get?"

"A-1 AT Lloyd's," I said. "A popular expression denoting superexcellence."

"You should have stayed with it to AALSMEER," Maud said. "A town in the province of North Holland."

"I'll get right back to it tomorrow," I said. "Tonight tell me why Ralph Mattlin was reading his way through Conrad."

"Does there have to be a reason?" she said.

"There doesn't have to be, but there is," I said. "I can tell from your delivery. You set things up like the pin boy in a bowling alley. You've set me up for a reason. Now deliver."

"You won't believe this," Maud said.

"Oh, my God," I said. "Bernie Yustin again?"

"None other," Maud said. "It seems Mattlin went into analysis after his mother died because he was troubled by his relationship to his uncle, Mr. Nachman. He had a sense of responsibility, an involvement with the old man that Bernie decided was a sense of guilt about a substitute father. Anyway, I don't know whether the analysis wasn't going well, or whether it was another one of Bernie's bright ideas. He's pretty unorthodox. The way he works, I mean. A lot of other analysts in this town think he should be arrested. I'm sure someday he will be. He takes a lot of chances with his patients, and one of these days his luck will run out. Anyway, he told Ralph Mattlin that Conrad had anticipated Freud in many areas, and if he immersed himself in Conrad he couldn't help finding some of the keys to his problem."

"Did he?" I said.

"That's the wild thing about Bernie Yustin," Maud said. "You think he's a fraud because of something he's done which seems absolutely insane, and then as a result of the absolutely insane thing something happens to make you wonder. Like here. From talking about *Lord Jim,* Ralph Mattlin and Gene Merritt learned they both hated what they were doing. Mattlin wanted to get out of Wall Street, and Merritt wanted to stop selling insurance. A little more talk, and they learned what they really wanted to do was publish the things they liked to read. The only problem was how, and how always means money. Mattlin had a friend who was rich enough to take a chance on a favorite bridge player, and Merritt had sold enough insurance policies to have laid down lines to a few people who could stand a few tax deductions. So they managed to scrape together about two thirds of their capitalization, and then guess what happened? Although if by this time you really still have to guess, out of the column headed 'Unstupid' you go."

I didn't want to get out of that column. Not so long as this dame had set it up.

"Bernie Yustin, of course," I said.

"Of course," Maud said. "He had a patient named Mrs. Applebaum. She was having trouble walking on New York sidewalks, because every place she went she saw or she thought she saw a great big grocery store with her husband's name on it. I would have thought the way to solve that problem is to change the name of her husband's chain of stores to Kelley, but in these matters my thoughts are not always completely sound. Anyway, Mrs. Applebaum was hitting the leather three times a week in Bernie Yustin's office. This led Bernie to introduce Mr. Applebaum to Ralph Mattlin and E. Spinoza Merritt. Thus the book-publishing firm of Mattlin & Merritt was born, except that they turned out to be not book publishers but manufacturers of jigsaw puzzles." Maud Eitner finished her drink, glanced at her watch and said, "My mother will positively blow a gasket. When the gong sounds, she puts the noodle soup on the table whether you're there or not. If you're not she opens fire the moment you show your face in the door. Before I go uptown to be nailed to the mast, however, it is now my turn to ask a question. Are you ready, bookkeeper?"

"Always," I said.

"Ted, darling," Maud Eitner said. "What are you doing here?"

"You invited me," I said.

"I don't mean the Walpole," she said. "I mean Mattlin & Merritt."

"I'm keeping the books," I said. "It's my job. I was hired."

"Oh no, you weren't," Maud Eitner said. "You hired yourself." She opened her purse, took out the small mirror and went to work on her face. "I want to know why, and just bring your eyebrows down from the middle of your forehead. It is a waste of time. The innocent act cuts no ice with me. I've known you for about twenty-four hours, perhaps thirty, but already I know this. When smarter cookies start getting made, they'll call them

123

seven-layer cakes and use the ingredients Ted Leff invented. You're not the bookkeeper type, is what I mean. Not that you don't know how to work with figures. But you're not the sort of lad who plans to spend his life hunched over a pile of ledgers. I've watched you operate these past two days. You're not interested in what I see and what everybody else sees. You see something in Mattlin & Merritt that nobody else has yet seen. Not even Ralph Mattlin and Gene Merritt. I want to know what it is."

There's only one time when the best policy actually is to be honest. That's before you've found a reason not to be.

"The reason why most people don't go into business for themselves," I said, "is they can't raise the capital. Raising capital is tough. I know because I once did it. You also know, because you've just told me how Mattlin and Merritt did it. They were lucky. Not everybody has a Bernie Yustin waiting in the wings. Or a loaded bridge-playing friend. I don't have the capital to go into business for myself. Until I walked into your office I didn't even know what business I wanted to go into. What hit me in the Mattlin & Merritt office was very simple. Here's a going concern, I said to myself. Except it's not going anywhere. Here's a setup that's crying to be used. But nobody is using it. This jigsaw-puzzle stuff isn't going to last. It's a fad. Like mah-jongg. How many firms do you know that used to make mah-jongg sets that are still meeting weekly payrolls? If any of them are, they've retooled to make something else, like maybe two-tone halvah. The point I'm trying to make, Maud, is that this Mattlin & Merritt outfit is marking time. With this fifty thousand bucks I've recovered for them, they'll mark time a little longer than they might have done otherwise. But the end will be the same. Unless somebody comes up with a way to use this machine they've put together that isn't being used now. What that way is, I don't know yet. But I can tell you this. I'm going to break my you-know-what to find out. And when I do, Maud, you're the first person I'll tell."

She gave me one of those looks. "How can I be sure of that?" she said.

124

"You can't be," I said. "All you can do is hope."

She stopped fussing with the mirror. She reached for her martini glass, saw it was empty, and left her hand palm down on the table. "You know what I want," she said.

"I know," I said.

"Have I got a chance to get it?" she said.

"You've got a better chance than you had before I showed up."

She shook her head. "I've helped you up to now," Maud Eitner said. "If I'm going to continue helping you, I want a better answer than that."

"You won't like it," I said.

"I don't care about liking it," she said. "I want to hear it."

"All right," I said. "Here it is. The way I figure him, he doesn't want from women what most men want. If he did, he wouldn't be this minute helping a two-hundred-pound stupid old satchel like Mr. Nachman to pack and taking the old idiot to Grand Central. He'd be lining up a piece of you-know-what for tonight. This boy, with his looks, he could have any dame he wants. But he doesn't want any dame. I think he's scared of the kind of dame most men want. I think what he wants from women, he feels he has a better chance of getting it from the not beautiful ones."

Maud Eitner lifted her hand from the table. She dropped the mirror into her purse. She pressed the catch shut with a sharp snap.

"You are a son of a bitch," she said. "But you are a smart son of a bitch. You know when to tell the truth." She stood up. "Is there anything else I can do for you before I go uptown for my weekly dose of heartburn?"

"Yes," I said. "I'd like you to lend me your key to the office."

11

" If You Want Hard Enough to Become a Spinoza, You Become a Spinoza"

When, on Monday morning, I gave the key back to her, Maud Eitner said, "How was Gertie Lawrence?"

"I don't know," I said. "I broke our date."

"You mean when you got back here to the office Friday night after our drink at the Walpole," Maud said, "you found something more interesting than Gertrude Lawrence?"

"I don't want to be unchivalrous," I said. "And with you and me, it's like George Washington and his father. I have to tell the truth. The Gertrude Lawrence I had a date with, she was born Gertrude Lebenbaum. She's the head model for the Divided Uplift Brassiere Company on Madison and Twenty-sixth Street. When that Arab two-liner Omar Khayyám wrote come fill the cup, Gertrude did. Both of them. I've seen her do it any number of times. Never spills a drop. It's a stirring sight. But I wasn't due to be stirred until seven o'clock, when I was supposed to meet her in front of her building. So I came back here for a while to put in the time studying the Mattlin & Merritt operation."

"You sound like you've learned something," Maud Eitner said.

"Enough to make me break my date with Gertie," I said, "and

126

spend all of Saturday and most of Sunday here in the office."

"What did you do with the balance of Sunday?" Maud said. "Write up your notes for teacher?"

"What I learned," I said, "I don't have to write down to remember. I've got it nailed down in my head. As soon as I was sure it was in there good and solid, I called Gertie and asked her to forgive me for Friday night. If she did, I said, I'd make it up to her right away."

"I take it from your smug look that she did," Maud said. "Or you did."

"Not right away," I said. "First she had to get rid of Alan Ellentuch."

"How did he get into this discussion?" Maud said.

"Well," I said, "he's not exactly in it, but he can't be left totally out of it. You see, Alan Ellentuch has just graduated from N. Y. U. Law School and he is taking a cram course for the bar exams. He has an interesting sex life, this Alan. It consists of eating dinner with Gertie three times a week while he tells her about the origins of the statute of limitations. Sunday night Alan had brought a steak that Gertie was just about to put on the fire when I called."

"How did she get rid of him?" Maud said.

"Gertie sent him out to get a can of Sterno for her hot plate," I said. "While he was gone, Gertie brought the steak over to my place."

"You make yourself sound like catnip to the ladies," Maud said. "Frankly, I don't quite see it."

"It's my supply of Sterno," I said. "I never have to send out for refills. Is this one of Mattlin's mornings on the leather with Yustin?"

"Yes," Maud said. "Why?"

"I want to keep the promise I made you Friday night," I said. "When I find out what it is I'm looking for here at Emandem, I told you, you'd be the first one to hear. So come on into the Bookkeeping Department and listen."

"I can't," Maud said. "You've got a visitor. Ring me when you're free."

127

She was off around the Ping-Pong table before I could ask any questions. So I went down to my office and opened the door. I almost didn't close it. Sitting in the chair at the roll-top desk, her hands folded patiently on the black patent-leather pocketbook in her lap, was a little old lady who could have been my mother.

Don't fall down. This is not a ghost story. But it's not a tall tale, either. It's an attempt to tell the truth about certain people and what happened to them. When, in the course of telling it, I run into certain things that other people have never told the truth about, that's not going to stop me. One of those things is Jewish mothers.

They've become a joke. Like Brooklyn. I think Jewish mothers began to go downhill when George Jessel started coming out on stage with a telephone to do the monologue that was supposed to be a conversation with Mama. The tip-off that it was a fake was in what he called her. No Jewish boy who was lucky enough to have the right kind of Jewish mother ever called her Mama. I called my mother Ma. I would no more have thought of calling her Mama than I would have thought of calling Rabbi Goldfarb, Berel.

The first quality that the right kind of Jewish mother used to have is dignity. She knew her place, and she expected her kids to know theirs. If you love someone and they love you back, you don't have to keep reminding each other of that basic fact every time you open your yap with little icky terms of endearment like Mama. Mothers and kids, husbands and wives, you watch and listen. The ones who call each other "Hey!" are making it. A guy who wants his shirt ironed, and he has to ask "Darling" to do it, start looking for the announcement that one of them is heading for Reno on Tuesday.

The next quality the right kind of Jewish mother used to have, she had strength. I don't mean strength like in weight lifting. I mean strength like in steel cable. The kind that holds up bridges. Good Jewish mothers were built to last. They had to be. And they did the building themselves. Learning to be a Jewish mother, in the places Jewish mothers had to learn to be

128

Jewish mothers, like East Fourth Street, for example, it makes this guy in the Bible, the boy who signed his checks "Job," it makes him look like Madame Pompadour in the days when she still had Louis eating out of her—well, this story is designed for the family trade—so let's say out of her hand.

The third quality the right kind of Jewish mother used to have, the only other person I can remember who ever had it was a boy named Stephen Decatur.

"My Teddy, may he always be in the right, but he's my Teddy right or wrong."

All the rest is crap. The jokes about "Eat! Eat! If you don't finish it I'll only have to throw it away." The big yocks about how chicken soup is a sure cure for a compound fracture. The way of talking English that gets a laugh because it's so different from the way Mrs. Cornelius Dressylhuys II talks. Write it off. All of it.

Because the truth is this: if Mrs. Cornelius Dressylhuys II had been driven out of her palace on Biscayne Boulevard because all of a sudden there were antigoy pogroms in Palm Beach, and she managed to escape to a ghetto street in Wolosh-onowa, Poland, where she was forced to sew by candlelight twenty hours every day to earn a few pieces of stale zwieback for her kids, none of the Jewish mothers on the street would have made fun of her because she talked Yiddish with a Palm Beach accent. If any kid did laugh at the immigrant Mrs. Cornelius Dressylhuys II, that kid would have got a shot in the mouth from his Jewish mother. Provided she was the right kind.

My mother was. When she died, after thirty years in this country, she still thought the IRT subway was a personal plot against her, and she'd never eaten a meal that had not been cooked in her own kitchen. But when she walked down the street, the kids playing potsy got out of her way. And if anybody had anything uncomplimentary to say about her Teddy, only the real dumb ones said it when she was around.

When I was a kid I remember reading in the papers about a writer named Jack London. He hated cruelty to animals so much that he started a campaign. He pleaded with people, when they saw an animal act come out on the stage, he begged the customers to stand up and walk out of the theater. Because he knew how the poor bastards were trained. When I see a TV show or a nightclub act in which the so-called comic is trying to lay them in the aisles with jokes about the girls who run Hadassah, I make one of my mental notes: don't tune this slob in again. I know about Jewish mothers. The right kind.

That's why, when I opened the door to my room in the Mattlin & Merritt offices on that day in 1937, I almost forgot to close it. Sitting at the roll-top desk, facing the door patiently, was one of the right kind.

"Come in, Mr. Leff, come in," she said. "I'm Mrs. Wishnick. Downtown here, all right, I'm Mrs. Merritt maybe, but what I'm called I don't care. I'm your boss's mother. How are you?"

I came across the room and took her hand. "I'm fine," I said. "How are you?"

"How should I be on a Monday morning?" she said. "Don't tell me. I'll answer myself. How I am? You want to know how I feel? I feel like this Benedict Arnold."

"Who?" I said.

A worried frown pinched the leathery old face down to half its size. "I got it wrong?" she said. "I mean that man he was a traitor? He sold the plans to this West Point to the other side in the war? The British?"

"I mean no, that's right," I said. "No, I mean yes, there was such a man, but I don't understand what you mean?"

"When we lived on Avenue B, my Gene, when he came home from school, he used to do his homework, he did everything with speaking," Mrs. Merritt said. "Out loud, so his father, either he was sewing or he was working on the pressing machine —so his father could hear, and learn. His mother too. Me. That was our school, our Gene's homework. You'd be surprised how much Mr. Wishnick and I, we learned that way. Ask me the first ten Presidents of the United States. Go ahead, ask me."

She sounded so much like my own mother that it never occurred to me not to do what she said. And do it fast.

130

"Okay," I said. "Who were the first ten Presidents of the United States?"

She took a new grip on the purse in her lap. She tipped her head back a few inches as though she wanted to make sure her voice was reaching the microphone. And she started to recite. "George Washington, John Adams, Thomas Jefferson, James Madison, James Monroe, John Quincy Adams, Andrew Jackson, Martin Van Buren, William Henry Harrison and John Tyler. I could give you more, maybe even up to twenty, but after John Tyler my head starts to hurt. How do you like that?"

Any Jewish boy who didn't know how to answer that question didn't deserve to face another plate of kreplach. "You must have had a wonderful teacher," I said.

Mrs. Wishnick beamed. I don't mean she smiled. Or looked happy. I mean all of a sudden her face looked like Luna Park when they used to throw the switch at sundown.

"I see already for a bookkeeper my Gene didn't hire a dope," she said. "Somebody else, a question like that, they would have said Mrs. Wishnick how smart you are. But you, Mr. Leff, you know it's not me that's the smart one, but my Gene, who taught me, he's the one that's smart. His father, Mr. Wishnick—someday you'll meet him—you know what he can do?"

"No, what?" I said, falling into the rhythm of *q* and *a* that I hadn't used since my mother died.

"Mr. Wishnick," she said, "he can give you the first ten *Vice*-Presidents."

"No!" I said.

The trim little figure in the swivel chair nodded solemnly. "An absolute fact," Mrs. Wishnick said. "And on days when he's feeling right, the Secretaries of State too."

"Mrs. Wishnick," I said, "I must tell you that's very hard for me to believe."

"Naturally," she said happily. "Even people they hear it they still don't believe it. That shows you what a teacher my Gene is."

"That's a nice thing to know," I said. "I mean it makes me

131

Jerome Weidman

feel better about working here. Not that up to now I felt bad. I was proud to get the job with such a firm. But to learn also that my boss is such a good teacher, it sort of—well, I mean, who knows what I can learn here?" All at once she looked troubled. My mind had learned all the shortcuts in a lifetime of conversations with my own mother. I picked up the thread where she had dropped it. "The only thing is," I said, "I don't understand why you should call yourself a Benedict Arnold."

Mrs. Wishnick sent a sharp glance toward the closed door. She pulled her Hudson seal coat more closely around her narrow shoulders. And she moved her small body forward to the edge of the chair. All at once she looked like one of the little old ladies who had been sitting around the slabs of mahogany in the almost total darkness of the Walpole Bar on Friday.

"Because my Gene doesn't know I'm here," Mrs. Wishnick said in a whisper. "I'm here like behind his back. So I'm what else if not a Benedict Arnold?"

If she was made of the same stuff they'd used to put together the late Mrs. Leff, the answer to her question could be anything from "Clara Barton" to "Henry Morgenthau, Jr."

"My own mother, she should rest in peace," I said, "I remember a few times she went to see my teachers in school without telling me. Sure, it was behind my back. But it never made me think she was Benedict Arnold. Because Benedict Arnold, what he did, he did it for money, but what my mother did, she did it for her Teddy. And I'm sure, Mrs. Wishnick, I'm absolutely positive that's what you're doing right this very minute."

The searchlight beam hit me again.

"Friday night, when he came up to eat," Mrs. Wishnick said, "I said like I always say, so what's new in the business? And my Gene he said we have a new bookkeeper. So what do you think my next question it was?"

I turned on a beam of my own. To be a success in American business, you can't depend on Con Edison exclusively. You have to have your own generators.

"Is he a Jewish boy?" I said.

132

She smiled back. "What else?" Mrs. Wishnick said. "And the second question?"

"How smart?" I said. "A lot or a little?"

Mrs. Wishnick laughed. "My Gene he said he didn't know yet but it looked like a lot. Now, this morning, from only these few minutes, I know he said right." The laughter went out of her face. "Your mother? She's gone long already?"

"Last year," I said.

Mrs. Wishnick shook her head. "To everybody it comes," she said. "When it comes for my Gene, I hope—"

She paused. I wondered if she didn't know how to say what it was she hoped, or if she felt she had said too much. So far as I was concerned, she hadn't. Not yet, anyway. I knew what she hoped. My mother had hoped the same thing.

Mrs. Wishnick shrugged. "Anyway," she said, "when he said Monday morning he has to go to the dentist, he won't get to the office till after lunch, I made up my mind I'll come downtown and take a look. Maybe I'll have a little talk with this new bookkeeper."

"I'm glad you did," I said. I was. What I'd discovered from working on the books and records over the weekend had excited me. But I wasn't sure yet what I should do about it. My thinking had gone no further than the decision to discuss it with Maud Eitner. Mrs. Wishnick's visit had interrupted that. It occurred to me that maybe the interruption could be useful. I'd known for a year that I missed my mother. It wasn't until now that I realized how much. I said, "I'm new on the job, as your son told you, Mrs. Wishnick. I don't know too much about the firm yet. If there's anything you can tell me that would help me do a better job for your son, I'd appreciate hearing it. I really would."

Her eyes moved the way her son's eyes had moved on Friday when he had been staring at me across the pile of sliced-up newspapers on his desk. I remembered the feeling that E. Spinoza Merritt was afraid of something. It didn't seem possible that this tough little old lady could be afraid of anything. And yet you never can tell. My mother had been afraid of one thing: that her Teddy would end up on the wrong side of the ledger. I had. On Seventh Avenue, anyway. And it had killed her. And nobody knew it better than her Teddy.

"Mr. Leff," Mrs. Wishnick said.

"Mrs. Wishnick," I said. "Just like to me you're not Mrs. Merritt but you're Mrs. Wishnick, so please, to you I'm not Mr. Leff. To you, you call me what my mother called me."

"Ted?"

"No, of course not."

"Teddy?"

"What else?"

"All right," she said. "So tell me this, Teddy. When you were a boy what did your mother want you should be when you grow up?"

I hesitated. She'd trapped me with her first question. Obviously I couldn't say my mother had wanted me to be the bookkeeper for a firm that manufactured jigsaw puzzles. Not to this little old lady, I couldn't.

"She wanted me to be a doctor or a lawyer," I said. "Like I'm sure you wanted your son to be."

Mrs. Wishnick shook her head. "No," she said. "What we wanted, my husband and I, we wanted our Gene he should be a teacher. That's why my husband gave him a middle name 'Spinoza.' You know Spinoza?"

Intimately.

"Only from what little I remember from school," I said. "And that wasn't much."

"My husband, Gene's father, when he was ironing a pair of pants in the store on Avenue B, with one eye he watched the pants, with the other he was reading in Spinoza. You know why our Gene his first name is Eugene?"

That's another quality the right kind of Jewish mother used to have. Without raising her voice, or leaving the kitchen table on which she was slicing her herrings down to the right-size pieces for her pickling jars, she could adopt the courtroom manner and tone of a prosecuting attorney driving a slippery witness to the wall.

"There's O'Neill," I said. "The man who wrote the plays.

And there's Sarazen, the man who plays golf. But they don't sound right."

"By my husband," Mrs. Wishnick said, "I can tell you this. No son of Morris Wishnick is going to get his name after a man who writes plays or a man who plays golf. Our Gene, he's named after Eugene Victor Debs. He was my husband's second great hero. First Spinoza, and then Debs. And our son he has both those names. Because all his life from the time he was a little boy he loved to learn and to read books and to teach. And the things he loved to learn and to teach, it was good things for other people. Like Mr. Debs. That's why he wanted, my husband, that's why we both wanted our Gene should grow up to be a teacher." Mrs. Wishnick paused, and she looked at me steadily for several silent moments before she said, "That you're not a doctor or a lawyer, it made your mother feel bad?"

I'd never been able to lie to her. I didn't even want to try to do it to this woman who could have been her twin sister.

"I'm afraid so," I said. "We were broke. After my father died, I had to go to work to support my mother as well as myself. So the idea of going to college for four years, and then law school or medical school for another four, it was—"

"I know, I know, I know," Mrs. Wishnick said quietly. "There's always reasons. They're good reasons. Nobody says no. But if you want hard enough to be a Spinoza, or you want hard enough to be a Debs, you become a Spinoza, and you become a Debs, reasons or no reasons. My husband and I, we don't know why our Gene, he was going to be a teacher, we don't know why he changed. We know only it hurt us both, my husband and me. It hurt us when we saw a boy like our Gene running around like a peddler, selling life insurance. That's why, when he met Ralph Mattlin, and they decided to go into the publishing business, my husband and I, we were happy. Books, these are things all my life my husband he loves. To publish books, it's like being a teacher. Maybe even better. Because a teacher can teach only a few people, but books, the things people can learn from books, books can teach the whole world. But it didn't last. I don't know why. We were so proud, my husband and I, three years ago, when those first books our Gene and his partner they published them. We were so—" The little old lady paused again. She pulled the Hudson seal coat tighter at the neck. "From a teacher, a publisher from books," Mrs. Wishnick said in a low voice, "now a manufacturer of puzzles. Puzzles with Jesuses on them yet. For children to play with. Children that they should be reading books and learning."

Her voice seemed to run down rather than stop. She dropped her glance to the purse in her lap. I took another look at it too. It wasn't patent leather. It was made of black alligator. The year before I went into bankruptcy I'd given one to Gertrude Lebenbaum for Christmas. So I knew what they cost. I saw also that Mrs. Wishnick was wearing something I'd never yet given to any girl, no matter how good a cup filler she was: a diamond ring. Gene Merritt's mother was getting her share of his profits from the sale of those puzzles with Jesuses on them yet.

"That's the reason I came downtown today like a regular Benedict Arnold," the old lady said. "Over and over again, these last three years, my husband and I, we ask our Gene what went wrong? Why they stopped publishing books? Always he says the same thing. We lost money, he says. If we didn't stop with the books and start with the puzzles, he said, Ralph Mattlin and I, we would go bankrupt. I believe him. My husband too. To us, our Gene wouldn't lie. But I still don't understand. So every time there's a new person to ask, I come and I ask. Now it's a new bookkeeper. A smart one, my Gene said. So I came to ask again. Maybe this new bookkeeper, maybe he knows the answer?"

I had a tough moment. It was like those times with my mother when I suddenly realized that she knew things she couldn't possibly have learned. She hadn't been there. She didn't know the people with whom I was dealing. She didn't even know what I'd been dealing in. And yet from the way she would suddenly be looking at me I'd know she knew everything.

"I only came on the job Friday," I said. "This is my second day in the office. I haven't had much time to learn anything yet." Mrs. Wishnick watched me quietly for a few moments. I knew I should keep my big trap shut, but I couldn't. "Give me a little time," I said. "I'll go over the records from the beginning and see if I can't find an answer for you."

The little old lady stood up. She came across the room toward me. "I know you will," she said. "You're not only a smart boy, Teddy. You're a good boy."

Before I knew what was happening she had dipped down and kissed me.

12

" When I Put All the Figures Together, I Made a Surprising Discovery"

Maud Eitner rang me at ten minutes after eleven.

"Mattlin just came in."

"How's his mood?" I said.

"Pretty good," she said. "It usually is, on mornings when he's had a session on the leather with Bernie Yustin."

"What about Merritt?"

"Not in yet."

"What's that dentist doing?" I said. "Fitting him for plates?"

"Probably for two sets," Maud said. "If his mother has anything to say about it. One for eating meat. The other for dairy."

"Did you tell Mattlin about the meeting?" I said.

"Not yet," Maud said. "You said you wanted both of them."

"I've got to have both of them," I said. "If I break it to only one of them the other boy might get sore or even suspicious."

"I don't understand what there is to be suspicious about," Maud said. "All you're doing—"

I knew what I was doing. My problem was to get them to do it with me.

"Maud," I said. "I've got a feeling about these two boys. I

138

know you think they love each other, but I don't. On the surface it's all what's mine is yours, and what's yours is mine, sure. Underneath, though, I'm telling you there's stuff going on. I think Merritt has his guard up about me already because it was Mattlin who hired me. I can't drop the ball on this thing just because I'm not bright in the way I handle it. I've got to have them both in the same room when I start talking."

"Well, you'd better start talking fast," Maud said. "Unless I say something to him soon, this being Monday, Mattlin will go up to the Panama Club for lunch."

"What's that?" I said.

"It's a group of publishers, authors, newspapermen, agents and actors who meet every Monday at some midtown hotel for a Dutch-treat lunch and shoptalk."

On Seventh Avenue it was Lou G. Siegel's delicatessen on Thirty-ninth Street, and the shoptalk would have made Fanny Hill blush.

"Wait a minute," I said. "I get the *p* for publishers, the *a* for authors, the *n* for newspapermen, the next *a* for agents, and the last *a* for actors, but there's a letter missing. What about the something for *m*?"

"When the club was organized," Maud said, "I'm told the movers and shakers couldn't think of any kind of members beginning with *m* except meat-loaf manufacturers, but they wanted to call it the Panama Club because they had the other five letters, so they decided to let the *m* stand for any publisher, author, newspaperman, agent or actor whose last name begins with *m*. These people don't have to pass the admissions committee. All they do is apply, and they're accepted. That's how Ralph Mattlin and Gene Merritt got in. Too bad your name isn't Meff, Mr. Leff."

"It will be mud unless I get those two boys into a room before—what did you say?"

Then I realized she wasn't saying it to me. Maud Eitner worked in a small room outside Mattlin's office. At the other side of her desk there was a door that led to a closet. It was used for coats and hats. It had doors on both sides. It was possible, therefore, to enter Merritt's office not only through his regular door down the hall but also from Maud Eitner's office by going through the coat closet. Somebody had obviously come into her room through her corridor door or through the closet. I could hear her voice.

"No, Mr. Mattlin hasn't said yet whether he's going to the Panama Club for lunch, but I'll check and ask him." Then there was a pause, I heard a door click, and Maud was talking to me. "That was Merritt," she said. "He just came in."

"How do his teeth look?" I said.

"I didn't get a clear view," Maud said. "He was hanging up his coat in the closet, so his conversation was directed to the collar. Shall I call the meeting?"

"Yes, please," I said. "And see if you can set it in Merritt's office."

"Any special reason?" Maud said.

I hesitated. I was thinking of the little old lady who had left the Bookkeeping Department less than an hour ago.

"It's that Grubensteller portrait in Ralph Mattlin's room," I said. "Every time I open my mouth to say something, the eyes keep following me with that look like I've raided the Israel Orphan Asylum pishke on the wall in my mother's kitchen."

"Would you?" Maud said.

"Not unless I needed carfare," I said.

"I'll try for Merritt's office," Maud said. A couple of minutes later she rang back. "You've got Merritt's office. Ten minutes okay?"

"Ten minutes fine," I said.

I spent them rechecking my figures. They checked. The phone rang.

"On the double," Maud said.

"Here I come," I said.

I picked up my equipment. The physical things you carry into a meeting can be as important as the figures you bring in between your ears. Most meetings, if there are more than three people, some secretary has seen to it that there's a small white pad and a stiletto-sharp pencil on the table in front of each chair. This is fine if you like doodling, and if all you're interested in is getting through the meeting fast so you can be sure not to be late for that tomato who's waiting to play a couple of hands of gin with you. I don't give a damn about doodling, and I don't go to meetings to fill empty holes in the day. I go to make a score.

To make a score, you have to carry the right equipment. I always carry a pad of analysis paper. You can buy them in any stationery store. They beat those long yellow pads of foolscap used by lawyers the way Dempsey beat Firpo. What does it are all those brown and black and green and blue lines, vertical as well as horizontal. You lay a pad like that in front of you, and all the other schmucks at the table start worrying. This guy ain't kidding, they all of a sudden start thinking. This guy knows figures. Especially if he follows through by disregarding the freshly sharpened brand-new pencil the efficient secretary left at his place and he pulls his own pencil from his pocket.

This should always be a cheap one, made of wood. Guys who use mechanical pencils at meetings, especially if they're solid gold, are not attending a meeting. They're showing off their Christmas presents. I always carry a two-for-a-nickel Eagle. If you can't get an Eagle any other brand will do. So long as it's yellow, and the eraser at the top is worn down, and half the wood has been ground away by a pencil sharpener, and the point resembles the end of a hot dog. The more it looks like a stub that's seen a lot of action, the more nervous it will make the boys with the platinum Eversharps.

"Yes, come in," Merritt said in a loud voice when I knocked on his door.

I came in. He was behind his desk, holding the long golden scissors like Clyde Beatty in the lion cage, holding the black whip. He blinked at me through the crooked eyeglasses. The cut-up newspapers on his desk billowed up under his Adam's apple like the whipped cream on top of an enormous charlotte russe.

"Good morning, Mr. Merritt," I said.

"Good morning," he said.

141

Mattlin was lying back in a black leather chair between the windows that faced Fourth Avenue. He was staring down his legs, through the V of his heels-together shoes, as though he were lining up a shot on a pool table. His legs looked about eleven feet long. "Good morning, Leff," he said around the cigarette smoke. It poured out of his mouth like he was Con Edison trying to keep up with a sudden peak load.

I noticed he left out the "Mr." That's all he left out, and that's all I did: I noticed. But sometimes when you think all you're doing is noticing, you're doing a lot more. Anyway, your guts are. On Friday I was Mr. Leff. Now it was Monday, and to Ralph Mattlin I was "Good morning, Leff."

"Good morning, Mr. Mattlin," I said. I turned to Four Eyes. "Where can I spread my papers, Mr. Merritt?" I said.

He blinked at me as though I'd asked him where I should chain the gorilla. "Your papers?" he said.

Mattlin lifted one leg and pointed with his toe. "Put them there, Leff," he said.

His toe was pointing to a low table covered with magazines in front of a black leather couch against the other wall. I walked over and moved aside a small bronze statue of a bald-headed guy who could have been either Julius Caesar or Jim Farley. I put my analysis pad on the spread-out magazines and sat down on the couch. I pulled out my five inches of beat-up Eagle and flipped back the cover of the analysis pad. I did it the way William S. Hart used to join a poker game in the Red Dog Saloon. He'd sit down at the table without a word and shove his sack of gold dust at the dealer. While the dealer counted out the chips Hart would pull a green Celluloid eyeshade from his pocket, slip it on his forehead, then drag his six-shooter from its holster and lay it on the table at his elbow. He always got a reaction. So did I. Mattlin sat up in his chair. There were so many numbers scribbled on that top page, it could have been a piece of flypaper on a hot day in a candy factory.

"It looks like you've been working hard," Mattlin said.

"It didn't seem hard," I said. "Work never is when it's interesting."

142

"Will it take you long to tell us how interesting it was?" Mattlin said.

You put that together with the way he left out the "Mr." and you could get the impression he was needling me. But the funny thing was, I didn't get the feeling he was needling me. Mattlin didn't seem to be able to look and talk in any other way. He reminded me all of a sudden of the kind of person about whom my mother used to say, "He's his own worst enemy." I wondered how Ralph Mattlin managed to get through an ordinary day without collecting a few raps in the mouth.

"How much time do you have?" I said.

Mattlin pulled out a gold pocket watch. I noticed it was attached to something I hadn't seen since I was a kid. A black silk fob.

"Mr. Merritt and I would like to be at the Park Lane by twelve-thirty," he said. "There's no point in going to the Panama Club for lunch if you're going to be late. The speakers start promptly."

I was looking at my own watch. "That gives me about a half-hour?" I said.

"Just about," Mattlin said.

"I'm sure you won't be late for your lunch date," I said. "This won't take me a half-hour." I turned toward the desk. "Mr. Merritt," I said, "Mr. Mattlin, I have a confession to make. I spent the weekend here in the office."

Merritt's eyes blinked, but it was Mattlin who said, "How did you get in?"

"I think Miss Eitner can explain that better than I can," I said. "You mind if she joins us?"

"Certainly not," Mattlin said. "Gene?"

Merritt poked at the glasses on his nose. "By all means," he said. "Let's have her in." He picked up his phone and said, "Would you ask Miss Eitner to come in, please?" He hung up.

Mattlin stabbed out his cigarette in an ashtray on the floor beside his chair. He was lighting the new one when Maud Eitner came in. "You want me?" she said, to nobody in particular.

"Mr. Leff does," Ralph Mattlin said.

143

To third parties, the "Mr." went in. Maybe there was a clue in that.

"I told Mr. Mattlin and Mr. Merritt I'd spent the weekend here in the office," I said. "Mr. Mattlin asked me how I got in."

"Simple enough," Maud said to Mattlin. "Late Friday afternoon Mr. Leff told me what he had in mind. He said it would take him two days to do the job, and would I lend him my key. I figured while he was new here, he was after all an employee, and it was too late to ask either of you if it was all right. So I gave Mr. Leff my key. It seemed a sensible thing to do, in view of what he told me he had in mind."

"What did you have in mind?" Mattlin said to me.

"Excuse me," Maud Eitner said. "Will that be all, Mr. Mattlin?"

"So far as I'm concerned, Maud, yes," Mattlin said. She went out, and Mattlin said to me again, "What did you have in mind?"

"I wanted to find out why the firm of Mattlin & Merritt switched from publishing books to manufacturing jigsaw puzzles."

Merritt did that thing with his eyes again. Mattlin gave me a long look, then jabbed out his cigarette and fished for a fresh one.

"I could say, Mr. Leff, what business is that of yours?" he said. "But I'm sure you'd say as an employee, especially as our bookkeeper, it's your business to find out everything you can about the firm, wouldn't you?"

And about you too, wise guy.

"No, I wouldn't say that," I said. "I'd say I'm puzzled. Or I was, on Friday. Every once in a while, for years, I pass Fifth Avenue and Twelfth Street. On the corner down there, there's a building it's as big as Grand Central. And over the door, in the stone arch, it says 'Macmillan & Company Book Publishers.' You can't look at a building like that without knowing the people that own it, they don't have to worry about whether they're going to be able to afford to have chicken next Sunday for lunch. I mean the place looks rich. It smells like money.

144

Then I come to work here, a firm that makes jigsaw puzzles, and only last Friday, the day I got here, you were still trying to borrow fifty thousand dollars to keep going. The contrast is what hit me. This Macmillan outfit, making with books, they own a building like that. This outfit, making with puzzles, you're borrowing money. You see what I mean?"

I said it to Mattlin.

"Not yet," he said.

Merritt's lips puffed in and out. More and more he reminded me of a guppy breathing.

"A man doesn't have to be a genius to figure out it's better to own a building like that than to borrow money," I said. "So the mystery to me, what I can't get through my head is why would you quit doing what this Macmillan outfit is doing, why would you stop making with books and start making with puzzles?"

Mattlin blew smoke at me the way I've seen people brush away panhandlers on the street. "Because we lost money on the first five books we published," Mattlin said. "If we'd continued to publish more we would have lost all our original capital, and then we would have been out of business. It seemed sensible to do something else. Does that answer your question?"

I hadn't asked it yet.

"Do you know why you lost money on those first five books you published?" I said.

"Of course we do," Mattlin said. The blue eyes began to get that *Watch Out!* look. "Mr. Merritt and I are not children," he said. "We lost money for the same reason everybody loses money. The cost of manufacturing our product was higher than the sums we were able to take in for selling them."

"Were you charging less for your books than these Macmillan boys with this great big fat building down there, what they charge for theirs?" I said.

The cigarette stopped on its way to his mouth. The look in the blue eyes got uglier. "No, of course not," Mattlin said. "All five of our books were novels. For a novel of standard length the price is standard for everybody. Three of them were priced at two-fifty. The other two, which were shorter, were priced at two dollars. Exactly as Macmillan would have priced them."

"But Macmillan has that building," I said. "And you're making jigsaw puzzles."

I waited. Mattlin pushed himself up a few inches in the chair. It was so quiet I could hear the tiny sucking sounds as Merritt puffed his lips in and out. Mattlin never took his eyes from my face. The ugly look was still there, but something else was coming up. Interest.

"Mr. Leff," he said finally. "During your weekend here in the office, what did you find out that Mr. Merritt and I don't know?"

"I found out a way to get you one of those buildings, " I said. I picked up my analysis pad. "What I did was make a cost breakdown on each of the five books. When I put all the figures together, I made a surprising discovery."

"Tell us," Mattlin said. "Let's see if Mr. Merritt and I will be surprised."

"On the five books you published you lost just a little under sixteen thousand dollars," I said. "And on those five books you paid out to the authors in royalties a little over eighteen thousand dollars."

Again I waited. I could still hear Merritt making those tiny noises with his lips. Mattlin still kept his eyes on my face. "In other words," he said.

So I gave them to him.

"If you had not paid out any royalties," I said, "instead of losing a little under sixteen thousand dollars on your first five published books you would have made a profit of a little over two thousand."

"There's only one thing wrong with your analysis," Mattlin said.

"What's that?" I said.

"Writers don't work for nothing," he said. "If you're in the publishing business you have to pay royalties."

"No, you don't," I said.

The concealed son of a bitch leaned his elbows on the window sills of his eyes and moved forward to look out at me more closely. "What's your solution, Mr. Leff, to this universal problem?" Mattlin said. You could have poured the sarcasm in his voice on a plate of blintzes.

"Very simple," I said. "Publish books by dead authors."

"Such as?" Mattlin said.

E. Spinoza Merritt stopped making noises like a guppy. "What's the matter with Spinoza?" he said to his partner.

13

" You've Made It into the Finals at Last. Now You'd Better Win"

Seventeen years later, facing my wife Evie across my second cup of black coffee at seven o'clock in the morning, I could still hear that special sound in Gene Merritt's voice.

"You know what it was like?" I said. "It was like Friday night when you were a kid and you came out of the synagogue. All week long, people talked in a certain way. You too. I mean the sound of their voices and your voice, they were sort of expected. Nobody sounded unusual. Then comes Friday night, and you go to shul, and there's that last final prayer, and everybody goes out singing *'Ein Keiloheinu.'* You feel wonderful, but in a funny way. Your heart is busting out of your chest and everybody's face is shining, because you know what they all know, that the week coming up is going to be a great week for you. You really know it. You can feel it from the voices singing that song, including yours. That's what was so funny about it."

"What was so funny?" my wife Evie said.

"I could hear that same thing in Gene Merritt's voice," I said. "That morning in 1937 in that Fourth Avenue office. It was as though he'd been traveling along in a dark tunnel for a long time, feeling his way, taking small steps so he wouldn't bump into anything or fall down in a hole maybe, and all of a sudden he'd come out into the light. *What's the matter with Spinoza?* It was weird the way he said it, this nutty-looking little guy with the skinny turkey-like neck, and his shirt cuffs hanging out over his wrists, and those glasses sitting crooked on his nose. He could have been a sort of Jewish Columbus peering through the night and saying, 'Hey, what's those lights over there?' I can still hear that *Ein Keiloheinu* sound in his voice. *What's the matter with Spinoza?* That was the beginning."

My wife Evie turned the page of the *Daily News* on which our names had not been mentioned in the account of the Walter Idleman funeral. "No," she said.

"What?" I said.

When my wife Evie says no, it's like you read in the papers the Supreme Court has denied an appeal. You're not involved, but you feel a small cold shiver in your gut for the poor unknown bastard who's just had the iron door slammed in his face.

"To say that was the beginning," Evie said, "it's like saying with Columbus, the discovery of America, the beginning of that was when Isabella said okay, take my pearls."

"I always thought it was," I said.

"No," Evie said again. In that same way. You could hear the key being rammed home as the iron door closed. "You thought wrong," she said.

I didn't like her tone. Ever since Walter Idleman had died two days ago I'd had the feeling she'd entered a phase. At her age it couldn't be menopause. So it had to be the only other thing she cared about. Money.

"Without the pearls," I said, "Columbus wouldn't have been able to buy those three rowboats."

"Without the idea for maybe I can find India by sailing west," Evie said, "Isabella would never had had a chance to get into the act with her pearls. Without the idea for the Library of Twentieth Century Classics, Gene Merritt would never have had a chance to get into the act with 'What's the matter with Spinoza?' "

I gave her a look. Most men I know, they've been married

149

sixteen years, at seven o'clock in the morning what they want to give their wives is a clout. Most days I'm no exception to this rule. Where I differ from most husbands, I know the mornings when all of a sudden I've become an exception. I pushed myself up a little higher in my chair. The time had come to listen. One of the things that's kept this marriage in the black for sixteen years is the fact that Evie and I don't trust each other. It keeps us both on our toes. This is an excellent posture for hearing straight-from-the-shoulder remarks. My wife Evie is not like Western Union. When she has a message for her husband she doesn't phone it in. She delivers.

"Okay," I said. "I'm listening."

"Mattlin & Merritt is so far behind both of us," Evie said, "I have to close my eyes and think hard to try and remember what everybody looked like." She did close her eyes and said, "I haven't even thought about any of those people for I don't know how long. I thought we were finished with them years ago. But now, because of this Walter Idleman dropping dead, and a new Sissenwein executor takes his place, I see we're not finished with those people." Evie opened her eyes and said, "So you'd better listen."

"I could do it better if I had another cup of coffee," I said.

"You've had two," Evie said. "You know what Artie Steinberg said about your blood pressure."

"If he says it again," I said, "I'm going to change doctors."

"No, you're not," Evie said. "Artie has known you so long he thinks you're part of the family, and he makes an extra effort to keep your liver chugging along. A new doctor might think you're just another bad-tempered smart aleck from the high-rent district and say to himself nuts to this boob and his blood pressure, let the idiot drink all the coffee he wants."

"I've got to be at Byram Noonan's apartment to meet the new executor at one o'clock," I said. "That gives me a little less than a mere six hours. If you don't stop with Artie Steinberg and how much coffee I'm supposed to drink, I'll never have time to hear your views on why we're not finished with the old Mattlin & Merritt crowd."

"Remember that girl who used to be Ralph Mattlin's secretary?" Evie said. "She was no beauty, but she had stuff. Maud Eitner?"

Hearing that name out of the past did more for my hangover than the Empirin tablets. The old almost-forgotten syllables gave me a funny little feeling in what other people would probably call their hearts. I couldn't. My wife Evie says I don't have one. "What about Maud Eitner?" I said.

"Something she once said about you," my wife Evie said. "Maud Eitner said you'd go far if you'd only shut up and listen once in a while."

"It's too late," I said. "I'm over forty."

"Maud Eitner said you mustn't shrink from a new experience," Evie said. "Look what listening did for those women at Delphi."

"Why don't you just tell me what it's going to do for your husband?" I said.

"It will help you handle this new executor of the Sissenwein estate," Evie said.

"You gave me your views on the subject two days ago," I said. "When we discovered Walter Idleman had dropped dead."

"I gave you my views," Evie said. "Now I'm going to give you something else."

"What's that?" I said.

"An ultimatum," Evie said.

"Like in a war?" I said.

"That's what most marriages are," Evie said. "Aren't they?"

It's a funny feeling to have your own wife take you by surprise in your own study at seven o'clock in the morning.

"Evie," I said, "I never knew you cared so much about this Sissenwein deal."

She gave me another one of those looks. Then, speaking slowly, giving out with each word as though she was inventing it on the spot, the way Miss Wien used to read aloud to the class in P.S. 188 a sentence she was chalking up letter by letter on the blackboard, Evie said, "The things you don't know, Ted darling, are what has kept this marriage going for sixteen years."

Next time you're feeling sort of phnyeh, and what you need is a change of pace to jolt you out of your rut but you can't afford the plane fare to one of those hot islands where the native girls have four of everything, why don't you ask your wife to drop a little statement like that in your lap across the morning coffee?

"Evie," I said. "Do I understand you correctly?"

"You'd better," she said. "You've made it into the finals at last. This Sissenwein deal is the play-off. Now you'd better win."

"Evie," I said.

"Pipe down," she said. "By and large, I've had no real complaints about this marriage. Sixteen years ago, when you said how about it, I knew what I was getting into. I'd been married long enough to a piece of sponge cake to know that next time out I wanted something I could get my teeth into. If I've almost cracked a molar two or three times, like during the war when you were in London and I found out about that little English tomato, and three years ago, my old school chum Molly Kanervogel, the bitch, I figured okay. Those are the risks I took when I signed on with a tough little East Fourth Street number like you."

"Molly Kanervogel," I said. "For Christ's sake, Evie."

"Yes, for Christ's sake, Evie," my wife Evie said. "In case you're still wondering why all of a sudden she and her husband moved to California, it's because when I found out about you and darling little Molly, the bitch, I didn't waste any time with her or with you. I went to the center of the action. Meaning, in case you don't know what I mean, my old man. I said to my father, as of today you take your account out of Kermit Kanervogel's office."

"Oh, Jesus," I said. "So that's what happened to Kanervogel & O'Hare."

"You bet it did," my wife Evie said. "Next time you get to thinking about a little extracurricular pisha-paysha, you think about something else. Like what my father can do to her husband's business, whoever he is."

"Evie darling," I said. "You know what you're doing? You're suggesting I start chasing unmarried Radcliffe freshmen."

"Why not?" Evie said. "At your age the only thing you can really handle is middle-aged nymphomaniacs. They're sedentary, and New York is full of them, so I'd rather have you trying for vices which cause shortness of breath, like Radcliffe freshmen, because boy in your age bracket, you're beaten before you start. I don't mind you being beaten by a Radcliffe freshman, because then it's your pride that's involved, not mine. But if you get beaten on this Sissenwein deal, if you don't pull it off, it's my pride that the bruises are going to show up on."

"I don't see why," I said. "I never heard you say a good word for Hubert Sissenwein."

"Why should I?" Evie said. "He didn't deserve one, but that's not the point. The point is here." She tapped the *Daily News*. "The people who were at Walter Idleman's funeral yesterday, the important ones in this town, they got mentioned. Mr. and Mrs. Theodore Leff did not."

"So what?" I said. "I'm like Ivy Ledbetter Lee."

"Who?" Evie said.

"Poison Ivy Lee they called him," I said. "When I was a kid he was the press agent for the Rockefeller family. The legend was, they paid him a fortune every year to keep the Rockefeller name out of the papers. I've been doing the same thing for myself for years. Your name in the papers can only help you if you're a stripper looking for bookings, or you're a schmuck running for alderman. I'm not. I don't want my name in the papers."

"I do," my wife Evie said.

The tone of her voice was an eyeopener. I looked at her carefully. She was closer to forty than thirty, but she didn't look it. Why should she? She spends more time at Elizabeth Arden's than Rabbi Goldfarb used to spend in the synagogue. Not that I'm complaining. Just the opposite. I don't give a damn how other women look. But the woman I'm married to, I want other guys to look too. I've banged many a homely broad, but I've never been able to walk down the street with one of them on my arm. I'm told this is a flaw in my character. If it is, call me pisher. I'm too old to pretend to be anything I haven't found out I am by going at it the hard way.

I learned long ago that to me a wife has to be a lot of things, and she'd better be good than just okay at them, but the one thing she's absolutely got to be is a medal. Evie always has been. That's why, when she takes me by surprise, I pay attention. Looking at her now, I saw the things I was accustomed to seeing. She still had the figure she had when I met her, which was two years after she got out of Vassar. Her hair still looked like my favorite nickel candy bar, a Mary Jane, when you break through the stiff yellow molasses on the outside and get to the creamy peanut butter in the middle. And if it still looked that way because of the bills I paid at Elizabeth Arden's, who cared? And she had that face.

Only two other women I've ever known have had that kind of face. My mother and Miss Wien back in P. S. 188. And for both of them there was only one thing I wouldn't do: a Steve Brody off a high place. My philosophy is simple: Don't die. Even for people you love. When you're dead, you can't wear medals. What happened to me on Seventh Avenue, the bankruptcy, it killed my mother. I was sorry about that, but I would have been sorrier if it had killed me. You take what you get, and you balance it off against what you want.

I wanted Evie the minute I saw her. When I found out how loaded her old man was, I wanted her more. I got her. After sixteen years of having her, looking at her carefully because she had taken me by surprise, I saw why. It was the way she was holding her mouth. The way I imagine Marie Antoinette held hers when some wise guy said, "Yes, Your Majesty, but there's no cake around for them to eat."

"Evie," I said, "this is a surprise to me. I never knew you wanted your name in the papers."

"At the beginning I didn't," she said. "After my first husband, just watching you in action was enough, and I must say there has been plenty of action. But after a while action stops being enough. You want the rest of the world to know you're scoring. I think what hit me hardest about Molly Kanervogel was not finding out that you and she were meeting at the New Trelawney three or four afternoons a week to play anagrams.

What killed me was that every time I picked up the paper there she was, Mrs. Kermit Kanervogel, wife of the prominent stockbroker who has recently been appointed Commissioner of Museums, chatting with the Mayor and Senator Lehman during the entr'acte."

"If you want to meet the Mayor," I said, "I can arrange it. As for Senator Lehman—"

"No," Evie said, "I don't want to meet the Mayor. I want the Mayor to want to meet me. So when like yesterday, he goes to a thing like Walter Idleman's funeral, it's me that he's chatting with when they start taking pictures. This Sissenwein deal is the biggest thing you've ever tackled. If you pull it off you won't be able to remain behind the scenes any more than Charlemagne could remain behind the scenes."

"What has Charlemagne got to do with it?" I said.

"You'll be like him," Evie said. "The head of an empire."

"Oh," I said.

"If Oscar Wilde had heard the way you say that 'Oh' he would have turned green with jealousy," Evie said. "And if you're the head of an empire you know what that will make me. I've waited sixteen years, and I'm not waiting any longer."

"All right, all right," I said. "Stop nailing notices on my door. I want to close this Sissenwein deal as much as you do. Idleman's death threw the car in the ditch for a while. Maybe for no more than a few days. I'll know better when I meet with the new executor. Maybe I can have the whole thing back on the rails by this afternoon."

"Not if you go up there to Byram's apartment with the idea in your head that the beginning of the whole thing was in 1937, the day Gene Merritt said *What's the matter with Spinoza?*"

I suddenly felt like a character in a comic strip when, in the balloon over his head, an electric light bulb begins to flash on and off to indicate the yoineh has begun to catch on. "Evie," I said, "I think I'm beginning to dig."

"High time," she said. "The point is this. Everybody who was involved from the very beginning, all the way back there in 1937, we all know that what really put Mattlin & Merritt on their feet and into the real money was the Twentieth Century Classics Series. Therefore, we can all trace a direct line from that fairly small beginning to this huge Sissenwein package you and Byram are trying to wrap up. Outsiders may not see that direct line. The other executors you've been working on these past four months, for instance, like Walter Idleman. One of the things that made it simple for you to work on them is that they had no reason to see the direct line. They were just outsiders who were tapped by a multimillionaire friend named Hubert Sissenwein to be executors of his estate. The lady waiting for you up at Byram's apartment, Ted darling, she's not an outsider."

"Evie," I said. "If the boys who run IBM knew as much about how your brain works as I do, they'd start unloading their stock. But in seventeen years you must have learned a little something about how your little helpmeet's brain works. Did you really think I'd go up there at one o'clock and start bragging about how I started the whole business because the Twentieth Century Classics Series was my idea?"

"No, of course not," Evie said. "But when you said Gene Merritt's remark 'What's the matter with Spinoza?' was the beginning, I began to wonder if you could be trusted alone with that new executor."

"Evie," I said, "it's not my fault Hubert Sissenwein did not choose for his first alternate executor a Radcliffe freshman."

"That's what I mean," Evie said. "I mean this meeting you're heading for, the discussion of who was responsible for doing what, that might be more important than what actually was done."

"Don't worry about it," I said. "Only one person in the whole wide world knows who was responsible for what, and you happen to be married to the boy."

14

" Ted, Here, Has Come Up with Something Big"

You don't always know when you're getting a medal. If you're summoned to Washington, and they make you stand up in front of the cameras while the President reads a citation, fine. Under those conditions if you don't know you're getting a medal you'd better turn yourself in. But there are other conditions. Moments of time. Combinations of words. Maybe even nothing more than a glance. Things that don't look like bits of shiny metal with scraps of colored ribbon attached to them for hanging around your neck. For example: what Ralph Mattlin did and said, all the way back there in 1937, after Gene Merritt came through with "What's the matter with Spinoza?"

What Ralph Mattlin did was turn to me. And what he said was "Ted, do you have a lunch date?"

For a few moments the question threw me. What did my having a lunch date have to do with what we'd been talking about? On Seventh Avenue lunch dates meant goosing a buyer into an order. Or a model into the sack.

"No," I said. "I don't usually go out to lunch."

"Why don't you come along with me and Gene to the Panama Club?" Ralph Mattlin said. "I think you'll enjoy it. Don't you think he will, Gene?"

Gene Merritt massaged the nosepiece of his glasses for a couple of moments. From this he apparently drew the inspiration for his reply. "I would certainly think so," he said, and he looked at his wrist watch. "It's twenty-five after twelve."

Next thing I knew, I was walking up Fourth Avenue between Gene Merritt and Ralph Mattlin, and I was doing some thinking of my own. Something about the sequence of events was suddenly bothering me.

I'd asked these two boys to a meeting. I'd told them something about their business they'd apparently never known before. It was something that looked though it could make a lot of money for them. I don't know even now exactly what I had expected to happen next. But I think in a general way I expected them to ask me questions. Or at least kick it around in a conversation that would dig into the problems of how to get my suggestion rolling as a practical proposition. This did not happen. The only reaction I got was an invitation to lunch. That's all I did get until we reached Thirty-fourth Street. Standing on the corner, waiting for the traffic light to change, Ralph Mattlin seemed to surface out of his thoughts.

"Gene," he said. "What's the program today? I forgot to look at my card."

Merritt pulled a post card from his pocket and examined it. "They've got this British fellow," Gene Merritt said. "Charteris? Amory Charteris? The book about Queen Victoria?"

"Oh yes," Ralph Mattlin said. "Harcourt, Brace. It's number three on the list."

"Four," Gene Merritt said. "It dropped this last Monday. Number three is that Harper book about the fascist philosopher. Vilfredo Pareto. The man Mussolini says he based his whole program on. And then let's see what else?" Merritt poked at the glasses on his nose and peered at the post card. "Yes," Merritt said. "Gypsy Rose Lee."

"That's interesting," Mattlin said.

It sure was. I didn't know Gypsy. But in my days at Thomas Jefferson High, I'd seen a lot of her. In fact, almost all of her. Professionally speaking, that is. The Irving Place Burlesque

Theater was just around the corner from the school. I wondered what she was doing at the Panama Club. With someone named Amory Charteris who had apparently written a book about Queen Victoria.

"I hear Gypsy has done a book for Simon and Schuster," Gene Merritt said. "A mystery story."

Ralph Mattlin didn't answer. He had sunk back into his thoughts. The light changed. We stepped off the curb and moved on uptown. I felt like one of those boys in a Warner Brothers movie who is being walked from the death cell to the hot seat. Both Ralph Mattlin and Gene Merritt seemed to be aware I was between them, but they didn't seem to be very excited about it. I had the feeling they were performing a duty and they'd be glad when it was over. They were clearly more interested in what was going on inside their own heads than they were in me. It seemed to me that I should be too. But I didn't know how to get into their heads. After a while it occurred to me that these two boys didn't know how to get into the Panama Club.

"Are you sure?" Mattlin said.

We had stopped under the marquee of the St. Francis Hotel at Park and Forty-sixth. Merritt was staring at his post card. "It says St. Francis Hotel," he said.

"But I don't see anybody going in," Mattlin said. "One minute." He stepped across the sidewalk to the doorman. "Excuse me," Mattlin said. "Is the Panama Club meeting here today?"

"Yes sir," the doorman said. I could see and hear that he liked talking to a man who looked like Ralph Mattlin. I wondered if underneath all that gold braid there was a boy from East Fourth Street. "The Forty-sixth Street entrance, sir."

The Forty-sixth Street entrance did not have a doorman, but it could have used one. Or even two. From the way men kept coming up the block from Lexington and disappearing through the doors, a stranger in town might have thought he'd stepped off the train in the town of Hamelin on the day that piper was doing his stuff. Inside the Forty-sixth Street entrance there was a table at one side and a few long rows of coat-check racks at the other. On the plum-red carpet between the table and the racks a couple of hundred men were reenacting the battle of Bull Run.

Some were tall. Others were short. Some were fat. Others were thin. Some were young. Others were old. Some were in tweed. Others wore worsted. Some had mustaches. Others were clean-shaven. Some had creases in their pants. Others were rumpled. Some were handsome. Others ugly. In short, a representative cross section of the human race, male division.

I would have thought a steam shovel, dipping down into any crowd of men, anywhere in New York City, would have come up with a group pretty much like the men milling around in the lobby just inside the Forty-sixth Street entrance to the St. Francis Hotel. Watching them, however, I knew my thinking was wrong. I had never seen a group like this on Seventh Avenue or on East Fourth Street.

Maud Eitner had said the Panama Club was made up of publishers, authors, newspapermen, agents and actors. Why should that make them look alike? As though they were all wearing the same invisible badge?

Following Ralph Mattlin and Gene Merritt, who were pushing their way through to the table on the left, I asked myself what this invisible badge was. There are people whose questions I do not bother to answer. I am not one of them. When I ask myself something, I come up with a reply. By the time we reached the table I had it. What made all of these men seem special, as though they belonged together, like members of the same family gathered at the funeral or wedding of a relative, was that they all looked as though they ate kippers for breakfast.

"I'll pay for Ted," Ralph Mattlin said.

We had reached the table. Behind it two gray-haired women were seated in front of a couple of green tin cash boxes. They kept snatching money from the kipper eaters, making change, and handing it back with blue and white tickets. A man in a

tweed jacket snatched a ticket from around Mattlin's right
shoulder. As it slid past my nose I gave it a fast look. On the
ticket was printed: PANAMA CLUB. ONE LUNCH. $2.00.

"Hello, Ralph," the man said. "Gets sort of hectic, doesn't
it?"

"Hello, Scudder," Mattlin said. "Sure does."

"Why don't I pay for myself?" I said. If you're going to be in
debt to people, I learned on Seventh Avenue, don't do it for two
bucks.

"Only members are allowed to pay," Gene Merritt said. A
guy with a mustache grabbed a ticket. Merritt said, "Hello,
Quincy."

"Nice to see you," Quincy said. "Great turnout, Gene."

"On second thought," Mattlin said as he fished for his money,
"I think maybe we should split it, Gene. What do you think?"

"Good idea," Merritt said. "That makes Ted the guest of
both of us."

Lucky Ted, in the middle again. I remembered the feeling I'd
had in Mattlin's house that when it came to money he scared
easy. I added a footnote: no sums were too small for Mattlin to
worry about, not even half of a two-dollar lunch.

"Three tickets, please," Mattlin said to one of the gray-
haired women. "Here's my three dollars. Mr. Merritt will give
you his three. Hello, Kingwood."

"Hello, Ralph," Kingwood said. Kingwood wore a tab collar.
"Things going well, I hope?"

"First-rate," Ralph Mattlin said. We backed away from the
table. "Hello, Clayborne," Mattlin said. "How's DeVere?"

"Ask him yourself," Clayborne said. He pulled forward a
little guy wearing a polka-dotted bow tie. "DeVere, you know
Ralph Mattlin?"

DeVere laughed. "Ralph," he said. "Nice to see you."

He headed for the green tin boxes. Ralph Mattlin and Gene
Merritt headed for the eye of the storm. It proved to be a large
poster sitting on an easel. On the left was a picture of Gypsy in
mufti: a mink coat buttoned to her chin. On the right: a picture

of a man who was a dead ringer for Anthony Eden except that his teeth didn't stick out. Between them a couple of hand-lettered lines read:

PANAMA CLUB
Today's Guests

Sticking with Ralph Mattlin and Gene Merritt, I got close enough to see the two words under Gypsy's picture: "Guess Who?" Under the other picture the words were: "Amory Charteris." With Mattlin's six-feet-four running interference, we managed to get through to the entrance of a big dining room.

"I was just making for Jocelyn's table," a fat man said. "Join us?"

"Thanks, Fowler, fine," Mattlin said.

We followed the fat man to a round table directly in front of a platform. A thin man was sitting at the round table with a red-faced man. They were both breaking rolls in half with the kind of ruthless authority I've seen oyster shuckers use in seafood restaurants.

"Look what I've brought," the fat man said. He tapped Mattlin on the shoulder.

"Good show, Fowler," the thin man said. He pounded a square of butter onto the end of the broken roll and shoved the roll into his mouth.

"Nice to see you, Jocelyn," Mattlin said.

"You look fine, Jocelyn," Gene Merritt said. "This is a friend of ours, Ted Leff. How are you, Staunton?"

"Never better," said the red-faced man. He pasted two squares of butter on the end of his broken roll before he shoved it into his mouth. "Nice to meet you, Mr. Leff."

"Same here," I said, and brushed his damp bread crumbs off my lapels.

"Mind if I join you?" a man said behind us.

"Not at all, Hamish," the fat man said. "A pleasure."

"I see you've got room for one more," another voice said.

"We've been saving it for you, Terence," the thin man said.

We all sat down. Ralph Mattlin and Gene Merritt went at their rolls like a goalee in an ice hockey game snatching at the puck before anybody else could reach it. I wanted to do the same. Not because I was hungry, but because I didn't want Fowler, Jocelyn, Staunton, Hamish and Terence to think I didn't know how to conduct myself properly at a two-dollar lunch in a hotel dining room. The trouble was I couldn't see my roll. With Ralph Mattlin and Gene Merritt joining Fowler, Jocelyn, Staunton, Hamish and Terence in the attack on the rolls, the air over our table was suddenly replaced by a mist of bread crumbs. I decided to wait until the air cleared. Peering through the crumbs, I saw that there were about forty or fifty tables spread around the big dining room. They were filling up with men coming out of the lobby, carrying blue and white tickets, and calling greetings to each other.

"Tickets, gentlemen? Tickets, please?"

A waiter had come up behind me. Fowler, Jocelyn, Staunton, Hamish and Terence handed over one blue and white ticket each. Ralph Mattlin handed over three.

"Thank you, gentlemen, thank you," the waiter said. He headed for a couple of swinging doors like Paavo Nurmi sighting the finish line.

"Too bad about Cathcart," Jocelyn said. "I hear it's a compound fracture."

"Did you?" Hamish said. "I heard it was his heart."

"No, that was Irving," Staunton said.

My epiglottis flipped. Irving? What was a guy with an unusual name like that doing in a crowd like this?

"Oh no!" Terence said. "Don't tell me Irving's had a heart attack? Not Irving Whitelaw?"

Apparently there are Irvings and there are Irvings.

"No, no," Fowler said. "That was Irving Hershkovitz. People tend to confuse them because they both publish medical texts. What Irving Whitelaw had, according to what Claude Demarest told me, anyway, was a slight palpitation brought on by that unprecedented heat wave down in Palm Beach. I hear it was a hundred and two yesterday. But he's fine now."

"Well, I must say Bosworth is a jolly good substitute chairman," Jocelyn said. "This promises to be a very good program."

The waiter appeared over his head with a line of plates stretched out on his arm.

"Low bridge," Terence said.

Jocelyn bowed his head over his folded hands.

"Thank you, sir," the waiter said.

Swinging them out like a discus thrower in the newsreels, he unloaded the line of plates from his arm so fast that I had the feeling somebody was holding a stopwatch on him. It was a beautiful performance. In a matter of seconds he had set a plate in front of Fowler, Jocelyn, Staunton, Hamish, Terence, Mattlin, Merritt and me, and the only damage was a splash of gravy on Jocelyn's hairpiece and two dislodged peas on my left arm. These rolled free onto the tablecloth, where I stabbed them up with my fork before they hit the pepper mill, so they didn't really count, and Jocelyn didn't seem to notice the splash of gravy. It was the same color as his rug, and just sank quietly into the color scheme under which he faced the world.

"Chicken again, I'm afraid," Fowler said.

I examined my plate. Fowler was right, but I didn't see what there was to be afraid about. The bird was dead. My quarter of it, anyway. Although it was still fighting back. I discovered this when I tried to cut off my first forkful. At two dollars for the entire lunch I figured that was worth at least a dime, so I chewed thoroughly. In P. S. 188 we used to get regular lectures from Miss Wien on a thing called Fletcherism. She must have had the Panama Club in mind. By the time I got the first mouthful down, a man who looked like Buster Keaton came out on the platform and started fooling with the microphone.

"Bosworth is looking well," Terence said.

"Why not?" Gene Merritt said. "This is his field."

I gave him a quick look. I smelled a joke. I leaned close to him. "Did I miss something?" I whispered.

Merritt giggled. "Wars of the Roses," he whispered back. "Battle of Bosworth. Where Richard the Third got it in the neck."

164

"Oh, him," I said. I turned back to the table. Nobody else was looking at Merritt. They were all chewing chicken like Juicy Fruit and looking at Bosworth on the platform.

"Since I am merely substituting for poor Cathcart," he was saying, "I feel I have the right to dispense with the witty preface to these introductions that have been for so long his inimitable signature to the Panama Club's weekly meetings. He's doing well, by the way. I talked with Cathcart's wife on the phone before coming over here, and she said he should be back with us in a couple of weeks. Aside from the pleasure this will give all of us, I'm sure it will also give me personally a great deal of relief because, as usual, I seem to have mislaid my reading glasses and I can't make out the name of our first speaker." He squinted at a card in his hand.

"Charteris!" somebody called politely from a table behind me. "Amory Charteris."

I had no way of knowing, but I remembered what Ralph Mattlin had said out in the street about who was this Amory Charteris' publisher. I would have given even money that the polite caller was a boy from Harcourt, Brace.

"Yes, of course," Bosworth said. "I'm sorry. And so, without further ado, fellow members of the Panama Club, I give you our distinguished guest from England, Mr. Amory Charteris. He has written what I am told is a most distinguished and moving book about Queen Victoria. I am told this by my wife, who has been utterly absorbed in it for the past two weeks. Until she finishes and allows me to get at it, here is its author, Mr. Amory Charteris."

The handclapping spread across the room like a nice soft blanket of rain. Watching the platform, I had the sudden feeling that there was a hole in the blanket. I looked around my table. Fowler, Jocelyn, Staunton, Hamish, Terence and Gene Merritt were all doing their bit. Only Ralph Merritt was motionless. He was staring down at his chicken. Not eating it. Just staring. I wondered what he was thinking about. I wondered, and I worried.

The last time he had looked alive was in his office, maybe

forty-five minutes ago, when Gene Merritt had said, "What's the matter with Spinoza?" Now here we were, at a round table in a square dining room, eating a two-dollar chicken lunch with people named Fowler, Jocelyn, Staunton, Hamish and Terence, waiting for an Englishman named Amory Charteris to do his stuff about Queen Victoria, and I had not yet received even a hint from Ralph Mattlin about his reactions to the idea I had put on the table in his office. I didn't like that. I like action. I hate pauses. I thought my idea was a good one. During the meeting in Mattlin's office I'd got the impression he and his partner thought so too. But it was only an impression. Before it could become more than that Mattlin had sidetracked us into the St. Francis Hotel. Now, while I was trying to figure if I'd made my score, I had to watch Mattlin staring at a vulcanized slab of chicken.

Was he doing it to shake me up? I'd seen enough of the s.o.b. leaning out of the windows of those blue eyes to realize this was a possibility. But I didn't really believe it. Because money was involved, and I knew how he felt about money. Inside my head I did one of those quick rebroadcasts for the West Coast. I went over my plan. I ran through what I'd said to Mattlin and Merritt an hour ago. It all checked out. I figured screw him. The next move was his.

I turned back to the platform. Bosworth had disappeared. In his place, talking away at the room, was the man from the poster out in the lobby who looked like Anthony Eden but, now that I saw him in person, also looked as though he had come out of the same cookie jar with Fowler, Jocelyn, Staunton, Hamish and Terence.

"She was above all a human being," the man was saying. "I find almost nothing in all political discourse so moving as her heartfelt statement to Lord Halifax as the ceremonies approached that she wanted to be married not as a queen but as a woman."

I took another look at the faces around me. Even Gene Merritt, with his Fahvel the Flicker profile, had begun to look like Fowler, Jocelyn, Staunton, Hamish, Terence and the boy on the platform. It seemed to be caused by the way he was listening. As though he were hearing a confidential briefing from a fellow member of a secret society. It upset me a little. I'd suddenly realized that even though they were all being polite to me on the surface they would never offer me a membership. I felt better when Bosworth came back on the platform to introduce Gypsy. She spoke a language I understood. Or so I thought until she got going.

"I must confess that this is a most unusual experience for me," she said when Bosworth finished and went tottering back to his slab of chicken. "An experience not only unusual," Gypsy said, "but one that I find deeply moving. I never realized a year ago when I sat down to write my first book that I was embarking upon an experience, indeed that I was entering a land not far removed from the one opened to the novitiate when she takes her first hesitant steps toward the role that has been so aptly described as becoming the bride of Christ. I do not mean to imply that publishers, writers, editors, the people who work with books, the men assembled in this room, are one with the great religious leaders like Jesus and Moses and Mohammed. But I do mean to say that my recent experience with some of the men in this room, men who have helped me bring my book from the crude manuscript I delivered to the beautiful object now available in Doubleday shops, has made me aware that these men are something special, members of a unique fraternity —engaged in commerce, yes; for after all, the rent must be paid whether you run a grocery store or a publishing firm—but they are dedicated men who do not think only of rent."

I gave her the hairy eyeball. Was this the girl who had kept me and my classmates at Thomas Jefferson High from eating lunch two or three times a week so we could pony up the price of a ticket to the Irving Place Burlesque? What had happened to the girl I had once given my heart to? All right, so at fifteen and sixteen it wasn't much of a heart. But whatever it was, it was all I had to give, and I gave it. Could this be the girl who had been on the receiving end? It was true, of course, that Gypsy at the moment was not wearing her working clothes. In fact, the trouble may have been that she was wearing clothes. She was wearing a blue dress with a high collar, but the color and the collar didn't interfere with anybody seeing clearly what she had to offer when she was working. This was one of the great girls of all time. What in God's name had happened to her? Could it be she'd started eating kippers for breakfast?

"Thus," Gypsy said, "I come here today humbly and with pride, because this private world of publishers and books, into which you have so graciously allowed me to enter, is so utterly, so completely, and so devastatingly different from the world from which I come, that—"

"Take it off!"

My epiglottis did it again. The voice had exploded a little to my left. I turned fast.

"Take it off!" Terence called again.

Everybody at our table laughed. Everybody except Ralph Mattlin. He was still staring at his chicken.

"Take it off!" a voice behind me called. Jocelyn on my right half rose out of his chair and cupped his hands around his mouth when he let go with his contribution: "Take it off!"

The laughter spread across the room the way the applause for Amory Charteris had spread. With one exception. There had been a hole in that applause that had attracted my attention. This time, if I hadn't taken a swift look at Mattlin before I looked at the rest of the room, I never would have noticed him. There was too much noise. It wasn't all yelling, either. In a few moments the voices chanting "Take it off!" were almost drowned out by the feet pounding under the tables to the rhythm of the voices. I looked back at the platform. Gypsy was standing there looking the way I must have looked when Staunton, at the other side of our table, had mentioned Irving. She looked as though she couldn't believe what she was seeing and hearing.

Her face filled up slowly with a blush that could have copied its purple color from an eggplant, but she never lost the smile. I looked around at the faces surrounding me, and all of a sudden the uneasiness I'd felt on the way in through the lobby disappeared. Those faces still looked as though they belonged to the members of a special club, but all of a sudden I realized the club was bigger than I'd thought. I could have been back in the Irving Place Burlesque with the kids who had followed me from Thomas Jefferson High to Seventh Avenue. I knew I wasn't going to have any trouble with these slobs on Fourth. I turned back to the platform. Gypsy held up her hand. Slowly the chanting and the shouting and the stamping died down.

"I want to thank you all," she said. The smile now looked as though it could have come out of a can of Karo. "For being so gracious."

She turned and walked off the platform. I wished she could have known she was carrying with her an old admirer's medal. Then I felt a hand on my shoulder. I turned. It was Ralph Mattlin. He had surfaced again out of his plate of chicken. He was talking to Gene Merritt.

"Ted, here, has come up with something big," he said.

15

" I'll Tell You What's the Matter with Spinoza"

Twenty minutes after we left the Panama Club we were back in Gene Merritt's office and Ralph Mattlin was pacing again. "Gene," he said, "just before we went out to lunch you asked me a question. You said, 'What's the matter with Spinoza?' Remember?"

"Of course," Gene Merritt said. "Certainly."

"I'm glad the Panama Club came up," Ralph Mattlin said. "Because when you asked the question I couldn't think of an answer, and yet I knew there had to be one. While we were having lunch at the Panama Club I thought it out. By the way, this English fellow? Charteris? Was he any good?"

"Didn't you hear him?" Merritt said.

"Frankly, no," Mattlin said. "I was thinking."

"Well, you missed something," Merritt said. "He was very good. Wasn't he, Ted?"

Not as good as Gypsy. But that was something they wouldn't have understood.

"Great," I said.

I was back on the couch in front of the table on which I'd spread out my figures before we went to lunch.

"Sorry," Ralph Mattlin said. "I'll buy his book and catch up. Now I'll tell you what's the matter with Spinoza. Ready?"

"Ready," Gene Merritt said.

"Nobody looks for him on the shelves of the A&P," Ralph Mattlin said.

There was something in his voice that reminded me of the way he had sounded Friday morning in his living room when I finished telling him about the fifty thousand dollars Mr. Nachman had siphoned out of the cashbox and he went to the phone to call Dr. Yustin. I got that same feeling as his chest heaved and he pumped the words out that he'd just run up several flights of stairs.

"But nobody goes into an A&P to buy Spinoza," Gene Merritt said.

"That's the trouble," Ralph Mattlin said. He moved across the room toward Merritt's desk as though it were a hurdle and he was coming down the track to take it in stride. "May I use your phone?" He snatched it from under Merritt's nose.

"Certainly," Merritt said, pulling the top half of his body away so fast he almost lost his glasses. "By all means."

"Send Miss Eitner in here," Mattlin said into the phone, and then he slammed down the receiver.

He held his hand on it. He leaned his whole long body on the hand, holding himself hunched over, exactly the way he had held himself on Friday morning after he hung up on Dr. Yustin. His eyes had gone blank, the way they had gone blank on Friday morning. He could have been staring at the wall over Merritt's head, or he could have been trying to stare through the wall into Fourth Avenue.

Then the door opened, and Mattlin seemed to come out of it. In the act of turning toward the door, he managed to get a cigarette out of his pocket and up to his lips. Maud Eitner must have known he'd be doing it. Before the door banged shut behind her she had struck a match and was carrying the flame toward him. When he dipped down, he took her wrist to steady the flame. I guess I was the only one in the room who saw the pink flush that came shooting up and out of her neck like water

171

from a broken hose. I'd known for almost five days how she felt about him. But until this moment I didn't realize how bad she had it.

"Thanks," Mattlin said. He sucked in smoke, and he whirled away from her like Fred Astaire leaving Ginger Rogers after completing a circling movement in one of their dance numbers. "Now then," he said. "Let's get organized."

"Ralph," his partner said.

Mattlin whirled back to Merritt. If he was annoyed by the interruption, which I felt he was but I couldn't prove, Mattlin didn't show it. "Yes, Gene?"

I recognized that doctor-dropping-in-on-the-patient voice.

"What you just said," Merritt said. "I said nobody goes into the A&P to buy Spinoza, and you said—"

"I said that's the trouble," Ralph Mattlin said. "It just struck me. People go into the A&P to buy cornflakes. But where do they go to buy Spinoza? To a bookstore. Let's assume it's the same person. What do you think he or she does more often? Go to the A&P for cornflakes? Or to a bookstore to buy Spinoza?"

"Well, obviously to the A&P to buy cornflakes," Merritt said. "Cornflakes get eaten up. He goes to buy another box. But once he buys a copy of Spinoza he's probably got it for the rest of his life."

Mattlin nodded. "Okay," he said. "Take another man. He's never heard of Spinoza. Or maybe he's heard of Spinoza but was never interested enough to go to a bookstore and buy a copy. Did you ever watch a person shop in the A&P?"

Merritt poked the glasses up on his nose. "Sure, yes, of course," he said. "What do you mean?"

"Say it's a woman," Mattlin said. "She goes to the cornflakes shelf. She takes down a box. Next to it, or under it, she sees a shelf of baked beans. Maybe she remembers back home she's out of beans. Perhaps she remembers she likes beans and hasn't had them for some time. Maybe she never ate a bean in her life, but she's always meant to try them. She buys a can. She had no intention of buying that can of beans when she came into the A&P. The intention was formed when she saw it. Suppose

172

instead of a shelf of beans under the cornflakes shelf, suppose there had been a shelf of Spinoza?"

"Good God," Maud Eitner said.

Mattlin whirled on her. "What does that mean?" he said. Not angrily. He sounded tense and curious. He prowled closer to her in a stooped-over, nervous series of steps. "Come on, Maud," Mattlin said. "I really want to know. What did you mean by that?"

She took a step backward. She put her hand up to the side of her neck. If she did it to cover the blush she was too late. It was climbing up the side of her face again. She was looking directly into Mattlin's eyes. "I meant good God it's an astonishing idea but—" Her voice stopped.

"But what?" Mattlin said. "Come on, Maud. But what?"

Without taking his eyes from hers, he fished another cigarette from his pocket. I wondered if he carried them loose like marbles.

"But," Maud said. She stopped again and flipped back the cover of the matchbook she'd brought into the room. She struck a light and then did a funny thing. She reached out and took the burned-down cigarette from his left hand. Apparently Mattlin didn't know when he fished out the fresh one that he still had one fired up. He put the fresh one to his lips, took her wrist again and sucked in a light. Maud turned. She went back and she punched out the old cigarette in the ashtray on the floor near the chair he'd been sitting on. When she straightened up, I knew why she'd gone through the funny little ritual. It had given her time to pull herself together. She wasn't even blushing when, in her normal slow-motion delivery, she said, "What I meant was it's an astonishing idea. But a can of beans costs only a few cents, probably no more than the box of cornflakes she came in to get originally. But a volume of Spinoza. I don't know. I imagine that would cost a couple of dollars. Perhaps more."

Mattlin snapped his fingers and did that whirling little dance step. "Exactly," he said.

"Exactly what?" Maud Eitner said.

"You've put your finger on the main problem," Ralph Mattlin said. "But there are others. I'm sure we can solve them. I know we can. I feel it. That's why I want us to get organized."

"Organized for what?" Maud said.

He was staring at her suddenly as though he had never seen her before. I thought he was going back into one of his trances. But I guess it didn't work unless he had a telephone to lean on, and he was about ten feet from the one on the desk. Anyway, he shook his head slightly, like a dog coming out of the water, and he did something I suddenly realized I had never seen Ralph Mattlin do before. He smiled.

"Yes, of course," he said. "Sorry, Maud. You don't know what happened just before we went out to lunch." Mattlin looked around the room, and his eyes stopped on me. He scowled slightly, as though he was trying to remember who I was, and then the scowl sank back into the smile. He came across the room. He put his hand on my shoulder, and he said to Maud Eitner, "Ted, here, has come up with something big."

I can still remember the small warm feeling that started in my gut when he called me by my first name. I can also remember the feeling of shame that started in the same place and came right along with it. To my mother the world had always been divided into aristocrats and serfs. Her son did not like learning at the age of twenty-four that for a boy from East Fourth Street, it still was. What I hated was knowing why I wanted Ralph Mattlin to like me: I'd always hated Jews who broke their backs to make it with the gentiles.

"What's happening?" Maud Eitner said.

"We are going back into the publishing business," Ralph Mattlin said.

174

16

" You Never Heard
of Us, But We Want
Three Minutes
of Your Time"

If you live where I live, on the upper East Side anywhere near Fifth Avenue, you may not know it but you're part of every travel-agency brochure that's printed outside the United States. What the streets around the Louvre are to Paris, and the approaches to the National Gallery are to London, the stretch of sidewalk in front of my apartment building is to New York.

From ten in the morning until sundown, winter and summer, spring and fall, the only English you'll hear when you come out in the street is your own doorman's "Good day, sir." On their way up from the Frick on Seventieth to the Guggenheim on Eighty-eighth or back, with stops at the Met on Eighty-second and a side job to the Whitney on Seventy-fifth and Madison, the culture-hungry hicks from overseas are reading aloud their guidebooks to each other in their native tongues.

They could be wearing leather pants and talking German, or sweeping the sidewalk with gold-embroidered saris and dropping pellets of Bombay Oxford behind them. Or showing off the latest in zoot suits from the Thirty Yen Tailors on the Ginza as they hiss Japanese at the natives like me. It doesn't matter. There are two things that this tzimiss of visitors from all parts of

175

the world have in common. Almost every one of them has a camera slung around his neck, and pretty nearly two out of every three are carrying one of the small pocket-size volumes bound in the pale blue leather that has become the international trademark of the Twentieth Century Classics Series.

I'm talking about today. A lot of years after that moment in 1937 in Gene Merritt's office when Ralph Mattlin put his hand on my shoulder and said, "Ted, here, has come up with something big." I haven't had anything to do with Mattlin & Merritt, Inc., as a going concern for years. I mean as a place to which I used to report every day. As a result, it wasn't until four months ago, when with the help of Byram Noonan I started putting the pieces of the Sissenwein estate together for our offer to the surrogate, that I realized how big that word "big" had become.

Mattlin & Merritt, Inc., went on to other things. Some of them have changed the way the people of this country live. But that Twentieth Century Classics Series, it's like Henry Ford and the Model T.

They're making better-looking cars. And they're getting more money for them. And they're equipped with gadgets that will do everything from open your garage door when you're still around the corner to brush your teeth after you've taken them out and put them in the Polident bath for the night. But none of it would amount to a hill of farfel if the old man hadn't taken out the basic patent on a thing called the clutch. The same with the Twentieth Century Classics Series. You can buy them in every country in the world except maybe Tionga, which was born only yesterday on the doorstep of Kenya, and it wouldn't surprise me before long to see Tiongan translations being carried past my apartment house. What that series grosses every year, worldwide, could finance another one of our quiet little preventive wars on one of those chop-suey continents. But even as a boy who thought up the idea, I can't say honestly that I had any more to do with it than the other two men involved. And the crazy thing about it is that what they did was done in exactly five days.

If you want to learn something about a man, don't sit and ask him questions. Jog him into taking you for a fast ride in his car, and then watch him handle the cop who pulls up and wants to know where's the fire. Or lead him into a kitchen at midnight and say I'll open the beer while you make the sandwiches, and then see how he makes out with the stuff you've got in the icebox.

A man who tells you "I am smart" could be. A man who invents a reason that convinces a motorcycle cop, is. A guy who gives you a monologue on his manual dexterity might be able to jockey a briefcase through a revolving door. A man who puts together a couple of workable chicken sandwiches without making the floor between the icebox and the kitchen table look like it's been hit by the fallout from a giant case of dandruff, him you can trust to candle the eggs on your poultry farm with a minimum of breakage.

What I'm getting at is something I learned that first week in 1937 after Ralph Mattlin and Gene Merritt took me to my first lunch at the Panama Club.

"Hey now, wait a minute," I said to Maud Eitner late in the afternoon when she dumped a coal scuttle full of cost charts on my desk. "I haven't even sorted out the stuff you gave me an hour ago."

"I suggest you start sorting faster," Maud said. "Mattlin wants you to have dinner with him tonight to discuss the preliminary figures, and he's calling a meeting in his office for nine o'clock tomorrow morning, at which he wants you to have all the figures ready so he can nail Bud Knisel to the mast."

This would not have been difficult to do. It wouldn't have had to be a big mast, either. Bud Knisel, the head of the Mattlin & Merritt Production Department, weighed ninety-two pounds. I know because a few months later, when we'd worked until almost eleven o'clock one night, I rewarded him with a visit to a joint on Twenty-third Street for a petty-cash zetz, and two of the broads were so astonished by what was left after he peeled off his clothes that they insisted on putting him on a scale.

"Good morning, Ted," Ralph Mattlin said when I came into his office the next morning with my analysis pad and my five inches of worn-down Eagle. "This is Bud Knisel, our production man. Bud, this is Ted Leff, our new bookkeeper."

When Knisel put out his hand I almost expected it to be a paw. He looked like a dachshund standing up in a double-breasted blue number from the $22.50 rack at Howard's. I said hello to Merritt. He was on the couch between the windows with a black loose-leaf notebook on his lap. I greeted Maud, who was in the chair beside Mattlin's desk with her steno pad and pencil. Mattlin was smoking, of course, and he must have been at it for some time because the eyes that looked out at me from the Grubensteller portrait seemed to be peering through a haze. Luckily, Mattlin was also pacing, so the smoky haze kept moving.

"Bud," he said, "I have news for you. We are about to embark on the publication of a series of books drawn from all fields of literature. Classics of fiction. Poetry. Philosophy. Science. Anything and everything that has over the years made its mark with the reading public. All the material will be drawn from the public domain, since the purpose of this series is to sell the book buyer not an unknown quantity, a work by a writer who has not yet proved himself, but something that has an accepted and known market value. To take an example, the writings of Benedict Spinoza are a known quantity. *David Copperfield* is a known quantity. The poetry of John Keats, that's a known quantity. When the reader picks up one of these books he'll know what he's getting. Exactly as he knows what he's getting when he goes into the A&P and picks up a box of Kellogg's cornflakes or a can of Heinz baked beans."

Bud Knisel scratched his ear nervously. "You mean a reprint series?" he said.

Ralph Mattlin nodded as he lighted a fresh cigarette. "A reprint series with a difference," he said. "In fact, several differences. The overall title for the series will be the 'Twentieth Century Classics.' How do you like it?"

Bud Knisel looked more nervous. "Mr. Mattlin," he said. "The woods is full of reprint series."

"I didn't ask you that," Mattlin said. "I asked how do you

like the title? The 'Twentieth Century Classics Series'?"

"It sounds okay, I guess," Knisel said. He sounded about as enthusiastic as a guy being asked to choose the kind of type face he wants used on his tombstone.

Maud Eitner spoke up. "I think it's terrific," she said.

Mattlin said, "Thanks, Maud." He gave her shoulder a light pat. "Gene," he said. "You like?"

The glasses on Merritt's nose got their little tap from the owner of same. "Well," he said, "it's the first time I heard it, so I haven't really had time to think."

"The first time a book buyer sees it on the spine of one of our books," Mattlin said, "he won't have time to think, either. It will either hit him right, or it'll hit him wrong. Or worst of all it won't hit him at all. It came to me this morning while I was shaving, and I rang you at home, Gene, to try it out on you, but you'd already left for the office. So I'm trying it out on you now."

Merritt's performance on the couch was practically a lesson in how to kvetch. He looked as though somebody were poking a live wire toward him with a stick and he was trying to get his feet out of the way. I decided to make a small score.

"Would you be interested in a bookkeeper's opinion?" I said.

"I would, Ted," Mattlin said. "I would indeed. Very much interested."

"It hits me right," I said.

Behind Mattlin's back Maud Eitner sent me a small wink.

"I agree," Gene Merritt now decided. "Me too, Ralph. It hits me right."

"I'm glad," Mattlin said. "I've got instincts. Instincts that work for me. I don't mean I'm smarter than anybody else. Just the opposite, probably. How I got through Yale, I don't know, because basically my instincts, my feelings, you could say my tastes, they're very ordinary. I feel what the average plumber feels. The average truckdriver. The man in the street. I think that's my strength, because if I feel it, then I think a lot of average people will also feel it, and that's how you rack up sales. So when it hit me this morning, the 'Twentieth Century

179

Classics Series,' I knew right away it was right, and naturally I'm pleased that everybody in this room shares my feeling. Especially you, Gene."

"Yes, I do," Merritt said. "It's a brilliant title for a series. It says the whole thing simply and directly. Now we have our handle, and we don't have to say what the fellow in the poem said when he was asked the name of his girl."

"What was that, Gene?" Ralph Mattlin asked.

I admired the way he did it. In that keeper-of-the zoo voice.

Through his nutty grin Merritt began to recite. "She doesn't drink. She doesn't smoke. She doesn't like a dirty joke. You ask her name? Why, that's a wow. She's not a dame. She's just a cow!"

Maud Eitner gave it a lips-together smile. I gave it one medium hock. Bud Knisel looked as though he had just learned the date that was going under the words on his tombstone tomorrow. Ralph Mattlin released another one of those things I've seen mentioned only in Dickens. A chortle.

"Very good, Gene," he said. "Excellent. One of your best. Well now. So the name of the series is settled. The Twentieth Century Classics. You getting all this, Maud?"

"Every word," she said.

"Good," Mattlin said. "A lot of things get said in a meeting that sometimes get forgotten. A lot of first-rate ideas are lost that way. All right, Bud. As I said, there are several things that are going to make this series different from any other previously published, and I'm going to get right to the one that affects you, Bud. Are you ready?"

"Oh yes," Bud Knisel said.

He sounded as though the captain of the firing squad had asked him to take a couple of steps forward, please, because some of his men were near-sighted.

"The books will all be uniform in size," Ralph Mattlin said. "Four and a quarter inches by six and a quarter. So they can fit into a man's pocket or a woman's purse. And they will all retail for the same price. Seventy-five cents."

"What?" Bud Knisel said.

180

I've never seen a dachshund change expression except, maybe, at the sight of his food. But that was not what happened to Knisel's face. Come to think of it, nothing happened to his face. It was lower down that things were happening. He seemed to be strangling.

Mattlin stabbed out his cigarette in the tray on the desk. He reached Knisel with two long strides, bent over him and began to slap his back. "Bud," he said. "What's the matter?"

After a few gasping inhales that were close to whistles the little guy said, "I must've swallowed wrong. I'm sorry."

"You all right now?" Mattlin said.

"Yeah, fine, thanks," Knisel said. "I'm sorry." He ran his hand across his mouth and looked worriedly at Mattlin. "Mr. Mattlin," Knisel said, and he stopped. He couldn't seem to say any more. He sucked in some more breath and tried again. "You say this series," he said. "The books. They'll sell for seventy-five cents?"

"Yes," Mattlin said.

"Retail?" Bud Knisel said.

"Of course retail," Mattlin said. "Everything in this series, size, color, price, everything will be designed for its impact on the buyer. When it comes to price, to the buyer it's always retail. He doesn't care how much it cost to make what he's buying. What he cares about is how much he's paying."

"But, Mr. Mattlin," Bud Knisel said. "Seventy-five cents retail, forty percent off to the bookseller, the normal discount, it means we have to produce these books for forty-five cents."

"Not forty-five," Mattlin said. "Thirty."

"Thirty cents?" Knisel said.

"Thirty cents," Mattlin said. "We're not running an eleemosynary institution, you know."

"A what?" Knisel said.

"A charitable organization," Mattlin said. "We're in business. We want that extra fifteen cents for our overhead and profit. We can make it too. Because one big cost that goes into most books will not be involved here. Since we plan to use only material in the public domain we will not have to pay royalties."

"Even so, Mr. Mattlin," Bud Knisel said. "To manufacture a book for thirty cents—"

"You won't have that whole thirty cents for manufacturing," Ralph Mattlin said. "That thirty cents must include advertising."

"Mr. Mattlin," Bud Knisel said. "It can't be done."

Mattlin did his whirling pirouette. He came out in a sort of crouch practically under the little guy's nose. "You mean *you* can't do it?" he said.

"Comes to production," Bud Knisel said, "I can do anything anybody can do. I mean *nobody* can do this."

Mattlin straightened up. He went to work on a new cigarette. He grinned around the match flame. "Bud," he said, "you don't know your own strength. Mr. Leff has prepared a cost schedule that will change your mind. Ted?"

I handed over the six sheets of clipped-together analysis paper. "Mr. Knisel," I said.

"Call him Bud," Ralph Mattlin said. "This is a moment in his life when he needs affection."

Maud Eitner laughed. Mattlin gave her a short, quick, side-swinging grin of appreciation. I began to have the feeling that her chances were better than I'd thought. He liked her.

"Bud," I said. "Why don't you take this to your office and study it for a while? You'll find a lot of it is familiar. I took the liberty of stealing from some of your own cost schedules on your first five published books. As soon as this meeting is over, I'll come along and go over the rest with you."

I was sending the words at him, but I was talking to old Ralphie. Nobody was sending me out of any rooms the way Bud Knisel had just been sent out. When the sender thought I'd heard all that concerned me. Not on this project. This particular sender didn't even suspect all that concerned me.

"Okay, sure," Knisel said.

"Study hard," Mattlin said as he led him to the door. "I went over those figures with Mr. Leff last night. Especially your fixed production estimates. I'm sure Mr. Leff's changes and additions will work." When he closed the door Mattlin leaned back

182

against it and grinned. "Poor Bud," he said. "We've handed him the toughest part of the job."

"No, we haven't."

Turning toward Merritt, I saw two things: Maud also turned, and the grin fell off Mattlin's kisser. "What do you mean, Gene?"

It looked like they were both fond of poetry.

"I know you and Mr. Leff worked late last night on the cost figures," Merritt said. "And nobody knows better than I do, how important that is. But it's just as important to choose the right titles that these cost figures will be turning out at the proper price. I'm sure you'll agree with that, Ralph."

"Of course I do, Gene."

Merritt made another hopeless attempt at getting the glasses straight on his nose.

"I think you should take down everything I say in this meeting, Miss Eitner," he said. "Just as you take down everything Mr. Mattlin says."

Maud's pencil jumped. It jolted me. The thing about her was her control. When she spoke, it was like someone reading from an instruction book on how to change a tire: aye, you grasp the ratchet in your right hand; then bee, you turn the dingus to the left; and see, you twist the gookle counterclockwise ninety degrees. Until she got to the end of her sentence. It was a shock to see that Merritt had rattled her.

"I'm sorry," she said. Then she recovered. "I was so interested by what you were saying that I forgot I was supposed to take it down." She lifted the pencil over the steno book as though she were walking out on the high board to do a double jackknife. "Would you like to repeat the part I missed?" she said.

His eyes did that thing. I decided he couldn't be as big a boob as he looked. At least he knew when he was getting an umbrella shoved up.

"No, that's all right," Gene Merritt said. "That was just preliminary. It's what I have to say now that I feel is important." He turned back to Ralph Mattlin. "I've given the matter a lot of thought," Merritt said. "Perhaps not as much thought as you and Mr. Leff."

"Please," I said. "Ted."

Why should he be less close to me than his mother?

"Sorry," Merritt said. "Perhaps I haven't given as much thought to this new and exciting project, Ralph, as you and Ted have. But I did stay up all night, and I've got something I think you both might find interesting." He flipped open the black loose-leaf notebook on his knees. "When you were just talking to Bud Knisel, Ralph, you mentioned Spinoza and you mentioned Dickens and you mentioned Keats. All well and good. They are all what you call known quantities. But I wonder if they're not too well known."

"How do you mean?" Mattlin said.

He sounded sore. Besides his nervousness about money, I was learning something else about Ralph Mattlin. He didn't like to be criticized.

"I'm thinking of the woman in the A&P," Gene Merritt said. "She's reaching for a box of cornflakes. Well and good. She sees a shelf of Dickens and Spinoza and Keats, all priced at a figure she can afford, and I ask myself why should she pick up one or all of them? If she's a Dickens or a Spinoza or a Keats fan, she's probably read them already, at some time in her life, and she probably owns other editions of these books. What I'm getting at, Ralph, is simply this. It's not enough, in my humble opinion anyway, it's not enough to place the books in that woman's reach at the right price. It's also important that the book fill a need."

"A what?" Mattlin said.

"A need," Gene Merritt said. "The book should be a need-filler. Just like that woman needs the box of cornflakes because she's hungry, it fills one of her basic needs, I feel before she reaches for the book on the next shelf she should have the same feeling, the feeling that the book will fill one of her needs."

"Such as?" Mattlin said.

"Well, a woman who shops in the A&P," Merritt said, "I'd say—and it's only a guess—but I'd say she's not a rich woman.

184

I'd say she lives on a small or middle-sized income earned by her husband, let's say. People like that, pennies count. I know, because that's how it was in my family when I was growing up. People like that, if cornflakes cost a penny or two less in the A&P than in, say, Applebaum's, that would be enough to bring this woman to the A&P rather than to Applebaum's. To such a woman anything that would show her how to save more pennies would be interesting because saving pennies is for her a need-filler. So if, instead of a book by Spinoza on the shelf under the cornflakes, suppose it was a book that told her how to make the equivalent of a steak dinner out of what's left in the bottom of her cornflakes box? The crumbs? I'm using a far-fetched example, but I think it shows what I mean. You understand, Ralph?"

If Mattlin didn't, I did. All of a sudden the weird little nut with the long turkey-like neck and the crooked glasses who reminded me of Fahvel the Flicker reminded me of something else: the kid Herbert Bayard Swope had called potentially the best editorial writer he had ever known. What had done it was movement. On Friday, when I met E. Spinoza Merritt, he was a nervous boy sitting behind a desk, slicing up newspapers with a pair of golden scissors. Now, on Tuesday, he was a guy with brains who had gone into action.

"I certainly do see it," Ralph Mattlin said. He seemed to have forgotten he was sore, because he thought he was being criticized. Now he was interested. "That's good thinking, Gene," Ralph Mattlin said. "Very good thinking. Go on, please."

"Thanks, Ralph," Merritt said. "I was sure you'd see it. There's not much more to go on about." He touched the loose-leaf notebook on his knees. "I won't bother you with the lists now at this meeting," he said. "They're still tentative, and they're pretty illegible, since I scrawled them hastily last night. But now that I have your approval, now that I know I'm on the right track, I'll polish them up, then have Miss Eitner type them and you can study them at your leisure."

"That's great, Gene," Mattlin said. "I really mean that. Now, let's see. Is there anything we've left out?"

Just one thing. Me.

185

"May I make a suggestion?" I said.

"Certainly," Mattlin said. "By all means, Ted."

"What Mr. Merritt just said—"

"Please," Mr. Merritt said. "Gene."

In the race for my affections he was now neck and neck with his mother.

"Thanks," I said. "What Gene just said about need-fillers reminds me of something. The last time I was in a bookstore was nine years ago. I was sixteen years old and I went down to Barnes & Noble to get a trot for *Tartarin de Tarascon*. For my French class in Thomas Jefferson High. That's my idea of need-filling. All the way down to Eighteenth Street to get a specific book. Why? Because I wanted to pass that course, that's why. My thought is this. With a minimum amount of research we ought to be able to find out the books that teachers are assigning as outside reading in high schools all over the city, and then we—"

"Why only high schools?" Ralph Mattlin broke in. He was pumping the words out again as though he'd run up another few flights of stairs. "Why not colleges too?" he said. "That's terrific thinking, Ted. Terrific."

"And why only all over the city?" Gene Merritt said. "Why not all over the entire country?"

"Why not all over the world?" Ralph Mattlin said.

"Gentlemen, please," Maud Eitner said. She grinned at all three of us. One at a time. "I can't keep up with you."

For the next four days nobody could. It was like the first time I tried to boil rice. I couldn't believe I was seeing straight as the stuff started to get bigger and bigger, climbing out of the pot, then across the stove. Luckily the five big things on which the series depended, the foundation that was so solid it could support the years of growth that were later piled up on it, those five things were set in those first four days.

By Tuesday morning we had three of them. First, the seventy-five-cent price. With the help of my cost breakdowns Bud Knisel came through.

"You're right," he said to Ralph Mattlin at the Tuesday morning meeting. "It can be done."

The second thing we'd had first: the idea to get the series out of the bookstores. To sell them in places like the A&P and drugstores where people went regularly to replace things they consumed regularly. And the third thing, the titles that would be need-fillers not only to the general reader but also to students so that we had a textbook series built into the Twentieth Century Classics, that third thing was ready on Wednesday when Gene Merritt presented what he called with a giggle his first "definitely tentative" list. It has never been changed. Added to, yes. But never changed.

Wednesday morning was one of Mattlin's days on Bernie Yustin's couch, so it wasn't until eleven-thirty when he came into the office as though he'd come off the rubber band of a slingshot that we got the fourth thing.

"A uniform binding," he said. "Every book looking exactly the same. This will not only make it cheaper for Bud Knisel because he'll be able to buy his binding materials in enormous quantities, but it will allow us to add the collector's slant to our advertising. Build up a serious and good library. Buy the Twentieth Century Classics one at a time, two at a time, three at a time, whenever you have an extra seventy-five cents to spend. And if we pick the right color, we'll be establishing a trademark that will grow in value. I sort of like pale blue leather. It came to me this morning while I was shaving."

I don't remember when he got the fifth and final idea on which the series was founded. But I do remember that he gave it to us late Friday afternoon because Gene Merritt was already heading out of the office on his way to the Bronx for his weekly dose of noodle soup with Ma and Pa.

"Gene!"

I was down the hall, in Bud Knisel's office, when I heard Mattlin's yell. "Be right back," I said to Bud, and stepped out into the hall.

Mattlin was standing in the open door of his office, waving

one hand toward the reception room. "Could you come back for a minute?" he yelled. "I've got something I want to show you."

"Of course," Merritt's voice called.

Mattlin turned and saw me coming up the hall. "You too, Ted," he said.

I went into his office behind Gene Merritt. Maud Eitner was in the chair beside the desk. The steno notebook was on her lap. Closing the door behind us, lighting a fresh cigarette, getting rid of the old one, lunging around the room in his excitement, Mattlin reminded me of a swimmer underwater trying desperately to come to the surface.

"Read, Maud, please," he said. "Read what I just dictated."

She read.

"Probably since the publishing business began, books have always been sold by direct-by-mail advertising. It seemed to me from the moment the Twentieth Century Classics Series was conceived that it was a perfect product for this form of merchandising. The problem was merely how to approach the people to whom we will be mailing our circulars and addressing our coupon ads. I have studied enough of these to know that the battle for the unknown customer's attention is won or lost in the headline of the circular or ad. If you don't get him with the headline, he'll turn the page to another ad or he'll throw the circular in the wastebasket. After a four-day struggle I think I have come up with a headline that should pull them in like a vacuum cleaner."

Mattlin whipped up his hand like a traffic cop. "Hold it, Maud," he said. Her voice stopped. "Don't read it," Mattlin said. "I want to speak it." He spread his arms high and wide, like a preacher in the movies letting his flock know he has come to the meat and potatoes of the message. "Think of a sheet of paper," Mattlin said. "Down below it's got a lot of copy about the series. A picture of a few of the books. The coupon to be filled in and mailed back. All that we'll work out later. This is what I want you to hear. The headline. The words in big type the reader of the circular will read first. Ready?"

"Ready," Gene Merritt said.

188

"Ready," I said.

Mattlin pulled in a lungful of smoke and poured it out around the words as he slowly said: *"You never heard of us, but we want three minutes of your time."*

When you consider how many copies of the Twentieth Century Classics have been sold by direct mail, and when you bear in mind that the only thing on the circular that has changed in seventeen years is the list of titles, it would be nice for me to say here that I recognized that handful of words at once as one of the great come-ons of all time. It would be nice, but it would also be a lie. I've stuck with my determination to tell the truth up to this point. I might as well go the distance on the same fuel.

Here's what happened. Gene Merritt blinked and tried to straighten the glasses on his nose. I blinked and suddenly wondered if this guy Ralph Mattlin kept a bottle in his desk. And Maud Eitner spoke up.

"I'm going on record," she said quietly. "Years from now, when they're putting together the textbook out of which college kids will be learning how to write direct-by-mail advertising copy, those thirteen words will be included among the classics in the field."

I've never seen one of those textbooks, so I've never had a chance to test whether that particular prediction by Maud Eitner came true. I know only this: if we had not found the five items I have just mentioned—the five stones, you could say, out of which the foundation of the Twentieth Century Classics Series was built—the series would never have got off the ground. Because that night, whatever the motor was inside Ralph Mattlin out of which his ideas for the series had been coming during the past five days, that motor conked out. I learned it at eight minutes to six that afternoon.

I was back in Bud Knisel's room. I was explaining why the cost of binding a book, speaking purely in terms of using the money sensibly, was no different from the cost of trimming a dress. Bud was a pretty smart boy, so I was puzzled by why he couldn't get it through his head, when I realized it was psychological. To Bud the book business was something clean and elegant, the way those men had looked to me in the foyer before the Panama Club lunch, but the dress business was something shitty and low-class, the way those same men had looked to me when they opened up on Gypsy. I was just beginning to make progress, by comparing Seventh Avenue for Bud with Fourth, when Maud Eitner stuck her head in.

"Bud," she said. "You mind if I borrow Ted for a minute?"

I went out. She walked down the hall to Mattlin's office and went in. From the way she did it I knew there was trouble. She didn't knock. I followed her in and closed the door. "Where's Mattlin?" I said.

"On his way to Lakewood," Maud said.

"Oh, Jesus," I said. "He's not starting that again?"

"No," Maud said.

Then her voice caught up with me.

"Okay," I said. "Tell me why he went to Lakewood."

"He just had a long-distance call," Maud said. "A few minutes ago."

"From Honest Abe?"

Maud shook her head. "No," she said. "From the police."

"The Lakewood police?"

She nodded. "Mr. Nachman just killed himself," Maud Eitner said.

17

"As I Recall My Mother's Womb, It Was a Drafty Place Compared to This Turkish Bath"

The entrance was on Seventy-third Street. About thirty feet down from the Madison Avenue corner. I hadn't realized when Maud Eitner gave me the address that it would be a maisonette. I pressed the bell. The door was opened by a girl wearing a felt hat like Greta Garbo in *Anna Christie*. That's where the resemblance stopped. She had a purse tucked under one arm. I'd apparently caught her in the act of pulling on a glove.

"Mr. Leff?"

"Yes."

"Come in, please."

I came into what looked like a living room. To me, anyway. By me a living room is anyplace that has pictures on the wall, a rug on the floor, and chairs in which, when you sit down, your tail sinks lower than the level that greets the eye. The girl closed the door. She walked across to another door at the other side of the room and opened it. "Dr. Yustin," she said into the next room. "He's here."

"Good for him," a voice said. "I'll be right out."

It was one of those voices you hear at the end of the movie

travelogue: *"And So to the Strains of Nathaniel Shilkret's Orchestra, We Say Farewell, Cuba, Pearl of the Antilles."*

"I'm going now," the girl said.

"Go slowly," the voice said. "Peering ahead carefully as you do. The town is full of pitfalls. Good secretaries are hard to find. I should hate to lose you to a Consolidated Edison excavation. Have a good weekend."

"Thanks," the girl said. "Good night, Dr. Yustin."

She closed the door. I looked around. I had always wondered about maisonettes. I figured doctors rented them because they gave the patients a feeling of privacy. No doorman to stare at you on the way in and wonder whether what you're coming to have fixed is an ingrown toenail or a backed-up postnasal drip. It seemed to me an ideal setup for a riding academy. Then the door opened, and what came out to join me made me think maybe it was one. Dr. Yustin looked like a madam dressed to relax after the night's work was over. "Mr. Leff?" he said.

I went over to take his hand. "It's very good of you to let me come here like this, Dr. Yustin," I said.

I did my best to sound like a member of the Panama Club while he was still out in the lobby.

"Not at all," Yustin said. "You told me it was an emergency. Besides, I was curious to meet the new young financial genius Ralph Mattlin tells me he's just hired. You will excuse my attire, I hope. My day is a long one. My work is wearing. I always take a hot bath at six o'clock sharp."

Fast as I'd been moving, it had still taken me almost a half-hour from the moment Maud gave me the news. I had to get her set, make the call, find a cab and ride uptown. It was now twenty minutes after six. This boy certainly took long baths.

"It's worse than an emergency," I said.

Yustin laughed. "I know, Mr. Leff, I know," he said. "Oh, dear God, how I know. It's a matter of life and death."

First I hadn't liked him because he was a hunchback. I know this is not a very Christian attitude, but they give me the creeps. Then I hated him because of the way he was dressed. A bright red bathrobe with black satin trim. Made of that heavy quilted material you see in newsreel shots of Chinese soldiers freezing their filberts off while they listen to Chiang Kai-shek tell them beginning next Monday it's going to be strawberries and cream three times a day. In addition, Dr. Yustin was wearing a pair of what in the layette ads they call booties. The sheepskin linings curled so high up his legs the fuzz touched the hem of his bathrobe. He was either afraid of drafts or he'd pulled on the robe and the booties without bothering to dry himself when he stepped out of the tub. Around his blubber neck, tucked into the heavy shawl collar of the robe, was the sort of cream-colored Turkish towel you find only in joints where the prices start at ten bucks a throw. In the middle of all this red robe and creamy toweling sat a great big round face. It looked as though somebody had taken the man in the Admiration Cigar ads and tried to turn his kisser into a roulette wheel. The attempt was a bomb. The lines running out in all directions from the button nose and the slot mouth did no more than take what had been to start with a fairly reasonable facsimile of a garbage-can cover, and turn it into a sort of Sessue Hayakawa version of Wallace Beery. If this wasn't enough to turn your stomach, the noises that came out of him were guaranteed to do the trick. Dr. Yustin sounded like a cow making her way across a muddy field. He didn't talk. He glugged. I could see right away Mrs. Leff's shy little son had just found himself a brand-new hero.

"You mean you know that Mr. Nachman just committed suicide?" I said.

When I started the sentence he had just turned his back on me and was waddling his way across the room toward a red leather chair. By the time I finished the sentence Yustin had stopped, turned and looked nailed to the floor. "Mr. Nachman what?" he said.

I wrapped the next one around a rock and I aimed for his center spread. "I thought that's what you meant when you said I know, Mr. Leff, I know, it's a matter of life and death."

The color started coming back into his face. "I'm sorry," Yustin said. "It was just a figure of speech. In my profession the people I deal with they live on the edge of hysteria all the time. They never start let's say writing a check and have their fountain pens run dry. Oh no. They always find they have suffered complete paralysis while trying to pay the monthly telephone bill. The people I deal with are never harassed by troubles. Oh no. They are hounded. They are victims of conspiracies. They are bombarded by disasters. Everything to them is a matter of life and death. If a doctor allowed himself to be swept up in the emotional climate of his patients he would soon be incapable of giving them any help. I did not know Mr. Nachman has committed suicide. If I had known, you can be assured, Mr. Leff, I would not have found it an occasion for levity. Please tell me all."

He turned again and heaved himself across to the red chair. He sank into it like a coal truck, backed up to a cellar, dropping its load.

"I don't know all," I said. "That's why I came up here practically on the run. About a quarter to six, according to Ralph Mattlin's secretary, he had a call from the Lakewood police. Miss Eitner didn't take the call, so she doesn't know what was actually said. All she knows is what Mattlin told her when he hung up. He said Mr. Nachman had killed himself. He grabbed his hat, said he was going to Lakewood, and beat it." I looked at my watch. "That was at ten minutes to six. Maybe a couple of minutes earlier. I mean it was ten minutes to six when Miss Eitner reported what had happened, and she came to tell me the moment Mattlin left the office."

Dr. Yustin heaved one foot up onto his other thigh and pulled off the bootie. This did about as much to improve his appearance as it would have improved the appearance of Jean Arthur to drop her into a tub of boiling oil. The toes of Dr. Yustin's naked foot didn't seem to like each other. They were all heading in different directions. I could not find it in my heart to blame them.

"May I ask, Mr. Leff, why Miss Eitner felt she must report this unfortunate event to you the moment Mr. Mattlin left the office?"

"Sure you can ask," I said. "Since you know about the new

194

young financial genius Ralph Mattlin has just hired, I guess you know about the Twentieth Century Classics Series. I mean he seems to tell you everything."

Dr. Yustin smiled as he reached across to the drawer in a small table. He pulled out what looked like a box of absorbent cotton.

"In the relationship between a doctor and his patient," he said, "I would like to point out to you, Mr. Leff, there are no secrets."

If this boy got any more repulsive it could be there soon would be one less doctor to have secrets from.

"Then you also know how hard we've all been working this week," I said. "Nobody has worked harder, and nobody's ideas have been more brilliant than Mr. Mattlin's. This afternoon he came up with a direct-by-mail merchandising idea that is the most brilliant of all. We were all there when he came up with it, and he later told Miss Eitner he's going to use it for our kickoff ad. All of us—Mattlin, Gene Merritt, Miss Eitner, me—everybody was there. So when this thing happened, the call from Lakewood, Merritt had already left the office, Miss Eitner came and told me. That's all. She was upset. She didn't feel she had to tell me. There was no had to about it. She was upset, and I was the only one around. So she told it to me. Anything wrong with that?"

"I didn't say anything was wrong with it," Yustin said. "I merely made a polite inquiry."

He tore off a piece of cotton and squeezed it into a small ball. He wadded the ball between his big toe and the one next to it that was trying to go over the hill.

"Anyway, Miss Eitner and I talked it over," I said. "Neither of us could figure out what to do, so I thought I'd come up here and ask you."

Yustin tore off another piece of cotton and rammed it between his second and third toes. "Does my doing this upset you?" he said.

Just because I was sitting on my stomach so it wouldn't start heaving, this was a reason for him to think I was upset?

"Of course not," I said. "Everybody I know stuffs cotton

between their toes after they take a bath and while they're receiving visitors."

Yustin laughed. "I'll bet I'm the only one you know who does it in front of visitors who also happen to be total strangers," he said.

"You win," I said.

He laughed again. "I suppose you're wondering why I do it?" he said.

Obviously to live up to the nickname by which he was known in society circles: the Aristocrat.

"Not really," I said. "I assume you like the color combination."

"The what?" he said.

"Pink toe, white cotton," I said. "Crooked toe, white cotton. Toe with ingrown nail, white cotton and so on."

"Not at all," Dr. Yustin said. "It prevents athlete's foot." He pulled off his other bootie and went to work on the second set of toes. "Do you find it hot in here?"

"A little," I said. "You mind if I open a window?"

"Very much," Dr. Yustin said. "I am extremely susceptible to head colds. Why did you come here, Mr. Leff?"

To learn how to avoid athlete's foot.

"Since they started three years ago," I said, "Mattlin & Merritt have not been a very successful firm. All of a sudden, the company is on to something that could make it very successful. A lot of that success will depend on Ralph Mattlin. His ideas, his feel for the public, you know what I mean."

"I do, Mr. Leff," Yustin said. "Oh, indeed I do. I've known Ralph Mattlin since he got out of Yale."

Having stuffed his crooked toes full of cotton, Dr. Yustin now put his ugly feet out in front of him on the coffee table.

"If Mattlin conks out on us," I said, "it could be the end of the Twentieth Century Classics Series before it even gets off the ground. I know Mr. Nachman meant a lot to Ralph Mattlin, so I know the news of his death must have hit him pretty hard. Miss Eitner says he looked like a ghost when he put down the phone. The next few hours, the next couple of days, they could

196

be very important. Miss Eitner agrees with me. She was the one suggested I make the call and come to see you."

"About what?" Dr. Yustin said.

"How to help Ralph Mattlin," I said.

Dr. Yustin grinned and wriggled his toes. One of the cotton wads fell out. He picked it up, squeezed it into what he obviously felt was a better shape, and shoved it back into place.

"Mr. Leff," he said. "Would you care to take another try at that?"

"At what?" I said.

"Your explanation for why you're here," Dr. Yustin said.

"I've just told you," I said.

"Now let me tell *you*," he said. "Mr. Nachman's suicide is obviously connected with the discovery made last week that during the past three years he stole over fifty thousand dollars from the firm of Mattlin & Merritt, Inc. When Ralph Mattlin recovers from the shock of the old man's death, tomorrow, next week, a month from now, no matter when, he's going to remember who it was that discovered what Mr. Nachman had done. You, Mr. Leff. And when he does remember, Ralph Mattlin is not going to like you, Mr. Leff. When an employer doesn't like an employee he usually does the usual thing. He throws him out on his ass. I don't think you want to be thrown out on your ass, Mr. Leff. So you've come up here to ask me how you can save your job. Am I right, Mr. Leff?"

Not quite, gorgeous.

"Suppose you are," I said. "Mattlin is a patient of yours. He sees you three times a week. Sometimes more. He's part of your income flow. I'm sure you want your income to continue flowing. Flowing in, I mean. The best way for it to do that is for your patients to be solvent. If Ralph Mattlin falls apart and the Twentieth Century Classics Series doesn't get off the ground, I may lose my job, sure. But you could also lose three or more nice fat fees every week. You'd have to find some other slob to lie down on your couch and pay for the cotton you stuff between your toes. Besides, the reason for Ralph Mattlin falling apart may get around. I'd certainly do my best to see that it did, and I could get others to help in the good work. When me and my friends get through with spreading the word, you might have trouble finding a few patients."

"Are you threatening me, Mr. Leff?"

No, I'm hand-lettering a valentine for you, you great big fat schmuck.

"Let's not use unpleasant words," I said. "Let's look at it this way, Dr. Yustin. We're in this together. Ralph Mattlin pays my salary, but he also pays a very nice piece of yours. I came up here for some advice. Instead of trying to show me what a smart ass you are, Dr. Yustin, I recommend that you make a stab at being really smart. I'd stop worrying about athlete's foot for a while, Dr. Yustin, and give me a little of what I came up here to get. Advice."

The hunchback did a little more laughing. But this time the glug-glugging was not so gluggy.

"I like you, Mr. Leff," he said. "You are a real smart little son of a bitch. It is the smart little sons of bitches who run the world. I like to watch them doing it. When they fall apart, which they always do, I like even better to soak them fifty bucks an hour to explain what's wrong is not that they're jealous of Harry Luce, but what's wrong is that deep down underneath, they love their maiden aunt, Iphigenia, and when Iphigenia is not around, they are terrified of pitted prunes. Okay, then. Since you are obviously headed for my couch one of these days, here's what I think you should do now. Are you ready for the word, Mr. Leff?"

"You just take off," I said. "I'll manage somehow to keep up with you."

"Here's the word," Dr. Yustin said. "Do nothing."

"Do what?" I said.

"Nothing," he said. "*N-o-t-h-i-n-g*. Absolutely nothing. Just sit on your rump and think about how smart you obviously think you are."

"I'm as smart as you are, Doc," I said. "So you just put it into words of one syllable, if you don't mind."

"Don't look like that, Mr. Leff," he said. "Yours is not the kind of face that improves in appearance when it registers astonishment. Go back to your normal sneer, Mr. Leff. When I say do nothing, I mean do nothing. *Rien,* as we used to say in the Bronx. *Gar nichts* as we say today at the Racquet Club. The situation is ludicrously simple, Mr. Leff. Ralph Mattlin has been involved emotionally with Mr. Nachman for many years. It's an old family thing that happens on all social and financial levels. To Hapsburgs as well as Mattlinbergs. We needn't go into it now. Especially since you are as smart as I am, Mr. Leff. You can take my word for it, however, that Ralph Mattlin really never liked the creature. Mr. Nachman was foisted on him. When I say foisted, I don't mean like in seconded, Mr. Leff. I mean Nachman was to Mattlin what a barnacle is to a ship. The old man grew on him because the old man had been in Mattlin's father's business. Mattlin had nothing to do with it. All he had to do was accept it and then start getting nervous about it. Therefore, as soon as he gets over the initial shock of Mr. Nachman's death, when Mattlin comes awake and realizes the old man is dead, gone forever, out of his life, he will feel a sense of relief. That's why I advise that you relax and let nature take its course. Once Mr. Nachman is buried, Ralph Mattlin will return to the Twentieth Century Classics Series with renewed vigor, lead in his pencil, ideas in his head, and ink in his fountain pen. Do you follow me, Mr. Leff?"

"Yes," I said.

"Then why are you perspiring," Yustin said.

"It's hot in here," I said.

"Not for me," Dr. Yustin said. "The way you are perspiring, so heavily, Mr. Leff, do you know what that means?"

"You should open a window," I said.

"Not at all," he said. "It shows, Mr. Leff, that you are trying to return to your mother's womb."

I stood up. "Dr. Yustin," I said, "as I recall my mother's womb, it was a drafty place compared to this Turkish bath."

18

" I Don't Expect You to Look Like Pola Negri, But There's No Reason Why You Should Look Like Louise Fazenda"

When I groped my way to North Northeast in the Walpole Bar, Maud Eitner was waiting. "I've signaled Gregory to bring you a double," she said. "Most people need something strong after their first meeting with Bernie Yustin fresh from the bath."

"You mean he really does it all the time?" I said. "That stuff with the cotton and his toes?"

"Always," Maud said. "It's his way of taking control. By revolting you. Did he offer you a drink?"

"No, but I didn't expect one," I said. "I didn't get the feeling that he was crazy to have me there."

"Then you missed the best part of it," Maud said. "It's quite charming if you've been invited for a drink and there's a platter of cheese and crackers and olives on the coffee table. Bernie keeps pushing the platter toward you with his bare feet. How did you like the Hoffritz act?"

"What's that?" I said.

"If you have to ask," Maud said, "then you didn't see it. Bernie thinks he can improve on anything, especially if God had a hand in producing it in the first place. This includes his own appearance, and I'm sure you'll agree he can use some improving. So he keeps buying all these gadgets made of Swedish steel that Hoffritz sells to commuters in Grand Central. Tweezers. Scissors. Blackhead removers. You've seen the things. Bernie owns all of them. It's quite a sight after he's finished stuffing cotton between his toes to watch Bernie using a gadget that looks like the silver bullet Eugene O'Neill gave the Emperor Jones, to clip the excess hairs out of his nostrils as he urges you to pour yourself another drink. Here's yours."

"Miss Eitner?" Gregory said.

"No," Maud said, "I think I'll coast along with this one for a while." The waiter went away. "If you left before the Hoffritz act," Maud said, "it means Bernie gave you the advice you went up to get and you left in a hurry so you could pass it on to me."

"That's pretty much right," I said. "Dr. Yustin's habits make sitting with him pretty rough, but he also makes a lot of sense."

"Stupid Bernie is not," Maud Eitner said. "How did he take the news that Mr. Nachman had done the Dutch?"

"He was so badly upset," I said, "he missed the space between the two middle toes on his left foot."

Even in the Walpole gloom I could see the funny little look Maud gave me. "Are you sure?" she said.

I figured it was going to work. She could have said, "Are you lying?"

"I don't know how I could be wrong about it," I said. "He looked like I'd punched him. He stood up and started pacing back and forth across the room in his bare feet. I don't know how long it was. A few seconds, maybe. But he looked, well, I had a feeling he was in shock. Really belted. You know? He looked scared. I had the feeling old Dr. Bernard Yustin felt he was responsible for it. Or maybe only he might be accused of being responsible. You told me yourself he's considered a reckless son of a bitch. The way he practices what's supposed to be medicine. Anyway, whatever it was, I could see he'd been badly hit."

Maud scowled down into her half-empty glass. "That's funny," she said.

"Why?" I said.

201

"It doesn't sound like Bernie," she said.

Why should it? Since the sounds were being made by Teddy?

"I could try to give you an imitation of the accent," I said. "Except I'm not very good at glug-glugging."

"Be grateful for it," Maud said. "First time out, Bernie is as good as anything they used to have at the Hippodrome. Now you come back and tell me he was upset. And it's made me feel the same way."

"Why?" I said.

"Because Bernie Yustin is not the type that gets upset," Maud said. "He's a cold fish. Cold and savage. To him people are just a series of ant hills. He enjoys watching them, especially when they're in trouble. Best of all when he can get them to pay for entertaining him. The way I had it thought out, he'd think Mr. Nachman killing himself was the best thing that could happen to Ralph Mattlin. It ends the whole emotional involvement mess with his father and family who saddled him with the old man. Yes, it's true, Mattlin's upset when he gets the news. But when he calms down he'll realize it's been a break for him. That's the way I had it thought out, and that's the way I thought Bernie Yustin would think it out."

But it wasn't the way Ted Leff wanted it thought out. "Just the opposite," I said. "He thinks Mattlin might do the same."

Maud Eitner turned to give me a look. "You're joking," she said.

I hung up my solemn look. It's not hard to do in that light. "I wish I were," I said. "Yustin thinks we ought to move fast, and by we he meant you."

"Me?" Maud said.

The brightest of them flicker a little when the ideas coming along are too new.

"You," I said. "Yustin thinks you ought to go out to Lakewood right now. Tonight. Without calling in advance. Just show up at the hotel where Mr. Nachman was staying and where Mattlin will be standing around or falling apart, probably both."

"What good will that do?" Maud said.

"Look," I said. "You want this boy, don't you?"

She hesitated. I didn't think she hesitated because she wasn't sure of the answer. I had the feeling she hesitated because she didn't think it was proper to make the answer. I don't know why, but it made me like her better.

"Yes," she said finally.

And that, the direct way she said it, made me like her even better. I didn't know why it should, but I knew I was certainly involved with a curious broad.

"Well," I said, "here's your chance to get him. There are things to do. Funeral arrangements. Police interviews. Newspaper reporters. God knows what else. All his life Ralph Mattlin has had women doing things for him. Don't let the process stop. You show up and continue doing them. If he doesn't know by now that you're as efficient as an IBM machine he doesn't know anything. Another demonstration at this moment in his life when for the first time he must be feeling alone and abandoned and scared, and he'll turn to you like iron filings going for a magnet. Do I have to spell it out any more clearly?"

Maud hesitated, then nodded. "I'm afraid so," she said.

"What's the part that bothers you?" I said.

"You," she said.

"Me?"

I've said wittier things in my life, but I sensed this was no time for going after Oscar Wilde's crown.

"Yes, you," Maud said. "Up to now I've more or less grasped what you're doing. Most of it, anyway. You're hung up. You've stumbled into a bakery. You have no money, but you've got brains. So you show the baker how to make a bigger loaf of bread cheaper, sell it for less, and thus make a larger profit. The baker is delighted, so he feeds you and gives you a job so you'll be near him when you come up with other good ideas about rolls and hot cross buns. All that makes sense. This new development—" She paused.

"What new development?" I said.

"Wanting to marry me off to Ralph Mattlin," she said.

"Didn't you just say that's what you want?" I said.

"Yes, but that's not the point," she said. "The point is why

203

should you want it? Putting it another way, up to now you've been a smart boy, and I haven't minded, in fact I've enjoyed helping you because smart boys are more fun than dumb ones. But now suddenly you sound more than smart. You sound like a, well, try not to feel too hurt by the word, but all of a sudden now you sound like a crook."

It was my turn to pause for station identification. I didn't pause long. I sensed that if I didn't convince her she wouldn't go to Lakewood, and if she didn't go to Lakewood, then old Ted Leff might just as well head back to Seventh Avenue.

"It's simple," I said. "I'm surprised a smart girl like you doesn't see it without me having to point it out. I don't want to just sit around the bakery, drawing a salary and thinking up ideas for hot cross buns that will make the baker rich. I want to own a part of the bakery. My chances of getting there are better if the baker has a wife who happens to be my friend."

Maud Eitner took down the bottom half of her drink in a single swallow. "When's the next train for Lakewood?" she said.

"No trains," I said. "Can you drive a car?"

"I can drive anything on four wheels except a Baldwin loco-motive," she said. "And that has eight."

"Good," I said. "Because I've rented one for you. After you bury Mr. Nachman, I want you and Ralph Mattlin sitting cozily side by side on a front seat on the long drive back to New York."

"You know," Maud said, "if you don't make it in the publishing business I think you've got a great future writing an advice-to-the-lovelorn column. Lead me to that rented car."

"First we're going to stop off and see a friend of mine," I said.

"Which one?"

"Gertrude Lebenbaum."

"The cup filler?" Maud said.

"She knows how to do other things too," I said. "She's sending Alan Ellentuch out for a Sterno refill while she gives you some of her expert attention. I want her to fix your hair a little different, and I think she can show you a few tricks with powder and lipstick that ought to help when you get to Lake-wood."

"Now, listen, Mr. Leff," Maud said.

"Not until you come back as Mrs. Ralph Mattlin," I said. "To do that, I don't expect you to look like Pola Negri, but there's no reason why you should look like Louise Fazenda."

19

" I Have a Feeling When I Open the Door My Mother Will Say Ralph Mattlin Just Called"

Sunday night, when I turned the corner into my block, the rented Chevy was parked in front of my building and Maud Eitner was sitting in it.

"These surprises are bad for a man's heart," I said. "I didn't expect you back until tomorrow morning."

"Neither did I," Maud said. "But it turns out that in Lakewood they bury people on Sundays, and if you slip them a few dollars extra they even do it early in the morning."

I could tell from the hop, skip and jump in her voice that she had come out ahead. "Come on upstairs and watch me shave and change my shirt," I said. "While you give me the round by round."

"Not this lass," Maud said.

"I've been holding hands with Gertrude Lebenbaum all week-end," I said. "You're perfectly safe."

"Not a chance," Maud Eitner said. "In this town you never know who sees you going in and out of buildings."

"I take it from that remark that you feel you're so close to home you don't want to risk blowing the ball game?"

She laughed. It was the kind of laugh that tells you more than

206

words. This one told me my new friend was about to become
the baker's wife. It gave me a funny feeling. When I realized the
feeling was jealousy, I also realized I was lucky she was now out
of the way. This was not the kind of girl I was accustomed to
being jealous about.

"It wasn't much of a game," Maud said. "Ralph Mattlin is
not exactly a lazy man but he hates detail, and as you pointed
out, all his life he's had things done for him. So when I showed
up at the hotel late Friday night he was more pleased than
surprised. He'd had the police and the local press on his neck
for a couple of hours, and the funeral arrangements were coming up next. When I said I'd come to help he just moved over
gratefully. Because of the paper work with the police the under-
taker couldn't actually do his stuff until today, so on Saturday
when Ralph and I met in the hotel dining room for breakfast I
said as long as I had the car and it was such a nice day why
didn't we drive over to Atlantic City for lunch and get some nice
fresh sea air."

I laughed. "I think you could have done it without Gertrude's
hairdo and padded uplift," I said. "After all, you carried to
Lakewood what you've always carried around New York.
Brains."

Maud Eitner did that thing I've seen other women do when
they feel they're one up on you. It takes three moves. She
cocked her head to one side. She gave me a slanted look. And
she touched the back of her head as though she was tapping an
invisible nail into her skull.

"Now that Mr. Nachman was out of the way, yes," she said.
"Or maybe I should say not yet but maybe. With him around,
nobody had a chance. Ralph Mattlin's mind was so loaded with
guilt about the problem his parents had dumped on him that he
had no time to think about marriage. Now I think he has time,
and that's where you come in."

I was leaning on the car door. My hand was on the rolled-
down window. If there was any way to measure the extent to
which my hand moved, it would have had to be done with a
slide rule. Yet Maud Eitner saw it. She was looking up, talking

to me through the open car window, but she saw my hand tighten under her nose. "Don't be nervous," she said.

"I'm not nervous," I said.

"Oh yes, you are," Maud Eitner said. "I wormed out of you on Friday night that you weren't sending me to Lakewood because you only go around masquerading as a bookkeeper, whereas actually you're Irving Cupid the Grand Concourse matchmaker."

If this broad had looks I could have gone for her myself. There are times when I don't know what I like better. Big brains or high casabas.

"Listen," I said. "A matchmaker is entitled to a fee."

"You got yours," Maud said. "That's what I meant by this is where you come in. Toward the end of the day yesterday Mattlin and I were driving back to Lakewood, he was feeling pleasant and relaxed, and he suddenly said if Ted Leff hadn't discovered what Mr. Nachman had been doing with the books he'd be alive today. I didn't waste time. I knew that was the place to attack. Not only for you, but also for me. I told Mattlin he was looking at it the wrong way. If it wasn't Ted Leff who discovered it, I said, Applebaum's accountant would have discovered it, and that would have been much worse. The way to look at it, I said, was if it wasn't for Ted Leff, Mr. Mattlin, you'd still be trapped in an association that I know has been a problem to you for years. Thanks to Ted Leff, I said, you're free, Mr. Mattlin. That's what you can thank Ted Leff for."

I reached into the car. I gave her cheek the kind of pinch Rabbi Goldfarb used to give me when I translated a *Sidrah* correctly. There was a little hollow in her cheek. It pulsed up and down.

"I'll bet I can tell what happened next," I said.

"No, you can't," Maud Eitner said. "Because I'm not Gertrude Lebenbaum, and Ralph Mattlin is not you. He may look like a great big squash-playing harp from the Yale Club, but deep down he's a Nice Jewish Boy, and Nice Jewish Boys don't marry the girls they've been sleeping with. When we got back to Lakewood, Mattlin had that look. But I saw to it he carried it up to his room, and I spent the night in my own room. This morning, after the funeral, on the drive back to New York, he said let's stop somewhere for dinner. I said I couldn't because I'd promised my mother I'd be home before it got dark. So I took him right down to his house, where I got a nice, antiseptic kiss while I was still in the car, and I drove uptown to tell you the good news. When your bell didn't answer I thought I'd wait around awhile. After all, when Gertrude was doing my hair Friday night I looked over her little nest pretty carefully. There was no sign of a razor in the medicine cabinet or a pair of men's pajamas in the closet or a clean shirt in the dresser, so I assumed you'd have to come out into the open sooner or later for supplies."

"If you don't want to risk what sounds like your official engagement to Mr. Ralph Mattlin by being seen entering my apartment house," I said, "how about waiting down here while I clean up, and then we can both go back to Gertrude Lebenbaum's and eat one of Alan Ellentuch's steaks? Gertrude liked you."

"I liked her too," Maud Eitner said. "But I'm afraid you'll have to count me out." She tapped the starter. "I'm going home," she said. "I have a feeling when I open the door my mother will say Ralph Mattlin just called. He wants you to call him back. See you at the office in the morning."

The next morning, when I walked into the office, I was surprised to see Maud Eitner sitting behind the billing-machine fort. She was leaning forward, hunched around the mouthpiece of the telephone. What stopped me dead was the sound of her voice. The hop, skip and jump had gone over the hill.

"How soon can we have her?" Maud was saying into the phone. "Is that the best you can do? No, no, the salary is fine, but we'd like to have her right away. All right, yes. As quickly as possible, then. Thank you."

She hung up.

"What are you doing?" I said.

"Hiring a new billing clerk and receptionist," Maud Eitner said.

"What's the matter with Benita?" I said.

"She just got married."

"Now?" I said. "You told me she's getting married on Decoration Day?"

"That's what she told me too." The door opened behind me. Maud Eitner leaned out of the fort. "May I help you?" she said.

I turned. What had come in was one of those kids you see all day long coming down the steps of the main branch of the public library on Forty-second Street. They're always carrying an armful of books. And all the clothes they're wearing can be picked up for the price of a pair of Kolmer-Marcus slacks. And they're always heading for some waiting broad reading T. S. Eliot as she leans against one of the lions. This kid looked worried.

"Yes, please," he said. "I'm looking for Miss Adler? Benita Adler?"

"So are we," Maud Eitner said.

"I don't understand," the kid said. "I always pick her up at her place in the morning and walk her to work. But this morning she wasn't there."

"Who are you?" I said.

"Miss Adler is my fiancée," the kid said.

It struck me as a funny way to put it. On East Fourth Street kids had girls. Only people in the Sunday supplements had fiancées.

"Not any more," Maud Eitner said. "Your fiancée eloped with Mr. Ralph Mattlin late last night." Maud swung the hair from her forehead. All of Gertrude Lebenbaum's work had been wasted. Maud Eitner looked the way she'd looked when I first met her: like hell. "Mr. Mattlin called me at home at seven o'clock this morning from Elkton, Maryland," she said. "Mr. Mattlin and your fiancée had just been married a few minutes before he made the call."

20

" I Won't Help You, But I'm Perfectly Willing to Join You"

After all these years I can still remember the sound of Maud Eitner's voice as she got rid of the kid who had been engaged to Benita Adler.

The boy went out, dragging his ass and his armful of books. Maud and I were alone in the Mattlin & Merritt reception room. I was staring at that framed sentence on the wall: THE REWARD OF THE GENERAL IS NOT A BIGGER TENT, BUT COMMAND. I pretended to be studying the words, as though I were trying to think my way through a problem, but actually I was watching Maud. I didn't know which way she was going to jump. Maybe she didn't know herself. It was hard to tell from the way she was fooling with the keys of the billing machine. Then she laughed. That's what I remember. The sound of that laugh.

"What's funny?" I said.

"Oliver Wendell Holmes," Maud said. "Junior."

She laughed again. I wondered why. It wasn't the sort of noise anybody would want to hear twice. Not even the person making it. "Or maybe Oliver knew a different kind of general," Maud said.

"Different from what?" I said.

"You and me," Maud said. "We have just been outmaneuvered by a little butterball with stars in her eyes and the joy of life tinkling in her voice who knows more about tactics than Von Clausewitz."

"If you're saying Benita Adler planned this thing a long time ago," I said, "I think you're letting the way you feel get in the way of your thinking. Putting the time sequence together, Benita Adler must have left the office without knowing anything about what happened to Mr. Nachman. Because I left at ten minutes to six to go see Bernie Yustin, and by that time nobody was sitting behind that billing machine. I remember it clearly. On my way out the reception room was empty. Benita was gone for the day."

"Yes," Maud said. "But where?"

"How do I know?" I said. "Where most people go when they leave the places where they work. Home, I suppose."

"No," Maud said. She shook her head slowly and said it again. "No," she said. "I don't think so." She paused and looked up for a few moments at the words of O. W. Holmes, Jr. "Remember a week ago Friday? The day you were hired? When you and I had our first drink in the Walpole Bar?"

"And you gave me the key to the office," I said. "Naturally I remember."

"I gave you something else," Maud said. "I gave you a piece of information, but I didn't know I was giving it to you because I didn't know myself at the time that it was information. Can you make a guess?"

I pressed the button on the memory box. The proper slide dropped into the slot. I examined all the details of my first visit to the Walpole Bar. I went from my first impression of the hotel's architecture. Through my stumbling over all those little old ladies in the darkness. To my conversation with Maud over drinks at North Northeast. I was hunting for anything that touched on Benita Adler. I found it.

"South Southwest," I said to Maud. "You were ordering a second drink for us and you told that waiter Gregory, you said

212

you just saw Miss Adler come in and she was heading for South Southwest, the darkest part of the bar. You said you wouldn't go in there yourself without a flashlight or a guide, so would he see that Miss Adler didn't trip in the dark, on account of she was getting married on Decoration Day and it wouldn't look good if she had to be carried to the altar with a broken neck."

Maud nodded grimly. "As my mother used to say," she said, "and unfortunately still does, you are smart like seven colleges. So you surely will be able to answer my next question. That kid who just walked out of here. That dazed little cluck with an armful of schoolbooks and a torn sweater. If he makes a date to meet his girl, where will it be?"

"One of the lions in front of the public library," I said.

"Eight colleges," Maud said. "Maybe even nine. Absolutely correct. Young Lochinvar on his way out of Economics Two at the Twenty-third Street Branch of City College does not make dates to meet his lady love in a residential hotel for ancient widows where martinis go for sixty-five cents a piece. So obviously sunny, fun-loving, life-is-a-bowl-of-cherries Benita was on her way to meet someone else."

"You're falling off the sled again," I said. "She couldn't have been meeting Mattlin in the Walpole Bar a week ago Friday."

"Why not?" Maud said.

"Because at that very moment Mattlin was heading for Thirty-eighth Street," I said. "To help Mr. Nachman pack so he could take the old man to the train for Lakewood."

"How do you know that?" Maud said.

"You told me," I said.

"Which only proves you shouldn't believe everything you hear no matter how brilliant your informant," Maud said. "I told you that because that's what Ralph Mattlin told me. Now I see something I never saw before. I see that Friday night a week ago was not the first time I'd seen Benita Adler heading for South Southwest. I'd seen her doing it many times. In fact, now that I think of it, I saw her doing it every time I've stopped in at the Walpole after work for a drink with somebody. I always assumed she was meeting the boy she was engaged to, and so they liked to sit in the darkest part of the saloon. My assumption, Ted dear, was wrong. She's been seeing Mattlin regularly, not only in the Walpole Bar, and they've been keeping it a secret. This last Saturday and Sunday, when I was out there in Lakewood, handling the details of burying Mr. Nachman, he was probably on the phone, talking to darling little Benita."

"Then how come Saturday night out in Lakewood he asked you to spend the night with him?"

Maud Eitner gave me a cool look. "Under the circumstances," she said, "wouldn't you?"

As Byram Noonan would have put it: *Oy!*

"I don't see the connection," I said.

"What you mean is no," Maud Eitner said, and she shrugged. "Maybe someday, when you've been shipwrecked on a desert island long enough, you'll say yes. But let's leave you out of it. You don't know about desert islands. You seem to have an inexhaustible supply of Gertrude Lebenbaums lying around, waiting for you to drop in and light up their cans of Sterno. I don't think Ralph Mattlin had. For him, there was only Benita Adler."

"Nope, I'm sorry," I said. "Benita is an N.J.G. I can smell them all the way from over the hill, and when I say hill I mean everything from Everest to Popocatepetl. Nice Jewish Girls do not put out until the rabbi says it's kosher."

"You're proving my point," Maud said. "He wanted to get it from Benita darling, but she was too smart to accommodate. What she wanted, I see now, was what she got this morning. The word 'Mrs.' Saturday night, in Lakewood, I also see now Ralph Mattlin wanted it from anybody."

There are times when even *Oy!* doesn't help.

"You're sore," I said. "So you're saying things you don't mean."

I got a couple of bars of that so-called laugh. If Billy the Kid had been at the receiving end, he would have gone over the border.

"You're the one who's saying things you don't understand,"

Maud said. "I went to school with a lot of girls who made it to the Jewish altar. So I know that when they're pregnant the husbands who did it, no matter how they loved their N.J.G.'s that they'd done it to, when they couldn't do it for a while because of for obvious reasons, these gentlemen songsters off on a spree would do it to anybody, and did. This is Monday morning. I'm thinking better than I was thinking Saturday night. Why not? What else have I got to do? That little wide-eyed bitch has got him. Anyway, funerals are like pregnancies. They don't stop a man's you-know-what. In fact, I think it arouses them. Saturday night I think Ralph Mattlin would have slept with anybody available, and I was available."

"How about Sunday night?" I said. "When you got back to his house? And he wanted you to have dinner with him?"

"As long as I'm seeing straight at last," Maud said, "I might as well see that one too. He was getting rid of me. It was I who was getting a brotherly kiss. The stewing was going to be with darling little Benita."

The phone on the reception desk rang. Maud picked it up. "Mattlin & Merritt, good morning," she said. "No, Mr. Mattlin is not in, I'm sorry. No, I can't give you his secretary because he doesn't have a secretary. Don't scream, whoever you are. Mr. Mattlin had a secretary, but she just quit." She slammed down the phone and said, "That's that."

If it was, your correspondent had pitched a no-hitter and wasn't even going to be suggested as a future possibility for Cooperstown.

"No, it isn't," I said. "You've lost a battle. This doesn't mean you're going to lose the war. The only way you can do that is by quitting."

Maud Eitner stood up and she came through the small mahogany swing gate of the billing machine fort. "You know," she said, "you ought to write greeting cards. You sound like this Walter B. Pitkin. Never open second-class mail. Rubbers will keep your feet dry, but they will also keep you out of paternity suits. I don't like people who talk in capital letters or quotation marks. That goes for O. W. Holmes, Jr., and his thoughtful

215

remarks about generals, and it goes for tough little nuts from down on East Fourth Street who are trying to stake out a claim uptown with pie-in-the-sky promises."

It was like sticking your finger in your mouth and then holding it up to see which way the wind was blowing. She had just showed me the way to jump. "I didn't make any promises," I said.

"You said I had a better chance than I had before you showed up," she said.

"You still have," I said.

Maud Eitner said, "That's what they told Marie Antoinette when she stepped into the tumbril."

I caught her arm as she started to push through the reception room door, and I pulled her around. "Listen," I said.

"Not to you," she said.

"You'd better," I said. "Nobody else is talking in your direction." Her arm stopped fighting my hand. "I never said I could deliver Ralph Mattlin," I said. "So I'll say it now."

"How?" Maud said.

"I got rid of Mr. Nachman, didn't I?"

She shook her arm free. "Mr. Leff," Maud Eitner said, "you are as full of waste material as a robin in the springtime. Murder, Inc., was put out of business by Tom Dewey."

"I didn't say I killed Mr. Nachman," I said. "But I did turn up the evidence that gave him the idea to do it. I'm not talking about killing Benita Adler."

"Benita Mattlin, if you please," Maud said.

"What I'm talking about is this," I said. "If she's as good a schemer as you say, if behind that peaches-and-cream look and that standing-on-tiptoe-to-life heavy breathing, if back of all that there's a tough operator, she's met her match."

"You, I suppose?" Maud said.

"Who else?" I said. "She's Benita Mattlin as of now, sure. That doesn't mean she'll be Benita Mattlin as of next month or next year."

"What are you doing to do?" Maud said. "Sell her on a divorce?"

216

"No," I said. "Arrange it."

The lines in her face did that trick of rearranging themselves. "You little son of a bitch," Maud Eitner said. "You certainly are something new in my experience."

She wasn't the first one who had made that discovery.

"Why not take advantage of it?" I said. "You want Ralph Mattlin. What difference does it make if you get him after the death of his father's old partner or a little later, after a divorce from his ex-wife?"

"Divorces come high," Maud said. "Especially when you're trying to get them from shrewd little cookies like Benita Adler. She'll squeeze him dry, and I don't think Ralph Mattlin has much to be squeezed out of."

"He will have," I said. "Very soon. I think this Twentieth Century Classics Series is going to go. One thing I can smell is money, and this thing has the smell. Everybody connected with this series is in a position to make himself a nice fat bundle."

"Including you?" Maud said.

I looked her right in the eye. "Not under the present setup," I said.

Her head tipped to one side. "What you're after is a new setup?" she said.

"You said it yourself that night in the Walpole," I said. "You said I'm not a guy who intends to sit hunched over a set of ledgers all his life. I said it last Friday night. I said I'm not going to sit around in the bakery shop at a salary and think up profitable ideas for the baker about hot cross buns. I've just handed these boys the equivalent of like in the automobile business you've handed a couple of not very successful boobs a little invention called the clutch. I'm not going to stand around and watch them get curvature of the spine from carrying the money to the bank while I collect eighty-five a week every Friday."

"How are you going to change that setup?" Maud said.

"I'll show you after you agree to help me," I said. "I can't do it alone and I sure as hell can't do it if you quit your job and walk out of here."

217

She didn't waste much time thinking it over. But during that little time I could see the hollow in her cheek pulsing. It was like seeing a butterfly in the park fluttering on the petal of a flower. I wanted to reach out and touch it.

"I won't help you," Maud said. "But I'm perfectly willing to join you."

"What's the difference?" I said.

She tipped her head the other way. "I want a cut," she said.

I was surprised it hadn't occurred to me before that she'd ask for it. I could see where to a smart dame it would occur at once. It certainly would have occurred to me.

"You're getting Ralph Mattlin," I said. "You'll get your cut as his wife."

"I may never get to be his wife," Maud said. "I've already missed the boat once. I want my consolation prize in the form of cash before I miss it again."

"All right," I said. "It's a deal."

21

" What We're Going to Need From Now On Is Two Ping-Pong Tables"

As soon as Mattlin came home from the honeymoon, it became clear that Maud and I had made a good deal. Between Ralph Mattlin and the Twentieth Century Classics Series, it was like when the first slice of ham finally met the first fried egg. They'd been waiting for each other.

It was a pleasure to watch him in action. He never raised his voice. He never added a wrinkle to his Savile Row suit. He never mussed his mink-colored hair. He never stopped smoking two cigarettes at a time. And he never stopped churning out the ideas that kept gold-plating the five basic points that fell into place during that first week after he put his hand on my shoulder and said, "Ted, here, has come up with something big."

The funny part about it was that I don't think anybody had any doubts. The feeling that we were cooking something big went right down the line. Even to the shipping clerks in the West Thirty-seventh Street loft who were given a demonstration by Mattlin, at a meeting he asked me to attend with him, on how he wanted the books slipped into the specially designed cartons. That was the day when two new things about Mattlin came clear to me: one, no detail was too small for him either to overlook or handle personally; and two, he liked me. He asked me to go to every meeting with him, in the office or out, and he started inviting me to have lunch with him. This was fine. He was using me to bounce ideas off of. Bounce, bounce, I figured. When I started swinging, being in his confidence would make it easier to land the haymakers.

During those first months there was only one tense period: the few days after the first full-page ad appeared on the back of the *New York Times* under Mattlin's caption: YOU NEVER HEARD OF US, BUT WE WANT THREE MINUTES OF YOUR TIME.

The ad ran on a Monday. Nothing much happened on Tuesday. Wednesday was a little better. Then on Thursday we had our trouble with the Ping-Pong table.

"We bought the thing soon after the firm got going," Maud Eitner told me. "Because Bernie Yustin told Ralph Mattlin it might help with his emotional problems if he could get his blood circulating a little faster, and Mattlin hated to go to a gym for his exercise. For a while he used to play a couple of games out here every afternoon with me or Bud Knisel or anybody else who was around, but it didn't last long, and pretty soon we started using it to sort out the mail in the morning."

That's what we continued to use it for during those first months when we were getting the Twentieth Century Classics Series off the ground. The Mattlin & Merritt mail had always come in the form of three or four neat little bundles delivered by a mailman with a shoulder bag who worked his way through the building from floor to floor. On the Thursday following that first Monday ad in the *Times,* a mailman none of us had ever seen before came into the reception room and asked for someone in charge. The new receptionist rang me. I came out to see what it was all about.

"We gunna need some help," the mailman said.

"With what?" I said.

"You come see," he said.

I went down to the street with him. The Mattlin & Merritt mail for that day had arrived by truck.

"I'll give you a hand with the first bag," I said, trying to sound calm. My blood was suddenly jumping. I knew what was in those bags. "Then I'll send down a couple of boys," I said.

When the mailman and I carried the sack through the front door, across the reception room, and out to the Ping-Pong table, Maud Eitner was coming down the hall from Bud Knisel's office. She stopped and stared. I gave her a big fat grin. "We gunna need some help," I said.

"What?" she said.

"I'm using the accent of the United States Post Office Department," I said. "We gunna need some help. Ask Bud to send a couple of his kids down to the truck in front of the building."

Maud went back into Bud's office. I went up front to Mattlin's office. He had not come in yet. I pushed through Maud's office to Gene Merritt's office. He had already made a pretty good score in his morning attack on the *New York Times*. He stopped slicing and looked up at me across the golden scissors.

"Come on," I said. "I want to show you something."

"Let me just finish this clipping," he said. "Cordell Hull said at his press conference in Washington yesterday that the swiftest traveler is he that goes afoot. You know whom he was quoting?"

The Leather Institute of America, obviously.

"No," I said. "But come on. I want to show you something."

"In a moment," Merritt said. He took a swipe at the crooked glasses on his nose and stabbed the scissors at the *Times*. "Henry David Thoreau, that's whom he was quoting," Merritt said. "We need Thoreau in this series, Ted."

"We'll get him," I said. "Right now I want to show you something."

He came out from behind the desk. I took his arm and led him out to the hall. Two of Bud Knisel's boys were just setting another big mail sack on the Ping-Pong table. Maud Eitner was coming back up the hall. She let out a yelp of warning. But she was too late. The legs of the Ping-Pong table buckled. The mail sacks slid to the floor. I heard the door snap shut behind me. I turned. Ralph Mattlin had just arrived.

He pushed past us to the collapsed table. He dropped to his knees and pulled apart the knot in the rope of the nearest mail sack. He shoved the top open, grabbed a handful of envelopes and thumbed open a flap. Maud and Merritt and I moved closer. Mattlin tore open another envelope. I grabbed an envelope. Maud did the same. Even Merritt caught on. We were tearing envelopes open in a kind of nutty way, nobody saying a word, dragging out the coupons that had been clipped from the ad in the *Times,* when Bud Knisel's boys arrived with another sack. Mattlin looked up. "Is that it?" he said.

"No sir," one of the boys said. "Two more sacks down in the truck."

Suddenly Mattlin started to laugh. He stood up. We all stood up. Mattlin dusted his knees. He looked down at his pants as he did it. As though he didn't exactly understand what he was doing. Then he turned to the boys. "See that the other two sacks come up," Mattlin said. "Then start opening and sorting."

"Yes sir."

They went out to the reception room. Mattlin went up the hall to his office. Maud and Merritt and I followed. We did it single file. Like the Indians trailing Art Acord in *The Oregon Trail.* We couldn't have come into Mattlin's office more than four or five seconds behind him, but he already had one cigarette going and had started to fish for a second. He wasn't laughing any more. But there was a smile on his face. A solid sort of smile. "Well, team," he said. "Do you know what we've just done?"

"If those bags are all full of returned coupons asking us to send the first ten titles we ran in the ad," Maud Eitner said, "I'd say we've pulled it off."

"They can't be full of Christmas cards," Mattlin said. "Those bags are full of returned coupons, and the chances are they'll keep coming for quite a while. The *Times* is read all over the country, and it takes time for mail to get here. I've done some research on mail-order response. I've learned something about how to judge it from bulk. Just from counting those bags out there, it looks to me like we've just made ourselves a little piece of history."

"In what way?" Gene Merritt said.

"We've probably racked up the largest response to any single coupon ad in the entire history of the publishing business," Ralph Mattlin said.

It looked as though the time had come for me to start swinging. "Let's go out and start counting," I said.

"Me too," Maud Eitner said. She moved with me to the door. "Let's get our hands on this stuff and see how much history we've made."

"Maud," Mattlin said. She stopped and turned. He said, "Call Macy's first. What we're going to need from now on is two Ping-Pong tables."

22

" She Now Says Matoor When She Means Mature"

By the time we bought a third Ping-Pong table, the Twentieth Century Classics Series was spreading out beyond the direct-by-mail field. We signed contracts with Applebaum's and the A&P to put wire racks near the cash registers in all their stores, and Mattlin's prediction about the success of this aspect of our distribution proved to be his only mistake. His estimate of our sales in this area was doubled in six months. When the series started to catch on in regular bookstores all over the country, Ralph Mattlin began making sales trips to the more important central outlets. The day he was leaving on the midnight train for his Baltimore–Cleveland–Chicago swing, he took me by surprise. Mattlin asked me to come down to Thirty-eighth Street and have dinner with him and his wife.

It was the first time I had been inside the house since the morning when I hit him with the news about Mr. Nachman. It was also the first time I had seen the ex-Benita Adler since the Friday afternoon when I went steaming uptown to Bernie Yustin's maisonette with the news about Mr. Nachman's suicide.

Maud Eitner and I had done plenty of guessing about why Ralph Mattlin was keeping his bride out of sight. But none of it added up to anything with which you would have wanted to walk into a court of law and call evidence. What bothered me was that it was slowing me down. You can't pitch a winning game unless you're on the mound facing batters. I couldn't move until I started making contact with Benita the Former Billing Clerk. And I couldn't do that until I was invited.

"I think I've got a clue," Maud Eitner said late that afternoon. I had joined her in the Walpole Bar for the drink she'd asked me to have with her before I went down to Thirty-eighth Street. "I may have stumbled on something," Maud said.

I gave her a look. Maud may not have had the shape of Toby Wing, but a stumbler she wasn't. If it had been Maud instead of Eliza crossing the river on the ice, Harriet Beecher Stowe would have had to change the plot of *Uncle Tom's Cabin*.

"You sound like me," I said. "That first day we met. When we were knocking back the lasagne and I told you what I'd found in the cash-payments book about Mr. Nachman's weekly postage checks."

"It's something like that," Maud said. "Except it's on a smaller scale and it's not crooked and it might be very funny."

"Better make me laugh fast," I said. "Ralph Mattlin said if I want a drink before dinner I'd better get there at six-thirty, because they always sit down at seven sharp. By this I guess he means he and Benita are different from common schlumps like you and me, who eat standing up."

"You're closer than you think," Maud said. "You've never been a secretary, so you probably don't know all the things a secretary does for her boss."

"Maybe I should get one and begin boning up," I said.

"Mattlin & Merritt is doing fine," Maud said. "But not so fine that we can afford a full-time secretary for the Bookkeeping Department. Not yet, anyway. What's the matter with our new receptionist's part-time shorthand?"

"She writes Pitman," I said. "I'm a Gregg man myself."

"I'm surprised," Maud said, "that a boy like you, your head as stuffed with facts as the head of Oscar Levant and all his *Information, Please!* cronies put together, yet you don't know

225

that one of the services of a secretary is that she pays her boss's bills. I mean she prepares the checks for his signature that pay Brooks Brothers for his button-down shirts, and Equitable Life for his insurance, and Dr. Bernard Yustin for his three hand-holding sessions each week, and the City of New York for the real estate taxes on his house, and so on. You get used to the bills that show up every month. You don't pay much attention to them. You just pay them. When something new shows up, you find yourself paying close attention. I suddenly found that every Monday morning since Ralph Mattlin got married, I was writing a check for fifty dollars to something called Milton Merkin."

"What's Milton Merkin?" I said.

"Judge for yourself," Maud Eitner said. "Here it comes now."

Out of the darkness that surrounded all those little old ladies in hats came Gregory. He was playing Chingachgook for the kid in the torn sweater who had come into the Mattlin & Merritt reception room looking for his girl, on the morning Maud Eitner and I learned Ralph Mattlin had eloped with Benita Adler.

"This gentleman says he has an appointment with you," Gregory said.

"He has," Maud said. "Won't you sit down, Mr. Merkin?"

"Thanks," Milton Merkin said. He sat down.

This made North Northeast a little crowded. It was, after all, a table for two. But Milton Merkin did not take up much room. Even in his torn sweater he had looked about the size of Benny Leonard in his prime. Or maybe Lew Tendler on a day when he had no trouble making the weight. Milton Merkin, however, was not wearing the torn sweater in which I had first seen him on that Monday morning five months ago. Milton Merkin was wearing a neat double-breasted blue suit from either Howard's or Crawford's. I could tell by the shoulders. There wasn't that much Milton under those pads. What there was, however, looked prosperous. The tip-off was his shirt. It was white. In 1937 the only guys who wore white shirts were those who didn't have to worry about the size of their laundry bills. Milton

226

Merkin's shirt had one of those Trubenized collars that didn't need starching. That added at least half a fish to the price. And even if Milton wore his shirts two or more days in a row before he turned them over to the laundry, with the one he was wearing now he was on his first day. All in all, he was no longer the kid who had dragged his tail and his armful of books out of the Mattlin & Merritt reception room on that Monday morning. Something had happened to Milton Merkin since I'd seen him last. He said, "To what do I owe the honor of this invitation?"

"You remember Mr. Leff?" Maud said. "He was with me on that dreadful Monday morning when you walked into the Mattlin & Merritt waiting room and it became my painfully unpleasant duty to break the appalling news to you that your beloved fiancée had without warning eloped with an older and wealthier man."

When Maud Eitner stopped to gulp for a little air, I wondered all of a sudden if she was bucking for the role of Portia in Maurice Schwartz's production of *The Merchant of Venice*. Milton Merkin gave her a suspicious look. Maud kept a straight face.

"Yes," Miltie said. "I remember Mr. Leff."

"What will you drink?" I said.

"A vermouth cassis," Merkin said.

I gave him another look. I didn't know what a vermouth cassis was, but it didn't sound like the sort of thing a kid I'd last seen in a torn sweater should be ordering.

"Yes sir," Gregory said, and went away.

"The reason Mr. Leff and I want to talk to you may seem silly," Maud said. "I mean it may seem silly to you, Mr. Merkin, but you've been worrying us."

"In what way?" Merkin said.

"That day I broke the news to you," Maud said. "You looked as though you were going out and cut your throat."

"I almost did," Milton Merkin said.

"But you obviously didn't," Maud said.

"You bet I didn't," Milton Merkin said.

"Would you mind telling us why?" Maud said.

"When I got out into the street," Milton Merkin said, "I asked myself why should I die? Just because I've been betrayed by a woman? That's Anna Karenina stuff. Other men before me have been betrayed by women. They hadn't all gone out and cut their throats. Some had said okay, I'll show her. I decided instead of cutting my throat I'd live and show her."

This, unlike the vermouth cassis, was more the sort of thing I expected from a kid in a torn sweater with an armful of books. The trouble was Milton Merkin was no longer wearing a torn sweater.

"Have you?" Maud said.

A funny thing happened. Milton Merkin started to laugh. "You're his secretary, aren't you?" he said. "Ralph Mattlin's?"

"Yes, of course," Maud said. "I told you that in my note when I asked you for a drink."

"Then if you're his secretary," Milton Merkin said, "you must know about the checks."

I turned to Maud. "Those checks you told me about?" I said.

"Exactly," Maud said. "A week after the happy newlyweds came home from their honeymoon, Ralph Mattlin gave me Mr. Merkin's address and said, 'Every Friday from now on I want to send him a check for fifty dollars.'"

"What for?" I said.

"That's what I asked Mr. Merkin to come tell us," Maud said. She turned to Miltie. "Will you?"

"There's not much to tell," Milton Merkin said. "Mr. Mattlin is paying me for tutoring his wife."

Gregory arrived with a tall glass and set it down. Milton Merkin tasted it. *"Magnifique,"* he said.

Gregory disappeared.

"Is that what you're tutoring Mrs. Mattlin in?" Maud said. "French?"

"Among other things," Milton Merkin said.

It was those other things I was suddenly interested in. "You mind a personal question?" I said.

"If it's not too personal," Milton said.

228

It's always struck me as being foolish to waste your time on any other kind.

"I'm puzzled by what happened," I said. "You're engaged to marry a girl. She runs out on you and marries another guy. From one day you want to kill yourself, a couple of weeks later you're willing to take this guy's money."

"For services rendered," Milton Merkin said. "And you mustn't take my engagement to Benita too seriously."

"How serious do you want us to take it?" Maud said.

"Not very," Milton Merkin said. "It was my mother's idea to begin with. About a year ago, when the Adlers moved in across the hall from us, she started pushing me and Benita together. My mother felt it would do me good to go steady with a nice Jewish girl."

"Did it?" I said.

Milton Merkin shrugged. "She's very beautiful," he said. "And a lot of the boys on the block were jealous of me, which was pleasant, of course, but what mainly attracted me to Benita was her brain."

It was like hearing Helen Wills say what attracted her to the game of tennis was the shape of the balls.

"I never noticed it," Maud Eitner said.

There were, of course, other things that caught the eye first.

"Because it wasn't well stocked," Milton Merkin said.

"Well what?" Maud said.

"Stocked," he said.

"Stocked like in a store?" I said.

"Goods on a shelf?" Maud said.

"Exactly," Milton Merkin said. "Benita has had very little formal education. The family is pretty poor, and to help out at home, she's been working at all sorts of odd jobs ever since she was fifteen. She quit high school during her second year. But she's highly intelligent. Very smart, actually, as well as quick. What I mean is she has an excellent brain, so I enjoyed filling it up."

"You mean after Ralph Mattlin married her," Maud said,

"he made the same discovery you made? That there wasn't very much on the shelves?"

"That's exactly what happened," Milton Merkin said. "Unlike most men, however, Ralph Mattlin decided to do something about it. After all, he's the head of a publishing firm. The visitors to his house are probably the sort of people who expect a publisher's wife to know Proust is not a cut of beef. Or you don't eat marmalade with a fork. Or when you say Yeats at her she shouldn't think you've muttered something dirty in Latin. Or when someone sets a fingerbowl in front of you, you don't salt and pepper the water to taste. Things like that. A receptionist is one thing. But a publisher's wife, that's something else. When Mattlin discussed the problem with her, Benita said she agreed that she could use some brushing up and she knew just the man to do it."

"How did Mr. Mattlin take to the arrangement?" I said. "I mean assuming that his wife told him she had been engaged to you when she married him?"

"You don't have to assume," Merkin said. "She told him. There's nothing devious or two-faced or underhanded about Benita. She's one of the most honest people I've ever known. She told her husband all about us."

"How did Mr. Mattlin take it?" Maud Eitner said. "If you know, that is."

"What do you mean if I know," Milton Merkin said. "Of course I know. I come to the house five days a week after I finish my own classes. I work with Benita from four to six. Mr. Mattlin almost always comes home before I leave. When he does he offers me a drink, and we all three have a talk. Sometimes Mr. Mattlin asks me to test Benita. Last night, for example, he insisted that we talk French for a while. His is quite good, by the way."

"How's hers?" Maud said.

Milton Merkin laughed. "It's getting better," he said.

"You sound like you're enjoying your work," I said.

"It's the greatest thing that ever happened to me," Milton Merkin said. "And I owe it all to Benita. I barely made it through high school, and I've had trouble staying in college because my father doesn't earn enough at pants-pressing to put a crease in his own. Now I'm earning more than he does by running what you might describe as a small college of my own."

"I've got a question that may hurt your feelings," Maud said. "It's not intended to do that. I'm merely curious to know how a young man of your, well, your background, how you managed to learn enough about all this to be able to tutor somebody who, as you yourself put it, is a publisher's wife."

Merkin laughed again. "I went to Macy's and bought a book on etiquette," he said. "What I do is keep one lesson ahead of Benita. I learned about vermouth cassis last night. This afternoon Benita learned about it. As for the French, it's strictly DeWitt Clinton High School."

"Aside from French," Maud Eitner said, "is your student making any overall progress?"

"Mr. Mattlin told me the other night he was very pleased with my work," Milton Merkin said. "I was putting Benita through a sort of general quiz while the three of us were having a drink, and when I finished Mattlin said he thought I'd turned his consort into quite a sophisticated woman."

My ears went up.

"He called her his consort?" Maud said. Obviously hers had too.

"No," Milton Merkin said. "But it was in the tone of his voice."

"How about Benita?" I said. "Does she think she's sophisticated?"

"She most certainly does," he said. "She has passed what I call Merkin's test."

"What's that?" I said.

"Benita now says matoor when she means mature," Milton Merkin said. "And she makes firm little speeches about you must never wash the salad bowl, but you should always wipe it out with a paper napkin."

23

" Don't Say Anything, Darling.
Not Even Thanks"

Ninety minutes later I saw her doing it. With Milton Merkin's warning under my belt, it came as no surprise.

Without Milton Merkin's warning, however, I might have been shaken up a little by what happened during the hour that led up to the wiping of the salad bowl. When I rang the bell, the door was opened by a butler.

I knew he was a butler because he looked like all the actors who in 1937 were opening doors for William Powell in those movies directed by Gregory La Cava. He looked at me as though he expected me to hand him a subpoena.

"Mr. Leff," I said. "I'm expected."

"Yes, of course, sir," he said. "This way, please."

I put down my briefcase on the table in the hall and followed him into the living room. But he didn't stop. He kept right on going. He moved slowly and steadily and relentlessly toward the back of the house. Like Spencer Tracy on his way to the chair in *The Last Mile*. Following behind him, I took a quick look around. Something had happened since my first visit.

It was as though somebody had hacked a few portholes in the walls. Maybe to let in more light. Everything certainly seemed brighter. Then I saw what was doing it. Since my last visit the room had been filled with chintz. But I mean filled. It looked like the upholstery shop in Macy's caught in a hurricane.

Green and red flowers on a bright yellow background. The stuff hung around the windows. It covered all the furniture. It seemed to be creeping off the walls. I had the feeling that if you turned your head it would sneak up and wrap itself around your legs. If rooms had ears this yellow and green and red gook would have been coming out of them. I felt as though it was coming out of mine.

One thing, however, had not changed. As I followed the butler, the Grubensteller eyes of Ralph Mattlin's mother followed me. With a leather collar, what a watchdog this dame would have made. German shepherd, of course.

"Mr. Leff," the butler said. He said it through a couple of open French windows. He stepped aside to let me pass, and I saw he'd said it into a backyard.

"Herein!" Ralph Mattlin called.

So I knew he was in a good mood. I walked out into the yard. Mattlin was unwinding his long body from a beach chair that looked familiar. When he was halfway out of it I saw why. The chair was covered with the same yellow chintz that was churning away in the living room. Mattlin finished unwinding and stood up straight. "You know Benita, of course," he said. "But I don't think you've ever met my wife. So may I present Mrs. Ralph Mattlin?"

"Oh, Ralphie," she said with a giggle. She started to unwind herself from a matching deck chair of her own. I wondered if the backs were marked "His" and "Hers." She had less to unwind, so she got to me faster. She threw her arms around me. "Darling," she said. "How nice to see you after all these months." And she gave me a kiss.

Now then. There are kisses and there are kisses. Anybody who needs footnotes to that statement should go right out and get himself a paperback reprint of *What Every Young Boy Should Know* and start working his way all over again up from *Maggie and Jiggs* to the marriage manuals. I am talking, of course, about kisses without an audience. Two people alone in a room. Or a tent. Or even a telephone booth. We now come to another type of kiss. We will leave out the kind of thing that goes on at smokers. I refer to the kiss in front of an audience that has about as much to do with yentzing as brushing your teeth. You're seeing somebody off in an airport. You're welcoming somebody home at Grand Central. You go uptown to see your old lady on Friday night. It's not exactly a kiss. It's a peck. The kind of thing you give a friend's wife when you come to their house. It's also all you expect to get from her. With her husband standing right beside her, I mean. It was certainly all I expected to get in Mr. and Mrs. Ralph Mattlin's backyard that night. Come to think of it, I don't think I even expected to get that. After all, she was a billing clerk I'd known in an office for a few busy days before she disappeared, and I hadn't seen her for almost six months. A handshake would have done it. A peck would have been what they call gracious. Showing the help that just because she'd become the boss's wife, it didn't mean she considered herself any different from the days when she had been plain, simple, just-like-you-and-me Benita. Sitting behind the reception desk. Cheerfully fielding visitors for one and all. What made me come alive was that I did not get a peck.

I got a kiss. And I mean a kiss. Right smack on the mouth. Wet as a washcloth after a hot shower. With suction.

Benita's husband was like maybe thirty-six inches from the clinch. Even the manager of Loew's, a couple blocks away, could have heard the sucking sounds. Why not Ralph Mattlin? I swung my eyeballs to the left. He looked like the chandelier in the Paramount when the lights come up after the feature. He was beaming. I wondered about that. Couldn't he see what was happening? Or didn't he mind? His wife unhooked her suction cups from mine. I made one of my mental notes. Next time I came here I'd bring a windshield wiper.

"It's so nice to see you here in our house," she said.

I stopped mopping my mouth. It looked like Milton Merkin had overshot the mark. His pupil had just sounded like the wife of George the Five making the new ambassador from Washington feel at home on his first visit to Buckingham Palace.

"It's nice to be here," I said. I didn't need no Milton Merkin to teach me my lines.

"I hope you don't mind our dining alfresco," Benita said.

It looked like it wouldn't hurt, though, if I talked to Milton about getting a rate on a few lessons for myself. "It's your house," I said. "You have a right to feed anybody you like."

The smile took a funny slant. Like Gene Merritt's glasses. As though she'd been poked in home base.

"Huh?" Benita said.

Her husband laughed. "Ted is making a joke," Mattlin said. "As though al is short for Alfred."

"Oh," she said. The smile came back into position. "Alfred Fresco. That's terribly funny, Ted. On an evening like this with the weather so pleasant the patio looks quite lovely, don't you think?"

I looked around. The difference between a backyard and a patio seemed to be three deck chairs and a yellow canvas awning. It matched the chintz inside and the chairs outside. I took my time looking. Not because there was much to see. I was trying to work something out in my mind. When I'd first seen Benita Adler on the day I came into the Mattlin & Merritt office with Arnold Zohn, she'd made me think of one of those girls in the rotogravure sections who weave daisy chains on the Vassar campus. Soon after that I decided she was a N.J.G. with better equipment than most. Now, all of a sudden, she was the gracious lady of the manor. Like Billie Burke in a big-budget movie, wearing a green velvet hostess gown. Probably to bring out the flowers in the chintz, as we used to say on Seventh Avenue. Which of these three dames was the real Benita? Because it was the real one I was going to have to deal with.

"It certainly is nice," I said, turning back. "Especially the flowers. It doesn't look like you're in the city."

"Whenever the weather is fine, Ralphie and I just sit out here by the hour," she said. "Don't we, darling?"

235

From the look Mattlin gave her you'd have thought she'd just invented trigonometry.

"We certainly do," Mattlin said. "You don't know what you're missing, Ted. What you ought to do is get yourself a wife and a patio and just sit out under the stars. It's the most wonderful thing in the world."

Five would get him ten it wasn't even the second most wonderful.

"I'm too young," I said. "I'm still loaded down with unsown wild oats."

"Oh, Ted," Benita said. "You're not nearly as wicked as you want people to believe."

So who was talking? The Vassar undergraduate? The N.J.G.? Or the lady-in-waiting? It was like looking at her through a prism. Every time you moved your head, you saw something different. What I saw now was the cut of the hostess gown. High neck. Hemline down to the floor. Double-bias width so it swept and billowed with every move the wearer made. When I had them as part of my Seventh Avenue line, garments of this type went for sixty-five and over wholesale. Which meant one-three-oh or better at Bergdorf and Bonwit's. Prism or no prism, and no matter which one was the real Benita Adler, it was clear that she had come up with the box lunch. For her, Ralph Mattlin obviously didn't mind shelling out.

"Some wicked," I said. "You know what I do after I finish up at the office every night? I go down to the Christadora House and run a boy scout troop."

"If you said girl scout troop," Benita said, "I might believe you. What would you like to drink?"

I decided to hit one out for old Milton Merkin. "Do you have any cassis?" I said.

"Any what?" Benita said.

Mattlin stepped in like Lou Gehrig one-handing a hard-line drive. "Jeremy," he said. "Do we have any cassis in the house?"

The butler was standing behind me. "Certainly, sir," he said.

"I'd like a vermouth cassis, please," I said.

Jeremy bowed and went through the French windows into the house.

"Funny," Mattlin said. "I would have thought of you as a martini man."

"Not when I'm going back to work," I said. "I've got some things to finish at the office."

"Oh no, not tonight," Benita said. "It's a celebration."

"Celebration of what?" I said.

A fourth Benita came out of the wings. The frightened little girl. Peering up worriedly at Daddy. Hoping he won't punish her too severely for having dropped and broken his favorite meerschaum pipe.

"Oh, dear," she said to Mattlin. "I've been naughty."

He laughed and put one arm around her. "Not at all, silly," he said, and he kissed her. A peck. "We asked you to dinner tonight, Ted, because Gene and I and Benita had a long talk about you out here on the patio last night. Since I'll be out of town for a few days on this Baltimore swing, it seemed sort of nice to break the news to you before I left. Gene wanted to be here too, but it's Friday night, and as you know, on Friday nights he goes up to see his parents. So I'm doing the honors for both members of the firm."

Jeremy came out of the house with my drink. I could see this Milton Merkin was no boy who painted only in broad strokes. He filled in the details. The glass was sitting on a small silver tray.

"Thanks." I took the drink and lifted it a few inches. "Well," I said, "here's to whatever it is we're celebrating."

"Wait," Mattlin said. He stepped to a small glass-topped table between the chairs. He picked up two glasses and gave one to his wife. "Ted," he said, "I know this is long overdue, but Gene and I wanted to be sure the Twentieth Century Classics Series was really on its way before we added to our overhead, and we now feel there's no doubt about it. As of next payday, your salary goes from eighty-five to a hundred and fifty dollars a week."

237

All of a sudden I was no longer looking at Benita Mattlin through a prism. All of a sudden I knew who the real girl was. The girl I would have to deal with. What did it was the way they were looking at me. Both of them. In exactly the same way. The Czar and his Czarina had just announced the freeing of the serfs.

The girl I would have to deal with was not a Vassar undergraduate. She was not an N.J.G. She was not the lady of the manor. Not any more. Benita had come into focus. From here on in, she was Mrs. Ralph Mattlin. I was going to have to deal with a team.

Knowing that, I knew what to do.

"Gosh," I said. I tried for the Gary Cooper touch. Kicking the sunbaked turds in the ranch-house yard as he tries to tell the girl in the gingham dress who is flinging corn to the chickens that he'd like her to go to the square dance with him on Saturday night. "I mean," I said, "I don't really know what to say."

Drop dead seemed singularly inappropriate.

"Then don't say anything, darling," Benita Mattlin said. "Not even thanks. Because Ralphie and I feel you've earned it. Don't we, Ralphie darling?"

24

" I Think You'll Remember That Fact Without Writing It Down"

Later that night, after I took Ralph Mattlin up to Penn Station in a taxi, I came back to Thirty-eighth Street. It was almost twelve-thirty when I rang the bell. The door was opened by Benita. She looked at her wrist watch. "I'm disappointed in you, darling," she said.

"Why?" I said.

"Well, I figured it this way," Benita said. "The train leaves at midnight. Ralph would make sure to be on board ten or fifteen minutes early. So if you took a cab, that would mean you'd be back here by about ten minutes after twelve. Or let's say a quarter after at the latest." She smiled. "What took you so long?"

I smiled back. It looked as though I was going to get the kind of cooperation that made this sort of work feel like a vacation. "I wanted to be on the safe side," I said. "I waited until I saw the old choo-choo pulling out."

"Come in," Benita said. She stepped aside, then closed the door behind me.

The butler came out from under the stairs. He was wearing a

maroon bathrobe with a black-and-white-checked collar. "Is anything wrong, madam?" he said.

"No, it's all right, Jeremy. Mr. Leff forgot his briefcase." She picked it up from the hall table. "Ted," she said. "Would you like a drink before you go?"

"Why yes, thanks," I said. "That would be very nice indeed." The "indeed" was for Milton Merkin.

"Another vermouth cassis?" Benita said.

"I think maybe not at this hour," I said. "Scotch and water, if it's available?"

"Of course," Benita said. She turned to the butler. "Jeremy, would you?"

"Certainly," he said. "Would you care for something too, madam?"

"Yes," Benita said. "The usual."

Jeremy bowed and went back under the stairs. I had a picture of him sleeping on an old mattress near the furnace. I followed Benita into the living room. The French doors at the back were closed. The moonlight came in through the glass. The chintz was huffing and puffing. Benita snapped on the two lamps at both sides of the fireplace. She sat down in the small couch at the left. "You sit there," she said.

She pointed to the chair facing her across the coffee table. It was the same arrangement Ralph Mattlin had made on the morning when I came to see him for the first time.

"You sound just like your husband," I said. I sat down.

"They say married people get to think and act alike," Benita said. "Sometimes if they're married long enough they get to look alike."

"If that happens," I said, "Ralph Mattlin is certainly due for a spectacular improvement in his appearance."

"Why, Ted darling, you're quite a hand at the dashing-compliments game, aren't you? Just put them there, Lydia."

A heavy-set woman had come in with a silver tray. It was about twice as big as the one on which the butler had brought my vermouth cassis into the backyard. Two things Ralph Mattlin seemed to have plenty of: Grubensteller portraits of his

240

mother, and silver trays. The woman wore a bathrobe exactly like the one the butler had been wearing out in the hall. Maybe they took turns lying on the mattress near the furnace and wore the bathrobe when one of them had to come upstairs. Her hair was dark brown shot with gray. It hung down her back in two thick braids. They whacked back and forth on her watermelon-shaped tail as she walked. She took a highball from the tray and set it in front of me. Then she crossed to Benita and set the tray in front of her. On it was a thick white mug with a silver handle, a teaspoon, two saltines, and a folded napkin about as big as an R.S.V.P. envelope with embroidered lace edges.

"Will there be anything else, madam?"

"No, that's just fine, Lydia, thank you," Benita said. "You can go to bed now."

"Will you be all right, madam?"

Benita laughed. "Now, stop worrying," she said. "Mr. Leff works in my husband's firm, and we've known each other since we were children. We think of ourselves as brother and sister."

Not if I was going to keep my promise to Maud Eitner.

"Very good, madam. Good night."

"Good night, Lydia."

"Good night, sir."

"Good night," I said. Her can took a drubbing from the braids on her way out. When she was gone I said, "Who's that?"

"Jeremy's wife," Benita said.

"I'm glad to hear that," I said.

"Why?"

"I'd hate to think of you all alone in this house with a man," I said. "I mean when Ralph is out of town."

"Is that all you mean?" Benita said.

"Not exactly," I said. I reached over and pulled out the light on my side of the fireplace.

"Does the glare bother you?" Benita said.

"I can see you better this way," I said.

"I prefer to have you see me the way I want you to see me," she said. "Put the light on, darling."

I hesitated. The voice didn't match the windshield-wiper job she'd given me when I came out on the patio earlier in the evening. "Suppose I said no?" I said.

Benita laughed. "Darling," she said, "you wouldn't say no to your boss's wife, would you?"

I stood up. "That's why I came back," I said. "Not to say no."

I came around the coffee table and sat down beside her. She smiled up at me. I reached down with my kisser and across her shoulder with my hand. The second light went out as we made contact. The slobbering had just got under way when something hot hit me between the legs. I let go with a yelp. She reached up and pulled on the light. In her other hand Benita was holding the white mug with the silver handle.

"Jesus," I said. I jumped up and looked down at my pants. "What the hell was that?"

"Hot milk, darling," Benita said. "Now be a good boy and go back to your chair and pull on that light."

I did all those things plus one more. I got out my handkerchief and started a wiping job. "Well," I said, "that shoots the ass out of about twenty bucks' worth of Kolmer-Marcus tailoring."

"Nonsense, darling," Benita said. "We use only Grade A milk in this house. Half a dollar's worth of dry cleaning will make you as good as new."

"Not if you'd poured a little more of that stuff," I said. "You were in a dangerous area."

"So were you, darling," she said. "But I didn't want to damage you permanently. I merely wanted to set you straight."

"About what?" I said.

"You're not a briefcase-forgetter," Benita said. "And I'm not a dumb little receptionist who managed to marry the boss because she has a large and well-distributed bosom."

"Is that the way for a new bride to talk?" I said.

"To you, yes," Benita said. "I want you to get it absolutely clear, so I'm using your frame of reference. As soon as you and Ralph left and I saw your briefcase in the hall, I knew you'd be back. I've been around grown-up boys long enough to know what you'd be back for. So instead of asking Jeremy to answer the door and tell you I'd gone to bed, I thought I'd do it myself. After all, I watched you in action in the office for a full week before Ralph and I got married. I knew if I didn't set you straight tonight you'd be back to try again, and I don't want any of Ralph's important executives to be wasting the precious time that they should be devoting to the business."

At eighty-five a week I was a bookkeeper. At one-five-oh I was an executive.

"I wasn't thinking of it as a waste of time," I said. "From the way you stuck your tongue down my throat when I showed up to eat with Alfred Fresco, I got the idea you wouldn't consider it a waste of time, either."

"That's the trouble with men," Benita said. "They get ideas, most of them wrong. I wanted you to come back so I could teach you a lesson. You mustn't read more into a kiss than the kiss itself. A matoor person understands that. I always thought you were matoor. If nothing else, I would think what you went through on Seventh Avenue would have had a matooring influence on you."

I managed to keep my voice on the level where it had been for a while. "How do you know what I went through on Seventh Avenue?" I said.

"A little bird told me," Benita said.

"You want to watch out with this talking to birds," I said. "There's no future in it."

"Oh, I'm not so sure," Benita said. "Look what it did for St. Francis of Assisi."

"Do I know the name of this bird?" I said.

"Probably," Benita said. "But it's not important. As soon as I saw you come in the office that first day with Arnold Zohn, I smelled garment center. That Kolmer-Marcus suit and that way of looking at girls. I used to be a model in fourteen ninety-fives. I still have some friends there. I made a few phone calls."

"Why?" I said.

"Self-protection," Benita said. "Just in case."

"Just in case what?" I said.

"Just in case you started acting like other citizens of the garment center I'd known," Benita said. "Which you started to do at once. When I saw the direction you were taking, I decided I was safe. Tonight proves it."

"How?" I said.

"I like you, Ted darling," Benita said. "Even though I regret to see you're not as matoor as I thought. And when I like someone I am so overjoyed when I see them that I give them a kiss, and that's all I give them."

"Is that all Milton Merkin got?" I said.

"Less," she said. "Milton is not interested in girls. He's interested in becoming a dentist. I would like you to know that when I married Ralph I was a virgin."

"Wait till I get a pencil and make a note of that," I said.

"I think you'll remember that fact without writing it down," she said. "Now there's something else I want you to remember. Ready?"

"Ready," I said.

"I'm as smart as you are," Benita said.

As Samson had said to Delilah.

"I never said you weren't," I said.

"Just so you never will have to say it," Benita said, "I'll let you in on a little secret. Ralph didn't marry me. I married him. I set my cap for him the minute I saw him. I am going to land this boy, I said to myself. I landed him, and I'm crazy about him, and I intend to hold onto him. I'm not going to risk that for a little wrestling match now and then with Hot Pants Teddy. Even you are not as good as you think you are. Is that clear?"

"All except why you want to tell it to me," I said.

"Because I'm a humanitarian," Benita said. "I don't like to see people going through life in a state of confusion. I don't want you to be confused, Ted darling. I think Mattlin & Merritt is going places, and I think a lot of those places will be reached because of you. So does Ralph. He thinks you're the best thing that's happened to the firm since it got going. I want it to work. I don't want it to get mixed up with your glands."

"How are you going to do that?" I said. "As long as you keep

244

wagging around those things you just nicknamed, I believe, your well-distributed bosom?"

She laughed and wagged them a little harder. "Ralph has removed temptation from your path," Benita said. "Even if you were Ramon Novarro, Ted darling, the boss's wife is out of the running. For about six months, anyway."

"Why?" I said.

"Milton Merkin informs me that the period of gestation in the matoor human female is nine months," Benita Mattlin said. "And I've already missed three of my periods."

25

"Fish Are Funny. You Have to Catch Them Before You Can Fry Them"

Maud walked across my one-roomer to the dresser. It doubled as my bar. She poured more whiskey into her glass, took a sip, then shook her head.

"No," she said. "I'm not upset. Married women get pregnant the way dogs get worms. There's nothing very unusual about it. What's unusual is that you should persist in thinking you can still get Benita into trouble that will lead to Mattlin divorcing her without getting yourself into worse trouble. I think you'd better forget the whole thing."

I was way ahead of her. I'd already forgotten it.

"You mean you don't want to be Mrs. Ralph Mattlin any more?" I said.

"I mean I'm doing something I wish you'd do," she said.

"What's that?" I said.

"Face the facts," she said. "One of my services as secretary to Ralph Mattlin is a simple one. I put through all his telephone calls. He tells me to get her on the phone four or five times a day. Sometimes six and seven."

"To say what?"

"My dear Ted, you are accusing me of eavesdropping."

246

"On Seventh Avenue we used to call it monitoring a call," I said. "Answer the question."

"I don't know why he calls her four or five or six or seven times a day," Maud said. "Because he doesn't really say anything. Neither does she. They just make noises at each other. Like great big dollops of syrup dropping out of a maple tree into the bucket. I think your trouble in this situation is you're underestimating the extent to which our leader is stuck on this little butterball."

"Maybe I am," I said. "Just the same, I made you a promise and I intend to keep it."

"Your conceit is, of course, one of the wonders of the age," Maud said. "But I like you and I have your interests at heart. So you don't have to be ashamed of picking up a lesson or two from a member of what you obviously consider the inferior sex. I won't tell people it was Maud Eitner who had to wise you up to one of life's basic truths. It's this. Men do not divorce women on whom they are stuck like mustard plasters. End of lesson."

"Mustard plasters get unstuck," I said. "It's just a matter of time."

"Don't waste it," Maud said. "I've set the automatic pilot in a new direction."

"Well," I said, "whoever the new guy is I hope he deserves you."

"He probably doesn't," she said. "But I'm willing to overlook that."

"Anybody I know?" I said.

"Not as well as you should," Maud Eitner said.

"Who is he?" I said.

"You," she said.

In the pig's eye, honeybunch, and I don't mean eye.

"You're kidding," I said.

"Not any more," Maud said.

"Isn't this sort of sudden?"

As the Mayor of Pompeii said to Vesuvius.

"I don't think so," she said. "We've been trying each other on for size for about six months. I like the fit."

247

I didn't. Not with the word "Mrs." in front of it.

"I guess only a louse would forget at this point to say I'm flattered," I said.

"I'm waiting for you to say something else," Maud said.

Wait, wait, baby. Keep on waiting.

"Like the word 'yes'?" I said.

"That's the word," she said.

"You've got a deal," I said.

She raised her glass. "Here's to us," Maud said. "Now say when."

When Hitler makes a public announcement: *I Take It All Back.*

"As soon as I can afford a wife," I said.

"According to your report of what happened down on Thirty-eighth Street last night," Maud said, "I understand you're now an executive earning one hundred and fifty dollars per week."

Here comes the rebroadcast to the West Coast.

"I wouldn't marry a woman," I said, "who thought so little of herself that she'd hitch her future to a slob who got to earning a yard and a half a week by accepting a tip that a snooty bastard like Ralph Mattlin tossed him the way he'd throw a nickel at a shoe-shine boy."

Maud sat down on my one good chair. She crossed her legs, which were good enough to stand in for Claudette Colbert. Then, very deliberately, she sat the glass of whiskey and water on her kneecap, which was just standard. Don't hold this against her. Nobody has ever made it into the history books on the basis of kneecaps. Not even Cleopatra.

"Well," Maud said in her best a, b, c with footnotes voice. "A number of things are finally coming clear."

Before I finished they'd have to do better than that. They'd have to come across.

"Like what?" I said.

"I didn't know how much you hate Ralph Mattlin," Maud Eitner said.

"I don't hate him," I said. "I resent him."

248

"I don't see the difference," she said.

She would if she'd come from East Fourth Street.

"He's not a bad guy," I said. "In fact, compared with most of the walking cruds you meet in the course of a business day in this town, he stacks up pretty good. The trouble is just that. Pretty good means pretty good and rotten. It's easy to handle a son of a bitch. You simply give him as good as you get or better. What drives me up the wall is the basically nice guy who doesn't know he's being a son of a bitch. Ralph Mattlin. On the surface? Richard Barthelmess. Underneath? Father Coughlin."

"Take your foot off the accelerator," Maud said. "It's true Ralph Mattlin hasn't written to Jim Farley in Washington and said let's put Mr. Leff's profile on the new two-cent stamp. But neither has he called up Abe Reles at Murder, Inc., and said put an ice pick into this Leff's duodenum and send me a bill. What Ralph Mattlin has done is give you a sixty-five-dollar-a-week raise. There are people who would say that's a nice gesture."

There are people who would say Herbert Hoover is a sexpot.

"I'm not one of them," I said. "This outfit was dying on its feet. No. Excuse me. It wasn't even on its feet. It was on its ass. I came along and did two things. First, I got them back from a crooked bookkeeper fifty big ones that saved them from Seventy-seven B."

"What's Seventy-seven B?" Maud said.

"A section of the bankruptcy act that you're better off being innocent enough not to know about," I said. "Not only did I save these boys from that, but I came up with a publishing idea that already looks as though it's saved the firm, and anybody with brains can see is going to put the major stockholders on easy street before the calendar warns us it's time to switch from pumpernickel to matzos. So what does one of the major stockholders do? He gives me a pat on the head and says good boy, Rover, here's the bone from the nice juicy steak we just finished."

Maud lifted the glass. She uncrossed her legs. She recrossed them the other way. She took a sip. She set the glass back on her other kneecap. I don't know why. All of a sudden she looked sexy. "Oh boy," she said. "I'm just beginning to understand something I never understood in my high-school French class."

"What's that?" I said.

"A proverb," she said. *"Il n'est pire eau que l'eau qui dort."*

"We had that," I said. *"Still waters run deep.* What's that got to do with the price of Indian nuts?"

"A good deal," Maud said. "If I've learned anything about you these last few months I've learned this. You're the lad who for me has given a new dimension to the old phrase. Biding your time. Has it come?"

"I'm pushing it," I said.

"How hard?" Maud said.

"Depends on how hard you're willing to help me."

"As your bride?" Maud said.

She should live so long.

"As my wife," I said. "If we make it."

"We" as in "me."

"I've never before heard you use the word 'if,' " Maud said.

"Pretend I never did," I said. "Let's just say we will make it."

"How?" she said.

"By letting Ralph Mattlin and Gene Merritt carry the ball on this Twentieth Century Classics Series. I've done as much for them as I can on that one. From here on in, it's up to them to do what they can for me."

"In what way?"

"Make the series a success," I said. "So that when the time comes for me to say to them: *make like an apple pie, boys, and show me my cut,* it will be worth something. While they're doing that, you and me, honeybunch, we'll be frying our own mess of fish."

"Fish are funny," Maud said. "You have to catch them before you can fry them."

"Listen to what I've caught," I said. "Those boys downtown on Twelfth Street? With the big building? Macmillan? They're no different from Mattlin & Merritt."

250

"You try telling that to a bank from which you're trying to borrow a small sum," Maud said.

"I wouldn't waste the time," I said. "Bankers are as dumb as publishers. Macmillan has a building and a bigger cash balance than Mattlin & Merritt only because they started earlier. Not because they're smarter. They're both still using the same old tools. Let Macmillan keep their wheelbarrows and wooden rakes. You and I are moving in with tractors."

"Ted," Maud said. "Have you been drinking?"

"No," I said, "something worse. Reading."

"Good God," she said. "What?"

"The first five books published by Mattlin & Merritt," I said. "Those five novels that almost put the firm out of business. Have you read them?"

"Not since we first unleashed them on an apathetic public," Maud said. "Three and a half years ago. Almost four."

"What do you remember about them?" I said.

"Nothing stimulating," Maud said. "Some received good reviews. Some bad. Some mixed. None of them set the Thames on fire."

"Forget the Thames," I said. "We're cooking this deal between the banks of the Hudson and the banks of the East River, which isn't even a river. It's a tidal estuary. I throw that in just to show you I'm cultured enough to discuss these five novels. You remember anything about the stories?"

"Not much," Maud said. "I think one was about a coal mine. That was the one Lewis Gannett liked. On the *Tribune.*"

"Like the lawyers say," I said, "let me refresh your recollection. Yes, one was about a coal mine. It was called *Pit Pony.* By the time you finished it, if you made an effort and tried hard to remember what you'd read you might know a lot or a little about how to dig coal out of a mine in Wales. Take that piece of information down to your bank, honeybunch, and try to make a deposit."

"Maybe I'd better not," Maud said. "My credit is pretty good there at the moment."

"Let's go on," I said. "The second novel was called *So Rose the Red.* It was about a district leader on the Lower East Side of New York who becomes a Communist. By the time you finished that one, you maybe knew how crooked politicians buy votes from ignorant immigrants. Right?"

"I think so," Maud said. "Actually, I never finished it. Viking Press turned it down, I'd heard, and I remember thinking while I was reading it how smart they'd been."

"The third novel was a fantasy about the opening up of the American West," I said. "It was called *Jonathan Jethro's America,* and when you finished it you knew less than you'd learned in public school. Except that maybe the West was opened up by people who spoke in little poems."

"I suggest you move on to the fourth number in this gallery of American fiction," Maud Eitner said. "You don't sound like the proper judge of that author's prose style. As I recall, it had charm."

"Charm, yes," I said. "Punch, no. But I move on gladly. Not because I can't wait for the fourth item. I mean gladly just to get away from the third. The fourth was called *The Checker.* This one was all about life in a big Chicago mail-order house subtly disguised as Sneers Roeduck & Company, and by the time you finished reading, assuming your wind was good and you made it to the end, you never wanted to see a postage stamp again."

"I don't recall that this was my reaction," Maud said. "I remember being puzzled by the fact that Ralph Mattlin was so eager to have the manuscript. Little, Brown offered a five-hundred-dollar advance. We got it for seven-fifty. Anyway, I think you've got the plot right. That's one, two, three, four. What in God's name was the fifth about?"

"The fifth and last item on our list," I said, "was a novel called *Mott Haven 2.* Here I want you to listen carefully. This number dealt with a nymphomaniac from Grand Concourse who meets a bookie from Bronx Park South, near Tremont Avenue, and as a result he never gets to the track again. Because from then on, they're always in the sack. Have I given a fair description of the five novels Mattlin & Merritt published?"

252

"Fair enough," Maud said. "Now tell me why all of a sudden you're giving me a one-man blitz course in American literature?"

"Because after I finished reading these books," I said, "I went to the sales records. Have you any idea how these five novels sold?"

"Yes," Maud said. "Appallingly."

"That's true," I said. "But appallingly in an interesting way. So I give you an interesting statistic, Miss Eitner. The book called *Mott Haven 2* sold two hundred forty-nine copies more than all four of the others put together."

"What's interesting about that?" Maud said. "Sex has always sold better than coal mining. Even *The Scarlet Letter* did better in the stores than *Areopagitica.*"

"*Mott Haven 2* did not sell," I said. "It merely sold better than those other four. From this I conclude that *Mott Haven 2,* like Gene Merritt says, was a need-filler. Learning about coal mining in Wales, or buying immigrant votes on Broome Street, or getting the lowdown on Custer's last stand through a schmohawk named Jonathan Jethro, or boning up on how mail-order houses ship their milk separators and imitation fur coats, this the average person can live without. But sex, this nobody can live without."

"Don't judge everybody by yourself," Maud said. "Millions of people are too young or too old to do anything about it."

"But nobody is too young or too old not to read about it," I said. "Or at least look at pictures."

"Then why didn't the firm of Mattlin & Merritt sell more copies of *Mott Haven 2?*" Maud said.

"For the same reason you didn't sell more copies of those jigsaw puzzles showing Pocahontas saving Captain John Smith," I said. "Because they were available only in bookstores."

"Are you trying to tell me if we'd put *Mott Haven 2* on the shelves in the A&P under the cornflakes we'd have had a best seller?"

"No," I said. "People buying cornflakes would probably be ashamed to buy right out in the open in front of their neighbors and A&P clerks a book that describes the act of sex in exactly the same way that the instruction book that comes with your Meccano set describes how to build a bridge or a derrick. I don't think the I-Bit-Her-Tit School of Fiction is A&P stuff."

"I suddenly remember something," Maud said. "The scene where the girl and the bookie stand in front of the mirror and, well, you know."

"Who wouldn't remember it?" I said. "I'll bet most of them told somebody else about it, which is why the book had as much of a sale as it did. The trick, I feel, is to make this sort of garbage available to a nation that is clearly sex-crazy without making them ashamed to be seen buying it. Now, Maud, my love, you're a smart girl. I've led you by the hand thus far. Tell me the next step?"

" 'You Never Heard of Us,' " she quoted. " 'But We Want Three Minutes of Your Time.' "

I laughed. "It won't take that long," I said. "What we've been building up these last few months, those coupons that come in from ads for the Twentieth Century Classics Series, we've been building up a sucker list. They don't know it, but they're just sitting there waiting to be picked off. All we have to do is mail out a circular."

"Which I can tell from the look in your eye you have already had written," Maud said.

"Not had written," I said. "If we're not paying royalties on Spinoza and Dickens, why should we pay royalties on a subject where every man is an expert? Or thinks he is? This one I wrote myself."

I took the typewritten sheet from the dresser drawer and handed it over. Maud took a short, quick glance at the headline, then looked up. "Ted," she said. "Are you crazy?"

"No," I said. "But I can see you think I am."

"Let me read this headline aloud," Maud said, and she did. " 'Nobody But Your Sexual Partner Will Ever Know You Purchased a Book That Contains One Hundred and Ninety-Six Photographs of Different Coital Positions.' " She looked up

254

again. "If I handed you a circular with that headline," Maud said, "wouldn't you think I'm crazy?"

"No," I said. "I'd sit down and fill in the coupon and write my check and have it in the mail before you could say nookie. Or I'd think to myself Maud here has come up with something big. As our leader said a few months ago about Ted here. Read the rest of it."

She did. When she finished Maud looked up. In the tone that this French boy at Verdun must have used when he let go with *"Ils ne passeront pas,"* she said, "Ted, you can't send this through the mails."

"Send what?" I said. "The circular? Or the book?"

She scowled at me for a few moments. The funny thing was that her scowl was better than her smile. Like a stained bolt of cloth or silk from Forstmann or Cheney. At least you knew the stuff came from a good firm.

"Well," Maud said finally, "I see your point. There's nothing illegal about the circular. It's what the circular promises that will get you into trouble."

"One thing at a time," I said. "Let's stick to the circular first. If we send out a mailing to the people on the lists we've accumulated through our Twentieth Century Classics ads, will we get a response?"

"Of course," Maud Eitner said. "What I'm afraid of is that you'll also get arrested."

"One thing I learned on Seventh Avenue," I said. "Only dopes get arrested for sending things through the mails."

26

" You've Got Yourself
One with a Whistle"

Two months later we sent out the first mailing. By "we" I don't mean Lindbergh and the *Spirit of St. Louis*. I mean me and Maud.

She was excited and impatient. She wanted to get started. So did I, but I wanted to get the trouble out of town first. By sitting on her, I managed to hold off until two things happened. Or rather coincided. Ralph Mattlin went out on his first West Coast swing: Los Angeles, San Francisco, Portland, Seattle. And Gene Merritt took his parents on their annual visit to Miami. The next morning the circulars were in the mail. Before Merritt's family's sunburn started turning to tan, the returns started coming in.

"It looks as though we're going to need a third Ping-Pong table," Maud said on the morning when the returns from our *How to Perform the Sexual Act* circular filled half a mailbag more than the returns from our latest Twentieth Century Classics ad in the Montreal *Star*.

"Get the kids started on the sorting," I said. "I'm going over to the printer to have a look at the proof on the follow-up letter."

When I got back Maud said, "Guess who called?"

256

I didn't have to guess. I'd been expecting the call for almost a week.

"How did he sound?" I said.

"Like Nanook of the North the day he learned somebody had stolen his earmuffs," Maud said. "It's only when he's working that Ralph Mattlin gets excited. When he's angry he's cold."

Let him freeze. I was on my way.

"How did he find out?"

"One of the clerks in Hazen's bookstore out in Portland," Maud said. "He'd answered one of our first ads on the Twentieth Century Classics Series just to see what it was going to be like. So naturally he was on the list that the sex circular went out to. Mattlin finished in San Francisco yesterday, and he took the sleeper up to Portland. Hazen's was his first stop because it's the biggest bookstore in town. When he walked in the head buyer called over this clerk, and he showed the circular to Mattlin. They either kidded him about it or maybe they said they were surprised a dignified firm like Mattlin & Merritt would get involved in this sort of thing. It was hard for me to tell which because it was obvious Mattlin's main worry was not to look like a fool in front of a customer. I mean finding out by accident on the West Coast about something that his own firm was doing back in New York."

When I felt he was ready to handle it, he was going to find out a lot more.

"He ask any questions?" I said.

"Only one," Maud said.

"Was I the big brain behind it?"

"No," Maud said. "He seemed to take it for granted it was you who had cooked it up. The question he asked, he wanted to know if Gene Merritt knew about it. Don't you think that's funny?"

Not if my guess about their relationship was correct.

"I've heard better stuff on the Jack Benny show," I said. "Does Mattlin want me to call him back?"

"You can't," Maud said. She looked at her wrist watch. "He's in the air right now."

"I hope he's wearing a parachute," I said.

"He's wearing a TWA ticket," Maud said. "He canceled Seattle to fly home at once. He said he'd be getting in at nine-thirty, and he wants us to meet him at his house."

When we got there Jeremy opened the door. "Mrs. Mattlin is in the drawing room," he said.

As we followed the butler, Maud spoke to me out of the corner of her mouth. "Milton Merkin is obviously still on the job," she said. "If the room with the Grubensteller portrait is now called the drawing room."

We followed Jeremy. In the doorway to the drawing room he said, "Miss Eitner and Mr. Leff, madam."

"Darlings!"

Benita sent the word out from the couch near the fireplace like a greyhound going after the mechanical rabbit. She tried to get up, but she couldn't seem to make it. I was not surprised. Even allowing for the fact that a hostess gown doesn't exactly cling like a knockwurst casing, since I'd seen her last, Benita Mattlin seemed to have caught up with the general outlines of Kate Smith.

"Darling yourself," Maud said. She walked over and dipped down. She gave the new fatso one of those kisses women give each other so it won't spoil their make-up. In the air, about two inches north of the cheekbone. "You've put on weight," Maud said.

"If I haven't," Benita said, "I'm going to have twins."

Twins? She looked like a case for Dr. Dafoe.

"Never mind how many you're cooking," I said. "You look great, Benita."

"Jeremy," she said, "I think we must provide these two charming fibbers with something to drink."

"Of course, madam," Jeremy said.

"Ralphie called from the airport just a few minutes ago," Benita said. "His plane was late. He'll be here as quickly as a taxi can bring him. What will you have?"

"If I ask for Scotch," Maud said, "I suppose you'll think I'm a boor."

"Darling," Benita said. It suddenly occurred to me that she or Milton Merkin had taken the *r* out of the word. "Why should I think that?"

"All this chintz," Maud said. "It's practically ordering me to say I want some elderberry wine."

Benita made her squealing noise again. I wondered if Milton Merkin, when he gave the sound to her, remembered to ask Claudette Colbert's permission.

"Maud, you thing, you," she said. "I'm glad to see you haven't lost your sense of humor. Jeremy, do we have any elderberry wine?"

"No, madam," he said. "But I could call the liquor store and find out?"

"Don't bother," Maud said. "Scotch will do."

"Jeremy, would you?" Benita said.

"Yes, madam," he said, and went out.

"I wish I could tell you how nice it is to have both of you here," Benita said, and then she seemed to stagger and say something that sounded like "Oy!"

Maud stepped to her side and said, "What's the matter?"

"I've been having these pains for a couple of hours," Benita said. "I wonder if—?"

"Stop wondering and give me the doctor's number," Maud said. "Ted, you run and get a cab while I call him."

I snagged a cab in front of the movie house and told the driver he was about to push through the revolving door that led into every Young Married movie from Harold Lloyd to Jimmy Stewart.

"Don't tell Equity," he said. "I'm not a member. But this is a scene I've been reading about in the papers for years. I've never had a chance to play it before. Hop in."

By the time we got back to the Mattlin house, Maud and Jeremy were helping Benita down the steps. I was certainly glad Milton Merkin was not with us. All the way up to Doctors Hospital his student, who had learned to say "matoor," kept saying, "Can't this oy son of a bitch oy drive any oy faster oy for God's sakes oy the bastard?"

"By the way," I said to Maud after we'd dumped Benita into the arms of a nurse and an intern and we were sitting in the waiting room on the maternity floor, "I've been thinking about our meeting with Mattlin."

"So have I," Maud said, "but we'd better stop. Here he comes now. Ralph, how are you?"

I turned. Mattlin had just exploded out of the elevator. He came loping toward us like Groucho Marx on the prowl after Margaret Dumont. The knot of his tie was up under the wing of his collar. His jacket was unbuttoned and flopping out behind him. His hair looked as though someone had held his head in front of an electric fan. His eyes could have been borrowed from Fay Wray at the moment when King Kong was balancing her at the top of the Empire State Building. And he had a beard stubble that must have been painted on with Waterman's blue-black. Whoever had done it, he had done it well. Like Floyd Collins coming out of that Kentucky cave, Ralph Mattlin didn't look. He was Expectant Father from the two cigarettes he had going to the panted "How is she?"

"According to Dr. Blake," Maud said, "she's doing very well."

"Who is Dr. Blake?" Mattlin said.

"The obstetrician," Maud said. "While Ted was out getting the taxi, Jeremy called Dr. Harris. He was out, but Dr. Blake was covering for him. He was waiting for us here at the hospital when we arrived. Here he is now. Dr. Blake, this is Mr. Mattlin."

The doctor came up and shook hands. "She's doing fine, Mr. Mattlin," he said. "She's in labor, and everything is going according to schedule."

I wondered who made up these schedules.

"Is there anything I can do?" Mattlin said.

"Yes," Dr. Blake said. "Please don't burn down the hospital. You really should wait until you finish those two cigarettes before you light a third."

"I'm sorry," Mattlin said. He stamped out the two cigarettes he'd come in with, and he put the end of the new one to the

260

match Maud had lighted. "Thanks, Maud," he said. "How long do you think it will be, Doctor?"

"My guess is it won't take too long," Dr. Blake said. "All my patients should be built like your wife. Mrs. Mattlin has a beautiful pelvis. There will be no trouble, I assure you." He turned to Maud. "Keep him occupied," Dr. Blake said. "I'll check back as soon as I have news."

He went out. Mattlin turned to me and Maud. "First of all," he said, "I want to thank you both for getting Benita up here. Jeremy and Lydia had instructions to do it if she went into labor while I was away, but I'm sure she felt better about coming with you."

"Nothing at all," Maud said. "Glad to be of help."

"Same here," I said.

Like a carpenter brushing the shavings off his workbench so he could get on to the next phase of his job, Mattlin pulled from his pocket a copy of the circular Maud and I had sent out. "Now, Ted," he said. "I'd like to know what the hell you've been doing while Gene and I have been away?"

Why, Ralphie, I've been laying the foundation for one of those scenes where Edward Arnold, who came into the plot as a poor boy, now sits there in a glass office, thumbs hooked into the armholes of his hand-stitched vest, temples streaked with gray, staring out on the rows of belching smokestacks under the great big sign that says: THEODORE LEFF ENTERPRISES.

"Nothing much," I said. "Just trying to make some money for the firm of Mattlin & Merritt."

"With this?" Mattlin said. He read from the circular: " 'Nobody But Your Sexual Partner Will Ever Know You Have Purchased a Book That Contains One Hundred and Ninety-six Photographs of Different Coital Positions.' "

"I don't think it's as good a come-on as 'You Never Heard of Us, But We Want Three Minutes of Your Time,' " I said. "On the other hand, in this morning's mail this circular pulled in half a sack more coupons than our latest Twentieth Century Classics ad in the Montreal *Star*."

Mattlin stopped lighting a fresh cigarette, as though he had struck the match in a theater and an usher had tapped him on the shoulder. The blue eyes held mine for a moment, then rolled toward Maud. "Is he kidding?" Mattlin said.

Maud Eitner gave him the a, b, c look. "I went out and bought a third Ping-Pong table this morning," she said.

Mattlin put the flame to the cigarette, and he started pacing. Halfway during his third trip between the rubber plant and the magazine table, he stopped.

"But what do we do with these returns?" he said. "You can't sell a book with photographs of men and women actually engaged in sexual intercourse. Even if such a book existed, you couldn't send it through the mails. Look what the post office tried to do only a couple of years ago to that magazine, the one with all those men's clothing ads. *Esquire.* And all they were doing were cartoons of naked girls by a man named E. Simms Campbell."

"We've been mailing back a letter," I said. "Everybody who answered the circular and sent in their money, Maud and I we've been sending them a copy of this thing."

I pulled the sheet from my pocket and handed it over.

" 'Dear Customer,' " Mattlin read aloud. " 'Thank you for your order of blank copies of *How to Perform the Sexual Act: a Happier Sex Life through Photography.* Even though we are bending all our efforts to rush production on this historic contribution toward sexual freedom, we have encountered certain delays that we now see were inevitable. The doctors who are preparing the text are all European and Asian, with a sense of thoroughness and dedication somewhat different from ours, and we must wait on their approval of each paragraph, in many instances of each sentence. More important, the photographs, which are the heart of this revolutionary manual of the physical relationship between the human male and the human female, require the sort of attention hitherto lavished only on the camera work devoted to movie stars. The right man and the right woman must be found for each of the 196 coital positions.

" 'At this writing, therefore, we cannot say with any degree of accuracy when *How to Perform the Sexual Act: a Happier Sex*

Life through Photography will be ready for mailing. When it is, the book will be sent to you at once in a plain wrapper. Until your copy is ready, which may be a matter of months, perhaps years, we thought you might be interested in two volumes from our Twentieth Century Classics Series: Krafft-Ebing's *Psychopathia Sexualis* and *Man and Woman* by Havelock Ellis.

" 'You will note that the combined price of these two world-famous publications comes to the same price we will be charging for *How to Perform the Sexual Act: a Happier Sex Life through Photography*. We are taking the liberty of sending these two books to you and will consider the money you sent for a copy of *How to Perform the Sexual Act: a Happier Sex Life through Photography* as full payment for them. When *How to Perform the Sexual Act: a Happier Sex Life through Photography* is ready, we will send and bill you for your copy. If you do not want the Krafft-Ebing and the Havelock Ellis, please return them at once and let us know whether you want us to return to you the money you sent for *How to Perform the Sexual Act: a Happier Sex Life through Photography* or whether you want us to hold it until *How to Perform the Sexual Act: a Happier Sex Life through Photography* is finally ready for distribution to our subscribers.

" 'Thanking you for your interest in this frontier-smashing approach to the age-long problem of man's relationship to woman and vice versa, we beg to remain.' " Mattlin looked up and said, "Jee-zuzz Kee-rist!"

"From Him," Maud said, "we didn't get a coupon."

She swung a lighted match toward Mattlin's fresh cigarette. He sucked in smoke and blew it out around, "Okay, you two. Give me some figures. I know damn well you've got them. Nobody could have thought up a con game like this without breaking it down to statistics."

Maud laughed. "Speak up, Ted," she said.

"Out of every thousand coupons we've received," I said. "That's coupons with checks or money orders attached, you understand. Out of every thousand coupons plus money received, then, we got the following answers to this letter you just read." I pulled from my pocket the card on which Maud had jotted down the figures. "Total silence: nine hundred and seventy-four. Please send me my money back: twenty-six." I looked up. "Do you get the picture?"

"Clearly," Ralph Mattlin said. "We've always known that sex is the single greatest motivating factor in the sale of books. I never before realized how greatest. If we dared publish it, you know what would be the biggest best seller of all time? No matter what the book contained? Just from the title?"

"What?" Maud said.

"Asterisking for Pleasure," Ralph Mattlin said.

"My God," Maud said. She turned to me like Mr. Paul Muni playing Zola in the film of the same name, turning to the boys to whom he was addressing *J'Accuse!* "Why didn't you think of that?"

Why didn't the guy who invented the wheel think of the internal combustion engine?

"I did," I said. "But I was on Seventh Avenue at the time, and up there that's not a need-filler."

"Now look," Mattlin said. "Set me straight. You are saying, if I understand you correctly, that as a result of this mailing you've sold nine hundred and seventy-four out of a thousand copies of our Twentieth Century Classics editions of Krafft-Ebing and Havelock Ellis?"

"That is correct," I said. "The other twenty-six, we just sent them back their checks and money orders."

The fact that this broke my heart, this I left out.

"Is that all you had in mind?" Mattlin said.

It was like that moment in his office when the idea for the Twentieth Century Classics got through to his engine room and the motor started turning over. The cigarettes he carried loose in his side coat pocket, the matches Maud carried to keep him going, both were suddenly in action. Not to mention the carpet between the rubber plant and the card table. It started getting a new workout.

"I've come up with one hell of a gimmick," I said. "Isn't that enough?"

"Yes, if all you're interested in is gimmicks," Ralph Mattlin said. "I don't know what you've got in mind. Tell me your thinking, Ted."

"I'm new on Fourth Avenue," I said. "So everything I run into on this street seems fresh to me. And then when I think about it for a while it's not fresh at all. It's just done with kissing."

"With what?" Mattlin said.

"When I was a kid in high school," I said, "there were these guys who came around and sold dirty books for a nickel and a dime."

"What kind of dirty books?" Mattlin said.

"They'd take a well-known comic strip," I said. *"Tillie the Toiler. Bringing Up Father. The Gumps. Happy Hooligan. The Katzenjammer Kids. Winnie Winkle. Harold Teen.* Stuff like that. And they'd get somebody who could draw to make up a few strips. They'd imitate the characters exactly as they appeared in the newspapers, with two exceptions. Jiggs and Maggie, for instance. Instead of being seen in their dining room, arguing about the corned beef and cabbage, they would appear stark naked, banging away like jack rabbits, and in the balloons over their heads, using language that would make the author of *Mott Haven 2* blush. For this, as I said, we kids paid a nickel or a dime. When I got out of high school and I started going to Broadway shows, I made an interesting discovery. A lot of the jokes I heard on the stage were exactly the same as the jokes I used to read in *Maggie and Jiggs.* With one exception."

"What was that?" Mattlin said.

"In *Maggie and Jiggs* it was crude and raw," I said. "The talk was about screwing, and they called it screwing. In the theater it was the same joke, but they changed it just a little so the talk was about kissing."

"What's that got to do with Fourth Avenue?" Mattlin said.

"When I was a kid, working on Seventh Avenue," I said, "I used to think about people who publish books, if I thought about them at all, I used to think about them the way I used to think about teachers and professors and rabbis and doctors.

They were making their livings like everybody else, sure, including the butcher and the street cleaner, because everybody has to eat, or so I'm told. But they were earning their three squares in a much more noble way than I was. I was let's say cut from alpaca. They were cut from velvet. I was made from stuff that went for a dime a yard. They started at forty cents and over. Then I came to Fourth Avenue, and I began to take a look at the raw material. A novel you yourself published, for instance. This thing called *Mott Haven 2*."

Mattlin hadn't quite reached the rubber plant, but he came around anyway. "It happens to be a very good novel," he said sharply.

And *Maggie and Jiggs* was a very good comic strip.

"Let's say it is," I said. "That's not the point."

"What is the point?" Mattlin said. That look was beginning to come at me out of those eyes.

"The point is this," I said. "I never realized things like *Mott Haven 2* could be printed in hard-cover books and sold in stores along with Shakespeare and the Bible and Dickens."

"Forget Dickens," Mattlin said. "Keep going."

"I can't skip Dickens," I said. "He was one of the writers we read in school. That's why, years later, when I ran into this thing *Mott Haven 2,* a hard-cover book, just like the Dickens books we had in school, and I saw it sold in respectable stores like R. H. Macy and Gimbels and what's that outfit, yes, Brentano's, it made me think. And when I start thinking I can't stop. So I did a little investigating. You know what I found out?"

"Of course not," Mattlin said. "If I did, would I be asking you to tell me?"

"I found that everybody on Fourth Avenue is peddling *Maggie and Jiggs,*" I said. "Under different names, of course. They call them *Sane Guides to the Physical Side of Marriage.* Or *The Physiology and Technique of the Marital Act.* Or some sort of crap like that. But when you look through these books you find that's what it really is. *Maggie and Jiggs,* but with kisses. That's my thinking," I said. "No, correction. That's where my thinking started."

"So you came up with this idea," Mattlin said, tapping the sheet of paper I'd given him. "A con game to tap the nation's absorption with sex."

"No," I said. "A sales angle to sell one kind of book we've included in the Twentieth Century Classics Series. People who answer circulars like the one I wrote for *How to Perform the Sexual Act: a Happier Sex Life through Photography,* people like that when they get our follow-up letter saying the book is not yet ready, people like that are not going to complain to other people that they were screwed. They will take their licking in the form of two substitute books, the Krafft-Ebing and the Havelock Ellis, and they will shut up about it because if they complain, if they go to the district attorney, let's say, they'll merely be advertising the fact that they sent away for a book of dirty pictures."

"Which doesn't exist," Mattlin said.

"Of course not," I said.

"I take it, then," Mattlin said, "that you never had any intention of producing such a book?"

"I want to make money," I said. "I don't want to get arrested."

Mattlin suddenly laughed and stabbed his cigarette into the rubber plant. That's the Germans for you. Always making holes in defenseless victims.

"Ted," he said, "I think you're one of the brightest guys I've ever met, but I think you've missed the main point of this thing."

"What's that?" I said.

"Making money and not getting arrested are not mutually exclusive," Mattlin said. "I see a way how we can carry this thing one step further." He was making the turn at the magazine table when Dr. Blake came into the waiting room. Irritably Mattlin said, "Yes?"

"Mr. Mattlin," Dr. Blake said, "you've got yourself one with a whistle."

"What?" Mattlin said.

"I think he means it's a boy," Maud Eitner said.

Mattlin scowled at both of them as though he had never seen

them before, and this time I knew what it was. His mind was working on the idea I'd come up with. His motor was turning over. He couldn't hear any other sound.

"How is Mrs. Mattlin?" I said to the doctor.

That seemed to help. I could see Mattlin starting to come out of it.

"She's fine," Dr. Blake said. "So is the baby. Would you like to see them?"

"What?" Mattlin said. Then he was out of it completely. "Yes, of course," he said. "Could you hold it one moment though, Dr. Harris?"

"I'm Blake," Blake said. "Harris is out of town. I'm covering for him."

"Of course," Mattlin said. "One moment, please." He turned to me. He was smiling. "Ted, you continue to impress me," he said. "I feel I must get Gene and me to do something for you. The firm, I mean. I don't know just what."

I suppose he'd never heard of money.

"I do," I said.

"Name it," Ralph Mattlin said.

"I'd like you to meet a friend of mine," I said.

27

" Never Trust a Man Who Wears an Astrakhan Collar"

At that time Byram Noonan was not exactly a friend of mine. On the other hand, he wasn't exactly an enemy, either.

I had seen him only twice in my life. First, on the day Schmeichel & Zetzer took the bath and my career as a Seventh Avenue shipping clerk ended. Second, almost seven years later, on the day I was trying to collect for $3,600 worth of taffetas from a Grand Concourse crook and Byram sneaked the money out from under the nose of my own lawyer.

There are people who will say that these two contacts do not add up to enough to form a basis for either friendship or hatred. Especially since neither of us said a word to each other on both occasions. Those people will never make it on Fourth Avenue. It's a place that runs on instant friendship.

If your name is Oliver—which is already a mistake—and you meet a guy named Jasper—which on Fourth Avenue could happen—and ten minutes later you're not calling each other Ollie and Jazz, one of you should switch at once from publishing books to manufacturing mandolin picks. The reason for this is not that Fourth Avenue is more relaxed and unbuttoned than, say, Wall Street or the Bourse. The reason is that what Fourth Avenue deals in basically is ideas. And it's easier to steal an idea faster from a guy you call Bob than from someone you're still addressing as Mr. Fenstermacher.

Mattlin and I were Ted and Ralph to each other before the ink dried on my first week's Mattlin & Merritt salary check. By the time I saw the returns coming in on the first *How to Perform the Sexual Act* mailing, I knew the time had come for me to get on a first-name basis with a good lawyer, and I knew only one good one. I looked him up in the phone book and sent him a note.

The paper I chose was the Mattlin & Merritt, Inc., letterhead. For getting you through the fence of the average business office I can think of only one that might be more effective, and that one you'd have to aim at a special target: a sheet of stationery from the private papal apartments in the Vatican addressed to the cardinal of the Archdiocese of New York.

Under the Mattlin & Merritt firm name there were only two words: "Book Publishers." And under those two words there was a small steel engraving of that face from another century that I had first seen on the wall of the Bookkeeping Department: William Makepeace Thackeray. There was something impressive about it. Like the picture of the Smith Brothers on the cough drop box. Those two stern old men with their long beards, you felt you had to go out and get yourself a throat tickle just so they would stop frowning on you. I didn't frown at Byram Noonan. I borrowed two words from Thackeray and put them at the end of the single sentence that said I wanted to see Mr. Noonan on a matter of the "utmost urgency." I saw him seventy-two hours after I thumbed George Washington's profile to the envelope.

"You look familiar," Noonan said to me across his desk.

I told him why.

"Schmeichel & Zetzer," he said, squinting up at the ceiling, "Schmeichel & Zetzer. Yes. Remember them now. Went to prison. Sent false financial statement through mails. Damn fools." Noonan brought his eyes down from the ceiling. I noticed his eyes had no wrinkles around them. His large, handsome face looked brand-new. Like a pair of shoes when the

270

clerk first pulls them out of the tissue paper in the cardboard box. The only creases on Byram Noonan were in his pants. He said, "Looks like you've come long way since old Schmeichel days."

I thought he had a stammer. I didn't learn until later that it was the way he talked. Like a nonstop telegram.

"Four blocks," I said. "Seventh Avenue to Fourth."

"Like the change?" Noonan said.

"Not bad," I said. "It could be better. That's why I'm here. I need help."

"Explain," he said.

After I finished explaining, Byram Noonan said, "Help will be granted."

"Does that mean you're taking me on as a client?" I said.

"Members of bar grant help only to clients," he said.

"I'm not exactly loaded at the moment," I said. "But I'm not eating out of the barrels, either. If you'll send me a bill for a reasonable retainer I'll send you my check."

"No retainer necessary," Noonan said. "Looks like promising situation. We'll settle lawyer's remuneration after flow of money starts our direction. Call my secretary whenever you want appointment set up."

I called her the morning after Sacheverell Mattlin was born. A week later Ralph Mattlin and I showed up in Byram Noonan's office at 120 Broadway.

"Mr. Noonan had to go upstairs to meet someone in the club," the girl at the switchboard said. "He asked me to send you up when you arrived."

"What club?" I said.

"I know it," Ralph Mattlin said. "Come on, Ted."

Following him back out to the elevator, I had a funny little feeling. A warning, sort of. All Mattlin had said was he knew the club, but it seemed more important than that. As though the balance of power had shifted under the surface. I don't like people knowing things I don't know. We got back into the elevator.

"Club, please," Mattlin said to the operator.

"You seem to know this building," I said.

"My father's attorneys used to be here at One Twenty," Mattlin said. "Probably still are. Toward the end, when he was sick, I used to come down now and then to attend meetings for him. Sometimes his attorneys would take me upstairs to lunch. The food is quite good. Here we are."

What we were in, the moment we stepped out of the elevator, looked like a great big glass bubble. We were surrounded by the East River, New York Bay and the Hudson. All three of them seemed to be washing up and around our shoes. It made me feel a little seasick.

Under the glass bubble there were a lot of tables covered with starched white tablecloths. Around the tables sat a couple of hundred men. They came in all shapes and sizes, and they were wearing different-colored suits and shirts and ties. The same sort of variety I had noticed in the lobby outside the dining room of the Panama Club, except that these men all looked alike in a different way. These men all looked like Byram Noonan. A heavy-set guy came over and bowed. He had one of those faces you see on the con who is leading the prison break at Warner Brothers.

"May I help you, sir?" he said.

The feeling that I'd lost the edge grew a little deeper. He'd said it to Ralph Mattlin, not to me.

"Mr. Noonan?" Mattlin said.

"Yes sir," the headwaiter said. "This way, please."

He marched off into the tables like those guys on horseback charging the enemy guns in Tennyson's poem. Mattlin and I followed. No. Mattlin followed before I could break away from the barrier. So I had to follow Mattlin. The irritation that had started in the elevator grew a little bigger. What the hell was going on here? Had I brought Mattlin down to see Byram Noonan? Or had Mattlin brought me down to see Noonan?

The Statue of Liberty seemed to be standing right under my nose. It was pointing toward the left. I followed her torch with my eyes. There was Byram Noonan, standing near a table, talking to a small man with a neat little potbelly. Even at that distance his eyes made an impression on me. They seemed to be the color of chicken livers before they're cooked. Byram Noonan saw me. He said something fast to the little guy, who nodded, tapped Byram's elbow and walked away. There was something funny about the way he walked. As though he was rocking himself forward. Then I saw his shoes. They had elevator heels.

"Ted," Byram said.

We shook hands.

"This is Ralph Mattlin," I said.

They shook hands.

"Gentlemen," the headwaiter said. He helped Ralph Mattlin with his chair. Me, I had to fend for myself. I made a note of that. "Would you gentlemen care for a drink?"

"Not for me, thank you," Mattlin said.

"Ted?" Byram said.

"You having one?" I said.

"I never drink until evening," Byram said. "But you go ahead if you want to."

"Not on your life," I said. "This is a business conference. I do like my lawyer does."

Noonan said, "Just the menus, then, Oliver."

The headwaiter bowed and went away.

"You're kidding," I said.

"About what?" Byram said.

"Nobody with a face like that is named Oliver."

"I don't know what he was christened," Noonan said. "But that's the name he travels under in this place. Is anything wrong?" This last question was addressed to Mattlin.

"Sorry," he said. "I didn't mean to stare, but weren't you at Pierson in '23?"

"No," Byram said. "Sterling."

"Of course," Mattlin said. "It was Skidder Burke who was at Pierson." Mattlin reached his hand across the table. "I was there the day you ran thirty-seven yards against the Harvards. I never got a chance to give you my congratulations."

Byram Noonan smiled. He took Mattlin's hand. "Nice to get

them now, fourteen years later," Noonan said. "Were you '23?"

"No, '24," Mattlin said. "But I remember every one of those three teams you played on."

They beamed at each other like a couple of yentas in Klein's who had met in a battle over dollar-ninety-eight corselets and had just established that they used to live on the same block in the Bronx when they were kids and two of their grandchildren had the same names.

"By the way," Byram said, "is that a Tweak Sothill?"

Mattlin looked down at the front of his jacket. "Yes," he said. He looked more closely at Noonan's jacket. "Yours too?"

"Yes," Byram said. "I had a sports jacket made in that same weave, but brown. By the way, I had the annual letter the other day. Sothill's too old, apparently, to make the trip any more. So it's young Mr. Tweak who will be pleased to see us again in the usual suite at the Biltmore."

"I usually do," Byram said. "You going?"

"I don't know," Mattlin said. "Every year when I got the letter I'd mark a date on my calendar to go over. But I'm a married man now."

"Congratulations," Noonan said.

"Thank you," Mattlin said. "And I became a father a few days ago."

"Congratulations again," Noonan said. "Boy?"

"Yes," Mattlin said. "And thanks again. What I meant is that as a married man I think maybe I ought to go with my wife this time. She might not like a pattern I chose, or a weave, or even the cut I order."

"It's a problem I don't have yet," Byram said. "Or Ted, either."

I had a bigger one. Whose side was this Irish left tackle going to be on? Mine or his new-found buddy from Old Eli?

"Oh, thanks, Oliver," Byram said. The headwaiter had arrived with the menus. He handed them around like a guy with a green Celluloid eyeshade dealing blackjack.

"What's today?" Byram said.

"Thursday, sir."

274

"In that case it's corned beef hash, isn't it?" Byram said. "Which I recommend heartily. Best corned beef hash in town we think, don't we, Oliver?"

"Yes sir, Mr. Noonan," the headwaiter said. "It's very good, sir."

"I have never had a bum steer from a fellow alumnus," Mattlin said. "Corned beef hash it is."

"Two corned beef hash," the headwaiter said. He wrote it down. He bowed over me. "And you, sir?"

"Just go out into the kitchen and rummage around," I said. "See if you can find me a slightly toasted lawyer with mushroom sauce who didn't go to Yale and gets his clothes off the rack at Rogers Peet."

Noonan laughed. So naturally his fellow Yalie laughed too. "You're quite right, Ted," Byram said. "If you'll order the corned beef hash I'll get right down to business."

"Promise?" I said.

"Promise," Byram said.

"Corned beef hash," I said.

The headwaiter bowed and went away.

"It's not very difficult," Noonan said. "Or very complex. Ted has kept me abreast of his recent activities. So I'm fully aware of the Twentieth Century Classics Series and this new *How to Perform the Sexual Act* venture, as well as Ted's role in both of them. I gather that you and Ted work very well together."

"That's putting it with what you lawyers call an excess of caution," Mattlin said. "We work beautifully together. Is that a fair statement of the case, Ted?"

"Yes," I said. "Aside from the fact that your tone of voice makes it sound like a grand jury handing down an indictment."

Mattlin laughed. The guy was positively light-headed. Why not? Look at the week he'd had. I gave him a new moneymaker. His wife gave him a new son. And for dessert he goes ahead and meets an old Yalie.

"That's not my intention," Mattlin said. "What I mean is that Ted and I seem to complement each other. That's complement with an *e,* not an *i.*"

275

"I studied English usage under Sterling's great Soapy Sunder-strum," Byram Noonan said. "I know the difference between complement and compliment."

"Good old Soapy," Mattlin said. "Remember how he used to take out his glass eye and polish it on his sleeve like an apple?"

"Sure do," Noonan said. "It used to drive Billy Phelps crazy. Phelps used to say to his class how can a man compete with that? A man who has nothing to polish but his pince-nez and his prose?"

"Couldn't we climb out of this class reunion for a while?" I said.

"Sorry," Mattlin said. "Anyway, as I'm sure Ted told you, while the Twentieth Century Classics Series was his idea, the minute he came up with it Gene Merritt and I started coming up with refinements. The same thing with Ted's sex book. He planned it as a come-on, a way to hook the pornography market and make them take substitute books from our Twentieth Century Classics Series. Did Ted tell you my refinement?"

"Did you?" Noonan said to me.

"There hasn't been time," I said. "He told it to me only this morning."

"I wanted to check out a few things first," Mattlin said. "To make sure it's practical. Well, it's not only practical, it's hilarious. You've read Ted's circular? The first mailing?"

"With interest," Noonan said.

"It promises the subscriber a book containing one hundred and ninety-six pictures of men and women in the act of copulation," Mattlin said. "As a lawyer, Mr. Noonan, do you think such a book could be sent through the United States mails?"

"No," Noonan said. "Do you?"

"No," Mattlin said. "And neither did Ted when he wrote the circular. All he had in mind—"

"We know what Ted had in mind," Noonan said. "Move on, Mr. Mattlin, to what you have in mind. Here comes the corned beef hash."

The waiter set down the plates.

"My mind jumped to the next step," Mattlin said. "Ted's idea for selling copies of our Twentieth Century Classics Krafft-Ebing and Havelock Ellis was ingenious. But, I asked myself, these people who sent in their money, they really wanted that book of pictures. So why not, after we sell them Havelock Ellis and the Krafft-Ebing, why not make an additional sale? Why not sell them a book on the technique of sexual intercourse?"

"We all agreed moment ago couldn't send book like that through mails," Noonan said. "How's the hash?"

"Top notch," Mattlin said. "We agreed we couldn't send through the mails a book of pictures of men and women actually screwing. But what's to prevent us from sending a book like Krafft-Ebing or Havelock Ellis?"

"How much like?" Byram Noonan said.

"A little more than like," Ralph Mattlin said. "I went over to see Dr. Siegfried Krohn at New York Hospital. He's been lecturing on the subject for years. I asked if he would let us bring out a collection of his lectures illustrated with photographs of men and women, fully clothed, demonstrating his positions more or less the way books on calisthenics demonstrate various things like push-ups and knee bends. Dr. Krohn thought it was a great idea and said he'd do it. So there you are. Again, Ted has come up with a great idea. And again, I've come up with a topper. That's what I mean when I say we're a very good team I believe."

"So do I," Byram Noonan said. "Which is why I asked you to lunch today. Ted and you are a team, but Ted is not getting a teammate's share of the profits. He's going have great many more ideas. I want see to it Ted gets some more out of them than he's got out of these first two. What we have in mind, Mr. Mattlin, is a profit-sharing arrangement."

Mattlin laughed. "Isn't that odd?" he said. "That's exactly what I've had in mind for some time. My partner, Gene Merritt too. We talked about it just before I went off on my Western swing. In fact, last week in San Francisco I'd worked out some figures which I planned to show Ted when I got back, but when I got back my wife was in labor, so I forgot."

The headwaiter appeared at the table with a telephone.

"Excuse me, Mr. Noonan," he said. "Is there a Mr. Mattlin lunching with you?"

"Yes," Mattlin said.

"Call for you, sir." The headwaiter handed the phone to Mattlin, dipped down, and sank the plug into a jack in the floor under the table.

"Hello?" Mattlin said. "Yes, Maud? Oh, Christ." He looked at his wrist watch. "All right, Maud. I'll grab a cab and go right to the hospital." Mattlin hung up.

"Anything wrong?" Byram Noonan said.

"Not really," Mattlin said. "But the rabbi who is supposed to perform the circumcision this afternoon at four just called to say he'd forgotten he has a tax audit at four on his 1935 return, so he's going to have to do it at two." Mattlin looked at his watch again. "I can just make it," he said. He stood up. "If you'll excuse me," he said, "I'll run. Thanks for the lunch, and don't worry about the profit-sharing arrangement. You work out whatever you and Ted think is equitable, and I'm sure it will be all right with Gene Merritt and myself."

As Noonan and I watched him cut across the bubble-top room toward the elevator, I started working on the answer to the question I knew Byram was going to ask. He asked it.

"Tell me something," Noonan said. "You think he really had been planning give you a profit-sharing deal? Or did he just make it up right here at the table?"

"What do you think?" I said.

Byram Noonan chased the last scrap of corned beef hash across his plate, nailed it near the blue "120" printed on the lip of the china, lifted the fork to his mouth and chewed for a few moments. The way he did it, with all his jaw muscles going, you would have thought he was giving a going over to a couple of inches of dried ptarmigan.

"I think we took him by surprise," Byram said finally. "But not all Yale men are fools. I think he realized he had to cut you in, so why do it with reluctance? As though forced to wall? Have to shell out the cut anyway. Why not at same time get credit for generosity? Seems to me that's how smart man would work it. Mattlin struck me as being pretty smart."

"That's how I figured it too," I said. "But he did it so smoothly I thought he might be fooling you. All the way back in the Schmeichel & Zetzer days I knew I'd run into a smart lawyer. I'm glad to learn today that I've got that smart lawyer working on my side."

Somebody tapped me on the shoulder. I turned. It was the little guy with the potbelly and the chicken-liver eyes. He must have finished his lunch. He was buttoning himself into a beautiful cashmere coat with a heavy black fur collar.

"Young man," he said. "Pardon me for butting in, but I came over to say goodbye to Byram and I couldn't help overhearing your remark. I don't know what your side is, but you not only have a smart lawyer working on it, you have the smartest lawyer in town working on it."

Byram stood up. There was just enough extra speed in the way he did it to give me a picture. "Hubert," he said. "This is a new client of mine, Ted Leff. Ted, this is Hubert Sissenwein."

I stood up and took Mr. Sissenwein's hand. It was like picking up a raw fillet of flounder. "I'm very pleased to meet you," I said.

I wasn't kidding. Wouldn't you be pleased to meet the Federal Reserve Bank?

"The reason I came over," Mr. Sissenwein said. "Wasn't that Ralph Mattlin who was just sitting here with you?"

"Yes," Byram Noonan said. "He and Ted are in business together."

"Indeed." I gave Mr. Sissenwein a sharp look. He didn't have the sort of kisser out of which you expected words like "indeed" to come. "I used to know Mattlin's father," Mr. Sissenwein said. "A fine old gentleman. He was in optical goods. Well, I must go. Nice to have met you, Mr. Neff."

"No," I said. "Leff."

"Sorry," Mr. Sissenwein said. "Nice to have met you, Mr. Leff. Always do what Byram says, and you'll spend your declining years battling the Internal Revenue Service. Byram, I'm going to Palm Beach on Saturday, so you'd better get those New York Central papers to me by tomorrow at the latest."

"They're on your desk right now," Byram Noonan said. "I

279

sent them over this morning with my secretary, and she showed your girl exactly where you're to sign."

"You see?" Mr. Sissenwein said to me. He smiled, tapped my shoulder again and waved as he headed toward the elevators. Byram and I sat down.

"Is that *the* Hubert Sissenwein?" I said.

"There's only one," Byram said.

"And you represent him?" I said.

"Hard to say," Byram said. "He's in so many things, and he's got so many people working for him, that you never really know. Put it this way. I represent him on certain projects. Maybe I represent him on more things than other lawyers do. Why do you look like that?"

"Like what?" I said.

"Like you're trying to remember something."

"I've remembered it," I said.

"Remembered what?" Byram said.

"Something my father told me when I was a kid," I said.

"What was that?" Byram said.

"Never trust a man who wears an astrakhan collar," I said.

28

" You Know Who
Your Doorman
Just Kicked Out?"

I'm not so sure that my father was right. After all, Enrico Caruso wore an astrakhan collar. So did Woodrow Wilson and Douglas Fairbanks. Not to mention George V and Poincaré. I've seen the pictures. So maybe my father was being unfair.

This was one thing you could never be to Hubert Sissenwein. Being unfair to Hubert Sissenwein is like being charitable to the Ford Foundation. It wouldn't show. I once sat next to one of his wives at a dinner party given by my wife Evie's mother. That day the papers had been full of stories about a ten-million-dollar hospital Hubert had donated to the State of Israel as a Chanukah present.

"He seems to be mellowing," I said.

The ex-wife gave me the sort of look I imagine the casting director at Metro gave John Gilbert after talkies arrived and for the first time they heard his squeaky voice coming in off a sound track. "No, dear," the ex-Mrs. Sissenwein said. "He's not mellowing. He's rottening."

Hubie's record during the next few years, which happened to be the time when our paths crossed, would seem to indicate that his ex-wife was right.

"Thing to remember about Hubert," said Byram Noonan when we started pulling together the Sissenwein package for the surrogate after Hubie died, "is he had a tendency to give manure a bad name."

I wasn't surprised. Hubert Sissenwein was born and raised on Cannon Street. That's practically around the corner from my Old Kentucky Home. Hubie had twenty-two years on me. So a lot of the things he had to live with when he was growing up may have changed by the time I started growing up. But I don't think the age gap made much difference. Until very recently, when the hippies moved in and started calling it the East Village, the Lower East Side remained pretty much unchanged for half a century. Maybe more. Hubie once told me he never saw an automobile until he was nine years old. Well, I saw automobiles from the moment I was able to look out our tenement window. But I remember that the form of transportation we actually used when I was a kid was the horse-drawn trolley car that ran up and down Lewis Street.

I guess it's true that if you change enough things you change the people who use them. To a certain extent, anyway. But I think the change has to be pretty dramatic. A kid who jets to his arithmetic class is going to be a different kind of kid from the one who used to get there on the IRT. But the reason is not the difference between a jet plane and a subway train. The reason is that the kid who gets there by jet will be studying a different kind of math from the kind they taught me in P. S. 188.

In Hubert Sissenwein's day, being born on the Lower East Side was to an American boy what being born at Blenheim Palace was to Winston Churchill. The accident of birth had made them both part of the Establishment.

If you were born on the Lower East Side nobody asked if you had brains. It was assumed you had them. All East Side boys were as smart as seven colleges. If you were born on the Lower East Side, it never occurred to anybody that maybe what you wanted to do with your life was bang a tambourine for the Salvation Army. It was assumed you were driven by fierce ambition to corner the stock market. All East Side boys were fiercely ambitious. If you were born on the Lower East Side and someone learned you wanted to be a watchmaker or a type-writer mechanic, it was taken for granted you were lying about the place of your birth. East Side boys didn't fix watches or repair typewriters. They wrote songs like Irving Berlin, told jokes like Eddie Cantor, sang ballads like Al Jolson and gov-erned states like Al Smith. All East Side boys had talent.

Not any more.

Politicians don't get elected today just because when they address the public it comes out "My goil's name is Goitee Moiphey, and she lives on Toidy-toid Street." Today if you want that seat in Congress you'd better talk the kind of English taxi drivers expect big tips from. And when you do a little democratic outdoor noshing, you'd better do it with the kind of charmingly elegant awkwardness that only a member of Fence or Skull and Bones can bring to the consumption of a knish on a Delancey Street sidewalk. There was a time when Al Smith could put an election in his pocket merely by saying, when asked the name of his alma mater, "F. F. M." The voters would fall off their seats into the aisles. They knew he meant Fulton Fish Market. If he tried it today the voters would send him right back to scaling mackerel.

Which brings us to home base: Al Smith and Hubert Sissen-wein and I were overlapping contemporaries. As a result, while I hope to God I'm not as big a bastard as Hubie was, it wouldn't surprise me to learn that I am. We came out of the same cookie cutter.

There were some differences, of course. But they were minor. My father died in a pants shop on Allen Street. Hubie's father went over the bridge from a necktie factory on East Broadway. My parents were Galitzianers. The Sissenweins were Litvaks. Hubie had two brothers. I was an only child. I made it all the way through high school. Hubie had to quit in his sophomore year. Hubie was sixteen when he went to Seventh Avenue as a shipping clerk. I went at seventeen. Maybe that's why Hubie stayed there a year less than I did. The general opinion, how-ever, is that he left because of Sidonie Shvenger.

283

There was a time in this town when the name Shvenger packed as much weight as Schiff or Warburg or Lewisohn. Not because old Jake Shvenger came from Hamburg or was a banker. He actually came from Mainz, and he made his bundle in fabrics. Next time you're walking down Leonard Street, heading for Broadway, look to the right when you get to the Church Street corner. High up on the wall of the big gray building you can still make out the large gold letters nailed into the brick: J. SHVENGER & SON, INC., COTTON CONVERTERS.

Bankers probably make better copy than cotton converters. This may be the reason why when I was growing up, the Schiffs and the Warburgs and the Lewisohns were in the paper as often as Jane Gibson, the Pig Woman. But I never saw the name "Shvenger" in print until Sidonie got herself appointed by President Wilson as a staff member of the American delegation to the peace conference at Versailles in 1919. I was not much of a newspaper reader in those days. After all, I had just made it to my sixth birthday. But I had big ears, and I heard a lot of the talk by people around me who did read the papers. I remember they all seemed to be annoyed with President Wilson. Even my father, who used to read the *Jewish Daily Forward* aloud to my mother every night.

"A woman for such a job?" I remember him saying angrily. "And such a woman yet!"

Years later when I began putting it all together I realized what he meant. Sidonie Shvenger was one of these broads with galloping glands. She got people's backs up. Judging by pictures I've seen, her appearance didn't help. She was a real dog. But she was a dog with good intentions.

"If it's a good cause," Nicholas Murray Butler is supposed to have said, "the problem is not getting Sidonie to join it. That's simple. All you have to do is drop a hat. The problem is how to prevent her from leading it."

This was not easy. Sidonie Shvenger did not like back seats. She once told an interviewer that the power-behind-the-throne act was okay for this Frenchman, whatever his name was, Cardinal Something. Who was always telling Louis what cards

284

to play. Not for Sidonie. If she couldn't sit up on the box, driving the horses, she got herself another buggy. This was not difficult, since she used her own money. Her old man's money, anyway. He had plenty. Years later, when I met him, Hubie Sissenwein made no bones about the fact that it was Jake Shvenger's bankroll that attracted him.

"The trouble with Dick Whittington," Hubie Sissenwein said, "he didn't know how to think for himself. If he hadn't heard those Bow bells telling him to turn around and go back, some other boy would have ended up as Lord Mayor of London. Not me. I'd been on Seventh Avenue ever since I was sixteen. Like every other kid in the garment center who came from the Lower East Side, my thinking was about as original as Milton Berle's jokes. My ambition was to raise some capital so I could stop pushing a handcart through the streets and go into business for myself. After five years, when I was moving up on my twenty-first birthday, it occurred to me one day my thinking was unsound. I took a look around at some of the boys who had managed to raise a little capital and get themselves off the street and go into business for themselves. It was an interesting sight. Half of them had gone into bankruptcy with their first or second lines, and the others, the boys who were making it, what had they made? Enough to marry the girl whose books they used to carry home from P. S. 188, and live on Central Park West. Was this, I asked myself, the American Dream? Was this hitting the great American jackpot? Not to Hubert Sissenwein. I realized I was fighting in the wrong stadium. What I needed was a fresh approach. The day I came to this conclusion, I saw in the papers that President Wilson had appointed Sidonie Shvenger to the staff that would be attending the peace conference in Paris. The contrast hit me like a punch. From Seventh Avenue to the Hall of Mirrors in Versailles. To a man looking for a fresh approach, the hunt was over."

Hubie shaved, put on a clean shirt and went uptown to Jake Shvenger's town house on West Eighty-sixth Street. On the way he stopped off in a stationery store and for a dime bought himself one of those salmon-colored file envelopes in which lawyers carry their papers. The Shvenger butler looked Hubie over and said Miss Sidonie was not in. Hubie said he would have to wait because he was a State Department courier and he had just come up from Washington with some secret papers. His orders were to deliver them to Miss Shvenger in person. The butler disappeared. He came back a couple of minutes later with the news that Miss Shvenger had just come in and would see the man from the State Department now.

You never know, of course, what women will go for. I've talked to a few of the girls who put in some time going for Sissenwein. The reports conflict. This is due to the fact that people, especially women, felt only two ways about him. There were those who really worked on it and made a career out of hating Hubie. And there were those who hated him only a few hours of the day, when he happened to cross their paths or their minds. The former said all Hubie carried around in his pants was money. The others said if a girl was willing to work up a sweat she could get some action out of him.

"It was worth it only because Hubie paid well," one of these shy creatures once told me. "Aside from that, watching him rise to the occasion was like seeing someone spread both doors of a barn wide open to wheel out a bicycle."

There were no witnesses to what happened after the door of Sidonie Shvenger's third-floor study closed behind Hubie Sissenwein and his salmon-colored envelope. An hour later, however, when the door opened, she had hired Hubie as her secretary and she was on the phone to Washington about his passport.

Before the American delegation sailed for France, Sidonie bought Hubie an entire new wardrobe, and she had his upper front teeth capped. On the ship going over, Hubie studied shorthand out of a book Sidonie gave him, and he practiced on her portable typewriter. By the time they were settled in adjoining suites at the Ritz, for which Sidonie lifted the tab, Hubie could take a letter, if Sidonie didn't dictate too fast. This was not easy for her. Sidonie's ordinary conversation went at the approximate speed of a Gatling gun. But for Hubie Sissenwein she made the effort.

In fact, for Hubie Sissenwein no effort seemed to be an effort to Sidonie Shvenger. She took him with her everywhere. She introduced him to Colonel House. She sat him on her left when she gave a lunch for Lloyd George. She arranged for him to shake hands with Woodrow Wilson. She bought him a wrist watch at Cartier's. And when she became aware that members of the delegation were gossiping about them, to save Hubie's face, not hers, she married him.

Hubie was then twenty-one years old. Sidonie Shvenger was fifty-two. She had the good sense to die before she reached fifty-three.

There is enough in the record of the next thirty-five years to give a pretty clear picture of how Hubert Sissenwein treated people when he was through with them. Including his two subsequent wives. And he was through with Sidonie, of course, after she made a new will in Paris, leaving everything she owned to Hubie.

She died while they were on the honeymoon in Switzerland they had delayed until the peace conference was over.

"We were married exactly forty-six days," Hubie once told Byram Noonan. "If you divide forty-six into the sum I picked up after the lady cooled, you will surely realize at once that you are talking to a gentleman who got the highest price per bout since sexual congress was invented."

He also got something else. What I got the day I came out of the subway at Twenty-eighth Street with Arnold Zohn and had my first smell of Fourth Avenue. Except that Hubie got it in spades. I met Ralph Mattlin and Gene Merritt. Hubie met Bill Bullitt and Lord Curzon. They went to his head. He decided, when he got back to New York, to "organize myself for luxury."

In the early phases, this involved a certain amount of juggling. Hubie knew Sidonie's will had made him a rich man. But his wealth was all on paper, not in his pocket, and he didn't yet know how rich. Besides, it was all a little unsettled. The Shvenger family lawyers were suspicious of this kid with the chicken-liver eyes who had married Jake's spinster daughter six weeks before she died. They didn't say Hubie had killed her, of course.

But Hubie admitted later he got the feeling that it wouldn't have surprised them to learn he had. That the problem raised by the will would not be settled overnight seemed dead certain because most of Sidonie's estate consisted of her share of the J. Shvenger & Son, Inc., outstanding common stock. The "& Son" had been a bachelor with sexual habits that were a little advanced for his time who died in 1910 leaving his stock to his father. So that when Hubert Sissenwein returned to New York with the body of his wife, he knew only that he was now one of the two owners of J. Shvenger & Son, Inc.

"It was a nice spot to be in," Hubie told Byram Noonan years later. "But it still was a spot. My wallet was as flat as the chest of a John Held, Jr., flapper. I needed a place to live. And I needed money to start the way of life I had marked out for myself. So I moved in with old Jake Shvenger."

It was an ideal arrangement. For Hubie, anyway. Jake Shvenger was, in late 1919, a lonely old widower. He had never quite understood what Sidonie was up to. The only thing he really knew about was cotton converting. But he was proud of his daughter. He liked seeing her name and her picture in the papers. And he enjoyed having her in the house with him. When he received the news from Paris that she had married Hubert Sissenwein, he is supposed to have said to the secretary who read him Sidonie's cable, "I don't believe it. Postal Telegraph is notoriously unreliable. I will wait until I hear through Western Union." He never did. The cable announcing Sidonie's death also came via Postal Telegraph. The first time Jake Shvenger met his son-in-law was at the dock when Hubert Sissenwein came down the gangplank behind Sidonie's coffin.

"Naturally," Hubie told me and Byram Noonan years later, "I didn't tell the old man I was moving in with him because I was financially embarrassed. I merely said I wanted to be near Sidonie as long as possible. This was not long, since they buried her the day after the coffin arrived in New York. When Jake and I came back to the house from the funeral, the place was crowded with the sort of people I had met through Sidonie at the peace conference in Paris. They were Sidonie's friends. I woke up to this when I noticed a quiet, very thin lady talking to a handsome buck with white hair and I asked the butler who they were. Edna St. Vincent Millay, he said, and Max Eastman. By the time the place was cleared, I'd identified John Golden, Mayor Hylan, Jess Willard, Joe Tumulty, Bernie Baruch, Rabbi Stephen Wise, Fannie Brice and Uncle Joe Cannon. They'd all come to pay their respects. I figured if people of that caliber would come to West Eighty-sixth Street to do a thing like that for a witless old idiot like Jake Shvenger, why shouldn't they come to have a good time and entertain Hubie Sissenwein?"

The answer was not clear in the beginning. The only thing that was clear was that they did not come. Hubie made calls. They were not returned. He sent out invitations. They were not answered. He wondered for a while if it could be his father-in-law. I think I would have done a little of the same kind of wondering. I never laid an eye on Jake Shvenger. He was ninety-one when he died in 1923. But I don't think Hubie Sissenwein was overdoing it by much when he called the old man a witless idiot.

If you look at the lists of the world's movers and shakers, you don't find many cotton converters on them. It began to dawn on Hubie Sissenwein that people like Edna St. Vincent Millay and Bernie Baruch didn't go any old place they were asked just because they could load up for free on a shovelful of caviar and a couple of splits of Piper-Heidsieck. There had to be some sort of other attraction. If it wasn't Jake Shvenger, it seemed to be pretty obvious that the only other person in the big house on West Eighty-sixth Street wasn't much of an attraction, either. Which only pointed up the most obvious fact of all: the only reason people like John Golden and Fannie Brice had ever gone to the Shvenger house was Sidonie.

Just about the time all this was coming clear in Hubie's mind, Sidonie's estate was settled and he had a curious experience. Hubie tried to get into a Fifty-second Street speakeasy.

Just why is not clear. Hubert Sissenwein is supposed never in his lifetime to have taken an ounce of alcohol internally. The only things in which he seemed to have believed firmly were the things his mother drilled into him before he was nine. These were two. First, take the cash even if you have to steal it and let the credit go but only when nobody will advance it to you. And second, never put any liquid into your stomach stronger than buttermilk. So what he was doing trying to get into a speakeasy on Fifty-second Street at the age of twenty-three in 1921 may seem a little puzzling.

"Not at all," Hubie said years later when I asked him. "My mother taught me the importance of money. Sidonie Shvenger taught me how to enjoy it. Every day in F.P.A.'s column, in O. O. McIntyre, in all the papers, you could hear the echoes of the bright conversation I'd learned to enjoy in Paris. There were all these people making these nice noises, and where were they making them? In saloons. In those days of course they were speakeasies. And they were called Tony's, or they had numbers for names. I decided I'd take a look at one. I picked Abe & Iggie's."

Hubie got as far as the little foyer just inside the door.

"Yes?" the doorman said.

"What do you mean, yes?" Hubie said.

"I mean what do you want?" the doorman said.

"Some of whatever it is you sell," Hubie said. "I'm a customer."

"Who are you?" the doorman said.

"Who does one have to be to spend money here?" Hubie said.

"You have to be someone I know," the doorman said. "I don't know you, mister."

As he started muscling Hubie back through the door Hubie heard someone laugh. "Hey, Iggie," the laugher said. "You know who your doorman just kicked out? Mr. Sidonie Shvenger."

Telling me and Byram Noonan about it years later, Hubert Sissenwein laughed. But I happened to be looking into his chicken-liver eyes when the sounds came out of his face. If you looked into Hubie's eyes when he was amused, you didn't get laughter. You got scared.

290

"For the first time since Sidonie died," he said, "I got the idea. I had more or less accepted the fact that to Rabbi Stephen Wise and Joe Tumulty, Hubie Sissenwein was not as big an attraction as Sidonie Shvenger had been. But to be called Mr. Sidonie Shvenger was totally unacceptable. The next day I started correcting the image. I had my lawyer find out who owned the club. A boy named Iggie Zeitz. Then I had my lawyer trace the title to the building. In six weeks I owned it. As soon as I was Iggie Zeitz's legal landlord I had my lawyer tell his lawyer that as of that moment I wanted a table reserved for me in 51 on a permanent basis. Every day. And nobody could sit at it except me and my guests. I wanted a card with my name lettered on it placed on that table. Unless I got this, my lawyer told Iggie's lawyer, Iggie's lease was not going to be renewed. Late in the afternoon I got the confirming call from my lawyer. That night when my taxi dropped me in front of 51, the doorman must have been waiting and watching through the one-way peephole in the door. He opened it before I could knock."

The image didn't change overnight. But Hubie had a toe-hold. In the beginning a certain number of people came to sit at his table in 51 only because they remembered Sidonie Shvenger and were curious about this little guy who had inherited her pile. Then Hubie Sissenwein began to do things with the pile, and people started asking Iggie Zeitz to introduce them to Sidonie's husband so they could be seen sitting at his table.

"If you want to get some witty newspapermen to come and be witty especially and exclusively for you," Hubie told me and Byram Noonan, "buy yourself a newspaper."

The Brooklyn *Echo* wasn't much of a newspaper when Hubie bought it in 1921, but that's why he got it cheap. He hired Johnny "Speed" Marsillon away from the Chicago *Trib* by the simple process of doubling the hot young editor's salary. By 1923, when the Hearst organization offered him four million for the paper, Hubie was in a position to turn it down.

"Jake Shvenger had just died," Hubie said. "Aside from what Mount Sinai got here in New York and what the civic opera got back in Mainz, I got the rest. I didn't need Hearst's four million. Besides, I began to like the idea of having an organization of my own. So I bought a radio station. This was a time when you could buy a radio station for not much more than the price of a Hershey bar. The day after I bought my first one, Graham MacNamee stopped by at my table in 51 and brought with him a smallish chap named Lee de Forest. I asked Jack Dempsey and his wife, Estelle Taylor, to move over to make room for them."

By the time he cooled, nobody really knew how much Hubert Sissenwein was worth. Or how it was spread around. After four months of behind-the-scenes work, trying to stitch together a package to put on the surrogate's desk, Byram Noonan and I didn't really know, either. When I started working on the executors one by one, the first thing I discovered was that they were surprised by this.

"He's been in the papers so much these last thirty years," Bruce Tomkin, the president of Skidder, Coe & Ehrlich said to me the first time we talked, "I thought everybody knew everything about Hubie."

Actually the public knew only what Hubie wanted them to know. They knew when he sold the old Shvenger House on West Eighty-sixth Street and bought the two adjoining Millard Fillmore houses on Sutton Place, because there were a lot of pictures in the papers and he was beginning to enjoy being pointed out on the street. The same thing happened when he bought the Suddersby Kirkland estate at Huntington. On the other hand, not a word got into the papers about his art collection until his agent outbid J. P. Morgan's man for Turner's "A View from Iggleston" at Sotheby's and Hubie's press agents filled the papers with the news that during the past five years, working quietly through dealers all over the world, he had put together a collection in which the French impressionists alone were estimated to be worth ten million. Nobody knew for two years after he bought the *Chicago Century Encyclopedia,* and the *Chicago Century Magazine,* which came with the package, that Hubie was even interested in encyclopedias or magazines.

By the time he broke the news, he owned three of each and he wanted the publicity so the owners of *L'Oeuil,* the first and then still biggest picture weekly in France, wouldn't think they were being bought out by a guy who was interested only in turning them over for a quick profit.

"The quick profit never pays anything but yesterday's bills," Hubie said to me and Byram. "What people don't understand about money is that you must not let it stand still. If you sell something you can put what you get for it into your mattress. Or into a savings bank, which is practically the same thing. But if you put the money into something that's working, and you understand how and why it's working, the money will grow. So that pretty soon you are in a position to buy two things that are working and will grow."

Nothing about Hubie grew as much as his reputation. Leaving aside heads of state and people like generals who fought the wars these bright boys got us into, I'd say Hubert Sissenwein is as famous a name as this country has produced during the many years since my bar mitzvah. You could even make a case for going beyond this country. After all, his second wife was an Italian princess, and his third the daughter of an earl. There were days in these two short episodes in Hubie's career when the Italian press gave him more space than they gave Count Ciano, and Fleet Street had him on the British front pages more often than the Earl of Bewdley. There are people who say they don't understand this. I've heard them. I've also heard the arguments.

He wasn't much to look at, they say. All right, they say, so he could make with the jokes. But Will Rogers he wasn't. Money? No matter how much he made, Hubie still wasn't in the same league with Carnegie and Rockefeller. And as for the divorce scandals, his second wife was not the first Italian princess who was caught with a Russian shot-putter in the locker room at the Olympic Games. And the earl's daughter, let's face it, three men and one broad—as orgies go in the international set that's pretty low voltage, even if two men turned out to be devoted faggots Hubie had set up in the dress business on Seventh Avenue and who testified they had been brought in by Hubie's wife only to watch.

I never knew the answer to these arguments until Hubie died and Byram Noonan and I started work on the surrogate's package and I started my round of lunches and other meetings with the executors. What I began to put together, at first without knowing I was doing it, was a picture of the effect Hubert Sissenwein had on the people he was sore at. He hated being known as Mrs. Sidonie Shvenger. So he decided to make the big shots of Sidonie's world come to him. He did it by putting them in financial spots from which they could get out only with his help. When they got it, first at his table in 51, then in the palace he made of the two Fillmore houses on Sutton Place, and finally the Suddersby Kirkland place at Huntington, they found being there was fun.

A lot of these people had spent their lives going back and forth from their own houses to houses like the Shvenger house on West Eighty-sixth Street. They were good and sick of it without knowing they were sick of it. Then suddenly, or maybe not suddenly but slowly, they discovered the fun of sitting at a table in 51 with a character like Hubert Sissenwein and his, well, all right, let's use the word, his friends. The booze was just as good. The food was probably better. And the talk was a new and exciting experience. These stuffy schmucks with old money were suddenly having fun with the snappy makers of new.

To put the bottom line on it, before Hubie Sissenwein came along, the chances of a boy from Cannon Street or East Fourth Street splitting a bottle of Moxie in the same room with a Warburg or a Schiff were about the same as the chances of Queen Marie of Rumania endorsing not Pond's cold cream but Manischewitz's Passover Schmaltz. Hubie Sissenwein was the Jewish answer to Ward McAllister in reverse. He put the Four Hundred out of business. Hubie invented café society.

To keep his invention going, he kept moving into new financial areas. If you want to keep them coming after that mousetrap, you'd better get out a new model at pretty regular intervals. I didn't realize Hubert Sissenwein had become interested in book publishing until the morning after the day I met him on top of 120 Broadway when I was having lunch with Byram Noonan and Ralph Mattlin about my percentage deal.

"You must have more charm than I've been able to discover in you thus far," Byram said. "Hubert Sissenwein called a few minutes ago. Like to have talk with you."

"About what?" I said.

"Didn't say," Byram said.

"Didn't you ask?" I said.

"One doesn't ask with Hubert," Byram said. "Most people, when he wants to see them, they just grab their hats and go."

29

" The Only Way to Double Your Money Fast Is to Fold It in Half"

The man who opened Hubert Sissenwein's door was the second butler I had ever seen in the flesh. I could see right away that to put this boy in the same class with Jeremy, the Mattlin butler on Thirty-eighth Street, was like putting Rembrandt in the same class with a street cleaner just because they both used brushes. Hubie's butler wasn't even called a butler. Hawksmoor was known as Mr. Sissenwein's steward.

"Good afternoon, Mr. Noonan," he said to Byram. "This way, please."

We followed him down a long hall. The walls of the hall were lined with paintings that had small lights in the bottoms of the gold frames. The lights were all turned off. Not only in the frames. The ceiling chandeliers too. So that it was a little bit like making it through the IRT tunnel from the Lexington Avenue subway to the shuttle when there was a power failure. Except that the pictures on these walls were not advertising Sal Hepatica for the smile of Health and Ipana for the smile of Beauty. All these pictures had two things in common. They were big, and all the guys in them wore silk knee breeches and white wigs.

"Sir Joshua Reynolds," Byram said to me. "All of them."

296

"They must be very good friends," I said. "For Sissenwein to have so many pictures of him."

"What?" Byram said.

"Skip it," I said.

To lawyers I don't explain jokes.

At the end of the hall Hawksmoor pressed a mother-of-pearl button. A mahogany door slid open. Byram stepped into an elevator. I followed. Hawksmoor moved in and pressed another button. The door slid shut. The elevator started to move. So did Byram. He stepped across for a better look at a painting over the instrument panel. "This Manet," he said. "Is it new?"

"Hardly, sir," Hawksmoor said. "Manet died in 1883."

"I meant is it new in Mr. Sissenwein's collection," Byram Noonan said. He said it the way he might have said, "I meant Forty-third Street, not Forty-second Street." He didn't seem to be aware that the boy with the Frederick Lonsdale accent had just hung one on him.

"No sir," Hawksmoor said. "It used to be in the basement, but the laundress who does Mr. Sissenwein's shirts said the colors made her feel bilious and as a result she was putting too much starch in the collars, so he had it moved here into the lift. No laundry is done in the lift, you see."

I took another quick look at Byram Noonan. He still didn't seem to realize he'd been caught in a Wheeler and Woolsey rehearsal. The elevator stopped.

"It's one of the most appealing Manets I've ever seen," Byram said.

"As a matter of fact, it's a Monet," Hawksmoor said. "This way, please. He died in 1926, sir."

The upstairs hall looked exactly like the downstairs hall except that here, in all the paintings that lined the walls, it was women in those Marie Antoinette dresses who looked out at you from under white powdered wigs. Hawksmoor opened a door. "Mr. Noonan, sir," he said.

It looked as though I wasn't going to get any billing.

"Come in, gentlemen," a voice said.

Byram and I came into what looked like a barbershop. Why

shouldn't it? Since that's what it was. Hubert Sissenwein was sitting in a barber chair. He still looked as though he was wearing an astrakhan collar. But a white one this time. It was the sheet wrapped around his neck. The man in the white coat who was clipping away at Hubie's head looked as though he'd been told one of the hairs was the trigger of a dynamite charge, and if he so much as touched it he would blow the house, his boss and himself into a fine spray of dust. I've seen monkeys in the zoo picking insects out of each other's fur with less concentrated delicacy. But never with so much terror. It was a way, I learned later, Hubie Sissenwein had with servants. They moved around his various homes as though they expected to be arrested.

"Sit down, gentlemen," Hubie said. "Help yourselves to a cup of coffee."

He was reading the tape from a market ticker that stood near the barber chair. He kept pulling the paper strip up across his face, right under his nose, as though he were sniffing it. I wondered why he wasn't wearing glasses. He was obviously near-sighted. Or cockeyed in some other way. Or maybe he just liked the smell of ticker tape.

"Sugar?" Byram said.

For a moment I didn't realize he'd said it to me.

"No, thanks," I said. "Nothing for me."

On the other side of the barber chair a coffee service was sitting on a small inlaid table. It looked like one of those things you see in the display rooms at Parke-Bernet before an estate auction. The pot out of which Byram poured himself a cup of coffee had enough silver in it to keep the mint going until they take Washington's face off the twenty-five-cent piece.

"Sit down," Hubie said.

He said it the way Sergeant Quirt in *What Price Glory?* said "Forward march!" Hubie didn't bother to look up from the ticker tape. He expected to be obeyed. He was. Byram and I dropped into a couch that looked as though it had come out of a set for a movie about Catherine the Great. I wasn't too far off. I

298

found out later the thing had belonged to Catherine the Great.

"If you have any spare cash lying around today," Hubert Sissenwein said, "buy AT&T."

"Man of your financial acumen," Byram Noonan said, "I expect more original stock-market tips than that."

"Of course you do," Hubert Sissenwein said. "That's why you'll never be rich. You put your money on a tip, tomorrow the tip could disappear like Judge Crater. You put your money on AT&T, tomorrow it will be there, worth more than it was worth yesterday. Only fools look for hot tips. The hottest tip I know is ferryboat. It's the only thing you can be certain will come across. Don't you drink coffee, Mr. Neff?"

"Leff," I said. "My mother warned me against it. She said coffee rots the lining of your stomach."

"My mother told me the same thing," Sissenwein said. "But that service cost me six thousand at Sotheby's. I had my London agent watch until it came on sale. I like to buy things that belonged to royalty. This thing, the man who used to brew his coffee in it he was the third Duke of Sunderland. I don't know if there's a fourth duke. If there is, he's probably drinking his coffee out of a cardboard container. I like to have the thing near me so I can look at it once in a while. Besides, I get a lot of unbright people coming in to see me. You give them a cup of coffee, and the sipping process reduces the number of stupid remarks they make. Not you, Byram. You have my permission to go ahead and made as many stupid remarks as you like."

"Thanks," Byram Noonan said. "I like that new Vermeer behind you."

"You're starting early," Hubert Sissenwein said. "That's not a Vermeer. That's a Van Dyck. Do you know anything about paintings, Mr. Neff?"

"Leff," I said.

"Don't have hurt feelings," Hubie said. "My memory is extremely good on everything that costs money. On names it takes me time. I don't like to waste it. Byram, here—now, to me he was Coogan for almost a year. Then I decided he wasn't as

big a fool as he looked and sounded. Once I decided he was
smart enough to handle things for me, I learned his name fast.
When I decide that about you, Mr. Leff, I'll make an effort to
remember not to call you Neff. Right now what have you got to
lose if I get your name wrong? You're a bookkeeper in a
book-publishing house. What you make per year, it could perhaps add up to almost enough to put a new frame on the Turner
I have out there in the elevator."

"Hawksmoor said it was a Monet," Byram Noonan said.

"Did you tell him first you thought it was a Manet?" Sissenwein said.

"Matter of fact, yes," Byram said. "How did you know that?"

"The man works for me," Hubie said. "Men I don't know
everything about work for other people. Right, Lennie?"

"Yes, sir," the barber said.

"Lennie is the best barber to pick up a pair of scissors since
Monsieur Beaucaire," Sissenwein said. "Unfortunately, he has a
weakness. He bets on horses. That's as bad as hunting for tips
on the stock market. But there's no reason why a horseplayer
shouldn't cut hair well. So every week Lennie's salary goes to
his wife. By my own personal messenger. And Lennie stays
downtown here, trimming my curly locks. It keeps us both out
of trouble."

"If you'd let me put a sawbuck on Nelly's Bay last week," the
barber said, "I'd have doubled my money."

"You would have done no such thing," Hubert Sissenwein
said. "The only way to double your money fast is to fold it in
half. Hawksmoor has instructions. Any fool who takes my Turner for a Manet is to be told it's a Monet. This is a fun house. We
play these little games all day long. It helps pass the time. Now
tell me how much you know about painting, Mr. Neff."

"Not much," I said. "It's Leff."

"I think I'm beginning to like you, Mr. Neff," Sissenwein
said. "You're a determined chap. But you must not rush me.
You're still Neff. Also, you're stupid if you fool around with
paintings unless you know a good deal more than not much.

300

Unless you know as much about any racket as the racketeers who run it, you will in all likelihood get stuck like a pincushion by trying to invest in it."

"I won't invest in paintings," I said. "That's a promise."

"See that you keep it," Sissenwein said. "What sort of things do you invest in?"

"I haven't started yet," I said. "I'm waiting until I make my pile."

"You will," Hubert Sissenwein said. "You've got that look." he said. "When you do start, remember never to invest in anything that eats or needs repainting. How did you happen to get to know Byram?"

Byram got as far as "We seem to have met several years ago without my being aware that—" when Sissenwein cut in with "Not you. I asked Mr. Neff. Careful, Lennie. That's skin you're trying to work your way through."

"Sorry," the barber said. "You really ought to have the doctor look at this thing, Mr. Sissenwein. It's getting bigger."

"So is your mouth," Hubie said. "You take care of the hair. I'll take care of the rest of me. How did you happen to meet this big Yale football hero, Mr. Neff?"

I told him.

"So you're a Seventh Avenue boy too," Hubert Sissenwein said. "What a group we are. Us, this happy breed of men, this little world, this precious stone set in the rectum of the city, where if you have what it takes you come away fully equipped to take it from everybody else. How did you get from Seventh Avenue to Fourth?"

I told him that too.

"I had a hunch about you the moment I saw you at Byram's table in One Twenty," Sissenwein said. "I said to myself, there's a man I can deal with."

"From the top of the deck?" I said. "Or the bottom?"

"I'll let you judge," Sissenwein said. "You look smart enough to be able to handle it."

"I guess I ought to be flattered," I said.

"Not necessarily," Sissenwein said. "Some of the men I deal with are not allowed to cross state lines. Do you want to deal with me, Mr. Neff?"

"That depends," I said.

"On what?" Hubie said.

"On whether you get my name right," I said.

Sissenwein laughed. Oy! Even the barber winced. And he was standing behind Hubert Sissenwein, so he didn't see the eyes.

"That will depend on you," Sissenwein said. "Byram, did you tell him?"

"How could I?" Byram Noonan said. "You haven't told me yet."

"You see, Mr. Neff, what we brilliant graduates of the garment center have to put up with?" Hubert Sissenwein said. "We pay these Yale chaps great big fat fees, and we pay it so they will keep us out of trouble. So what happens? We have to explain to them how to do it. Byram, old chap. Pretend you're in there against the Harvards. Last quarter. One minute to go. The play is called. The ball has been snapped to you. What do you do?"

"Let me run through it," Byram said. He took a sip of coffee, stared at the Van Dyck that could have been a Norman Rockwell, and he said, "How's this, Hubie? You were attracted to Mr. Leff because you saw him sitting at table with me and Ralph Mattlin. You came over and said you knew Mattlin's father. Way I figure you, Hubie, you don't cross restaurants just convey piece of information that elementary nature. So you must have come over to learn relationship between me and stranger. Who turns out to be Mr. Leff. You learn that. Next thing happens you call and say you want me bring Mr. Leff to house. Why? Must be because of what Mr. Leff does. What does Mr. Leff do? He is in book-publishing business. You are not. You are in pretty near everything else, Hubie, but you are not in book publishing. Hmmm, I say to myself. Or rather hmmm, I hmmm to myself. My hmmming leads me to conclusion you want use Mr. Leff to get into book-publishing business. How's that?"

302

"Better than some of my other lawyers could have done,"
Hubert Sissenwein said. "What I like about you, Byram, is you
look gentile-stupid, but you think Jewish-smart. As a reward for
the rest of this visit, Byram, if you want to call my Van Dyck a
Vermeer, you have my permission to do so. Mr. Leff, are you
interested in working with me?"

Not as much as I was beginning to be interested in working
him over. "Yes," I said.

"Why?" Sissenwein said.

Because I like modest people.

"You finally got my name right," I said.

"Byram, this boy looks splendid," Hubert Sissenwein said.
"Mr. Leff, do you have a first name?"

No, I go by a number.

"Ted," I said. "It's not much but I got it for nothing, so I've
kept it."

"Ted," Sissenwein said. "Ted. It's not bad. Not bad at all.
Consider what I got for nothing. Hubert. My father wanted to
call me Hyman, but my mother said we were in America now so
it was only appropriate that I should have an American name.
She had a chronic cough. It finally killed her. She was always
taking large doses of Hubert's Catarrh Syrup. It didn't do her
any good but it was American, so she called me Hubert. You
must learn to count your breaks in this world. She could have
called me Catarrh. Now then, Ted, this is what I want. I want to
buy the firm of Mattlin & Merritt, Inc. But I don't want anybody
to know I'm trying to do it. Not yet, anyway. I want you to
handle this for me. Do you think you can?"

"I'll have to know the details," I said.

"Naturally," Sissenwein said. "But that's all details are. Details. They come later. The important thing at this stage is a
simple yes or no."

"If I say yes," I said, "what do I get out of it?"

"I can't say in dollars because I don't know what Mattlin &
Merritt is worth," Hubert Sissenwein said. "But let me put it
this way. I'm not a poor man, as you may have heard, and I'm
not greedy, no matter what you may have heard, and I'm not

going into book publishing for the money. It's a nickels-and-dimes business. I'm going into it for personal reasons. Therefore, give a moment's thought to this suggestion. Whatever I get out of the deal, you and I will split it down the line. How about that, Mr. Leff?"

He hadn't said down the middle. He'd said down the line. "Who decides where the line goes?" I said.

"Why not your friend, here, the art expert?" Sissenwein said. "This Yale right end who thinks a Turner is a Monet and a Van Dyck is a Vermeer? With an intelligence of those dimensions working for us, how can either of us lose?"

Mr. Hubert Sissenwein could be in for a surprise answer to that question.

"Okay," I said. "I trust Byram."

The next problem was to get him to trust me.

"Any further questions?" Sissenwein said.

"Yes," I said. "I'm interested in why you want to own a book-publishing firm."

"I don't want to own a book-publishing firm," Hubert Sissenwein said. "I want to own Mattlin & Merritt."

"Why?" I said.

Sissenwein laughed. Like a schmuck, I had to be looking into his eyes when he did it. It occurred to me I'd probably just cut myself off from chicken liver for life.

"Sixteen years ago," Hubert Sissenwein said, "I had an interesting experience. The owners of a speakeasy on Fifty-second Street wouldn't let me in because they didn't know me. As the bouncer evicted me, a man standing at the bar with the owner started to laugh and he said to the owner, 'You know who your doorman just kicked out? That was Mr. Sidonie Shvenger.'" Hubert Sissenwein laughed again. "The man at the bar who said that," he said, "would you care to make a guess who he was?"

I reached for a long one. "Ralph Mattlin?" I said.

Hubert Sissenwein turned to Byram Noonan. "You know something, Byram," he said. "This could be not unlike the day Abercrombie met Fitch. This young man has brains." Hubert

Sissenwein turned back to me. "No, Ted," he said. "It was not Ralph Mattlin. It was his father, Siegfried Mattlinberg, the president of Mattlinberg & Nachman. Unfortunately that old German son of a bitch is dead," Hubert Sissenwein said. "So all I've got to work on is his son Ralph."

30

" For Money,
Just for Money,
I Don't Want My Son
to Die"

I had more than that to work on. I had Gene Merritt as well as
Ralph Mattlin. Which is what gave me a few troubled moments.
I was pretty sure I could handle Ralph Mattlin alone, and Gene
Merritt ditto. I was not so sure I could do it if they were in a
room together. The reason is simple. It's like four-wall handball.
One man in a room with you is one player to handle. Two men
become more than two players. You've got to handle not only
the bounce from each one. You've got to handle what they
bounce off each other. Merritt seemed to me the easier of the
two. So the day after my meeting with Sissenwein, while Ralph
Mattlin was still uptown on Bernie Yustin's couch, I walked
into Gene Merritt's office and asked him to have lunch with me.

"Sure," he said. "Glad to, Ted. *At noon he bounded out for
food, and nothing less than roast lion would content him.* Thoreau. Anything special?"

"Just a business thing," I said. "I thought it would be easier to
discuss it over a hamburger and a cup of coffee."

"At your service," Merritt said. "Ralph too?"

"I don't want to waste his time," I said. "It's not really in his
department. Twelve-thirty?"

306

"Twelve-thirty fine."

"I'll pick you up."

A few minutes after twelve my phone rang.

"Ted? Gene. Listen, I'm afraid I won't be able to make the lunch. My mother just called. She's down in Klein's and she wants me to come over and help her pick out a spring coat. I told her I was supposed to have lunch with you, so she said today is Friday, why don't you bring him up to the Bronx tonight? He can eat with us. How about it, Ted?"

I thought fast. If I said no, I would lose three days. Since I didn't want to tackle Merritt in the office, the canceled lunch meant today was out. And if today was out, it meant I couldn't get to him until after the weekend, on Monday. Too long.

"That's swell, Gene," I said into the phone. "I haven't had a nice Jewish home-cooked meal for years."

At three o'clock in the afternoon it began to look as though I wasn't going to have one that night either. Merritt came into my room wearing his topcoat.

"Ted, do you mind going up to my mother's house by yourself?" he said. "My dentist's nurse just called. I forgot to put my three o'clock appointment on the calendar. He's waiting for me. Here's my mother's address." He put a piece of paper on my desk. "It's two blocks from the last stop on the 180th Street Bronx Park Express. Try to get there by no later than six-thirty. She lights the candles at quarter to seven. I'll meet you up there. The best way, take the express at Grand Central. Then when you get off, walk toward the park."

It was like telling Lindbergh how to get to Le Bourget.

"I know where it is," I said. "The last six years of her life, my mother lived practically around the corner."

"Swell," Merritt said. "See you at six-thirty."

He almost didn't. The moment he left my office, I found myself thinking about his teeth. They weren't anything to paint into the Pepsodent ads, but they seemed to get him out of the office at convenient times. It was because he'd had his teeth uptown in the dentist's office that Merritt's mother had been able to come in and look me over soon after I was hired. Now it was because of his teeth that Merritt was able to avoid being alone with me on the long subway ride to the Bronx. If it was true that he was trying to avoid me. Maybe I was overthinking it. He couldn't know why I wanted to talk to him in private. Yet all of a sudden, there seemed to be a connection between the broken lunch date and the broken date to ride uptown together. I decided to skip Merritt and his mother's home-cooked meal and tackle Mattlin.

"Too late," Maud Eitner said when I came into her office and asked if Mattlin was free. "He's just gone out to buy a Teddy bear for Sacheverell, and for Benita let's see now, what will it be today? Perhaps his weekly two ounces chipped off the Hope Diamond, or a package of Juicy Fruit. Anything I can do?"

Not yet. I hadn't told her about my meeting with Sissenwein. I wasn't sure yet that I would. I wanted to see first what I came up with.

"Not really," I said. "We've had two more offers for the subscribers' lists we're building up on the sex mailings. I think Ralph should make a decision soon. They're offering quite a lot of dough, but it'll keep till Monday."

"What are you doing tonight?" she said.

"Same as you," I said. "Eating kosher. Gene invited me up to the Bronx."

"If you survive," Maud said, "I'll have my mother ask you over next Friday so you can compare. My mother says she was twenty-seven, married, and pushing a baby carriage down to the park every single day like one of those hot-chestnut vendors before she learned that all meals don't end with a dose of bicarbonate. Take my advice and go up by cab, even if you have to charge it to petty cash."

I took her advice. When the taxi turned into 180th Street, I realized in all the thousands of times I'd moved up and down this street I'd never done it on wheels. This is something to call a special session of Congress about? Maybe not. But it's interesting. To me, anyway. I said at the beginning I'm writing this for the record. Part of the record is the way I felt when I was living through all the pieces of this story. The last time I'd been in the Bronx, I came up to bury my mother. You want to know how I felt?

Well, when I paid off the cab I felt pretty much the same way. Any putz who says you can't go home again is just that: a putz. The trouble with life is you not only can go home again, but inside your head you're doing it all the time. There are other troubles. Like for instance the bastards who run the Internal Revenue Service, and underwear that rides up on you, and grapefruit that fights back. But I'll take those troubles any day in the week in exchange for that trip you keep making over and over again. The trip you can't stop making because it happens inside your head. The trip back to the place where it was bad.

The places where it was good, you go back there too. Like with me, East Fourth Street. But when you go back there, you don't need it. You're feeling good to begin with. What gives you the old kvetch are those trips back to the places where it wasn't good. With me that was the Bronx. That's where we were living when the old man died. That's where I did my postgraduate work in How to Hang On. That's where my old lady finally threw in her hand. That's where I found myself, all of a sudden, on that Friday night when I came up to eat with Gene Merritt and his family. It hurt.

I went around the corner to Korngold's. The old man wasn't there. But the store was. And the kid behind the faded old marble counter could have been a Korngold. He looked snotty enough.

"You got any chocolate cherries?" I said.

"What size box you want?" he said.

"What size you got?" I said.

"Half a pound? A whole pound?"

In my day you bought them loose. Three for a nickel. Out of a big glass jar. If you bought three you took them in your hand and ate them on the street. If you bought six Mr. Korngold put them in a small paper bag and he folded the top very carefully. He knew you were buying them for a girl or for your mother.

"Let's see the pound," I said.

The kid slid back a glass panel behind him and brought down a red and white box marked "Schrafft's."

"You got anything bigger?" I said.

"I got a two-pounder," the kid said. "But it's shaped like a heart. It's left over from St. Valentine's Day."

"Let's see it," I said.

He had to go down the counter to get it off a shelf over the ice cream freezer. It was shaped like a heart, all right. And it was bright red. With a ribbon.

"That's what I want," I said. "Can you wrap it?"

"I can put it in a paper bag," he said.

"That'll be fine," I said.

It was a little better than that. By the time I climbed the stoop of the Merritt apartment house it still hurt, but in a different way. I'd never brought my old lady anything bigger than the one-pound box.

"But how did you know?" Gene Merritt's mother said when she opened the door and I gave her the box. "How did you know by me it's chocolate cherries?"

How did that Greek runner know by Atalanta it was golden apples?

"My mother was crazy about them," I said.

"Come in," she said.

It was like coming into our old foyer on Vyse Avenue. Except that we never owned a bookcase full of the *Encyclopaedia Britannica*. With us it was rubber plants. We had four of them. My father hated each one individually. As though they were people. My mother couldn't understand why. I did. They were tough. They didn't need doctors. They outlived him.

"This is Gene's father," Mrs. Merritt said. "Zisha, this is Gene's bookkeeper, Ted Leff. Look what he brought me. A two-pound box of chocolate cherries."

"For me this is a great pleasure," Mr. Merritt said. He was wearing a brown leather windbreaker with a zipper that came up to his Adam's apple. He looked like that actor in *Lost Horizon* who played the lama.

310

"It's a great pleasure for me too," I said. "Where's Gene?"

He came out of the front room. "Here I am, Ted," he said.

There was something about him that made me give him a second look. Then I saw what it was. For the first time since I'd met him, the glasses were sitting straight on his nose. Like those Cockney taxi drivers are always saying in Alfred Hitchcock movies, "It makes you think." Of what? Up here in the Bronx he was safe? So the glasses sat straight on his nose? Downtown where he was nervous they sat crooked? I felt like calling Bernie Yustin to come up and make a few remarks about this boy fighting his way upstream like a spawning salmon to get back into his mother's womb.

"So go in and sit down," Mrs. Merritt said. "It's time to bench licht."

Gene and his father and I went into the front room. Front rooms on the Lower East Side and the Bronx are like the female figure. They're all different, but they're all exactly alike. The important things are always in the same place. This front room was just a little bigger than our front room had been on East Fourth Street, but it had the same things in it. On one wall a picture of Gene in his bar mitzvah tallith and yarmulka. On the other wall a picture of Gene in his double-breasted blue-serge high-school-graduation suit. In both pictures the kid's glasses sat crooked. Between the two pictures a round mahogany table covered with an embroidered tablecloth.

"You sit here," Mrs. Merritt said to me.

I sat down and examined the design in the tablecloth. My mother's tablecloth had red scallops with small blue stars in each bend. Mrs. Merritt's tablecloth had small interlocked blue circles with red dots in the places where the circles crossed. There was only one thing different from my old Friday nights, and Mrs. Merritt fixed that when she came in with the candles.

"Here you're at home," she said. "So take off the jacket, please."

Gene Merritt and I both took off our jackets and hung them on the backs of our chairs.

"Me, I'll keep on," Mr. Merritt said. "I got a little bit a cold."

Mrs. Merritt put a piece of lace over her head and lit the candles. She covered her face with her hands and murmured the prayer. Then she went out to the kitchen, and Mr. Merritt started slicing the challah.

"This knife I have already forty years," he said. "A present it was from a street cleaner on Avenue B. He tore his good suit in a fight in a saloon, so he asked me to fix it his wife shouldn't know. When it came to pay he had no money, so he brought me this knife a present."

Mrs. Merritt came in with the plates of gefüllte fish. "That street cleaner," she said. "He was Jewish."

"Annie," Mr. Merritt said. "How can you say such a thing? First of all, he was a big tall goy with blond hair. Second, his name was O'Brien. And third, Annie, you never in your life saw him."

"Everybody is Jewish," Mrs. Merritt said to me. "You like the horseradish red or the plain white?"

"White horseradish is for goyim," I said.

Mrs. Merritt laughed. "You can say that again," she said. She sat down at her place. "So now," she said. "If you want to talk business, Teddy, you can start."

Luckily the lump of gefüllte fish I'd deposited in my mouth had not yet started south or I would have choked on it. As it was, I had trouble not losing it. "Business?" I said. "What business?"

"Friday night when the candles are burning," she said, "there's no telling lies by this table. I don't know yet what business because you haven't told us."

Gene Merritt poked at his glasses. "When I told my mother I was bringing you up here for supper," he said, "I explained that you'd wanted me to have lunch with you but I had to break the date because she wanted me to help her pick out a coat in Klein's. From this I assume she concluded there was some business matter you'd wanted to discuss with me at lunch. Is that right, Ma?"

"Of course it's right," Mrs. Merritt said. "Eat with challah. We're listening, Ted."

I took a bite of challah, did some fast thinking, and remembered whom I was up against. I'd never been able to think fast enough to keep ahead of my mother. The chances were better than even money that I wouldn't be able to keep ahead of this little old lady, who could have been her twin sister. Besides, I suddenly knew why I'd been suspicious in the office about Gene Merritt's teeth. I was also willing to bet his mother had not been downtown in Klein's that day, buying a coat. He hadn't wanted to be alone with me. The minute I said it was something I didn't want to discuss in front of Ralph Mattlin, Gene Merritt had known he wanted it discussed where all his decisions were made. At the old lady's table.

"There isn't really very much to discuss," I said. "Did you ever hear of a man named Hubert Sissenwein?"

"Sissenwein?" Mrs. Merritt said. "Zisha, wasn't there a Sissenwein around the corner on Seventh Street? He was a cutter by dresses? His oldest boy fell from the ice wagon? They told him not to hitch, but he didn't listen, so he hitched and what happened? He broke his leg?"

"No, that was Weintraub," Mr. Merritt said. "Abe Weintraub. He wasn't a cutter. He worked on the Fourth Street dock by the Forest Box & Lumber Company. And it wasn't his oldest boy. It was the daughter. Sheindle, her name was. She was playing potsy and she kicked it too hard, so when she ran out in the gutter to get it a taxi was coming the other way and she didn't see it. Not a leg. What she broke it was up here, the collarbone."

"So who is this Sissenwein?" Mrs. Merritt said.

"He's a very rich man," I said. "My lawyer does a lot of his work for him. That's how I met Mr. Sissenwein. My lawyer introduced him to me. And Mr. Sissenwein wants to buy Mattlin & Merritt."

I polished off my gefüllte fish and wiped up the last of the sauce with a piece of challah. I knew I'd get a good mark for that. I did.

"See how he eats?" Mrs. Merritt said to Gene. "It makes a person's heart feel good to watch such an appetite. Another piece, Teddy?"

"If you can spare it," I said.

"To a nice Jewish boy, a guest in my house, I shouldn't be able to spare a second piece of gefüllte fish?" Mrs. Merritt stood up and took my plate. "Don't speak till I come back."

It was a pretty useless piece of advice. I had no intention of opening my mouth while the boss was out of the room, and neither Gene Merritt nor his old man looked as though they dared risk it.

"Wow," I said when Mrs. Merritt came back with my plate. "That's some second piece."

"Eat it in good health," she said. "If you don't finish it I'll only have to throw it out." She sat down. "Why should this Mr. Sissenwein want to buy Mattlin & Merritt?" she said. "With challah eat."

"He owns a lot of other companies," I said. "But he doesn't own a book-publishing business. He feels if he owned a book-publishing company all his other companies would benefit from it, and so he's willing to pay a lot of money to get it."

"So another question," Mrs. Merritt said. "Why should my Gene and his partner, Ralph Mattlin, why should they sell something that all their life they wanted to own and that now it's beginning to be a success?"

"They wouldn't be selling it the way you sell a pair of pants or an automobile," I said. "I mean Gene and his partner, Ralph, they wouldn't be getting money in exchange and giving away their company. They'd still own Mattlin & Merritt, the company."

"This is a kind of selling I never heard of," Mrs. Merritt said. "Zisha, give him another slice challah."

The old man in the brown leather windbreaker went into action with the knife he'd been given forty years ago by a Jewish street cleaner named O'Brien.

"The way it works is this," I said. "Right now, all the Mattlin & Merritt stock is owned by three people. Gene, Ralph Mattlin and that Mr. Applebaum. Mr. Sissenwein is willing to give all three of you for every share of Mattlin & Merritt stock one share of stock in his overall company, which is called Hubert Sissenwein Enterprises, Inc. In addition, the name Mattlin &

Merritt, Inc., will remain unchanged. And on top of that, Mr. Sissenwein will give Gene and Ralph management contracts for life so nobody can interfere with the way they run their business, and they'll be paid salaries equal to whatever they have been drawing up to now or, if they want, whatever they decide they want to draw each year. In this way, Gene and Ralph Mattlin will still be in charge of their own company, and they will earn dividends on their Hubert Sissenwein stock, which is worth my lawyer tells me about twenty-two times as much as the present value of the Mattlin & Merritt stock."

I don't know if Gene Merritt and his old man got the picture. I wasn't looking at them. But I could see that the person I'd been talking to, she got it. The little old lady sat quietly for a couple of moments, looking directly at me, and then she stood up. "Don't speak till I come back," she said. She collected the gefüllte-fish plates and said, "Zisha, cut for Teddy another piece challah."

When she was out of the room I said, "A little thinner, please, Mr. Merritt."

"You don't know what you're saying," he said. "On my wife's table a thin piece challah it's by her like cut off and I put on the table a piece ham."

Mrs. Merritt came back with two plates of chicken soup thick with noodles. She set one in front of her husband and the other in front of me.

"Not yet," she said, and she went out again. She came back with two more plates. She set one in front of Gene, the other at her place, and sat down. "So all right," she said. "Everybody eat. Zisha, this you call a slice challah? Like a page from a book?"

"No, no," I said. "It's really thick enough, Mrs. Merritt."

"So all right," she said. "Eat it and you'll have another one with the chicken. Now if you'll excuse me, Teddy, for business I don't have a head, so if I ask stupid questions, blame it on an old lady she doesn't think so good any more."

"My mother used to say the same thing," I said. "Then she used to ask the only questions that made sense in our house."

315

For this I got a nervous giggle from Gene, who had not opened his yap since we sat down except to stuff it with calories, an empty stare from Mr. Merritt, and a dose of kvelling from the old lady.

"So all right," she said. "Then I won't be ashamed what I'm going to ask. It's like this. This Mr. Sissenwein, he's not crazy?"

I laughed.

"He could be," I said. "I've only met him once. But my lawyer says he's the smartest businessman he's ever met."

"I'm wondering like this," Mrs. Merritt said. "What he's giving to Gene and to Ralph it's like a great big present. They keep their firm, but they get stock that it's worth you say twenty-two times what their own stock is worth. Such a big present, either a man has to be crazy to give it away, or he has to be getting something out of it that we don't know he's getting. What is Mr. Sissenwein getting from this, Teddy?"

"An improvement in all his various holdings," I said. "For example, he owns a paper factory. By owning a book-publishing business, he can increase his profits from his paper factory by having a steady customer named Mattlin & Merritt, and Mattlin & Merritt can increase their profits by being able to buy their paper cheaper than they've been able to buy it up to now. Another example. Mr. Sissenwein owns some radio stations. He can throw book advertising to them, and Mattlin & Merritt can profit from a whole new way of advertising books, on the radio, at very low rates because Mr. Sissenwein owns the stations they'll be advertising on. That's why he doesn't want to change the name of Mattlin & Merritt or the way Gene and Ralph run their business. That's why nobody, the public, they won't even know that Gene and Ralph have sold their business."

I went back to my soup. It was worth going back to. The noodles were homemade. You can always tell. If you were raised on homemade, anyway. The trick is the width. Even when they're as thin as thread from a spool, if they're home-made they're not all the same width. Just in case someday you should have noodle trouble, you might jot that down.

"Gene and Ralph will know."

I looked up. "I beg your pardon?" I said.

What surprised me was not what I'd heard. What surprised me was where the words had come from.

"Gene and Ralph will know," the little old man in the brown leather windbreaker said again. His voice didn't sound any different than he'd sounded when he was describing how he'd got his bread knife. So it must have been the words he was using. They had an edge.

"They made a business," Mr. Merritt said. "Because they loved books. The business is beginning to work. I'm not talking money. I'm talking books. What people read. What makes people better people. What Gene and Ralph are doing. If they sell their business to this Mr. Sissenwein they'll be doing something different. They'll be doing something only for money. When you do something only for money you're not doing it from the heart. Every time you do something that the heart doesn't have anything to do with, you die a little. For money, just for money, I don't want my son to die."

When his voice stopped, it was all of a sudden like when I was a kid in the synagogue on Yom Kippur. The prayer where nobody raises his voice. Everybody whispers. And with each line they hit themselves a small whack over the heart with their closed fists. You feel scared.

"Ma," Gene Merritt said.

His voice hadn't been any louder than his father's. But it was the first thing he'd said since we sat down. The single syllable cut through the room. I knew I was licked.

"Ma," Gene Merritt said again. "I think Papa is right."

31

" Ralphie Darling, There's Always the Other Side of the Coin"

The next morning, I called Ralph Mattlin at home and said I wanted to see him about something important. I saw him in the room now stuffed with chintz where we first met. The night before, in the Bronx, it had taken me two helpings of gefüllte fish and half a tepple of luckshin soup to explain the Sissenwein deal. On Thirty-eighth Street, I got through it by the time Ralph Mattlin was lighting his third cigarette.

"What do you think of the offer?" he said. "I mean personally, Ted."

I turned so his mother's Grubensteller eyes were for a moment off my face and fixed on the back of my head. "I'm not a stockholder," I said. "I'm just an employee. I'm not entitled to an opinion."

Not yet, anyway.

"Pretend you're a stockholder," Ralph Mattlin said. "I'd like to know your opinion."

"If I were a stockholder in Mattlin & Merritt, Inc.," I said, "I'd have trouble looking and sounding calm."

"In other words," Ralph Mattlin said, "you'd accept Sissenwein's offer."

There were no other words.

318

"I'd grab it," I said.

Mattlin punched out the third cigarette and hacked a kitchen-match light to a fourth. He threw the match into the fireplace and started to prowl the room. "You'd be crazy," he said.

His rating with the boys at Bellevue I'd match against mine any day.

"Why?" I said.

"You'd lose control of your firm," Ralph Mattlin said. "Right now Mattlin & Merritt is two men. Me and Gene. We sell out to Hubert Sissenwein, and the firm is not that any more. It stops being two men who like books and enjoy publishing and selling them. It becomes a piece of somebody else's firm. It becomes one small corner of Hubert Sissenwein Enterprises."

A corner that could be to the owners of Mattlin & Merritt stock what the Atlantic Ocean is to a lawn sprinkler.

"Run by you," I said. "He's offering lifetime management contracts to you and Gene. Nobody will have the right to tell you what to do."

"Not the right, no," Mattlin said. "But they'll have the power."

"How?" I said.

"I don't know how," Ralph Mattlin said. "But I feel it. Sissenwein is worth millions. When money gets concentrated in doses as large as that, it ceases to be money. It becomes a force of nature. Like armies and navies. You don't know how a government is going to use them. All you know is they've got them. You can feel the power. You know what they can do to you with that power if you let yourself come into their orbit."

"Ralphie darling, there's always the other side of the coin."

I turned. Benita had come into the room. Every time I saw her, she looked more and more like a charlotte russe. She was all pink and white. Not fat. But cuddly. No wonder Mattlin went home for lunch two or three times a week.

"What did you say?" Mattlin said.

She came into the room. She was wearing a pink and white housecoat. I wouldn't have minded dropping in for a snack once in a while myself.

319

"I was coming up from the laundry," she said. "I heard what Ted said and what you said. I didn't mean to eavesdrop, Ralphie darling. It's just that I could tell from your voice this was not an ordinary business talk. You sounded—you sounded—I don't know, Ralphie. You sounded like—like—you sounded tortured."

"How else would I sound?" Ralph Mattlin said. "A man has just asked Ted to bring me a proposition. He wants to make me rich."

"But if that's all he's offering," Benita said, "why be tortured? If all he's offering is money, the answer has to be no. Neither one of us cares that much about money. Surely you know that, Ted."

What I knew was that when it came to hot air this broad could have kept the *Shenandoah* going until helium got invented.

"Keep me out of this," I said. "It's not my firm. I'm just the bookkeeper."

"Not any more," Ralph Mattlin said. "Byram Noonan and I have just finished working out the final details on your profit-sharing arrangement. In a way, Ted, you're now a partner."

Not in the way I wanted to be a partner.

"All right, you put it like that," I said, "I guess I have the right then to ask Benita what she meant when she first came into the room."

"When I first came into the room?" she said.

I was beginning to understand from whom Hetty Green took her lessons.

"You said there's the other side of the coin," I said.

"There always is," she said. "But as long as Ralph feels that way about Mattlin & Merritt it doesn't matter."

"Think of his bookkeeper," I said. "In a way I'm now a partner. It would matter to me."

"Oh, Ted," she said. "I'm sorry."

"For what?" I said.

"I shouldn't have said that about the other side of the coin."

No, of course not. The way the guy at Sutter's Mill shouldn't have said what's this yellow stuff I've just kicked up with my shoe?

"But you did say it," I said. "I'd like to know what you meant?"

She turned to look up at Mattlin the way those girls in the mistaken-identity movies look up at the guy in whose oversize pajamas they happen to be caught at the moment when he comes home from a sales trip and discovers she was lying to him when she first arrived in town and said he was her long-lost uncle. "Oh, Ralphie," she said.

"It's all right, honeybunch," old Ralphie said. "Tell Ted what you meant."

She turned the headlights on me. She worked a nice little quiver into her lower lip. "I meant only that the power of money can be used just as easily for good as for bad," Benita said. She sounded like Shirley Temple telling Bill Robinson why she wanted all those darling little pickaninnies at her birthday party. "If what you love is books and you love what books can do to make people better, then it seems to me a man like Mr. Sissenwein, with his millions, placing all that money at your disposal, why shouldn't it be used to publish more books? Reach more people? Do more good than a small firm like Mattlin & Merritt can do? That's all I meant, darling. It's probably a stupid little girl's idea and I apologize for interfering in your business discussions."

She turned and started slowly out of the room. She did it like Joan of Arc. She'd just heard that the governor had said nothing doing to a pardon. So she was heading for the old bonfire. She didn't get very far. Ralphie belted the cigarette into the fireplace, took two fast jumping steps, caught her hand and pulled her around. Tom Mix never headed the Indians off at the pass more neatly.

"Ted," Mattlin said. "I think Benita's right." He dipped down and proved it by kissing her. "You smart little honeybunch," he said. Then he nibbled her ear for a while. I was

321

about to ask if he'd like me to get him some A-1 Sauce, when he came back up for air and said, "I'd like to meet this Mr. Sissenwein, but first I'd better discuss this with Gene."

"That won't help," I said.

"Why not?" Mattlin said.

I told him what had happened the night before up in the Bronx.

"Maybe if Benita talked to him?" Mattlin said. "I mean, honeybunch, if you told Gene the things you just told me it might change his mind?"

Honeybunch looked bewildered. She did it by giving her eyes an Eddie Cantor spread and shaking her head from side to side as though she were a palm tree trying to loosen a few cocoanuts from her fronds. "I'll be glad to do anything you and Ted want me to do," she said.

Anything?

"I don't think either one of you has to do anything," I said. "Gene Merritt owns only one third of the Mattlin & Merritt stock. You own another third. If you say yes to Sissenwein and Gene says no, it's a Mexican stand-off. The guy in the driver's seat is the boy who owns that last third of the stock."

Mattlin said, "You mean you want me to talk to Earl Applebaum?"

"I think that might be a mistake," I said. "The last time you talked to Earl Applebaum you'd just drop-kicked his son-in-law, Arnold Zohn, out of here and told the old man you didn't want his loan or his audits. I don't think Mr. Applebaum is in a mood to listen to any suggestions you have to make about how he should handle his Mattlin & Merritt stock."

"You're right," Mattlin said. "And yet before we can accept Hubert Sissenwein's offer we must have Earl Applebaum's consent."

"I have a suggestion," I said. "Let me take a crack at convincing him."

"I didn't know you knew Earl Applebaum," Ralph Mattlin said.

"I don't," I said. "But I know somebody who does."

32

" Change to Shell and Feel the Difference"

I left Ralphie and Honeybunch nibbling each other's ears on Thirty-eighth Street and went up to Forty-second Street. But not into the Knickerbocker Building. Arnold Zohn had said on the day he hired me that he always went to his office at eight-thirty, discussed the day's plans with his assistant, and then they went to the client's office together. Because this made a better impression on the client than if Zohn and his employee came straggling in separately. So on this Saturday morning, I went into the coffeepot across the street from the Knickerbocker Building.

I had called Ralph Mattlin at seven-thirty. We were discussing the Sissenwein offer at eight. I started uptown at twenty minutes after. I was having a glass of milk at a table in the cafeteria window across the street from the Knickerbocker Building at a quarter to nine. At five minutes after, Arnold Zohn came out of the building.

He was carrying the same briefcase and he was loping for the subway entrance in the same Groucho Marx crouch. But he was doing it alone. None of the jerks who had taken his adding test on the morning I had won had apparently got hired after I quit.

This meant losing the Mattlin & Merritt account had meant the end of Zohn's dream to move onward and upward from his Seventh Avenue clients to something more classy and lucrative downtown on Fourth.

Anyway, this was how I analyzed the situation.

It's true, I could have analyzed it wrong. It could turn out Arnold Zohn now had three assistants. It could be he'd sent them all out on their assignments before I sat down with my milk at the table in the cafeteria window. It could be Arnold Zohn was racing down those subway steps because he had a date with Otto Kahn to take over the audit of Goldman Sachs. And it could be I was Sir Thomas Lipton.

The look of a loser is as unmistakable as a limp. Arnold Zohn was exactly where he was the day I met him: still trying to make it in the eyes of his father-in-law without looking as though he was begging for handouts.

I finished my milk, went out, crossed the street and took the elevator to the ninth floor. I stopped in front of the door marked in gold letters:

909–910

ARNOLD ZOHN

CERTIFIED PUBLIC ACCOUNTANT

ENTER THROUGH 911

For the second time in my life I did that. For the second time in my life I found myself in that outer office. For the second time in my life Mrs. Arnold Zohn looked up at me across her typewriter and that wooden rail.

I remembered the mental note I had made the first time to find the answer to a puzzling question: why would a twenty-year-old chick who looked like this marry a boob who looked like Arnold Zohn? The time had come to find out. "Good morning, Miss Applebaum," I said.

"The name is Zohn," she said. "Mrs. Arnold Zohn."

"Aren't you tired of it?" I said.

"What does that remark mean?" she said.

324

"It means you should read the ads and take their advice," I said.

"What advice?" she said.

"Change to Shell and Feel the Difference!"

"Get yourself out of here, smart aleck," she said.

"Not until I return something I owe you," I said.

"What is it?" she said.

"A black knitted tie," I said. "The first time we met, you made your husband take it off. You said it looked better on me."

Nothing happened. Except that underneath, everything was happening. I could tell. So could she. I could tell that too.

"It still does, Mr. Leff," she said. "Don't take it off."

"You mean it's a present?" I said.

"I mean you've had it so long my husband has forgotten he ever owned it," she said. "Now tell me why you really came here today?"

"I want to have a talk with you," I said.

"All right," she said. "Start talking."

"It's sort of personal," I said. "I'd rather not do it here in the office. Couldn't we go downstairs and have a cup of coffee?"

"Sure," she said. "But who's going to answer the phone?"

"If you agree with what I want to talk to you about," I said, "you'll never have to answer a phone again."

33

"What We Want for a Wedding Present Is a Few Shares of Stock You Probably Don't Even Know You Own"

This is the only promise I ever made to my wife Evie that I did not keep. Since that day in 1937 when I asked her to marry me she answered many a phone. But they were not office phones. From the day she gave Arnold Zohn the gate, she has never set foot in any of my offices except as a visitor. It isn't that my wife Evie doesn't know how to run an office. If her hair appointments with Horst at Elizabeth Arden's did not get in the way, she could run General Motors. And it isn't that I believe woman's place is in the home. It's just that there are things a man does in an office that he doesn't always want his home to know about. Arnold Zohn didn't feel that way. That's one of the reasons why he lost her. If she hadn't seen him during the day he could have come home at night and told her about all the killings he'd made while he was downtown. But she did see him during the day. She was part of his action. So there was nothing he could tell her when he came home at night that she didn't already know, and what she knew was that he was a boob. When I came along she was ready for a change. Even I was surprised at how fast Evie Applebaum made the change.

But even that didn't surprise me as much as her parents. You have to see the Applebaums to believe them, and even then it takes an effort. Whether or not the effort is worth making depends on what you're after. I made the effort.

What the Applebaums have going for them is surprise. I refer to Earl, the founder of the family fortune, and to Clarissa, his wife. On second thought, I wonder if "wife" is the correct word. People like Earl Applebaum don't have wives. They have what Milton Merkin called consorts. I do not refer to their daughter, who is my wife Evie. My wife Evie is a knockout. Her parents, Earl and Clarissa, are not. Which is why they always surprise people. Everybody who meets them for the first time says the same thing: "These two slobs are *the* Applebaums?" With a rising inflection. Sometimes even with a little scream of astonishment. Let's face it. My in-laws are not pretty.

In my initial contacts with them I was luckier than most people. I met the Applebaums one at a time. So I didn't scream. I gulped a little, true. But I didn't scream. Evie took me to her father's office to explain to him why she intended to divorce Arnold Zohn. It was a shock, I admit. For me, I mean. Seeing Earl Applebaum, I mean. But by the time Evie took me to the triplex in the Pierre to introduce me to her mother, I was prepared.

I was not prepared for the way Clarissa and Earl Applebaum think of themselves, but I soon adjusted to it. Earl thinks of himself as a duke. In Clarissa's eyes this makes her a duchess.

When Clarissa Applebaum invites you to dinner, and on that night your appendix happens to take it into its silly head to explode, you'd better talk sharply to your appendix and tell it to try some other night. Anything that interferes with Clarissa's personal plans she treats the way Woodrow Wilson treated the sinking of the *Lusitania*. As for Earl, when the traffic commissioner made Fifth Avenue one-way, Earl Applebaum dictated a letter to the Mayor which began, "Do you realize that when I come home from my office at the end of a hard day my car must now circle the block before it can pull up in front of the Hotel Pierre in which I have made my home for a dozen years?"

The day that Evie and I got married, Earl and Clarissa gave a

327

reception for us at the Plaza. It was quite a day. The weather-man, who had never been one of my warm admirers, decided to rub it in. He dumped twenty-two inches of snow on New York City and points north. I was in the room when the Governor called up in person from Albany to apologize for not coming to the reception. The field was socked in, and they wouldn't let his plane take off.

"I have no reason to doubt your word," Clarissa Applebaum said to His Excellency. "Just for the sake of the record, how-ever, you might be interested to know that in spite of the weather seven hundred and eighty-two people managed to get here."

She wasn't kidding. There was a man at the door with one of those little clickers. He counted. When it was all over, and Evie and I were having a nightcap with my new in-laws, Earl Apple-baum asked us what we wanted for a wedding present.

"Don't be hasty," he said. "Think it over. You can tell me when you come back from your honeymoon."

"We've already thought it over," my wife Evie said. "We know what we want for a wedding present, don't we, Ted?"

"You bet," I said.

If anybody thinks he could have made a wittier reply, let him wait till he hears the end of this.

"Speak up," Earl Applebaum said. "What do you kids want for a wedding present?"

"What we want," my wife Evie said to her father, "is a few shares of stock you've got tucked away somewhere that you probably don't even know you own."

"What stock?" Earl Applebaum said.

"It's something you invested in a few years ago," I said. "A publishing firm."

"I did?" Earl Applebaum said.

"You did," I said. "You put up one third of the capital and you got one third of the stock."

"What's the name of this firm?" Earl Applebaum said.

"Mattlin & Merritt," I said.

34

" Take It or Leave It"

The next morning Evie looked up from the bag she was packing. "I think this is a mistake," she said.

"What is?" I said.

"Going on a honeymoon," she said.

"But, Evie," I said. "I thought every girl dreamed of going on a honeymoon?"

"I've been on one," she said.

"Arnold Zohn doesn't count," I said.

"It was my first and it was his first," Evie said. "So it's got to count. But that's not the point. The point is what you married me for. My father's Mattlin & Merritt stock."

I put down my coffee cup. "Evie," I said. "That's not a nice thing to say to your husband on the morning after your wedding night."

"Of course it isn't," she said. "And if you're going to expect me to say nice things to you every morning, this marriage isn't going to last long. Nice things I can always say to you in public, in front of other people, and you better do the same. But in the morning, when we're alone, what counts is not nice things but true things. I'm glad you asked me to marry you and I'm glad I did. Up to now anyway. But I don't think you would have remembered to come around and ask me if my father didn't own that Mattlin & Merritt stock. In fact, if it weren't for that stock, I don't think it would have occurred to you to return that black knitted tie. You would never even have remembered I existed."

I turned to the Room Service coffeepot. We were staying at the Plaza until our apartment would be ready.

"I look at it this way," I said. "What makes a guy remember a girl is not as important as what happens after he does remember her."

"Now you sound much more like the Ted Leff I came to know during our whirlwind courtship," Evie said. "I'd forgotten all about you, too, until you showed up with that tie. So we're even and I'd like it to stay that way. Which is why I think we should stick to the point, and the point about us is not you taking snapshots of me in front of Niagara Falls. That we can do later. The point about us right now is you should vote the one third of the Mattlin & Merritt stock Father gave us as a wedding present with Ralph Mattlin's one third so you can close the Sissenwein deal fast."

"If you cancel the railroad tickets," I said, "I'll get dressed and go to the office right now."

"I already canceled them," my wife Evie said. "While you were in the shower."

When I got to the office I went right into Ralph Mattlin's office.

"Good God," he said. "I thought you were on your way to Niagara Falls."

"I decided it was more important to close the Sissenwein deal first," I said.

"How can we do that?" Mattlin said. "As long as Gene refuses to sell?"

"Gene's refusal doesn't mean anything any more," I said.

"Why not?" Mattlin said.

I told him what my brand-new father-in-law had given me and my brand-new wife the night before as a wedding present.

"So it's two to one," I said. "You and me against Gene. You

330

and I now own sixty-six and two thirds percent of the stock of Mattlin & Merritt, Inc. Gene with his thirty-three and one third has to go along, or else."

That thing started to happen to his eyes. The son of a bitch inside him came up to the window sill and looked out at me. "You sound pretty cocky," he said.

What did he expect me to do? Burst into tears?

"Why shouldn't I?" I said. "I've pulled off something big for both of us."

Mattlin ground out his cigarette and fired up a fresh one. "Suppose I change my mind?" he said. "Suppose I decide to vote my stock with Gene against you?"

He said it casually, through a small smile, but what was leaning out at me across the window sill of those eyes told me he was just crazy enough not to be kidding. But I knew his weakness. I knew where he scared easy. "What does that mean?" I said.

"I mean you've come pretty far in a short time for a boy from the Bronx," Mattlin said. "From Vyse Avenue, I think you said it was, to the Applebaum fortune."

Things were beginning to come a little clearer. I'd forgotten I was dealing with a German. To Ralph Mattlin I would always be a Galitzianer.

"What do you resent?" I said. "That I've come pretty far, or that I started from a place you don't like?"

The look in the eyes moved back a little, but I could still see it. I'd tagged him in a place he didn't like to be reminded about.

"I don't resent anything," he said. "I have nothing against the Bronx."

Except that he now had another equal partner who came from there.

"Good," I said, and I rammed it home. "Because you and I, we now stand on exactly the same level. I refer only to our financial position in the firm, of course."

"Of course," Ralph Mattlin said. "Perhaps that's why it seemed to me you sounded cocky."

"No matter how I sounded," I said, "it wouldn't be very

331

bright of you to worry about it or act on it. Because what you'd be doing, just to try and keep a boy from the Bronx in what you think is his place, you'd be turning your back on your only chance to make a fortune. Just by selling to Sissenwein, you become a rich man. What you become six months from now, a year from now, two years from now, there's no telling. Under the Sissenwein Enterprises umbrella it could be millions. You're not going to do anything as stupid as turn your back on that just to put a Bronx boy in his place."

"What makes you so sure?" Mattlin said.

"First," I said, "it won't do you any good. Nobody is going to keep me in what you think should be my place. I'm on my way and I've got the Applebaum money behind me. Second, you're not a stupid man, so you won't do anything stupid. And third, if you did I don't think Benita would like it."

The look sank back out of sight. Mattlin punched the cigarette into his ashtray. He stood up, laughed, came out from behind the desk and put his arm across my shoulder. "Let's go into Gene Merritt's office," he said.

When we came in, Merritt came up out of his attack on the *New York Times* with the golden scissors. "Gentlemen," he said through the wild little giggle. "Did you hear the one about the fat lady in the circus who married the midget?"

"Yes," Ralph Mattlin said. "Many times."

Merritt looked as though he'd been slapped. I took a quick look at Mattlin. The feeling I always had when they were together, the feeling that Mattlin was taking it carefully and gently with a difficult patient, that feeling was gone. Something new had come into the room. Mattlin had brought it in with him. Listening to him tell Merritt what the new setup was, I remembered the feeling I'd had from the beginning: that these two men didn't like each other. Listening to Mattlin lay it on the line, I began to understand something else: Mattlin had been storing this up for a long time. The opportunity had finally come. He was pouring it all out. Watching Merritt's face as Mattlin banged the words at him, telling the frightened little guy with the crooked glasses that Mattlin and I were going to vote against him and sell the firm to Hubert Sissenwein, I had still another feeling: guilt. This little guy with the crooked glasses was a Galitzianer, like me. I had taken sides against him with a German. I was suddenly glad my mother was dead.

"That's it," Mattlin said. "We're exchanging the stock of Mattlin & Merritt, Inc., for stock in Hubert Sissenwein Enterprises, Inc. You can go along with us if you like. If you don't, Ted and I will be glad to buy you out. Take it or leave it."

In the silence that followed, the little guy's lips puffed in and out, gently, like a fish breathing. He didn't look at Mattlin or at me. He stared down at his golden scissors. When he finally looked up, it was not at Ralph Mattlin. It was at me that Gene Merritt looked.

"Ted," he said in a low voice. "My mother is going to be very disappointed in you."

35

" Keep in Touch"

Maud Eitner was waiting at our table in North Northeast.

"The usual?" Gregory said when I sat down.

"Yes, except make it a double," I said.

He went away.

Maud said, "The least you could have done was invite me to the wedding."

"No," I said. "Gertrude Lebenbaum, maybe. But you, no."

Maud looked down into her drink. "I guess that's a compliment," she said.

"Don't guess," I said.

"What's she like?" Maud said.

"What difference does that make?" I said.

"It's been a bad year for homely girls," Maud said. "I didn't mind losing Mattlin to Benita, because she's a foolish little I Love Life nitwit, and besides I'd suddenly discovered I liked somebody else better. I'd hate to feel I lost you only because you wanted Earl Applebaum's Mattlin & Merritt stock."

It was the word "only." It stopped me. I'd been going so fast I hadn't had time to think about anything but keeping the car on the road. Now I was thinking of something else. Would I have done it if Evie had looked like Maud Eitner?

"I'm lucky," I said. "She's a knockout."

"That's good," Maud said.

"Why do you say that?" I said.

"You're a bastard," Maud said. "But so are a lot of people, and maybe it's as good a thing to be as any other if you want to get through the twentieth century in one piece. But you're a bastard I happen to like. So I prefer to see the damage you cause kept to a minimum."

"What's that got to do with the way Evie looks?" I said.

"You've got what you wanted," Maud said. "To get it, you'd have married even someone who looks like me. But later, when you got over the excitement of the money, you'd start looking at her the way I've seen you look at lots of women, including me. And if she looked like me and she loved you, she'd be in for a rough time."

Gregory brought my drink and set it down. "Miss Eitner?" he said.

"No, thanks," she said, still talking to the olive in her martini. "I'll wait a bit."

"Yes, ma'am." He went away.

"Look," I said. "I promised if you helped me you'd get your cut, and I intend to keep my promise."

"Oh, God," Maud said.

"What's the matter now?" I said.

"Don't you ever think about anything but money?" she said.

"Sure," I said. "But a guy can handle only one thing at a time. When I laid this out you said you wouldn't help me but you'd join me. Now that I've pulled it off and I want to see that you get your share, you sound as though I double-crossed you."

"Didn't you?" she said.

"On a couple of minor points, sure," I said.

"I guess you're right," Maud said to her olive. "Marrying a girl for her father's stock. What could be more minor than that?"

Wasting time in this kind of argument.

"How would you like to get it?" I said.

"Get what?" Maud said.

"Your cut," I said.

"Give it to the U.J.A.," Maud said.

She stood up. I put my hand on her arm and pushed her back.

"Quit that," I said. "And tell me. What are your plans?"

"I'm quitting," Maud said.

"Why?" I said.

"I don't think I want to continue working in an office where I'd have to see you come in every morning all aglow from your happy little love nest."

"Good," I said. "Then you don't have to quit."

"Why not?" Maud said.

"I'm not coming into the Mattlin & Merritt offices any more," I said. "I've got as much out of Fourth Avenue as I want or can use."

"Where are you going?" she said.

"Fifth," I said.

She gave me a long look. "Forgive me for being so slow," Maud Eitner said finally. "But I think I've got it at last. From now on you're a Hubert Sissenwein man."

Not exactly. I was what I had always been. A Ted Leff man.

"Right," I said. "What I'd like you to do is remain behind and mind the Fourth Avenue store."

"For you?" Maud said.

"For both of us," I said.

She picked the olive out of her glass and put it into her mouth. Even in the gloom I could see why she had been talking to her drink. It gave me a funny feeling. The only other eyes in which I had ever seen tears like that had belonged to my mother. "You are a son of a bitch," Maud Eitner said very quietly. Then she added, "But aren't we all?"

"Not you," I said.

I meant it. I could hear it in the sound of my own voice. That I meant it. She heard it too.

"I'm no different from anybody else," Maud Eitner said. She hesitated. She seemed to be trying to decide whether she should say something. Then she reached out and touched my hand. "Ted," she said.

"What?" I said.

"Keep in touch," Maud said.

36

" Better Call Before You Go and Check If It's Okay"

I tried. But I didn't make it. Maybe I didn't try very hard. This is still the biggest city in the world. Just the same, it's a small town. People who keep in touch are always getting tagged. For me it was no longer worth the risk. My wife Evie had made it plain right from the start how she stood on this point, and my wife Evie was my pipeline to the Applebaum vault. Besides, as a Hubert Sissenwein man I no longer had much interest in Fourth Avenue. It had served its purpose. The book-publishing business had done for me what the dress business had fallen on its face trying to do. I was on my way.

I didn't realize how far I'd gone until sixteen years later when I walked uptown from our apartment at Eighty-third and Fifth to meet the new executor of the Sissenwein estate in Byram Noonan's apartment at Ninety-sixth and Fifth.

Byram Noonan's apartment house was what he called "comfortably below the anchor." Byram's office did a lot of real estate work. One of his specialties was turning old apartment houses into cooperatives. The choicest items in this field were the Fifth Avenue buildings that faced Central Park. When Evie and I bought our apartment at Eighty-third Street, Earl Applebaum said we were crazy.

"It's too far uptown," he said. "Harlem is moving down so fast, by the time you get your mezuzah nailed to the doorjamb your neighbors in the building will be hitting you up for contributions to the NAACP."

Byram Noonan disagreed. "Fifth Avenue real estate is safe up to One Hundred and First Street," he said. "On its way downtown, Harlem will never be able to cross the barrier of Mt. Sinai Hospital. Look at me and Juliette. Even at Ninety-sixth Street, we're comfortably below the anchor."

They were also uncomfortably on the second floor. To me it doesn't make sense to shell out a hundred big ones for a place where you can lay your head, your wife and an occasional friend, only to find when you look out the front window that what you've bought yourself is one hell of a beautiful view of the Good Humor Man. He was unloading a Double Fudge Ripple on a kid in a St. David's blazer when the Noonan maid showed me into the living room.

"Ted," Byram said. "Hello."

So again I knew there was trouble. Since Walter Idleman had cooled, and Byram and I had gone two days before to see him properly tucked away at Campbell's, I had not had a single one-syllable "Hi" greeting out of my lawyer. I looked around the room for the cause of the trouble. At first I didn't see anybody. Not even Byram. This was not surprising. In addition to the other things she had, Juliette Noonan had a hobby. She collected tinsel prints. She felt about these the way she felt about the spectacular equipment with which nature had provided her. She liked to have it all on display at the same time. As a result, the Noonan living room looked as though it were papered with pages from a postage-stamp album in which all the stamps had been made from the tin-foil wrappers out of old packages of chewing gum. With the sunlight shafting in across the Good Humor Man, it was a little like peering through the golden jumping fizz thrown off by the sparklers we used to burn on the Fourth of July when I was a kid. Then a big blob stepped out of the sunlight, and I saw Byram.

"Hi," I said. Until I found out what the trouble was, there was no point in both of us wasting syllables.

"Ted," he said. "I know you know Mrs. Claude Wakefield, Jr.?"

She came out of the winking lights the sun was splashing on the print of a black and red vase full of purple and yellow flowers.

"No, I'm afraid not," I said. "I used to know a girl named Benita Adler who became Mrs. Ralph Mattlin."

She laughed. "Ted darling," she said.

I moved forward to meet her, and she took me by surprise. I was holding out my hand, but she used both of hers to pull me toward her. It was like that day when Ralph Mattlin invited me to Thirty-eighth Street for dinner for the first time. I got the windshield-wiper job.

"Well," I said. "One thing hasn't changed."

She laughed again. "No, it hasn't," she said. "You're still reading more into a friendly greeting than you should."

I wondered. If she was getting anything at all from Claude Wakefield, Jr., how come she had so much left over for former bookkeepers of her dead husband's firm?

"Maybe so," I said. "But a man can't help hoping."

Byram managed to get a couple of "Er ahem" notes out of his voice box. "Would you two like to be alone?" he said.

"Mr. Noonan," she said. "You're not arranging the grounds for a divorce. We're meeting to discuss a business matter. Surely we're all matoor enough to do that?"

That was another thing that hadn't changed. I wondered if she still made little speeches about never washing the salad bowl but always wiping it with a paper napkin.

"Hope so," Byram said. "Nothing much to discuss, really."

I suddenly wondered if he was right. I remembered the trouble I'd had, years ago, after she married Mattlin, in trying to decide with which of the several Benitas I was dealing. All I could tell from looking at her now was that there had been some changes. In seventeen years there were bound to be. In everybody. My morning session with the shaving mirror told me that.

340

The last time I'd seen her, she'd been a plump little charlotte russe. All pink and white curves that made it hard to keep your hands in your pockets. Some of the curves were gone now, but there were enough left to go around in the right places. Also, she still had that look in her eye. The one that made you feel if you ever got your hands on the reins she'd give you a ride you wouldn't forget.

The main changes, however, were what money had done to her on the outside. The last time I'd seen her she was still wearing her hair high up in a bun, and she had herself wrapped in one of those pink and white flouncy things with a zipper down the front that were known as hostess gowns. Now her hair was chopped off. Ragged and uneven at the edges. It looked as though she'd cut it herself in the dark with a pair of blunt cuticle scissors. One of those jobs that go for five quid on Old Bond Street in those joints where you've got to have a standing weekly appointment or they won't let you through the door, and when a woman can't keep her appointment because let's say her husband had dropped dead, her friends start bidding for the available hour like those Roman soldiers throwing dice for Jesus' robe. As for what Benita was wearing, it was one of those suits my wife Evie and her mother go over to Paris every year to pick up at what they call "the openings" for what before the war you could buy a Buick. With four-wheel drive, yet. Benita looked the way Milton Merkin must have wanted her to look when he started taking the *oy gevalts* out of her conversation and sticking in the *mais oui's*. The raw material had obviously been there, but Milton had not had the ass to swing it. I wondered what Claude Wakefield, Jr., had.

"What I'd like to discuss," I said, "is how a girl I once knew as Benita Adler became the daughter of a man called Walter Idleman."

"Oh, darling," Benita said, "I'm not really an Idleman except by adoption. What happened, it was Claude's first wife. He married Alicia Idleman, and Claude was terribly fond of her parents. After Alicia died he continued to see Mr. and Mrs. Idleman, and then when Claude and I got married I grew just as fond of them as Claude was. Four days ago, when we got her cable in London about Mr. Idleman's death, Claude and I both wanted to fly to Los Angeles at once but Claude couldn't get away, so I came on alone."

"Glad you did," Byram said. "Simplifies matters."

"For whom?" Benita said.

The xylophone in Byram's throat started bonging.

"Byram," I said, "if you had a drink I think it would improve that throat condition. I don't think it would hurt mine, either."

Benita brushed me with that look the way a martini nut sprays his slug of gin with a fast glimpse of the label on the vermouth bottle. I had a sudden feeling my chances had improved since I'd seen her last. I'm told most middle-aged men feel this. As a middle-aged man I can add something to that. Most middle-aged men are right."

"Sorry," Byram said. "Of course. What will you have, Mrs. Wakefield?"

What an opening. But she let me down.

"A drop of sherry," she said. "If it's available?"

"Of course," Byram said. "Excuse me."

He disappeared into the winking lights of the tinsel prints that filled the corner of the room in which Juliette had installed the bar. Benita and I were face to face. The look on hers changed. "What do you want, Ted?" she said.

She said it the way the shamus in the shul used to say in a low voice, "Stand over there, Teddy, on the other side of the Torah." I took a chance.

"What you wanted when you married Ralph Mattlin," I said.

"I don't think that's true," she said. "In those days we were both hungry. I wanted money. So did you. But now we're both beyond that. I know how much I have. It doesn't take an active imagination to figure out how much the husband of Evie Applebaum has. Not counting what you've piled up on your own. There must be some other answer."

"I can't think what it is," I said.

Benita touched the fringe at the back of her Old Bond Street haircut. "I can, Ted darling," she said.

342

"Tell me," I said.

"Remember the last time you and Ralph met?" she said.

I did and I didn't. The good parts came back right away. But they were fuzzy at the edges. Like one of those photographs that have had the bad parts air-brushed away. I wasn't surprised. In the beginning I'd been very interested in Ralph Mattlin. The moment I saw him that day when Arnold Zohn first brought me to Fourth Avenue, I knew I'd found the boy I could use to get me out of the hole into which my bankruptcy on Seventh Avenue had dumped me. For about a year, while I was working my way up out of the hole, everything about Mattlin interested me, including his wife. Then I made it with Hubert Sissenwein. I was out of the hole. I peeled off Ralph Mattlin and Gene Merritt and Fourth Avenue like the skin of a tangerine. I told them to get themselves a new bookkeeper, and I moved over to the Sissenwein Enterprises offices at Forty Rock.

Right from the start I liked the feel of Rockefeller Plaza. It wasn't just a place full of expensive offices and restaurants where a shrimp cocktail went for a buck seventy-five. It was an instrument panel. The boys who sat in front of it and moved the dials were running pieces of the world that on East Fourth Street had been to me just names on a map. Hubert Sissenwein's team controlled a nice fat share of those dials. He made it perfectly plain right from the moment I moved in that he had not signed me on as a bat boy. Hubie sent me out on the field. I started pitching immediately. Sissenwein liked my fast ball. I liked the sense of moving forward. And nothing stopped the expansion of the ball game. Not even the war.

I spent part of it in Australia. Most of it in England. Then a lot of it in France. I was in uniform, of course. But my orders were never cut in the Pentagon. Hubert Sissenwein Enterprises was fighting its own war. More accurately, Hubie was using the war everybody else was fighting. The Pentagon sent me where they thought they wanted me to go. But it was Hubert Sissenwein who did their thinking for them. About me, anyway. I'm positive Rabbi Goldfarb would have said this was wrong. My mother too. But who can say for sure? What counts is we won the damn thing. And a week after we did, I was back in New York.

The day I got home, Ralph Mattlin called up and asked me to have lunch with him. I looked at my calendar. It was so stuffed with dates put into it by my wife Evie at home and by my secretary in the Sissenwein office, I found I couldn't meet anybody for lunch for more than a week.

"I'd prefer not to wait that long," Mattlin said. "Could I come to your office?"

This surprised me. Before the war, in the days when I'd first known him, Ralph Mattlin had not been the sort of guy who went to other people's offices. Not unless it was the only way he could get something he wanted.

"You could," I said. "But we'd never hear ourselves talk. Hubert Sissenwein's general manager is reconverting the place to peacetime activities. We've got more carpenters banging away than Henry Kaiser had in his shipyards. How about if I come to your office?"

"Why, Ted, that would be very nice."

This time I was surprised because he was surprised. I could tell it in his voice. He had not expected me to come to him.

"What's a good time for you?" I said.

"You name it," Mattlin said.

So I knew he wanted something from me.

"How about four o'clock?" I said.

"Great," Mattlin said.

With warmth? No. Gratitude? Not exactly. Then inside my head I replayed the sound of the single word, and I had it. Ralph Mattlin had sounded relieved. As though he'd expected me to refuse to see him. For the first time since I'd left Mattlin & Merritt behind me, I realized I could have refused. I was annoyed by the fact that I hadn't. It's no fun to be reminded you're never going to stop being that Galitzianer kid from East Fourth Street who gets a kick out of being noticed by a rich German bastard from uptown.

As soon as I came into the Mattlin & Merritt offices I forgot my annoyance. It was like that day I'd gone to the Bronx to have Friday night supper with Gene Merritt and his parents, and I'd suddenly remembered what it had been like when I was a kid in the Bronx. Now I was suddenly remembering what it had been like that first day when I walked into this reception room with Arnold Zohn.

There was a new girl behind the billing-machine fort. And on the long table, instead of the display of cellophane-wrapped jigsaw puzzles, there was a double row of the Twentieth Century Classics. But out of the frame on the wall, O. W. Holmes, Jr., was still saying "The reward of the general is not a bigger tent, but command," and facing the frame was the same old fumed-oak sofa on which I'd waited to meet Ralph Mattlin, and a little piece of that first feeling came back to me. A feeling you didn't get at Forty Rock. A feeling that you'd stepped into a place not unlike an unmarked laboratory in a hospital, a place where things went on that you didn't quite understand but had to respect. They were doing whatever they were doing not only for their salaries but for humanity, whatever that was.

Only eight years had gone by since that first day. And I hadn't yet crossed the line of my thirty-third birthday. But all of a sudden I knew something I'd never known before. Not even in London when the German hardware was falling all around you. All of a sudden I knew I wasn't going to live forever. A nice fat juicy lump of my life was over. I could see where it had gone. You didn't have to be a whiz at arithmetic to see something else: the number of lumps like it was not endless. All of a sudden I knew what had happened to my mother was going to happen to me. All of a sudden I knew someday I was going to die.

"Is Mr. Mattlin expecting you?" the girl said.

All of a sudden I wished he wasn't.

"Yes," I said.

She picked up her phone, announced me, then said, "Go right in, Mr. Leff. First door on your left."

On my way in I noticed another change. The Ping-Pong tables in the large open space between the private offices had been replaced by desks. A dozen girls, maybe two dozen, were working at them. I knocked on Mattlin's door.

"Herein!"

It was like Cracker Jacks. A surprise in every box. This one puzzled me. The way I remembered Mattlin, he used that word only when he was in a good mood. How could he be in a good mood on the same day when he'd sounded relieved on the phone because I'd agreed to come and see him? I opened the door and went in.

"Ted."

He got up from behind the desk and came around to take my hand. All six-feet-four of him. Except that now he looked shorter. The slight stoop, the small round-shouldered bend that had once made him look like a Jewish Noel Coward, had become more noticeable. As though he'd been warned the mob had marked him for a rub-out job and he was trying to hide the height that made him conspicuous.

"Ralph," I said.

He held my hand for a long time and looked straight into my face. He did it with a sort of worried frown. As though he were reading the small print on the label of a bottle of British steak sauce made from the recipe of a gentleman in the country. I looked back at him. What else could I do? When the optometrist is examining your pupils you're going to study your toenails? Mattlin's eyes were still blue, but the hardness had gone out of them. As though the paint had been diluted by something neutral. His hair was no longer the color of good mink. Or even cheap mink. It was gray and it looked sloppy. As though he'd been meaning for a couple of weeks to get around to the barber but things kept getting in the way. But it was the jacket that told most of the story. It was one of his Tweak Sothills. The high-peaked lapels were practically tickling his ears. He must have lost twenty pounds since I'd seen him last.

"You look great, Ted," he said.

"So do you," I said.

It was the sort of lie even Rabbi Goldfarb would have told. Ralph Mattlin looked like a guy who had climbed out of a sickbed with a hundred and two against the doctor's orders because he felt if he missed this appointment he'd have to hang up his gloves.

"I feel better since I quit smoking," he said.

Sick men always assume the rest of the world has been keeping tabs on their condition.

"How long?" I said.

A man tells you he's quit smoking, and you don't ask when, you could get arrested for like what the divorce lawyers call cruel and barbarous treatment.

"Eight months," Ralph Mattlin said.

"Was it tough?" I said.

"The first few days," he said. "But when I began to feel better the way the doctor said I would it got easier. How was the war?"

I suppose when he made it back home to Carthage, Hannibal got asked the same dopey question.

"My part of it was okay," I said. "How's Benita?"

"Great," he said.

"Sacheverell?"

"Doing fine," Mattlin said. "He's at the Little Red Schoolhouse. He's got a brother now. Be four next month."

"Winston?" I said.

The lines in the tired face rearranged themselves. Surprise. "How did you know that?" Ralph Mattlin said.

I assumed he'd have enough brains not to name the kid Adolf.

"I must have heard it somewhere," I said.

"He's a nice boy," Mattlin said. "What are you looking for?"

"I don't know," I said. "Something's missing?" The room had more chintz in it than a Jane Austen novel, but the walls felt naked.

"Shortly after you left," Mattlin said, "Benita redid my office. It's attractive, I think. Don't you?"

"Great," I said. Then I knew what was wrong. "The Grubensteller portrait of your mother," I said. "The painting. It used to be up there."

He turned to look at the great big Audubon print. A black bird with a head like a hammer and a great big red sack under its beak. With chicken-liver eyes it could have been Hubie

Sissenwein's twin brother. Mattlin stared at it as though he'd never seen it before.

"Yes," he said finally. "It seemed a little—" He stopped and scowled down at the floor. He could have been an actor at rehearsal who had just forgotten a line. Mattlin drew a deep breath. "Benita felt it didn't go with the chintz," he said. He waved to the couch out of which eight years before he had jumped to say, "Ted, here, has come up with something big." Now he said, "Sit down, Ted."

I sat down. He went back to the chair behind the desk. I noticed he eased himself into it. He used both hands on the chair arms to lower himself slowly, as though he was afraid the seat might be too hot. When he made it, Mattlin stared at me out of those diluted blue eyes as though he couldn't seem to remember who I was or what I was doing in his office. I decided to help him. Why not? He'd once helped me.

"You said it was important," I said.

"What?" Mattlin said.

He was like a guy in a picture gallery who had been staring at a painting and a guard had come up and touched his elbow to tell him it was closing time.

"This thing you wanted to see me about," I said. "You said on the phone it couldn't wait a week."

Mattlin's mind came back into the room. "Oh yes," he said. "I meant I'd rather it didn't. It's about Gene."

"Gene Merritt?" I said.

I could have said Gene Tunney. But I had the feeling I was sitting next to a sickbed. I had to be careful with the jokes.

"Yes," Mattlin said. "He's not well, Ted."

Somebody must have stolen his golden scissors.

"I'm sorry to hear that," I said. "What's wrong with him?"

"Bernie Yustin calls it acute melancholia."

"What's that?" I said.

"Depression," Ralph Mattlin said.

I thought Franklin Roosevelt got us out of that.

"What's he depressed about?" I said.

"Mattlin & Merritt," Ralph Mattlin said.

348

"That's curious," I said. "I haven't been in close touch with your operation, because all through the war Sissenwein has had me working on other things. But I took a look at the figures before I left the office to come over here. The last fiscal year you did seven million gross."

Mattlin nodded. Like a fiddler keeping time to the opening bars of "Hatikvah." "And made a net of almost eight hundred thousand," he said. "Of which Gene and I got not a penny."

Hubert Sissenwein had not bought out Mattlin & Merritt to see that Ralph Mattlin and E. Spinoza Merritt had a nice steady flow of pennies.

"Because other elements in the Hubert Sissenwein Enterprises holding company are still fighting to find their feet," I said. "Cairo Productions lost a million two on its first picture because Hubert felt it was more important to blow a couple of million on promotion to establish the trademark than to come up with a black figure at this early stage. WKCTO in Omaha is still running at a loss, but a loss that's one third what the previous management was doing, and we're pretty sure to bring it into the black next year. The Washington newsletter can't be expected to make money for another couple of years. It's still too new, but it's sure to be better and bigger when it gets rolling. We don't know yet about the Toronto thing. It may have been the wrong moment to buy Canadian real estate, but Hubert feels—"

"Ted."

My name came out of Mattlin's face so quietly that I wasn't sure I'd heard it.

"Yes?" I said.

"I know how Hubert Sissenwein feels," Ralph Mattlin said. "I'm trying to tell you how Gene Merritt feels. He feels sick. He wants his child back."

Why didn't he call the Missing Persons Bureau?

"You mean Mattlin & Merritt, Inc.?" I said.

Ralph Mattlin nodded. Hunched down in the chair behind the desk, watching me out of those once hard but now watery blue eyes, he reminded me of beggars I'd seen in the park.

Sizing you up as they made the touch. Were they going to get that nickel? Or was this one of those wise guys whose approach to charity was a cold look across the head of the guy with the outstretched palm?

"Yes," Mattlin said. "Gene wants his firm back. The firm he and I founded."

It was like Gertrude Lebenbaum saying she wanted her virginity back. There are things when they're gone, they're gone.

"That's impossible," I said. "Mattlin & Merritt, Inc., is now owned by Hubert Sissenwein Enterprises, Inc. Gene Merritt swapped his Mattlin & Merritt stock for Hubert Sissenwein Enterprises, Inc., stock. Just as you and I did."

"Gene didn't want to do it," Ralph Mattlin said.

Neither did Gertrude Lebenbaum.

"But you and I did," I said. "We outvoted him."

"It was a mistake," Ralph Mattlin said.

So was Hitler's invasion of Russia.

"How can you say that?" I said. "Did you see what Hubert Sissenwein Enterprises common closed at in yesterday's market?"

"Of course I did," Ralph Mattlin said. "So did Gene. But he gets no satisfaction from it."

A new problem for the Federal Reserve Board to tackle. Giving schmucks like Gene Merritt satisfaction.

"He gets no satisfaction out of being worth almost two million dollars?" I said.

"It's only on paper," Ralph Mattlin said. "All those other things. Cairo Productions. The radio station in Omaha. The Washington newsletter. The Toronto real estate. All those things mean nothing to Gene. It's Mattlin & Merritt, Inc. The firm we started. That's the only thing that means anything to him. He wants it back. He wants to be what we started to be. Book publishers."

People have funny ambitions. Why didn't he want to be Clark Gable?

"You are," I said. "You've both got management contracts. You run this firm without any interference."

350

"But we're not running it for ourselves," Ralph Mattlin said. "We're running it for something called Hubert Sissenwein Enterprises. So that when we do something we enjoy, like the year before last, the Thoreau in three volumes for the Twentieth Century Classics Series, all we're doing it for is to bail out a movie company called Cairo Productions and a radio station in Omaha we never heard of and a Washington newsletter we had nothing to do with."

"You and Gene should have thought of that before you swapped your stock," I said.

Ralph Mattlin waved his hand in front of his eyes. He could have been brushing away a fly. Except that there were no flies around. Certainly not on me.

"I did think of it," Mattlin said.

"But you went ahead and swapped anyway," I said.

He looked up at the Audubon print. I had a feeling he wasn't seeing the black bird with the hammerhead. My guess was the Grubensteller portrait of his mother had been removed not because it didn't go with the chintz. It was those eyes. They didn't go with what he had done with his stock.

"Yes," he said in a tired voice. "I swapped, anyway."

"Why?" I said.

He shook his head. "I don't know," Ralph Mattlin said.

I did. I could see him downtown on Thirty-eighth Street the first time I'd met him. The morning I came to tell him Mr. Nachman had slipped fifty grand out of the kitty. I remembered the way his hard blue eyes had changed when he got the news. They had suddenly gone soft. As though something had been poured in to dilute the color. They had looked for a few seconds the way they now looked all the time. I remembered thinking this guy has stuff, but when it comes to money he scares easy.

"Benita said it was a good thing," I said. "She said with the Sissenwein money behind you Mattlin & Merritt could do a lot of good by bringing more books to more people."

For a second or so the eyes changed. The old color came back. The pupils were hard ice-blue. Mattlin even straightened up in the chair. "Keep her out of this," he said. His voice sounded like a kid's fingernails going down a blackboard.

"How?" I said.

It was like sticking a pin into a balloon. I could almost hear the air hissing out of him. The hard blue disappeared. The eyes became watery again. The long body curled down into the chair. "She didn't understand," Ralph Mattlin said. "Neither did I. Now we do. Now I want to save Gene. Because what's happened to him is my fault."

"You've got to be practical," I said. "Hubert Sissenwein is not the kind of man who backtracks. He wanted Mattlin & Merritt, Inc., in his complex. He's got it. There's no reason why he should give it back."

"He might if you asked him," Ralph Mattlin said.

It was the accent on the "you." It told me what had happened here on the home front while I was overseas saving the American way of life.

"What did Sissenwein say when *you* asked him to give it back?" I said.

Mattlin looked down at his desk blotter. He did it the way in P. S. 188 we used to look at the pictures Miss Wien handed out with instructions to find the hidden diagrams.

"Did Gene also ask him?" I said.

Mattlin shook his head. "He couldn't," Mattlin said. "Gene was too sick. But his mother went to see Sissenwein."

All of a sudden I felt sick. I could see that little old lady in that room with the Duke of Sunderland's coffee service and the barber chair..I could see her holding her purse on her lap with both hands while Lennie snipped away at Hubie's hair. I could hear her voice the way I could still hear my own mother's voice. And I could hear Hubie's answer. All of a sudden I knew why people made a career out of hating Hubert Sissenwein.

"No dice?" I said.

Mattlin shook his head again. "No dice," he said.

People who don't know how to figure odds shouldn't shoot craps.

"There's only one solution," I said. "If Gene is so crazy to get his own firm back again, I can arrange to buy his Hubert

352

Sissenwein Enterprises stock at current market value. Yours too, if you want, and with that kind of money you boys will have more than enough to start a new publishing firm."

And if Earl Applebaum didn't jib at ponying up the purchase price I'd have three times as big a slice of Hubert Sissenwein Enterprises, Inc., as I had now.

"That won't help," Ralph Mattlin said. "You know as well as we do that when we signed our management contracts with Sissenwein at the time of the stock swap we agreed never to use the name 'Mattlin & Merritt' on any other company. It's the name that Gene wants. Not the money. He wants his name back."

So did a boy named Judas.

"Maybe I'd better have a talk with Gene," I said. "Is he in his office?"

"No," Ralph Mattlin said. "You'll find him here." He pushed a card across the desk. "Better call before you go and check if it's okay," Mattlin said. "Sometimes when he's very bad they won't allow people to see him even during visiting hours."

37

" For You I'll Try"

Ten minutes later, following Gregory through the gloom of the Walpole Bar, I noticed something else that had not changed. The little old ladies in the funny hats were still getting stoned four to a table.

"They've been sitting here since Pearl Harbor?" I said.

"Except on V-E Day," Gregory said. "That afternoon they all came down early for an extra belt. Miss Eitner, your guest."

"Bring him a double," Maud said.

"Yes, ma'am," Gregory said.

He went away. I sat down facing her at North Northeast. For a few silent moments we examined each other the way I imagine prize fighters sneak guarded glances at the opposition during the weighing-in ceremonies on the morning before a bout. I don't know what Maud Eitner saw, but what I saw was very nice. The light in the Walpole Bar had always been kind to her. Now I realized something else. The passage of time was going to be even kinder. Only eight years had gone by since I had last seen her. Not exactly what my P. S. 188 history book called an era. But it was long enough to show the beginnings of a change that I could see was going to get better and better as she got older.

Kids have no charity. Only hot nuts. So a homely girl is something to laugh at. And avoid. But nature evens things off. As your cashews cool, your eyesight improves. Homely girls begin to look like handsome women.

"What are you thinking?" Maud said.

"The days before the war," I said. "When we were on the way up. What are you thinking?"

"That I just won a bet," Maud said.

"From whom?" I said.

"Me," she said. "When Ralph Mattlin told me this morning you were coming in to see him at four, I told Selma to catch you on your way out and ask you to meet me in the Walpole Bar at five."

"Who's Selma?" I said.

"The new billing clerk who gave you my message," Maud said. "She's new so she doesn't know what happened before Pearl Harbor. But I do, of course, so I made the bet."

"That I wouldn't show up?" I said.

"No," Maud said. "That you would."

She had more confidence in me than I had. "You almost lost," I said.

"But I didn't," Maud said.

"What Mattlin told me about Gene Merritt," I said, "I felt—I don't know how I felt. Not good is about the best way to put it. It was out of the past. I'd forgotten it. Then I left Mattlin's office, and the girl at the billing machine gave me your message. All the way down in the elevator I said to myself no, I'm not going around the corner to that goddamn saloon. But I did."

Maud smiled. "Never underestimate the power of a woman," she said.

"Some woman," I said.

"Stop pushing," Maud said. "That's over."

"Is it?" I said.

"No," she said. "Of course not. But that's the way I'm going to play it."

"Why?" I said.

"Two reasons," Maud Eitner said. "I don't want to get you

into trouble. From what I've been able to learn about your wife Evie, she's the Jewish J. Edgar Hoover. She'll find out. When she does you'll be right back where you were when you first walked into the Mattlin & Merritt offices eight years ago. She dumped Arnold Zohn without working up a sweat, and she'll do the same to you."

"What's your second reason?" I said.

"Only two men have ever meant anything to me," Maud Eitner said. "One of them is in bad trouble. I couldn't keep going if the other one was too."

"I'm the other one," I said.

"You're the other one," she said.

"I don't understand what kind of trouble Ralph Mattlin is in," I said. "It was Gene Merritt he kept talking about."

"He doesn't give a damn about Gene Merritt," Maud Eitner said. "You were right from the start about their feelings for each other. Ralph Mattlin has never had anything but contempt for that Galitzianer. Ralph was talking about himself."

Like an old lantern slide it came back to me. The impression I'd had eight years ago, when I first saw the two men in a room together. That morning when Ralph Mattlin had introduced me to his partner.

"You mean what Ralph Mattlin just told me is not true?" I said. "Merritt is not in this sanatorium?"

"No, that's true enough," Maud Eitner said. "Merritt cracked up about a year ago. First, his father died. Then, when it became clear that no matter how successful Mattlin & Merritt was, the profits would always be milked away by the other things under the Sissenwein umbrella, his mother got sick. I don't know if there was any connection, but it seemed to kick away the scaffolding that was holding Gene Merritt on his feet. We know of course that he was always something of a nut. Those golden scissors. Cutting up all those newspapers. The crooked eyeglasses. I don't know. If it wasn't the Mattlin & Merritt stock swap, I think something else would have got Gene Merritt. But Ralph Mattlin—"

She took a sip from her glass. The movement rearranged the shadows on her face. All of a sudden she looked a little like Greta Garbo in the movie version of *The Green Hat*. The way I remembered her at the old American Theater on East Third Street. For the first time since we had met, I knew what it was about this homely broad that had kept me interested: in her own plain way Maud Eitner had the kind of face my mother and my wife Evie had. I couldn't take my eyes from the small hollow under her cheekbone. It was pulsing up and down. I wanted to reach out and touch it. "What about Ralph Mattlin?" I said.

"He had a heart attack a year ago," Maud said. "A few days after they locked Gene Merritt away. I've talked to Bernie Yustin about it. He says if the present situation continues with Sissenwein Enterprises milking Mattlin & Merritt, Ralph will have another heart attack. Or something worse. Bernie may be exaggerating. Ralph is sick and he's not getting better. Maybe he would have got sick if he never heard of Hubert Sissenwein. Maybe he would have got sick if he was in the dress business up on Seventh Avenue. Or selling hot chestnuts. Or just clipping coupons. The point is, he never had any serious health problems until he sold the firm to Sissenwein. So it's an easy hook for Bernie Yustin to hang the blame on. My own personal feeling is that Ralph Mattlin has given up. He wants to die. So it's easy for Bernie to say, and I guess it helps Ralph Mattlin to believe that unless he gets his firm back he's going to die."

"And you want me to get it back for him," I said.

"Yes," Maud Eitner said, and then she said, "Please."

"It means that much to you?" I said.

"Of the two men I wanted," she said, "he's the only one I can still see every day. If he dies I'll have nobody. Do it for me, Ted." She paused and then again she said, "Please."

"If you answer one question," I said.

"Ask it," Maud said.

"If the firm meant that much to him," I said, "why did Mattlin agree to sell out? I thought Merritt, the kid from Avenue B, I thought he'd be the one who would grab at the money. But Mattlin, with his background, money wasn't all that important to him. Yet it didn't work that way. Merritt was against it. But it was Mattlin, Mattlin was the one who grabbed. Why?"

Maud shook her head. "All you boys who know so much about money," she said. "In the end you don't know anything. What it gets down to is this. If you do something just for money and for no other reason, you have nothing to fall back on when the money stops. Ralph Mattlin made a mistake. He didn't see anything but the money Sissenwein was dangling under his nose, and he was always shaky about money. A family weakness. Going back, probably, to his father's bankruptcy. Who knows? All I know is that later, now, when it hurts, he has nothing to fall back on." Maud Eitner paused. Then she said, "Except you."

"Not me," I said. "You."

"For him you wouldn't do it?" she said.

"For him I couldn't do it," I said.

"Why not?" Maud said.

"My mother wouldn't have liked it," I said.

"I don't understand," Maud said.

"She was born a serf," I said.

"Will you do it for me?" Maud said.

I reached out and touched the place in her cheek where the shadowed hollow was pulsing up and down. All of a sudden I was wondering how I could ever have been dumb enough to think she was homely.

"For you," I said, "I'll try."

38

" I Made Up My Mind I'd Pay You Back Someday"

Nine years later, in Byram Noonan's apartment at Ninety-sixth and Fifth, Ralph Mattlin's widow said, "You didn't try very hard, did you?"

I wondered if I had. I think I went through the motions. I don't have to think about how I went through those motions. My heart wasn't in it.

"I did my best," I said. "But Hubert Sissenwein was a tough man to handle when he was alive and kicking."

"Now that he's dead," Benita said, "I suppose you think you can handle him better?"

"With your help," I said. "Yes."

Benita laughed. "The shoe is on the other foot now, isn't it?" she said.

If she didn't watch out she might be surprised to find where the foot that was wearing the shoe was going to land.

"No," I said. "If this works out we'll all be helping each other."

Benita laughed again. "The picture isn't right," she said.

"What picture?" I said.

"You in your boy scout uniform," she said. "Standing on the corner, helping little old ladies across the street."

"That's not the sort of help I had in mind," I said.

"Maybe you'd better explain," Benita said. She looked at her wrist watch. "I promised to meet Mrs. Idleman at three. She's flying back to Los Angeles at five. I'm taking her to the plane."

Byram arrived with the drinks. "Told Mrs. Wakefield purpose this meeting?" he said.

"You better do it," I said. "She has me mixed up with little boys in khaki shorts."

"Quite simple," Byram Noonan said. "As you know, Mrs. Wakefield, since Hubert Sissenwein died, his will has been subject much controversy. Aside from minor bequests, he left entire estate to foundation named after him. His two brothers, both very small legatees, been contesting will on ground it is illegal method to avoid inheritance taxes. They say estate should go to them and they will pay inheritance taxes and thus government will get tremendous sum. Case has been in court now almost two years. This rate could be two more or even longer. Surrogate worried. Doesn't want to condone tax evasion. Same token doesn't want to act contrary intent of deceased. Ted and I have worked out a solution beneficial all concerned."

"All?" Benita said.

Every one of Byram's seventy-six inches moved in the small bow he dropped over her. "All, Mrs. Wakefield," he said. "Ted and I interested in contents of Hubert Sissenwein empire. Radio stations. Magazines, Newspapers. Publishing firms. Movie studios. So on. We have put together a syndicate that is willing to buy up entire contents Hubert Sissenwein Enterprises for sum comfortably in excess current market value Hubert Sissenwein Enterprises stock. When ready we plan to make this attractive offer to surrogate, who can then act in interests both government and Sissenwein brothers. Surrogate cannot accept our offer, however, without consent of executors of Sissenwein will. Ted and I have presented our plan to all the executors one by one including your father Walter Idleman."

"He not my father," Benita said. "Sorry. I'm beginning to

talk like you, Mr. Noonan. I meant to say Walter Idleman was not my father. He was the father of my present husband's first wife."

"Accept correction," Byram said with another bow. "Fortunately does not affect financial picture. Ted and I were ready to go to surrogate next week with our package offer, having consent of all executors, when Walter Idleman died three days ago. Necessary, therefore, present picture to new executor. You. Hence your presence here today."

"These executors," Benita said. "Now including me. They will get some rather substantial fees, won't they?"

"They'll cut up one hell of a melon," I said.

"And they'll cut it up now, Mrs. Wakefield," Byram Noonan said. "Soon as surrogate accepts offer. Not years from now, if ever."

"That's what I meant by helping each other," I said.

"I know what you meant," Benita said. "I even know how much you meant. Which may be something even you are not aware of. I didn't allow Hubert Sissenwein to put my name in his will as an alternate executor without asking him how much I'd be executing about."

"I take it, then," Byram said, "you knew him well?"

"Not until after my first husband died," Benita said. "Since I felt Hubert Sissenwein had been indirectly responsible for my husband's death, I made it a point to find out something about the man who killed him. This was not difficult. Hubie thought of himself as a ladies' man. It was during my second visit to his house that I met my present husband, and soon after that I got to know Walter Idleman and Mrs. Idleman."

"And now you're an executor of Hubie's estate," I said.

"I didn't know it was going to end that way," Benita said. "But I knew I was moving in the right direction."

"Good," Byram said. "Then Ted and I can count on you, Mrs. Wakefield."

"I don't think so," Benita said.

"I beg your pardon?" Byram said.

"Don't bother," Benita said. "It's possible, Mr. Noonan, that you're one of these clean crooks who takes the position that you're just a lawyer. You do what you get paid to do, and you don't ask any questions so long as what you're doing is within the law. If that's the kind of lawyer you are, Mr. Noonan, then you're worse than this creature you work for." She gave me the sort of smile she used to give me with the windshield-wiper job on Thirty-eighth Street. "I refer to Mr. Leff," she said. "Whom I can only describe as an utterly conscienceless son of a bitch."

"Benita," I said. "Think what Milton Merkin would say if he heard you talking like that."

"I know what Milton would say," Benita said. "He'd say you should have been put in the electric chair. You sent Gene Merritt to a mental home, and then, by refusing to help him, you killed Ralph Mattlin. The day Ralph died, I made up my mind I'd pay you back someday. I'm now in a position to do it. Don't waste your taxi fare going down to the surrogate's office with your attractive package," Benita said, and she smiled again. "One executor is going to unwrap it."

39

" It's Something We Used to Say on East Fourth Street When We Had Our Brains Knocked Out"

A half-hour later, when I came into our apartment, my wife Evie was sitting at my desk in the study. She was talking to somebody on the phone. "Here he is now," she said. "Good-bye." She hung up.

"Who was that?" I said.

"Byram Noonan," my wife Evie said.

"What did he want?" I said.

"He didn't," Evie said. "I did."

Thus at long last I knew something Miss Wien had tried but failed to make me understand in P. S. 188. How Caesar felt when he crossed the Rubicon. I knew it from the tone of Evie's voice. The way things had been for sixteen years, ever since the day I returned Arnold Zohn's black knitted tie, the way things had been only a few hours ago, when Evie and I had been drinking coffee and reading in this room the *New York Times* and the *Daily News* accounts of Walter Idleman's funeral, all that was finished. The referee had just said, "Ten!"

"You called Byram?" I said.

"I did," Evie said.

363

"Why?" I said.

"I told you this morning," Evie said. "You'd made it into the finals. Now you'd better win. I wanted to know if you had."

No matter how many words Byram had saved in making his report, she knew how the game had gone. Evie was a born scorekeeper.

"How was your lunch with Juliette?" I said.

"I didn't have lunch with Juliette," my wife Evie said. "After you left I called her and told her to take my hair appointment with Horst at Arden's because I'd had a sudden nosebleed and Artie Steinberg wanted to see me at once."

"You don't look like you've had a nosebleed," I said.

"Why should I?" my wife Evie said. "Since I didn't. What I had was a feeling that on this day of the finals I was lunching with the wrong person. So I sent Juliette to Arden's, and I called your old girl friend."

"Who?" I said.

What would you have said?

"Maud Eitner," my wife said.

As Byram would say: *Oy!*

"We had lunch," Evie said. "At Byram's corner table in Tony's."

"How is she?" I said.

"Expecting your call," Evie said.

"What?" I said.

"You're in a rut," Evie said.

I was also in trouble.

"She told me about your last meeting," my wife Evie said. "When you came home from the war. You never told me about that."

I thought of the hollow under Maud's cheekbone. And the way I'd reached out to touch it. How did you tell that to another woman? Especially if the other woman is your wife?

"We were trying to save Ralph Mattlin," I said.

"I learned what you never told me," my wife Evie said. "Why you never saved him."

"It wasn't me," I said. "It was Hubert Sissenwein."

364

"Ted," my wife Evie said. "You are talking to Evie Applebaum."

"No," I said. "I tried. I really did."

"But Hubie said no," she said. "Is that the version you're rehearsing for the jury?"

"Hubie didn't use that word," I said. "What you and Maud and Benita forget, Hubie Sissenwein got involved in the Mattlin & Merritt thing for only one reason."

"What was that?" my wife Evie said.

"Ralph Mattlin's father once laughed at Hubie in a nightclub," I said. "Over thirty years ago. On Fifty-second Street. Hubie destroyed people for less than that."

My wife Evie nodded. "I know," she said. "I even know some of the people. Or their survivors. But that's your tough luck."

In my time I'd had all kinds.

"Luck always changes," I said.

"Look me up when yours does," Evie said. "I dumped Arnold Zohn to put in with you because I like action. I warned you this morning. I'm bored with the ball park. You could keep me in it only by winning the play-off. You didn't. It was nice knowing you, Ted. Pretty nice, anyway."

"This is only temporary," I said. "I've scored before. I'll score again."

"It's not your score," Evie said. "It's that girl. Maud Eitner. She looks like the back end of a Mack truck. But she's got something. She sort of shines. I like her. She said she has nothing against you. She believes you really tried to save Ralph Mattlin."

The little hairs on the side of my jaw twitched. "I did," I said.

"I know better," Evie said. "But you go tell her that if you want to."

"I will," I said. I started toward the desk.

"Not from this phone," Evie said. "Or this apartment. It's in my name. You get out of here and make your phone calls to other women with your own dimes."

I gave it a moment of thought. Which means I didn't open my face until my guts stopped jumping. Then I realized it wasn't

Pearl Harbor. Not yet, anyway. I'd lost my pipe line to the Applebaum vault. But the tax-free municipals were in my name. And all of a sudden I felt the way I'd felt that day when I touched the hollow under Maud Eitner's cheekbone. After sixteen years of camping out, I was coming home.

"I guess I never should have returned that black knitted tie," I said.

"No," Evie said. "That was all right. It gave us sixteen years. Most marriages, they don't get sixteen months. But like everything else, even sixteen years come to an end. Ours ended at my lunch in Tony's today."

"Why?" I said.

"I don't want to stay married to a man who is loved more by another woman than I love him," my wife Evie said. "Don't be stupid, stupid," she said. "That's quite a girl."

"She's not a girl any more," I said.

"Neither am I," Evie said. "So we'd both better move fast."

"Is there another guy?" I said.

"There has been," my wife Evie said. "For some time."

"Anyone I know?" I said.

"Byram Noonan," Evie said.

I started to laugh. "I should have figured that," I said. "I guess I'll have to get myself another lawyer."

"For what you've got left," Evie said, "you won't need a lawyer. A new wife with a head on her shoulders will do. Better get going. She's waiting for you."

Suddenly I couldn't wait. I knew what she'd look like. The years were always kind to homely girls.

"I'll just pack my clothes first," I said.

"It won't be as big a job as you think," Evie said. "I started for you."

I was laughing again before I understood why.

"What's funny?" my wife Evie said.

"I just remembered something," I said.

"What?" Evie said.

"Something we used to say on East Fourth Street when we had our brains knocked out."

366

Evie gave me that look. I knew in my gut if I wanted to stay, all I had to do was touch her. But I knew also that from here on in, it was not Evie I wanted to touch.

"Tell me," she said.

"You may not understand it," I said. "It's an old Yiddish expression."

"Try me," my wife Evie said. "I'm as smart as Maud Eitner."

That was the first stupid remark I'd ever heard my wife Evie make. Nobody was as smart as Maud Eitner.

"Nil desperandum," I said. "Or screw it."

Jot that down.

About
the Author

Jerome Weidman, novelist and short-story writer, was born in 1913 on New York's Lower East Side. He was studying law at New York University when his first novel, *I Can Get It for You Wholesale,* was published in 1937. He quit law school at once to devote all his time to writing, and has been doing so ever since, except during the war, when he served with the Office of War Information in this country and overseas.

Mr. Weidman has traveled extensively in America and to the far corners of the world, from which he brought back raw material for many novels and approximately two hundred short stories, published in almost every magazine in the United States as well as in Canada, Europe, Australia, and Asia. His books have been translated into eight languages. His first play, *Fiorello!,* written in collaboration with George Abbott, was awarded the 1959 Pulitzer Prize. His third musical play, adapted from his own *I Can Get It for You Wholesale,* was produced in 1962. His comedy *The Mother Lover* was produced by Leland Hayward in 1969.

The Center of the Action, Mr. Weidman's twenty-eighth book was written in New York City, where he, his wife, and his two sons now live.